DEFIANT
LOVE

The Triumphant Hearts Series

Book One

Judith E. French

Cover by Kim Killion www.thekilliongroupinc.com
eBook design by eBook Prep www.ebookprep.com

January, 2018
ISBN: 978-1-61417-894-1

ePublishing Works!
www.epublishingworks.com

DEDICATION

For my loving grandparents, who opened the window to the past and told such magic tales; and for my children and grandchildren, who listen and remember what was and what may be again.

CHAPTER 1

Ohio River Country, 1703

A few pale stars hung suspended in the eastern sky as the girl crept silently from the wigwam and passed through the sleeping camp. She murmured softly to a tethered pony and received a gentle nicker in reply. She paused for a moment to stroke the animal's sleek, arched neck before moving on. Rustling sounds filled her ears, the stirrings of people not yet ready to greet the day. She smiled as the whimpers of a newborn came from her brother's lodge, then a sudden silence as, no doubt, the babe was soothed by a drowsy mother's full breast.

Already streaks of rose were beginning to illuminate the horizon. The girl quickened her steps. This was a special time of day, one she cherished, a time to be one with the inner voices of her heart and to communicate with all the living beings of the earth.

Star Blanket knelt on the bank of the creek and cupped her hands to drink of the cool, fresh water. The stones under her feet still held the night's chill, and she shivered, her brief deerskin skirt and sleeveless vest providing little warmth. Summer seemed late in coming this year. It was June, yet the wild strawberries were slow to ripen.

Swiftly, Star Blanket slipped out of her clothing and kicked aside her moccasins. She unbound her single, heavy braid, letting the dark hair fall in waves about her tanned shoulders. Then, with a running leap, she dove into the deep pool beneath the overhanging trees. She gasped at the shock of the cold water, unable to contain a small cry of surprise. Determinedly, she took handfuls of sand from the creek bottom and scrubbed her body until it tingled; then, having waded to the bank, she reached for a birch-bark container, intending to wash her hair with the herbs inside.

She paused, suddenly struck by the silence. She should be hearing bird calls, but instead not even a leaf or tree branch moved. A trickle of apprehension sobered her mood, and she climbed out of the water and dressed quickly.

Where was the village sentry? Cupping her hands, the young woman emitted the shrill, unique *pitty-pit-pit* of a nighthawk. She listened. There was no answer. She called a second time, and abruptly the silence of the morning was broken by the roar of a musket.

Before her eyes, the Indian camp dissolved into a nightmare filled with smoke and screams and blood. Dozens of bearded men charged out of the forest, their long guns spitting fire and death. The Shawnee scrambled from their wigwams, most with empty hands, to face cold steel and shot.

The children! Wrenched from her shock by a child's wail of terror, Star Blanket ran toward the village. A woman in front of her fell, pierced by a musket ball. Star Blanket leaped over the body and dashed toward her mother's wigwam. She saw her brother, naked, with only a skinning knife as a weapon, launch himself at a giant white man as his wife ran in the opposite direction, the baby in her arms.

"Star Blanket!" The woman's face twisted in pain as she thrust the screaming infant into her arms, then dropped to her knees. An English trade hatchet quivered in her back. "Take the baby," she cried. "Run!"

A musket backfired not a dozen paces away, the explosion shattering the face and chest of the white man who pulled the trigger. Blood spattered Star Blanket's cheek.

"Go!" her sister-in-law screamed.

A rough hand closed on her shoulder, spinning her around. For a heartbeat, she stared into the face of death. A bloody knife slashed down toward her throat. Instinctively she ducked, brought a knee up into the man's groin, and dodged away, running for her life. A musket ball passed so closely by her head that she heard the whine of its trajectory.

Clutching the child to her breast, she ran like a startled doe, splashing through the shallow creek and plunging into the thickest part of the forest. Branches raked her face and bare breasts, ripping at her unbound hair. Gasping for breath, her heart pounding, she dropped to the ground beneath the shelter of an overhanging pine bough. "Shhh," she warned, pinching the baby's nose between her fingers to stop his crying. The sound of shots coming from behind her and boots crashing through the trees told her she was not far enough away for safety. Star Blanket breathed deeply, trying to control her trembling, trying to erase the smell of blood from her nostrils.

The baby stared up at her from slanted black eyes. I have to think of him, she told herself. The dead are beyond help. A whimper caught her attention, and she pushed aside the boughs. There, only a few feet away, crouched a boy— Amatha. He was no more than eleven summers, and his eyes were glazed with fear. Blood trickled from his hair.

Star Blanket motioned him to silence. "You must be a warrior," she whispered. "Take the little one. He is my brother's child. Guard him with your life and carry him safely to Stone Bull's village. Do you understand?"

The child nodded, holding out bloodstained hands to take the infant.

"Inu-msi-ila-fe-wanu will protect you if you do not lose courage. Fail me and I shall send demons to haunt you."

She lay the baby in his arms. "His mother's sister lives there. She will care for him like her own." For an instant Star Blanket laid her hand against the boy's cheek. "Remember, you are Shawnee," she murmured. "Make no sound, no matter what you see or hear. And if you abandon the child, I will come back from my grave to seek revenge!"

Before she could lose her nerve, Star Blanket crept out from under the tree and inched her way through the brush. When she was a dozen yards from the hiding place, she leaped to her feet and began to run.

To her right she heard a shout and the snap of branches. She caught a glimpse of a white face.

"There goes one!" A musket cracked, and a piece of bark flew from a tree trunk overhead.

Star Blanket let out an ear-shattering scream. Her dark hair spread cut behind her like a silken wave as she sped down the faint deer trail. Like a pack of wolves the white men pursued her, howling in bloodlust, eager for the kill.

Their cries are no more than the wind, her soul whispered. She let the fear fall behind her as her moccasined feet flew across the hard-packed ground. The running became a glory, without beginning and without end.

Since childhood Star Blanket had prided herself on her ability to run swiftly and surely. The Shawnee honored those who showed great skill and stamina, and in races she had taken many prizes, including the tiny golden bells that hung in her ears. She had run against the young men as well as the women, but never had the potential prize been so great as now.

An Iroquois war party could run from the Great Lakes to the land of smoking mountains in five days' time…run without stopping to eat or sleep and yet fight when they arrived. If an Iroquois could do it, why not a Shawnee?

The pain in her side became an agony. She told herself that to feel pain one had to be alive, so pain was good. She concentrated on running, on placing each foot precisely where she wanted it; a slip now would bring about her death.

Ahead, the trees thinned, and the game trail led into a grassy meadow. The ground grew soft beneath her feet; her pace slowed despite her sudden burst of energy. She broke through the last of the hardwood trees searching frantically for cover. Sucking in great gulps of air, she dropped to her knees.

The whinny of a horse made her stagger to her feet. A memory teased her. Beyond the meadow—what lay beyond? Was there a sharp drop into a river? Ignoring the cramps in her legs, she forced her body to move faster.

She had crossed half the open space when two horsemen burst from among the trees. She turned to meet them, a Shawnee death chant on her lips, knowing she couldn't outrun the horses. She had lost the gamble. She would pay the price without tears.

With howls of delight, the militiamen lashed their mounts toward her, each eager to be the first. A red-bearded man pulled his tomahawk from his belt and swung it high.

Star Blanket stood frozen until she could feel the breath of the brown horse in her face, then she dodged swiftly aside. The blade went wide. With a curse, the man yanked hard on the reins, pulling the horse almost to his knees in the soft earth.

The second man dove out of his saddle and lunged for her. A hand closed around her ankle, pulling her to the ground. In a heartbeat, she twisted free, scrambling up and darting behind the horse. The white man cursed and circled the animal. Star Blanket scooted under the horse's belly, seizing the mane and throwing one leg over his back.

The horse, terrified by the strange-smelling creature clinging to his back, reared up, raking the sky with his forelegs. One hoof struck the man, instantly crushing the fragile bone above his right eye. The man fell like an empty sack, his life's blood draining out on the green grass.

Star Blanket struggled for control of the animal, leaning forward on the tossing neck and reaching for the elusive leather rein. The act saved her life as the red-beard's laughter turned to cries of rage. His musket ball grazed the back of her neck, like the sting of an angry wasp.

Then the hard butt of his musket slammed into her shoulder, knocking her from the horse and tossing her, breathless, onto the trampled grass.

With a whoop of triumph, the man threw himself down beside her, grabbed a handful of her dark hair, and yanked her head back. Instantly, the steel blade of his tomahawk plunged toward her head. The last thing Star Blanket saw was his horrible bearded face and a ribbon of blue sky framing his raccoon cap. Then there was only blackness....

In her dreams the blackness would grow deeper and then recede. Sometimes pain invaded her nothingness, but usually there was only the blackness: it was so much easier to float, carried by the tide of a dream river, safe from fear and sorrow, free from all the cares of life.

Yet something within her breast would not be stilled. A flicker of resistance ate at her passivity. The resistance hardened and strengthened until it would not be denied. The girl forced herself up from unconsciousness through clouds of pain and fear. Gradually her brain acknowledged signals...sounds and smells. A hint of light passed through the barrier of her thick, dark lashes.

Cunning bade her wait; she did not yield to the urge to open her eyes. Instead, she lay unmoving, listening, trying to identify the sounds around her.

The breathing of animals...horses. A sensation of movement. The creak of leather. Men's voices. The tongue...not French, English. English-*manake*. She was a prisoner of those who had brought death to her village!

Memories spilled over; all her control could not stop a tear from running down her cheek. So many dead...so many. Fire and shot and death brought by cold steel. Why had she not died with them? Wishemenetoo! Why? Why have you punished me by letting me live when all I love have crossed over?

The pain in her heart gave way to the pain in her flesh. Star Blanket's head pounded; every bone in her body ached. Her chest and belly hurt with every step of the horse across which she had been flung. Her arms...she could barely feel them; her fingers were numb. Her hands were tied behind her back, and she lay over the horse so that her face slapped against his belly as he walked.

Her despair passed with the fading of the day. At dusk, the English-manake reined in their horses and prepared to make camp for the night. Star Blanket waited, her eyes closed, her breathing faint and steady. She lived! When she learned why they hadn't killed her in the meadow, she would plan her escape. Wishemenetoo, the Great Spirit, would give her the cunning and courage needed to make the best of every opportunity. She began imperceptively twisting her wrists to free herself.

Rough hands pulled her from the horse and tossed her to the ground. Her head slammed against something hard. To her shame, a soft moan escaped her lips. She lay limp and unmoving.

"See! I told you," a voice said overhead. "I told ye she were alive."

The accents were strange, but Star Blanket knew the words. Her father had spoken English with her so that she would not forget. And once she had been the voice for her mother in trading with a Frenchman from the north country. His English had been funny too, but she had always had an ear for the tongues of other people.

Then another, deeper voice said, "Should of kilt her with the rest!"

"She be white, James. You can see by the skin. Them's no Injun features."

"Born white, maybe. But livin' with them like that, who knows how long, she's tarred with the same brush. She ain't fit to live with decent white folks. Them squaws is dirty! Like rabbits, all of them. Legs like she's got, she's warmed some buck's blanket. Live with them, die with them, I say!"

"After all them bucks, maybe she'd be grateful for a white man. What do you say, Harlan? I know your old woman ain't got tits like these!"

Coarse laughter filled her ears, and Star Blanket bit the inside of her cheek until she tasted the salt of her own blood. She would die before she lay beneath their stinking bodies! They called her people dirty. Phahh! These white dogs carried a stink like carrion on their unwashed flesh.

A hand gripped her ankle. "Come on, sweet thing. Open your eyes. Harlan's got something for you."

Star Blanket came alive in a churning tempest of fury. The bonds on her wrists that she had worked loose flew off, and she launched herself at her tormentor with a cry of pure rage.

The unexpected attack caught the bearded white man off guard, and he fell over backward with the girl on top of him. She struck his chin with her head and her nails reached for his eyes. A knee caught him in the groin even as his friends attempted to rescue him from her savage assault.

Hands grabbed at her as she cursed the man with every profanity she had ever heard in English or French. The words were interspersed with Shawnee, Fox, and Chippewa invocations, which, although not true curses, left no doubt of her feelings.

The man staggered to his feet, blood streaming from a dozen scratches on his face, and came toward her, his fists raised. Star Blanket struggled to break loose from the two white men who held her.

Suddenly a pistol shot sounded behind them. The laughter and yelling ceased abruptly as a big man shouldered his way through the crowd. "I waste no more pistol balls," he threatened, glaring at the men. "What goes here?" He held a flintlock pistol in each hand, one still smoking. "Well?" he demanded. His broad forehead was lined, his once yellow hair faded to near gray, yet there was no doubt of his authority; his tone and bearing told Star Blanket that this man was a war chief.

"Him!" She motioned her chin toward the bearded one. "He…" Her mind scrambled for the unfamiliar words.

The ice blue eyes turned on the man. "You know my orders." He raised the pistol until the barrel was level with the bearded man's forehead. "You challenging me, James Walker? We are Christian men, doin' God's work." His voice rose as he warmed to his message. "We have come into this wilderness to teach the red man a lesson, not to lie with his women! Not to sink to the level of beasts! And not to take advantage of this poor, unfortunate white girl. Have you no shame? Cover her nakedness!"

Flushing crimson, a man skinned off his smock and threw it toward her. "She kin have thet, Colonel. James didn't mean no harm. We was jest funnin'."

Star Blanket kicked the filthy garment away. "I do not need your skins! I need nothing of you! Let me go!" She turned her face toward the war chief. "You break the peace. You kill. You make war. If your God tells you to do this, he is as evil as you are."

"Silence, woman!" he thundered. "You can be forgiven much for your ignorance, but not for blasphemy. Cover your body from the eyes of my men, or I will not be responsible for their sins. You are white. You'll be taken back to the settlements, and someone will try to find out if you have any family left. Do you know your name?"

Her green eyes grew smoky with anger. "I am Alagwa Aquewa, Star Blanket, and I am Shawnee of the Wolf Clan. I am not white. And I will not go anywhere with you. Set me free or kill me."

The big man spat in the dust. "God help us, she is mad," he uttered quietly. "Tie her well and gag her again if she will not be still. Be she mad or not, we will do our duty." His fierce stare took in the watching men. "And I'll shoot any man who lays a lustful hand on her, so help me God."

* * *

Annapolis, Maryland August 1703
Sheffield Plantation

Thomas Bradford dropped into a chair and reread the thin, creased parchment for the third time. He swallowed hard and motioned to the serving girl. "Brandy!" he ordered.

She poured it and handed the goblet to him. Trembling, he took the glass and downed the amber liquid in a single gulp.

"Are you all right, sir?" the girl asked hesitantly. "Is it bad news? Should I fetch Master Adam?" The old master looked pale. With his bad heart, anything could happen. Suppose he keeled over right in front of her? Saints preserve us! Molly bit her lower lip nervously. "Do you want me to find Master Adam?" she repeated. "He's in the office. I seen him there just a few minutes ago."

"Yes…yes. Get Adam."

Molly ducked a hasty curtsy and dashed from the room. Master Adam would know what to do.

Thomas was just helping himself to a second glass of brandy when the younger man burst into the room.

"Sir! Are you all right? Molly said…" Adam put an arm around his stepfather and helped him back into his chair, noting the tears in the faded green eyes and the crumpled letter in his hand.

"I'm all right," Thomas said hoarsely. "They've found my Rebecca. After all these years." His voice cracked, and he wiped his eyes with the back of a gnarled hand. "Listen to me, sniveling like a kitchen wench! Damn it, boy, they've found her. Alive and well…my little Rebecca." He pushed the parchment into Adam's hands. "Read it yourself. This just came by rider from Annapolis."

As Adam read, suspicion drained from his square face and was replaced by unaffected joy. "It sounds like your granddaughter," he agreed, running a hand carelessly through his hair. Contrary to the custom of the time, when even servants wore wigs, Adam was content with his own plain brown locks pulled back into a club at the back of his neck and secured with a leather thong. The simple style of dark hair framing his face was as unpretentious as his high, wide forehead and sympathetic brown eyes, which missed nothing.

He was a big man, tall and broad of shoulder, with massive arms and hands. His clothes were as plain as his face, well made but of simple lines, without frills or artifice. Yet he moved easily, with none of the awkwardness of many large men. And the plain face softened with compassion as he turned toward the old man.

"She's the right age," Adam said, "and the scar would seem to indicate—"

"The Bradford eyes!" Thomas said triumphantly. "My son had them and both of the children. Green as the ocean off the cliffs of Dover. Bradford eyes! It's my Rebecca, I tell you. I knew she wasn't dead! Damn it to hell! I told them. I told them all. She's alive, Adam." He slammed his fist against the desk, sending a candlestick spinning.

"It says here she's in Pennsylvania, about a day's ride west of Lancaster. A place called Logan's Crossing." Adam walked to the window to catch the light. "Not a very good speller, is he, this Colonel Steiner?"

Thomas's thin lips pursed as memories of those he had lost swept over him. "October seventh, sixteen ninety-two," he murmured. "Mary's brother took up land three days west of here. I told him it was foolhardy. Indian country. No place for a white man. And then nothing would do but that Robert take Mary and the children to visit her family. I begged them to leave the little ones here." He sighed deeply. "Rebecca was only eight years old, little Tom not quite five."

Adam patted his stepfather's shoulder. He'd heard it all a hundred times before. "Don't trouble yourself with it, sir."

Adam and his mother had been bondservants on Sheffield at the time of the massacre, but he remembered little Rebecca Bradford well. He'd taught her brother how to swim in the creek. The deaths had been a blow to servant and master alike.

"They never had a chance…murdered in cold blood, the women and children along with the men. No reason to it. Bloodthirsty savages." Thomas blinked back tears. "They found Mary's body beside Robert's and little Tom's. But no girl child. Without a body, how could they be sure she was dead? I knew she wasn't. I knew it all along." He chuckled. "People thought I was just a crazy old man. This should show them, eh, Adam?"

"Crazy like a fox, maybe," the younger man conceded. If this girl was Rebecca, it was nothing short of a miracle. There were frequently tales of white children who'd been captured and raised by the Indians, but after eleven years, he'd believed the girl long dead and in some lonely grave. And if this girl was Rebecca Bradford, she was the rightful heiress to Sheffield. Adam swallowed hard at the sudden realization.

From the time Thomas Bradford had married Adam's mother, Martha Rourke, six years earlier, he'd treated Adam like a son. They'd worked the plantation together, and Adam had come to respect and love his stepfather in a way he'd never been able to care for his own father. During the long years of hard work, in the sharing of responsibility and danger, Adam had begun to think of Sheffield as his own. Thomas had even written a will naming Adam his sole heir. Now all that was changed by the arrival of this letter from the Pennsylvania frontier.

Adam shrugged. All that he had, Thomas Bradford had given him. Thomas had taught him to run a plantation and given him a sense of self-respect. If fate had returned to Thomas the granddaughter everyone thought dead, he could only share in the old man's joy. "Do you want me to ride up to Pennsylvania and bring her home, sir?" he asked. "It might be better if someone from the family went. After what she's been through, there's no telling what kind of mental state she might be in. Likely she's terrified."

"I was thinking just that," Thomas agreed. "I'd go myself, but I know I couldn't ride two hours on a horse." He chuckled again. "Besides, there's the matter of the reward, two hundred pounds in gold. I think it would be safer with you than with an old man. I don't think there's anyone in Pennsylvania big enough to take it away from you."

"When do you want me to leave?"

"At daybreak tomorrow. Take three of the best riding horses. You'll make better time if you travel alone. Servants talk. You'll be safer with that much gold if you don't have to worry about a loose tongue."

Adam nodded. "You're right. If she's well enough to travel, we should be back in a few weeks. I hope she can ride; I wouldn't want to travel by wagon. The roads are almost nonexistent up there." He paused thoughtfully. "I suppose I should take dresses and such, but I'm at a loss as to where to start. If my mother was alive, she'd know."

"There are things of Mary's packed away in the attic. They'll do until Rebecca is safely home." The seamed fingers tightened around Adam's arm. "Be gentle with her, boy. She's been through so much. And tell her how much I love her."

"Don't worry, sir, we'll get on. When she was a child, Rebecca used to trail me about like a puppy. She'll be so happy at the thought of coming home, I doubt there will be any real problems. You can count on me."

Thomas released his grip. "I know I can. You're your mother's son, Adam." Faded green eyes locked with brown. "I know I promised you Sheffield if Rebecca was never found, but you'll not lose by this, I swear it."

CHAPTER 2

Logan's Crossing, Pennsylvania
August 22, 1703

Day after day, Star Blanket had paced the shadowy confines of the log blockhouse, wearing a path in the bare dirt floor. Now she crouched in a corner, her arms folded across her chest, waiting. Her breathing was shallow, her green eyes patient in the darkness, the gloom hiding the fierce intelligence submerged in the depths of those catlike orbs.

Though her body was motionless, her mind was not. By her reckoning, it was nearly time for one of her captors to come with food and water. They were afraid of her, and their fear made them dangerous. Her cheek bore a bruise from a blow that had not faded in more than seven suns.

A smile softened her full lips as she remembered the day she had come close to regaining her freedom. The young buck who had come to bring the disagreeable corn mush had been careless. Tripping him and slipping out the door had been child's play. If the big man they called the Colonel hadn't ridden her down, she'd have reached the safety of the forest.

The pale-faced women were terrified of her. They hid behind their men, too cowardly to face her, content to whisper insults they thought she was too stupid to understand.

Phahh! They were contemptible; it filled her with shame to think that she had once been one of them. She could not imagine living in fear like these *s'squaw-o-wah,* who hid even their bone-white faces from the sun and cringed at the sounds of animals in the forest.

How they clutched their whining children to their breasts, as though she, Star Blanket, would wrench them away and eat them raw! They eyed her with hard, suspicious stares, their pale blue eyes dull and without intelligence. What kind of women were these, who loved their own children but sent their braves to cut the throats of Shawnee babies? They must be demons without a shred of compassion or sympathy in their bone-white hearts.

Iroquois, she knew, killed children. Perhaps these English-*manake* were kin to the eaters-of-men, the Iroquois. The Shawnee did not kill children, precious gifts of Him-on-high. The women and children of the whiteskins might be taken as captives, but they were always adopted into the tribe. Had they not so accepted her?

The *English-manake* who held her prisoner now believed she did not remember her white family or her white name. She did remember. The morning of blood was branded on her brain; dreams still threatened her sleep. Star Blanket, she who had been Beck-ka'bad'ford, remembered.

She had been playing with her small brother Thorn, feeding a pet raccoon, when her mother had called her back from the edge of the woods. The little boy had turned obediently, but she had chased the soft animal into the trees. She wasn't sure now how long she had followed it before it allowed itself to be captured. She was holding it in her arms when she heard the first blood-curdling yell—the Iroquois war cry. She had not recognized it then, but now she would never forget.

Her child's instincts had told her to run to her mother, but an older instinct had bade her lie still in the tall grass beneath the trees, as still as death. The scene of blood and terror that had unfolded before her remained frozen in her mind—the silver flashes of steel, the puffs of smoke from the muskets, and the sweet, cloying smell of blood. Blood was everywhere; it soaked the ground and turned the rich brown of the log barn to crimson.

Her father took two Iroquois warriors with him into death. He died bravely, as bravely as the woman who stepped between her small son and a gory hatchet. But in the end, they all died...cows and dogs, sheep and people. In the end there was silence, broken only by the chant of blood-crazed Iroquois braves and the crackle of flames that ate at the house and barns, filling the air with thick, black smoke.

And she lay in the shadows of the boughs, alone. Until then, she could not remember ever feeling afraid. What had there been to fear? Until then, when suddenly everything was gone, everyone. Even the warm, soft raccoon had fled into the woods at the first scent of blood.

She lay there through the heat of the day, her tongue dry, her head aching from lack of water. Even after she realized that the Indians were gone, she could not move. Her body and mind seemed turned to stone.

Slowly, she had become aware that she was not alone. A face, bronzed and unmarked by paint, loomed only feet from where she lay. She had seen no movement, and he was so still it was hard to believe the man was real. His eyes were brown and full of pity. It was impossible to be afraid of those eyes, even when brown fingers motioned her to silence.

It was comforting to have the man nearby. She dozed, sleeping for minutes or hours, until a featherlight touch on her shoulder woke her. The man still crouched by her side in the fast-fading light. He motioned her to rise and follow him. Without question, she obeyed. She could not have done otherwise. He was all she had.

Later, she learned that the man, Chaquiweshi, was a Shawnee scout. He had been following the enemy Iroquois war party, and he had seen all that had happened. Because he could not leave a child, even a white one, to die in the forest, and because he was afraid to return her to the nearest white settlement, he took her home to his sister at the Shawnee camp.

Chaquiweshi's sister, Co-o-nah Equiwa, had taken her without question. She had lost a girl child at birth and had always believed she was owed another. Despite her husband's warnings, she had made Beck-ka'bad'ford—renamed Star Blanket—her daughter, as dear and as greatly loved as though she had been born to her own lodge. And in time Cut-ta-ho-tha, her husband, had come to accept Star Blanket as his own.

Co-o-nah Equiwa and Cut-ta-ho-tha had replaced the parents who had died on that bright morning of blood. Shawnee had replaced English, and she had changed bit by bit until she knew that the white child Beck-ka'bad'ford had died that day along with the others. She no longer mourned her white family or the child she had been. She had been born again into a new life; she was Star Blanket of the Shawnee. And nothing these English-*manake* could say or do would change that.

The sound of footsteps outside the blockhouse drew her back to the present. Several people were coming. She let her eyelids sink lower until only a sliver of light passed through. With the patience of a hunter, Star Blanket waited. Her captors could not hold her forever, and if they relaxed their guard for an instant, she would be gone.

Adam Rourke tried to conceal the dislike he felt for these frontier Pennsylvanians. They were a rude, unlettered lot, and he had no doubt that Rebecca Bradford had been misused because of their ignorance. Colonel Steiner demanded the two-hundred-pound reward before Adam even laid eyes on the girl.

"She's touched in the head," Steiner warned. "Most are like that after the savages get through with them. Don't look for any gratefulness. The girl's stark, raving mad."

If so, you haven't helped, Adam thought. The gold was still safe in the saddlebag slung over his shoulder. He wouldn't part with a coin of it until he was certain this poor girl was Rebecca Bradford.

The dour German led the way across the enclosed compound to a log blockhouse. "Don't turn your back on her. She'll knife you in a minute." He paused with his hand on the wooden bar that secured the massive door. "'Twas my Christian duty to spare her life and see her returned to her own people. But, God help her, she might have been better off dead with the rest of the vermin."

Adam's muscles tensed; his hand crept to the pistol at his waist. He didn't trust this Colonel Steiner. If this was all a hoax, an attempt to swindle him out of the reward...Adam's brown eyes darkened to ebony. He had never considered himself a violent man, but he'd go to any lengths to keep from betraying his stepfather's trust.

The leather hinges squeaked as the door swung open. The German motioned him inside. Adam shook his head. "You first, Colonel."

The big Pennsylvanian stepped in, and Adam paused, letting his eyes become accustomed to the dim interior.

The dirt floor gave off a musty smell; there were no windows, only an opening in the ceiling that Adam supposed must be reached by a ladder. The blockhouse was built for defense, not for comfort; the rough log walls would give no solace to a young and frightened woman. A flood of anger surged through him. Mad or not, the girl did not deserve to be treated like a wild animal!

Adam glanced around the cell, noticing the bucket half full of water and the empty wooden bowl. Had she been fed like a beast without a table or chair, without even eating utensils? His eyes found the girl huddled in the darkest corner.

He breathed deeply of the damp air, deliberately controlling his tone of voice, hiding his anger. "Rebecca," he called softly. "Rebecca Bradford? I'm your uncle. I've come to take you home."

There was no answer, no sign that she had heard or understood.

"You, girl!" the Colonel snapped. "Come here." He took a step toward her. "She hears well enough. I told you she was mad." He reached out to grab her arm, but Adam stepped in front of him.

"Don't touch her." Rourke motioned toward the door. "Wait outside. I want to talk to her alone." The softness in Adam's voice nearly covered the steel. "Leave us. Now." Blood pounded in his temple as he saw the bruise that ran down the side of the girl's cheek.

Steiner shrugged. "It's your throat. Remember, I warned you."

When they were alone, Adam squatted on the dirt floor and spoke to her. "They say you are Rebecca Bradford. If you are, you should remember me. I'm Adam Rourke. I worked for your grandfather at Sheffield. I used to take Rebecca and her little brother swimming in the creek. And I gave you pony rides..." He made no effort to move closer. "Do you remember the pony, Rebecca? It was a black pony."

"No." Her voice came clear in the darkness, heavily accented but strong and unwavering. "Gray. Pony was gray."

"Yes." Adam tried to keep the excitement from his voice. "He was gray. Do you remember his name?" Nothing in Thomas Bradford's notices had ever mentioned the pony Rebecca and her brother had played with as a child. If she knew the answer to that question, there could be no doubt who she was.

"Dancer." Her eyes opened wide. "You *are* A-dam. But A-dam was not uncle. You lie," she accused.

He smiled warmly at her. "Yes, Rebecca. The pony's name was Dancer. He's still there, a little grayer, but as fat as ever. I'm not lying to you. I wouldn't do that. Do you remember my mother, Martha?"

"She was the..." Star Blanket struggled for the words. "Hoose..."

"Housekeeper. She was the housekeeper for your grandfather. Martha. She used to bake gingerbread. Do you remember? You always liked her gingerbread." Slowly, Adam extended his hand. "After you were lost, your grandfather married Martha. He was very much alone, and he needed someone. Can you understand that? Your grandfather married my mother. That makes me your uncle. It's the truth, Rebecca." Adam's legs began to cramp, but he was afraid to stand up. A sudden movement might frighten her. "I've come to take you home to Sheffield, home to your grandfather. Is that all right?"

"No." Star Blanket rose to her feet. "I not go. I not this Beck-ka'bad'ford. I Alagwa Aquewa, Star Blanket, of the Wolf Clan. I Shawnee. I no go with you, A-dam Rourke. I go back to my people." She moved gracefully along the side of the wall, her thick braid hanging over one shoulder. "Beck-ka'bad'ford is dead. Iroquois kill. Kill mother, kill father, kill Thorn. All dead. You A-dam Rourke, true, you set me free."

Trickles of sweat began to run down Adam's forehead. "Is it all right if I stand up? I won't hurt you, I promise." The girl nodded, and he unfolded his long legs.

Her unwillingness to go with him was the last thing he'd expected. "You must try to understand, Rebecca... Star Blanket. You're frightened now and upset. You're not thinking clearly. Once you're home at Sheffield with your grandfather, you'll feel much better." He sighed and ran a hand through his hair. "I think these people have treated you badly. I'm sorry. It was very wrong. But it won't happen again, I promise. I'm going to take very good care of you. You can trust me."

How easily they spoke of trust, these English-*manake*. Star Blanket's green eyes inspected him closely. He was a giant of a man, a head taller than any of the Shawnee warriors in her village. His hair was brown and slightly waving. Was it soft to the touch? she wondered. His face was fair, but not so fair as to be sickly. His nose was thin, too thin to be attractive. Co-o-nah Equiwa, her mother, said you could read a man's virility by the size and shape of his nose.

His eyes, at least, were the proper color—brown—and full of intelligence. But they showed none of the fierceness that should shine through the windows of the soul. This one was no warrior. Perhaps he was a digger of dirt.

She did not miss the clean, spicy scent of the man. Unlike her captors, this English-*manake* must bathe. She was glad to know that all of them were not swine who slept in their own sweat. Tobacco she smelled, a different kind than she was used to but definitely tobacco.

His hands were large and hard, lined from work, not soft and white like swollen mushrooms. Were they clumsy, these big hands? Could they draw a bow or throw a knife? She doubted it.

She searched her mind for memories of A-dam Rourke. She remembered laughter and kindness. There was nothing in this man, now or then, to fear. The corners of her lips curved upward in a faint smile. Nothing to fear.

"Will you come with me, Rebecca? Away from this place?" Adam asked. A ray of light, coming through the trapdoor in the ceiling, illuminated her smooth, heart-shaped face. The breath caught in his throat. Once she was washed and dressed in decent clothing, she would be a real beauty.

The ragged gown hung on her, but even the dirty folds could not hide the womanly curves of her high, firm breasts and compact hips. The bare feet that peeked out from under the muddy hem were small and shapely. But it was her eyes that drew him, large and heavy lashed, as wise and mysterious as a sphinx's. They glittered in the dark cell like fiery emeralds.

Any doubts he might have harbored were washed away in a wave of emotion. Bradford eyes. Even a fool could see the similarity to Thomas Bradford, could see the shadow of the child she had been. This was Rebecca Bradford, all right. Lord, but he was grateful! Going home empty-handed to face his stepfather was something he hadn't even wanted to consider.

"I will come away from this place with you," she answered. Shyly, she extended a hand. But I do not promise how far I go with you, A-dam Rourke.

Had he no ears to hear? He was a fool. He did not listen when she told him she was Shawnee. The white girl he sought was dead. She, Star Blanket, could waste no pity on her enemies. She must escape any way she could.

"Good." Adam grinned as he took her small hand. "I brought clothes for you, but I don't want to stay here a minute longer than we have to." Doubt crossed his face. "Can you ride a horse?"

"I can ride." Better than you, English-*manake*. She lowered her eyes to hide the cunning there. Does he know nothing of the Shawnee? she thought.

She decided she would not hurt him when she made her escape. It would be like hurting a big, foolish child. But she would take away his horses and perhaps the fine English pistol at his waist. The pistol was worth the pelts of many beaver. A digger man would have little use for such a weapon anyway. She doubted he could even hit anything with it.

"Rebecca?" He touched her cheek. "How did that happen?"

She jerked back, her fingers tracing the bruise. "Stei-her, the one they call the Colonel, he did it. I try to run away and he catch me."

Adam's body tensed as he turned abruptly toward the door. "Follow me. Don't be afraid. No one will hurt you again."

With feigned meekness, she obeyed. There was a time to fight and a time to run. This was neither. Wisdom lay in waiting for the proper moment to carry out her escape. She must wait until they were far enough away from the settlement to be certain that A-dam Rourke would have no help in pursuing her.

The sun was warm on her face as she stepped through the doorway into the compound. Too long had she been shut away in the dark. Gratefully, she breathed in the fresh air.

Upright logs formed a palisade around a half dozen cabins. At each corner of the rough square was a two-story blockhouse identical to the one used as Rebecca's prison.

One side of the enclosure was fenced off to act as a pound for the livestock. Dogs and children swarmed around the cabins, adding their noise to the squawk of chickens and the grunting of pigs.

Star Blanket sniffed loudly. Even the Iroquois had more order in their towns! And an Indian village was laid out sensibly; no Shawnee woman would cook her food in such squalor or draw her water from a spring where clothes were washed and animals stirred up the mud.

With great effort, she kept her eyes on the ground, following in the big man's footsteps. Stei-her and several other men were waiting for him. By the horse pen, a thin, dark man loaded his musket. Star Blanket felt the hair rise on the back of her neck. Suppose the Colonel's men would not let them go? She pressed close to A-dam Rourke. Didn't he see the hate in the eyes of these people?

Women stood in the doorways of their cabins, staring and whispering in a tongue she did not recognize. Even the eyes of the children were hard. A yellow-haired *s'squaw-o-wah* led a slat-ribbed cow to the spring. She drew back her skirts as though Star Blanket would soil them. "Indian bitch," she hissed.

Star Blanket bared her teeth at her tormentor and was rewarded with a squeak of fright as the woman dropped the cow's rope and jumped back. Laughter formed in her belly and seeped up the back of her throat until it was hard to control. If they had been alone, Star Blanket would have pulled every yellow hair from the woman's head until she looked like a vulture.

Startled by the white woman's actions, Adam turned back suspiciously. Star Blanket stopped short and lowered her head submissively as she had seen the white *s'squaw-o-wah* do. Her bare feet made circles in the dust.

"You have the woman. We want our money," the Colonel demanded in a loud voice.

"Hand it over," another said. "It should be more, by rights, as much trouble as she's put us to." He crowded close, so close she could smell the stale whiskey on his breath.

Star Blanket glanced sideways at him from under her lashes. It was the red-beard, the man she hated above all the rest. She would remember his face with its crooked nose and beady blue eyes. The Shawnee had long memories. It could be that he would live to regret being a butcher of children.

A pack of dogs ran out from behind a cabin, snarling and barking. The Colonel cursed and kicked them away. "We're waitin', Rourke. If you don't have the gold, it will go hard with you."

A brown-and-white hound circled around to nip at Star Blanket's ankles. She whirled on him, her eyes fierce, her lips forming a command in Algonquian. Its hackles raised, the animal backed away. "Call off your brother," she said in English.

The Colonel shouted a command, and a fat woman struck at the hound with a broom. More people were gathering. Star Blanket could hardly control her trembling. Was A-dam Rourke such a fool that he did not see the danger?

Calmly, he kept walking until he came to the gate of the compound. "You'll get what's coming to you," he promised. Deliberately, he raised the wooden bar and pushed open the doors.

Three horses stood outside the compound. Adam Rourke motioned and Star Blanket scrambled up on the nearest animal. He took the pistol from his waist and put it into her hand. She tucked her feet into the iron stirrups and took a firm grip on the reins, watching as he dumped the contents of the saddlebag onto the sand.

"As agent of Thomas Bradford, I've been instructed to give you this reward for the return of his granddaughter," Adam said patiently. "And, as his agent, I'm sure he'd want you to have this too." Before the German could gather his wits, a solid fist connected with his chin. The Colonel groaned and crumbled to the ground as Adam simultaneously swung up into the saddle of his horse and grabbed the lead line of the spare animal.

With a cry, Adam slapped the rump of Star Blanket's horse and they were off at a gallop. She leaned low over the horse's neck and dug her heels into the animal's sides. Behind them, the *English-manake* shouted futile threats.

A shot whistled over their heads, and A-dam Rourke's laughter joined with hers as they put distance between them and the settlement. She clung to the pistol. The big man might not know it, but getting it back from her would be harder than giving it to her had been.

CHAPTER 3

The horses' necks were white with sweat before their riders began to slow their breakneck pace. Adam reined his mount level with Star Blanket's and motioned to a gap in the trees to the right. "That way."

Single file, they left the narrow, rutted road and entered the forest. Adam pulled a brass compass from his saddlebag, studied it for a moment, and turned his horse's head south-southeast. "If they give chase, they'll expect us to follow the road."

"Do you know the way?" she asked in disbelief. A-dam Rourke did not look like a woodsman.

"No, but my compass does." He grinned. "I found you, didn't I?"

She concentrated on guiding her horse around a fallen log. It would not do to become too friendly with this English -*manake*. Who knew what she might have to do to make her escape?

They rode in silence among the towering hardwoods, the only sound the crunch of twigs and leaves under the horses' feet. The air seemed close, rich with the odors of decaying vegetation and the spicy scent of an occasional pine. Indian pipes thrust their waxen stems up from the forest floor, along with mountain laurel and low-bush blueberry.

The heat of the late August afternoon enveloped the two riders. Even the birds and small animals fell still, wrapped in a somniferous enchantment. Star Blanket felt her eyelids growing heavy, and she pinched the inside of her leg to rouse herself from her torpor.

After more than an hour, they reached a small creek lined with graceful hemlocks. Adam signaled for her to dismount, and they led the animals downstream, taking care not to slip on the moss-covered rocks. She gave silent approval to his decision; in the water they would leave no trail to follow.

"Moss grows on the north side of the trees," she said softly.

"What?" Surprised, he turned to stare at her. "What did you say?"

"I tell you moss grows on the north. A Shawnee has no need for your metal box with its flying arrow. That com...comp..."

"Compass." He grinned. "Suppose you were in an open meadow, or on the ocean, somewhere without trees—then what would you do?"

"Shawnee not go on o'cean, not need your compass."

"Well, I need it." He turned his back and continued down the stream. She followed a few feet from the lead horse.

The cold running water felt good on her feet and ankles; the air seemed fresher along the stream. Now and then, she spied a darting trout, its silvery body a flash of light against the mossy bottom. Her spirits rose, and unconsciously she began to hum a children's song. Her horse, a magnificent chestnut, flicked his ears and nudged her with its dark, velvety nose. She laughed aloud.

Adam glanced at her over his shoulder. "So you can laugh. I'm glad. That's the first time I've seen you smile."

"I smile when I am happy. I smile when you strike Stei-her."

Adam laughed, a deep, rumbling sound that shook his wide shoulders. He stopped and leaned against the bay gelding. "Are you tired?" he asked. "We can ride again if you like."

The green eyes narrowed suspiciously. "Why Star Blanket be tired? You think I am same as white-skinned *s'squaw-o-wah,* A-dam Rourke?" She glared at him haughtily. "Shawnee woman does not tire riding through woods in after-day."

"Afternoon," he corrected her solemnly. "And it's just Adam."

"A-dam," she snapped.

"Close enough." He climbed the bank at a break between the overhanging hemlocks and led the bay up the muddy slope. "I doubt Steiner and his men care where we've gone now that they have the gold." He offered her a broad hand.

Ignoring it, she struggled up alone, slipping to one knee when the chestnut balked at the stream's edge. Adam caught her arm and pulled her to her feet.

"Careful. We can't have you breaking a leg." He tugged hard at the chestnut's reins. "Gittup, there. Come on, boy. That's it." He patted the horse's neck, then handed her back the reins.

"If I break leg, you shoot me like horse?"

"It's a thought," he teased.

"You never shoot me," she scoffed. "You pay too much gold for me." She bent and gathered a few bright red berries from a low-growing plant and popped them into her mouth. "Tea berries," she explained. "You want taste?" She offered a handful.

Adam sampled them hesitantly. The plant with its shiny green leaves was unfamiliar. "They're very good," he finally admitted. "Tea berries, you say?"

She nodded, wiping her hands on the shapeless dress.

"I've got bread and dried meat in the saddlebags. This is as good a place as any to stop and eat something. I'll fill the water bags too, in case we make a dry camp tonight." From the spare horse he removed the supplies and a very wrinkled lady's riding habit. "I thought you might need something in the way of clothes. I hope this will do."

She wrinkled her nose. "Is it clean?"

"Of course."

"It will do."

To Adam's dismay, she pulled the worn gown up over her head and stood before him completely naked. With a gasp, he turned his back, suddenly painfully aware of the effect her perfectly formed nude body had on him. He swallowed hard, remembering the glimpse of dark, curling hair below the flat, tanned belly. Her breasts were round and firm with rosy nipples that begged to be teased to arousal. Shame flooded him as he realized what he was thinking. To take advantage of this poor girl, even to imagine doing so, was unpardonable. "You shouldn't do that!" he said sharply. "A woman…a lady doesn't undress in front of a man."

She struggled with the unfamiliar buttons of the crimson riding habit. "She does not? No man? Not even her husband?"

"Of course she can dress in front of her husband." Unconsciously, he started to turn back, then stopped. "There are undergarments in the saddlebag and slippers. I didn't bring boots. I didn't know what size you wore."

A smile tugged at the corners of her mouth as she saw the flush creep up the back of Adam's neck. "Is something wrong with my body? I am ugly?" She forced her voice into a childlike tone. "I be too ugly to find husband?" She sighed loudly. "You can look now. My ugliness is covered."

Adam faced her, his brown eyes clouded with confusion. "No, of course you're not ugly. You're very beautiful, but…"

"I do not understand this *but*. I am ugly or I am not. If you wish me to hide my body, it must be ugly. I know it is dirty. The English-*manake* do not give me water to wash. They are not clean people. I think they have bugs." She grimaced. "Shawnee are clean. Swim every day, even in time of snow." Her eyes pierced his soul with their intensity. "Do you wash, A-dam?"

He nodded. "Certainly."

"Then I will bathe now." With a tug, she pulled down the shoulder of the riding habit, exposing the top of her left breast. "I wash quick," she promised as the big man busied himself with the horses. "But I worry. Shawnee not think I am ugly. Star Blanket have many warrior who wish to join with her. I think I better with Shawnee than with white man who believe I ugly like old crow." The riding habit dropped to the grass, and she waded back into the stream.

Deftly she untied the leather thong in her hair and released the heavy braid. Even without soap, the water would wash much of the dirt and oil from her dark hair. She knelt in the water, scrubbing her skin with handfuls of sand until it tingled, remembering the last time she had bathed on the morning her people had been so brutally attacked.

The thoughts hardened her against A-dam Rourke. He was one of them. She must keep that thought uppermost in her mind. He was the enemy. She must outwit him to win her freedom.

She pushed the heavy hair aside and glanced in his direction. He was transferring the packs to the bay, carefully keeping his back to her. Was he a man who did not care for women? she wondered. Even among the Shawnee she had known men who preferred the company of their own kind. No, she decided, A-dam Rourke was not one of those. If her body had not affected him, he would not have shown such alarm. She must have broken a custom. But if so, it was a foolish custom. Did not all men and women have bodies alike? Did not Wishemenetoo make them all? Even the whites who called him by another name had reverence for the Creator. How could they worship the Creator and be ashamed of what he had created?

Rising from the stream, Star Blanket twisted her hair until rivulets of water ran from it, then shook it free. In this heat, it would dry quickly despite its thickness. She had always been proud of her hair, as heavy and glossy as a crow's wing. In the night, when her strange eyes couldn't be seen, she had always looked the proper Shawnee.

After drying herself off with the discarded dress, she quickly donned the clean clothing. "I cannot do these things," she admitted. "You will have to fasten them for me."

Composed once more, Adam turned to help her with the buttons. "I didn't mean to offend you," he apologized, "but when you are home, certain things will be expected of you. Even among your Indians, there must be rules of proper behavior."

"Yes. But the rules are not foolish."

Adam's big hands were gentle on the back of her neck. He was as guileless as a child. If he were not the enemy, she would have liked to have this man as her friend. The thought was disturbing, and she pushed it away.

Star Blanket decided not to wait for night. Slyly her eyes sought out the little pistol where it lay on a rock. She waited until he had finished with the dress, waited until he went back to the food. Then she crossed to the rock and picked up the pistol. "A-dam."

"You'll feel better if you eat something. The bread's a little crumbly but not bad." Smiling, he turned toward her. The smile faded as he saw the pistol leveled at his chest. "What are you—?"

Star Blanket tried to hold the gun steady. Her heart was pounding. "I told you, English-*manake,* I am Shawnee. You do not listen when I tell you I not want to go with you. I not go Mary-Land. I go my people. Now your fine horses go with me."

Adam's face creased with puzzlement. "I thought we were friends. I thought I could trust you." He took a step in her direction.

His musket was already strapped to the spare horse, the black. The girl moved toward the animal. "Stay where you are," she warned. "I shoot."

Sensing the tenseness between them, the horses snorted and shuffled their feet nervously. Adam took another step.

"I tell you no!" she screamed. "Not make me kill you!"

"You're going to leave me out here without a horse or gun? You might as well shoot me. My scalp will be hanging from a lodgepole by nightfall." He took two steps forward.

Star Blanket's hand trembled like an autumn leaf in the wind. "Please, A-dam," she begged. "I not want do this. I only want be free." Tears welled up in her emerald eyes. "I will leave you pistol upstream where you can find. You find white man, you be safe."

With a cry, she launched herself toward the black horse, setting a slim foot into the stirrup and swinging up into the saddle in a single fluid motion. In the same instant, Adam crossed the ground and caught the black's bridle.

"No!" he shouted.

Star Blanket pulled hard on the reins. The black reared, and one hind leg slipped on the damp leaves, nearly throwing them both to the ground. Adam clung to the bridle. In desperation, she brought the pistol within inches of Adam's head and pulled the trigger.

There was no explosion. Her surprise was so complete that she didn't even protest when an arm closed around her waist and pulled her from the saddle. She hit the ground hard and rolled, coming to rest at the base of an oak tree. She opened her eyes; Adam was standing over her, the pistol in his hand.

With a sigh, she shut her eyes. He would kill her now, and she deserved it. She waited for the blow.

"Get up from there!" Adam's voice was thick with anger. "I'm not going to hurt you, damn it. Get up!" He seized her shoulder and pulled her to her feet.

Shamed, Star Blanket kept her eyes on the ground, seeing only his black leather boots planted stubbornly before her.

"Look at me," he demanded. "You tried to kill me."

Green eyes met brown hesitantly. "The gun no fire," she said softly.

"Of course it didn't fire. It wasn't loaded."

White-hot fury stiffened her spine. "Not loaded! What kind fool are you? You give me gun at stockade to hold back English-*manake*. You give me gun without bullet?" She glared up into his face, her fists clenched.

"What kind of fool would I be if I gave *you* a loaded gun?"

Disbelief clouded her eyes. "You make me to face down the English-*manake* with an unloaded gun?"

"It fooled you, didn't it?" Steel fingers closed around her wrist and dragged her back toward the horses. "Your grandfather sent me to bring you home, and I intend to do it—with or without your consent." He pushed her down on a flat rock. "Sit there! No, don't say a word! Just listen."

A ribbon of fear wound its way up from her toes to tangle around her heart and close her throat. Her breathing became strained. She had misjudged this man. Badly. Controlled anger radiated from his huge body. Tensed muscles bulged under the linen shirt and stood out above the stock at his throat. Beneath the quiet surface lurked a cunning warrior capable of violence. She was suddenly afraid as she had never been afraid of the red-bearded Pennsylvanian.

"First, the militiamen who captured you, Colonel Steiner and the rest, are not English, they're Germans. German. Do you understand?" The brown eyes were shards of fire-hardened flint. "And *you* are not Shawnee. Your skin is white. You were born white. You are English-*manake* as far back as William the Conqueror and maybe before that. Put on all the paint and feathers you like, cover your body in skins, walk and talk like an Indian, but you're still English-*manake!*"

"I not." The stubborn chin quivered. "I am *equiwa*, woman." A hint of mischief danced behind her thick lashes. *"Manake* is Shawnee for 'man'. How can I be English-*manake?"*

"Second," he bellowed, ignoring her reply, "you've turned what should have been a pleasant journey into a tense and uncomfortable one. From now on, consider yourself a prisoner. You'll have to be tied to a horse to make sure you don't get away. It won't be easy for either of us, but you have only yourself to blame."

She shot him a defiant glance. "I am crazy Indian. Maybe I kill you after all."

"You're welcome to try." He turned toward the chestnut, slipping the bridle off and replacing it with a lead line around the animal's neck.

His back was to her. Star Blanket considered the possibility of running into the woods on foot, but hesitated. Would he follow? Could she reach cover and hide? Climb a tree?

As if reading her mind, he spoke in a tight, controlled voice. "If you move one muscle off that rock, I'll truss you up like a hog for butchering."

She sat still. "I not going anywhere."

"You're damn right you're not. At least not anywhere I don't want you to go." He turned his head in her direction. "I heard about what the militia did to your village, and I'm sorry. It was barbaric."

"What is this bar...barbar..."

"Inhuman. Cowardly. But you can't blame your own people for that. There are good and bad people, no matter what color skin they have. Indians killed your mother and father and your little brother. That was barbaric. Do you blame the Shawnee for that?" He led the chestnut over, put her in the saddle, and proceeded to tie her ankles under the horse's belly.

"I cannot ride like this!" she protested. "How can I make horse go where I want?" Her fingers opened and closed nervously as she reached for reins that weren't there. "Suppose horse falls?"

"You'd better hope he doesn't." Adam pulled the leather knot tight, then slid a finger between the thongs and her ankle to test the space between them. "If this rubs your leg too badly, I'll put something around it."

Star Blanket stared straight ahead. "Shawnee not kill. Iroquois kill. Shawnee scout save me, take me to people.

Iroquois barbar-bar-ick! Not Shawnee."

"If that's true, I guess we both have a lot to learn," Adam admitted. He mounted the black and headed off through the trees, leading the bay and her mount.

"You said we eat," she complained. "I am hungry."

"I thought Indian women were silent."

"You know nothing."

"I know you're not getting anything to eat until we stop for night camp." Adam's back was stiff, his voice still tinged with sarcasm. He bent low over the black's neck as they passed under a low-hanging branch.

Star Blanket ducked. "My grandfather would not want you to starve me." She tried to reach far enough to untie the leather thongs at her ankles. The bay nipped at her horse's rump, and the chestnut wheeled back, his teeth bared. Star Blanket grimly clutched the mane. "I do not like this!" she grumbled, feeling as helpless as a baby. She had not ridden this way since she was a small child.

Adam's black mood intensified, as they put distance between them and the stream. This girl was completely uncivilized! Bringing her back to Annapolis would be like turning a fox loose in a chicken coop. His stepfather was expecting a tender young woman, not an Amazon who could shoot a man in the head with a pistol from a foot away! The fact that she looked so innocent only made things worse. No one would believe his story. No matter what he said, it would look as if he were trying to discredit Rebecca Bradford to keep her from her rightful inheritance.

"Why you pay so much gold for me?" Rebecca asked, breaking the silence.

"I'll be damned if I know." If he'd had any sense at all, he'd have told the German they had the wrong girl. Thomas Bradford could have kept his gold, and he, Adam, would have been heir to Sheffield. It would have been only a matter of time before she gave Steiner the slip and returned to her precious Shawnee. Then everyone would have been happy.

He glanced back at her. She sat that damned saddle like some exotic princess, making even that wrinkled riding habit look like royal apparel. Thoughts of the smooth, tanned body beneath the garment disturbed him. You didn't get a tan like that with your clothes on. Adam's pulse quickened as he felt a familiar warmth in his loins. Damn it to hell! Why had the old man sent him on this errand? Why not somebody else? He ignored the fact that his role as rescuer and chaperone had been his own idea.

The girl's face was unmarked by pox, and her teeth were white and even. Those features by themselves would have made her a beauty in Annapolis or anywhere else in the colonies. Her chin was a bit too firm for a woman, but her lips were full and perfectly formed. Her brows were dark wings above expressive eyes, and it was hard to find fault with the slightly uptilted nose.

Adam dug his heels into the black's sides. What would it matter if Rebecca Bradford had the face of an angel—which she didn't—if she had the soul of a she-devil? Thinking about her only made his position worse. He pulled out his compass and checked his direction again. Once she was back at Sheffield, she would be someone else's problem.

Star Blanket's horse threw up his head and whinnied. From somewhere in the forest behind them came an answering nicker. "A-dam!" she called. "You hear that?"

He reined up tight. "What?" he asked suspiciously. Her face told him this was no joke. "What did you hear?"

"A horse, back there." She pointed in the direction from which they had come. "I hear something before, but I not sure. I think someone follow."

Adam ran a hand through his hair. "Indians, do you think?" He hoped not. What would he do if she had reinforcements? "Some of your Shawnee?"

Her brow became furrowed; she shook her head. "No Shawnee. Too far east. This Susquehannock land, or maybe Lenni Lenape. No use horse in forest. Man follow us on horse white man." Tendrils of hair had worked loose from the thick braid to curl about her face; she looked younger than her nineteen years. And she looked frightened.

"Can I believe you, or are these more lies?" He listened hard, hearing no sound except the soughing wind and the chattering of a gray squirrel.

"Man come. We go quick," she suggested. "Up there." She pointed to a rise of ground covered with large boulders. "Rocks hide horses. Hide us. We wait. See who comes. They not see us."

Adam looked unconvinced. "I don't hear anything. If this is another trick…"

"I hear."

Adam turned the animals uphill, urging them into a trot. When they reached the shelter of the rocks, he dismounted and tied the horses, then approached Star Blanket cautiously. "I'm going to let you down, but if you try anything, I'll knock you senseless," he said.

"Be quick. Horses come. Two riders," she whispered.

Adam untied her ankles and lifted her down. She sank to her knees and leaned against a rock. He pulled his musket from the saddle and loaded the pistol.

Seconds passed slowly; their breathing sounded unnaturally loud in Adam's ears. Star Blanket crept to the edge of the boulder and lay flat on her stomach beneath a concealing bush. Adam knelt beside her, one hand on the small of her back.

"Remember," he warned. "No tricks."

"Shhhh." She turned fierce eyes on him. "No talk. Listen."

The thundering *rat-a-tat-tat* of a pileated woodpecker echoed through the tall oaks. High in the trees, Star Blanket spied the flash of a black-and-white body. She lay a restraining hand on Adam's knee. Something had frightened the woodpecker.

Adam saw the first rider only a heartbeat later. The second rider was close behind. Two men wearing buckskins, each with a long musket cradled across his lap.

The horses stopped, and one of the men dismounted. He bent to examine the leaves.

"You see," Star Blanket whispered. "They follow."

The tracker looked vaguely familiar. "Can you make them out?" Adam asked softly. "Isn't that the redhead from Logan's Crossing?" The man was pointing in their general direction. At that rate, it wouldn't be long before they were trailed to their hiding place.

"What they want, these...these German?" Star Blanket breathed. "You have more gold?"

"No, but these horses are probably worth more than they'll see in a lifetime. And maybe they want you." Adam could feel the sweat trickling down his neck; his fingers tightened on the musket. He wished he'd brought another gun.

"You shoot," she suggested. "Before they see us."

Adam shook his head. "I can't. That would be murder. We don't know they mean us harm."

She gave him a look of pure disgust. "They take your scalp quicker than Susquehannock."

"Can you load a gun?" Adam dumped his powder horn and the bags containing ball and wadding on the ground. "If it comes to a fight, I'll need you to reload for me. Do you know how?"

She nodded. The fear he had seen in her eyes earlier was gone, replaced by a strange exhilaration. "I can shoot too, if you give me loaded pistol."

Overhead, there was an ominous rumbling. Branches swayed as the wind picked up. Leaves showed their underbellies, and the air suddenly turned cooler.

Star Blanket licked her lips and pressed close to Adam. A thunderstorm was coming; she didn't know if it would help them or make things worse.

The horses twitched their ears, their nostrils widening as they caught the scent of rain. Adam made soothing noises in their direction.

Below, the second man had dismounted and the two seemed to be arguing. Would the threat of the storm make them turn back? Adam considered firing a warning shot over their heads, then decided against it. It might be a waste of a bullet; it would also mean reloading and there might not be time.

The first drops of rain spattered against Star Blanket's face and arms. The wind gathered force as thunder sounded nearer. Saplings leaned, shedding their leaves before the gust. The raindrops made thudding sounds as they soaked into the dry leaves.

Adam thrust the pistol into her hand. "If we have to fight, just be sure you shoot them instead of me."

A flood of shame coursed through her veins, and she clutched the pistol in a death grip. Let the red-beard come within range, and I will show you a thing or two about shooting, she vowed silently.

Behind them, the chestnut raised his head and nickered. Adam leveled his musket and cursed under his breath as the Germans stared up the hill, then began to move toward them.

"What do you want?" Adam called, then ducked to safety as the redhead's musket roared an answer.

CHAPTER 4

"I tell you so." Star Blanket's faintly accented voice was accusing, yet held not a trace of fear. "If you shoot when I tell you, A-dam…" His hand shoved her hard against the ground, and she gasped as she got a mouthful of dirt.

"Get down! Do you want your head blown off?" Adam pinned her down with a knee and took aim carefully with the musket. Both men had taken cover behind a tree after the shot. The red-beard would be reloading, but the second man was an immediate danger.

Behind him, Adam heard the horses snorting in fear. He hoped the reins would hold, but he couldn't spare even a glance in their direction.

Something hard struck his knee, and he winced in pain, letting out an involuntary groan and grabbing his knee, seeing stars. The girl squirmed free, rolling away from him and coming to a catlike crouch just out of reach. Simultaneously, a musket spat smoke and fire and a rock exploded inches from Adam's head.

Adam felt the pain as rock fragments splattered his cheek and neck. A warm wetness trickled down his face just as red-beard leaned away from the tree and fired.

Adam squeezed off a shot, knowing he was high before the ball left the barrel. He cursed softly as he heard

Rebecca crawling away down the hill. Her betrayal would cause both their deaths. The certain knowledge that numbed his brain didn't stop his swift, methodical reloading of the musket. Grimly, he sheltered the pan with his body as he dumped in the proper amount of powder, his lips forming an unspoken prayer that the rain wouldn't prevent the powder from igniting.

Red-beard moved off to the left as the first man charged up the hill, then dove behind a low outcrop of sandstone. Adam finished reloading and waited. His next shot must count. If he was going to die on this nameless hillside, damned if he would be the only one.

Maybe the girl had been right to run; with luck she would escape, Adam thought wryly. His hands tightened on the musket stock. If she'd trusted him enough to stay and reload, maybe they both would have made it.

One of the two men would try to draw his fire, knowing that when he did, the other could rush him. Why had he been fool enough to hand over the pistol? If he still had it…But it was useless to surmise what might have been. His eyes narrowed as he peered through the misty rain for any sign of movement.

The forest was surprisingly clear of undergrowth; the tall trees blocked the light from the sun, making the forest floor almost parklike. Adam sighed, remembering the forest he had played in as a child on his father's estate. The gamekeeper, William, had taught him to seek out rabbit trails and to gauge the interval of time since a herd of deer had crossed the stream by the freshness of their delicate hoof-prints in the dark, wet soil.

A twig snapped with the crack of a gunshot. Adam swung the barrel of his musket toward the sound. Red-beard's musket boomed, followed immediately by the reverberation of a pistol. A man screamed as Adam's target moved into view.

He waited for what seemed a lifetime, his eyes sighting down the barrel, his finger squeezing the trigger gently, almost caressingly. Adam threw himself sideways even as the Pennsylvanian staggered and fell forward like a giant, broken puppet, his musket ball spending itself uselessly in the treetops.

Without stopping to reload, Adam hurled himself down the hill toward the remaining frontiersman. The man lay half reclining, his fingers swiftly reloading, tamping down the ball of his own musket. Blood soaked one knee of his leggings, and his scarred face was pale above the red beard.

From the corner of his eye, Adam spied Rebecca running for the shelter of the rocks. The grace of her movements proved she was unhurt.

Shale slid beneath Adam's feet as he plunged down the hill toward the man. For an instant, Adam's eyes made contact with the German's. "Don't do it!" Adam screamed.

Red-beard brought the musket up to fire point-blank. Instinctively, Adam smashed the butt of his own gun against the German's head. The sickening crunch of bone filled his ears, and he turned away in disgust as the man's blood ran out on the thick mat of pine needles.

Adam leaned against a tree, trying desperately to control his nausea as his gorge rose. He had never killed a man before. Now he had just taken two lives. The senselessness of it seized him, and he shook with a violent chill that ended only when he fell to his knees and was quietly sick.

"A-dam. A-dam." A woman's voice penetrated the blackness. "You are hurt, A-dam?" He felt a hand on his forehead, the touch warm and alive. Without thinking, he pulled her into his arms and held her against him, his heartbeat gradually slowing to normal, eased by the comfort of a living human body.

Star Blanket's first reaction to Adam's bear hug was fear. Her muscles tensed, then relaxed as she realized it was his pain that was in his mind. First blood. This had been A-dam's first kill. She had heard the women speak of it around the campfires.

She uttered a soothing sound, giving willingly of herself to heal his wound, as she would for any companion. Only minutes before they had been comrades, united against a common enemy. He had fought bravely, and she would not hold this shock to his soul against him. To take first blood was a step through a mystical doorway, a doorway that could not be entered twice, and one through which there was no exit.

Unconsciously she fell into the Shawnee tongue, whispering to him as she might a frightened child. For the space of a dozen breaths, he clung to her. Then his ragged breathing slowed, and he loosened his grip.

Star Blanket stepped away, watching intently as the earth brown eyes lost their glazed stare and the light of reason returned.

Adam dropped his eyes and wiped his mouth with the back of his hand, flushing when he realized what he had done. His body remembered the feel of her embrace and the clean smell of her hair even as his mind rejected the action of holding her so close. "I'm all right," he said hoarsely, "except for my knee. Why did you hit me?"

"I am no use on the ground. My aim is better than yours, English-*manake*. You shoot twice, hit one time. I shoot one time, hit him." She wrinkled her nose in disgust and kicked the prone body of the red-beard with her toe. "In the knee. Pistol no good from far away. I must get close. I better shot than you, A-dam."

"You nearly got us both killed." Adam rubbed at his aching knee. "Suppose you had broken my leg?"

Star Blanket shrugged. "I did not think you would break so easy. You push me, I push back." Her brow creased in a frown. She should have taken the horses and made her escape when Adam was sick. She was too soft. At first she had believed he was hurt. She glared up at him. "If you shoot when I tell you, I not need to hit your knee with pistol. Your fault, not mine."

Adam crossed the rugged ground to where the first man lay. Any hope that he was still alive vanished as Adam knelt beside him and placed a hand on his neck. Already, the German's flesh was cooling. The musket ball had taken him through the heart. "We'll have to bury them," Adam said, more to himself than to Rebecca. "Although how we can dig through these rocks with our hands is more than I can tell you."

"No." The girl shook her head. "No bury. You bury, German people know for sure who kill. Maybe come after us some more. Leave them where they lie. Take guns. Take horses. Steiner come, he think they killed by Indian. Lenni-Lenape. Susquehannock." She shrugged again, a faint rippling of her shoulders. "Only you fool enough to dig hole in rocks to bury enemy." She spat on the ground. "These not men, not warriors. They kill babies. Fit only for wolf bait."

"I suppose you want me to take their scalps too," he said sarcastically.

She considered his suggestion seriously, then shook her head. "No need. Unless you want scalp." She looked at him quizzically. "Is white custom?"

"No." Adam bent and retrieved the man's musket and powder horn, then forced himself to unstrap a belt with a sheathed hunting knife. The belt was stained with blood, and he wiped it on the leaves.

He couldn't deny the good sense of her suggestion. He didn't want to ride the rest of the way to Sheffield looking back over his shoulder, but the thought of leaving the bodies unburied was unnerving. How could he ever convey to his stepfather how much of a savage Rebecca had become? Any white woman would have been terrified by the attack, would have been sobbing with hysteria instead of comforting him.

"You're right," he admitted reluctantly. "But we'll let the horses go when we've put enough distance between us and this." He motioned toward the dead man. "I've no mind to put my neck in a noose by being caught with stolen horses."

Star Blanket's eyes widened incredulously. Abandon the horses? A-dam must be very rich if he could willingly lose two fine riding animals. She still clutched the pistol, hoping he would forget to take it from her. He didn't.

"Hand it over."

"I need pistol," she answered stubbornly. "I shoot better than you."

"You shoot nothing without ball and powder. Give it to me."

The threat in his eyes was enough. Sullenly, Star Blanket handed it over. He would not keep it long, she vowed. The pistol and some of the horses would return with her to the Ohio country. He owed her that much for saving his life.

Adam did not tie her to the saddle this time, but he did keep the lead line on her horse. They rode in silence through the dusk of early evening.

Gradually the rain ceased, and ghostly patches of fog rose from the forest floor. Sound became magnified; the soft footfalls of the horses beat a steady cadence against the carpet of decaying leaves and branches.

Even Adam's eyes began to fail him. It was more than the failing light—trees loomed before them, then seemed to vanish in the fog, only to appear again farther away. They passed a lightning-scarred oak and then, a short time later, another. Was it the same tree or not? He pulled out his compass and stared at the needle. It was too dark to see.

Star Blanket broke the silence. "You ride in circles, English-*manake*. Is this a plan to con...confoose the German warchief?"

"Confuse. The word is 'confuse,'" Adam snapped, jerking his horse up short. "Are you certain we're riding in circles?"

Her softly tinkling chuckle was the only answer. He could barely make out her features in the semidarkness. She pointed gracefully to the ravaged tree.

"The same one?" he asked, certain of her reply. The chuckle became a giggle.

"Same." She held up her fingers. "Three time."

"Damn!"

"Is better we stop for night, I think. More rain come soon. No one chase us tonight."

"Nobody but ghosts."

"No ghosts! No make laugh." Star Blanket looked nervously over her shoulder and spoke in a louder voice. "English-*manake* have powerful spirit friends."

Adam's eyes widened in surprise. "My God, Rebecca! You're serious. You actually believe in ghosts!"

"Ghosts real. Spirits real." There was no amusement in her tone now. "Bad night to ride. We make camp, build a fire. Shawnee no hunt tonight. Shawnee know about night spirits." She urged her horse up close beside Adam's mount and pointed to a rise on the left. "We go that way. Rocks...maybe shelter for camp."

The rain had become a drizzle before she found what she had been looking for—an overhanging rock with a deep enough recess to form a small cave. The niche in the rock was small, not high enough to allow Adam to stand upright, but there was enough room for them both to lie down and still build a fire at the front.

The horses were tied to stout trees and hobbled as a double protection. They would have to weather the rainfall as best they could. Star Blanket busied herself with gathering wood for the fire while Adam secured the animals.

No humans had taken shelter in the rough cave for many years, and a thick carpet of branches and twigs provided dry fuel for the fire. It took only a few seconds for Star Blanket to strike a spark from Adam's flint and steel, and a few more to coax the tiny embers into a glowing flame.

"You're handy to have along," Adam admitted good-naturedly as he squatted beside the fire and held out his hands to the welcome heat. "It would have taken me a lot longer to do that."

"Of course." Patiently, she fed the fire larger sticks until she was certain the fire would burn the damp log Adam had carried in from outside. Her spirits seem to rise with the flames, and she smiled at him as she spread blankets in the back of the cave. "Now we be dry and warm," she assured him. "No rain tomorrow. Tomorrow sun."

"I won't argue with that." He handed her a saddlebag. "There's a little food yet and water to wash it down with." He positioned the log so that the fire would ignite the edge and it would burn through the night. "I'm not used to making a fire without an axe, but I guess this will work."

"It will work. This is Indian fire, little fire. We stay warm, fire keep away bad spirits. Keep away wolf."

"If it keeps away wolves, that's all I ask," he teased.

She was beautiful in the firelight; a man would have to be made of wood not to notice. Flickers of light illuminated the lines of her face and body, and Adam felt the familiar tightness in his loins. He dropped his eyes for fear she would read the lust in them and only succeeded in noting the shapeliness of her legs and ankles beneath the hiked-up riding habit. A pulse pounded in his brain, and he forced himself to take deep, slow breaths. With a start, he realized Rebecca was holding out a handful of dried apples. He took them, painfully aware of the touch of her hand as it brushed against his.

Adam seized the goatskin water bottle and gulped down the warm liquid, spilling some carelessly down his chin in his haste. It was only the closeness of the shelter, the intimate confinement, he told himself. He was no sixteen-year-old boy to become suddenly tongue-tied at the nearness of an attractive female! A fresh wave of shame coursed through him. She was little more than a child and completely at his mercy. No, the devil within him whispered. Not a child, a woman…a very desirable woman. An image of her undressed body rose to haunt him, and his mouth went dry. He nervously ran a hand through his hair. He was acting like a fool, and he knew it.

"You are not hungry, A-dam?" Star Blanket settled on the blanket cross-legged and carefully ate her own portion of fruit and dried meat. She forced her face to remain expressionless, her eyes to reveal none of the plans forming in her head.

Tonight, when the English-*manake* was sleeping, she would make her escape. The precious muskets leaned against the rock—she would take all but one. And she would have the little pistol if it cost her life! It had become a symbol between them. Because they had fought the red-beard together, she would do A-dam no harm if she could help it.

She would leave him a horse and the means to defend himself.

She considered her decision, all the while watching him subtly through downcast eyes. Perhaps her white blood did make her soft, as a Shawnee girl had once accused. This man, A-dam, a man who should have been her enemy, tugged at the thongs of her heart. Was it weakness to feel compassion for him? She shrugged, a movement so slight that he did not seem to notice. A human should hurt no living thing without reason; it was against the laws of Wishemenetoo. She would spare the big English-*manake* that he might live to dandle his grandchildren on his knee and remember the gift of a Shawnee woman, the most precious gift that can be given—life.

Relieved that the decision which had been troubling her all day was resolved, Star Blanket moved over to share the sleeping space. She smiled at him with her eyes and said softly, "You will be wet if you stay on that side of the fire. There is room here, even for you. Come, A-dam. Sleep. We have come far this day."

His plain face shone with an inner light, brighter than that of the flames. *How could I have believed him ill-favored?* His eyes were a deep brown, as deep and as rich as a beaver pelt. *How tenderly they gazed at her.* He was as eager for a sign of friendship as any child.

Star Blanket motioned toward the blanket. "If you take the fever, you will be too sick to ride."

His huge bulk filled the rock shelter as he stepped over the log and folded himself into a sitting position, carefully avoiding contact with her. She stifled a chuckle. *Did he think she would bite?* No flicker of emotion showed on her face as she handed him another blanket. "The ground is hard. If it not rain, I make proper bed with pine..." She searched for the English word. "Leaf."

"Needles. Pine needles."

"No." She shook her head. "More than needle." The dark brows drew together as she struggled with old memories. "Bough! Pine bough! Make good bed. Clean. No bugs. No cramp in neck," she pronounced triumphantly "Boughs."

Adam's fingers itched to trace her feathery brows. His skin looked as soft and as smooth as silk, the tan no longer strange but natural and intriguing. Her lower lip was full and moist, shell pink...made for a man's lingering kiss.

Ruthlessly, he drove the traitorous thoughts to the deepest corners of his brain. Rebecca's grandfather had entrusted her to his care. She was his niece, for God's sake How could he tolerate such thoughts about her, even for an instant?

And even if he could sink so low, common sense should tell him she wasn't to be trusted. Hadn't she tried to kill him once? If the pistol had been loaded, she would have blown his brains out without blinking an eye. She was savage—as dangerous as a wild animal! If he made a mistake with her, it would be his last.

"Rebecca."

She eyed him suspiciously. Something in the tone of his voice caused the hairs to prickle at the back of her neck Although the sound of the name was strange, alien, she responded. "Yes?"

He forced his speech to brusqueness. "I don't want to do this, but I'm going to have to tie you."

"No!" Her muscles tensed for flight even as his hand shot out with a speed she would have thought impossible. As his iron fingers tightened around her wrist, she struggled fiercely against him, striking out with her free hand and uttering cries of fury.

One fist struck his mouth, splitting his upper lip and sending a trickle of blood down his chin. In desperation, he pulled her against him, entrapping her against his massive chest and pinning her flailing arms to her sides.

"Stop it! Stop it, Rebecca!" he ordered. "I don't want to hurt you!"

"Coward!" she spat. "English dog!" Viciously, she sunk her teeth into his arm.

Adam let out a cry of pain and pushed her down onto the blanket, flinging himself on top of her. "Stop it, I said!"

"Let me go!"

"Rebecca." Anger washed over him in black waves. "You're making me hurt you!" He held both her wrists above her head and blocked her thrashing legs with his own. "Lie still, damn it! I'm not going to hurt you."

Her breath came in ragged gasps; her heart was pounding so hard she could hardly make out the English words A-dam was saying. The thick taste of fear was like old copper in her mouth. "Let me go," she repeated futilely. No amount of inner control could stay the tears that welled up in her green eyes.

"Rebecca," he repeated, panting. He eased the pressure on one wrist, and she nearly wrenched it free. Her wiry strength amazed him. His lip stung, and it required all his concentration to hold her without hurting her. "For God's sake, Rebecca," he pleaded.

The scent of him was overpowering. The sheer male power filled her nostrils. His face was barely inches from her own; his breath was hot on her cheek.

Star Blanket blinked to clear her eyes of the hated tears and forced her panic to recede. If the *English-manake* meant to ravage her body, he would have done so by now. The thought calmed her, and she shut her eyes and went limp.

"Rebecca? Rebecca, are you all right?" Strong hands gripped her shoulders and shook them. The strange-sounding name was shouted in her ear over and over.

Deep within the secret recesses of her mind, she heard the loud voice, heard and ignored it. He could not touch her there. He did not even know where to look.

There, her spirit voices could give her wise council, and she could rest and prepare a new plan of action. The borders of the shadow world enfolded her. A-dam faded away until his touch on her body was only a memory and his pleas an echo on the wind.

"Damn it, Rebecca." Her breathing was shallow but steady. She's fainted. What did you do for a fainting woman? Adam searched his brain for the answer. Fainting had been common enough in social circles in England, but there had always been maids and clucking women to tend to the victim. He hadn't thought Rebecca to be the fainting type. He knew he hadn't hurt her, at least not enough to cause this. Could the girl be having some kind of spell?

If she was having a spell, you couldn't give water. She might choke on it. Could it be another trick? Gently he lay her back on the blanket and pulled her skirts down over her legs. She seemed almost in a deep sleep, with none of the paleness he associated with fainting or a fit.

"Rebecca?" he called softly. There was no reaction; she might have been carved of stone, except stone didn't breathe. If it was a trick, it was a damned good one.

He murmured her name again. God, but he felt rotten. He wiped at his bloody lip with the back of his hand and swallowed the lump in his throat. "Rebecca, please."

From far away she watched him, her heart touched by the concern in his voice. She felt vaguely ashamed…guilty to worry A-dam so. What was wrong with her that she could not remember he was the enemy?

Puzzled, she felt him take hold of her left wrist and bind a leather thong about it. Then he cradled her body against his and pulled a blanket over them both. How strange it was to feel the rise and fall of an enemy's chest, to feel the pulse of his blood.

Curious, she allowed herself to rise a little from the deep trance. His arms were around her…she felt their strength…felt the tickle of the golden brown hairs on the back of his wrist. Were all white men as hairy as bears? she wondered.

Adam felt the change in Rebecca's breathing. "Rebecca? Are you all right?" He couldn't see her face. "You don't have to be afraid. I'm not going to hurt you." He spoke slowly, as though to a child. "Only your wrist is tied to mine. Do you understand? To keep you from running away in the night."

She released a deep sigh, coming back into her body. "I am not afraid," she lied. "Why should I fear you?" But she did fear. She was glad her face was turned away from the fire so he could not see it. She was confused, bewildered. But the fear was not of A-dam; the fear was of her own heart. Never had her thoughts been so disturbing. She could not accept A-dam as her enemy. And if he was not...If he was not her enemy, then it followed that all English-*manake* were not her enemies. Did she feel this way because she had been born white? She had believed herself to be a true daughter of the Shawnee. If she was not Shawnee and not white, then who was she?

"I do not like this," she said.

Relieved that she sounded so natural, Adam's spirits lightened. "I didn't think you would. But once I was asleep, the Lord only knows what mischief you would have gotten into. I am taking you home to Sheffield, and the day will come when you'll thank me for it."

Her answer was quick, a rapid-fire discourse in Shawnee. For once, Adam was almost glad he didn't comprehend the Indian tongue.

"I don't know what you said, but I guess I understand your meaning," he admitted. He was beginning to wish he had tied her like a hog for slaughter. Then he could have put the fire between them at least.

As it was, Rebecca's head was under his chin, her soft, woman-scented hair brushing against his throat with every breath she took. Her round bottom nestled against his midsection, bringing more warmth to his loins than he needed even on a wet, damp night. He was even more acutely aware of the curve of her breasts beneath his arm.

A light sheen of moisture broke out on his forehead as he tried to move as far away from Rebecca as possible yet still keep her encircled by his arms.

Mystified by his contradictory behavior, Star Blanket settled into a comfortable spot. Her mind continued to analyze the situation even as her muscles relaxed. A-dam's actions made no sense at all. He was treating her gently, speaking to her as though he cared for her, yet his body was withdrawing from her as though she were something unclean. Did he hold her in contempt for living with the Shawnee? Did he think the People were less than human? His attitude did much to still the confusion in her own mind. They were not alike! He was English-*manake*. She was Shawnee. She must conquer the softness in her heart for him. Tomorrow or the next day she would make good her escape. There were many days' ride between this place and the waters of the Chesapeake. She would watch and wait. Her chance would come. And this time, she must not fail.

Star Blanket shifted a little on the hard ground and the back of her thigh accidently brushed against A-dam's manhood. A flash of comprehension burst across her mind with the brilliance of a shooting star. He desired her! It was not disgust that made him pull away but desire. With great effort, she choked down a chuckle. There was no mistaking what she had felt.

With a sleepy sigh, she nestled down, allowing her body to mold to his in seemingly innocent sleep, certain he could not see the smile that turned up the corners of her mouth. It might not be such a bad thing, she decided, if she were well rested in the morning and her enemy was not.

CHAPTER 5

Star Blanket noted with great satisfaction the swollen lip and dark smudges under A-dam's eyes as they saddled the horses the next morning. She had slept well enough herself; A-dam's great body had kept her as warm and snug as a bear in its den.

"We'll ride an hour or so before we stop to eat," he announced. "I'd like to put as many miles as possible between us and those bodies."

He had unfastened the bonds that held her fast to him but had given her orders not to move an eyelash until they were ready to ride. Dutifully, she obeyed, sitting meekly with her hands in her lap and her eyes downcast.

Her acquiescence lasted until Adam began to loosen the halter on the nearest of the dead men's horses. "No!" she cried. "What do you do, English-*manake?*" She jumped to her feet, crossed the distance between them, and squeezed between him and the animal. "Why you do this?" she demanded.

"I told you, I'm going to let them loose. I'm not going to be charged with both murder and horse stealing if I can help it." He reached for the halter again, but she grabbed his hand.

"No, A-dam! You cannot!" She searched for a reasonable excuse to give him. "Wolves. If you let these fine horses go, wolves will eat them. You cannot be so...so cruel." Passionately, she threw her arms around the gelding's neck. "He too fine an animal to die for no thing!"

Adam dropped his hand. "I hadn't thought about the wolves," he admitted. "But we've got to do something with them."

"Yes," she agreed. "You must do something." She stroked the bay's neck. "You will think of something, A-dam. But you cannot let them die." She looked up at him, her lower lip quivering faintly. "Please, A-dam."

He shrugged. "All right. We'll keep them with us for now." He hoped he wouldn't live to regret the decision.

Once again, he tied her ankles under the horse. Even though her hands were free, Star Blanket's horse was guided by a lead line with no reins she could reach. She knew it was A-dam's revenge for her victory over the captured horses, and she didn't let it trouble her. If he was suspicious over her lack of protest when he tied her on the animal, he had given no sign of it. Perhaps he thought she had given up her attempts to escape. If so, all the better. She would not be fool enough to give him reason to be on guard again.

The rain had stopped, and rays of sunshine spilled through the verdant roof of the forest. Birds trilled bright melodies overhead, and there were flashes of rust brown and dull red and sometimes a brilliant red as birds fluttered from branch to branch.

Squirrels and chipmunks raced up and down the trunks of trees with a complete disregard for life and limb, often pausing to chatter angrily at the human intruders. One squirrel, his silky coat so dark it was almost black, had his cheeks so crammed with nuts that he looked to Star Blanket like an old man.

"Oh, A-dam," she called, "look at him." As her horse passed close to the tree, the squirrel scampered up and dove into a hole, immediately bobbing his head back out to glare at them.

Adam laughed. "Right now I'd rather see him grilled or even served up in a stew with biscuits. I'm starving." He continued gently, "It's not A-dam, Rebecca. Listen to the way I say it. Adam, not Ad-damn."

She wrinkled her nose in distaste. "Adam."

He shook his head and repeated the syllables again.

"Adam."

"Better," he said. The soft Indian pronunciation was more musical, not so plain and hard. "You'll have to listen and try to make your speech more like mine."

"Why? You do not like my words?"

"It's got nothing to do with my liking or not liking. But people will expect...Oh, never mind, Rebecca. Your grandfather will explain it to you." He clicked to his horse, pretending to give all his attention to the faint trail ahead. How could he admit the thrill he felt each time she said his name in a way no one else had ever said it? Better to cut short the torture even at the risk of hurting her feelings. It was for her own good, after all. People would expect her to act and speak like a Bradford, not an Indian squaw.

"But, Adam, I—"

Adam's horse shied as an arrow plunged into a tree beside him. "Rebecca, get down!" he yelled, bringing his musket up to fire.

Star Blanket yelled something in Indian, then switched to English. "No, Adam! Don't shoot!" She spoke again in Shawnee and pointed to a low-hanging cedar. "There, Adam. See. Is only a boy."

Adam's black horse snorted and half reared as a child stepped onto the path ahead, a drawn bow in his small hands.

"Put down your gun," Star Blanket insisted. "He is alone."

"Maybe, maybe not. Tell him to lower his bow." Adam's eyes searched the forest for signs of movement. His mouth was dry, and the hair on his neck prickled. A little closer and he might have been killed by a brat who hardly looked old enough to be of school age!

Star Blanket argued in Shawnee with the boy for a few minutes; then he released the tension on his bowstring and removed the arrow, dropping it into the quiver on his back.

He stared at Adam, frowned, then motioned for them to follow him.

Star Blanket smelled the smoke of a campfire long before they reached the edge of the clearing. The boy led them around a cornfield that was as yet unharvested, toward a low, bark-covered shelter.

An old woman squatted beside the fire, turning corn cakes on a cast-iron griddle. She looked up in surprise at the riders, then called out a greeting in the Delaware tongue.

"We bid you peace," Star Blanket answered loudly in the same language. "Blessings on you and on this house."

The wrinkled face split into a toothless smile. She stood up slowly and directed questions to the boy.

"What's he saying to her?" Adam asked. "Do you understand them?" He thought the speech was much like Rebecca's Shawnee language, but he couldn't be certain.

"They are Lenni Lenape, what you call Delaware. They are of the Wolf Clan." Rebecca asked a quick question in Algonquian, then waited patiently as the old woman answered at length.

"They're not Shawnee?" Adam drew his horse close to Rebecca's. "Are there men about?"

"No, not Shawnee, Delaware. Shawnee, Delaware, Fox." Rebecca motioned with her hand. "Many tribe speak same tongue. We are..." She searched for the correct word. "Cousin. The Shawnee are cousin to the Delaware." She smiled reassuringly at the woman. "Her name is Ma-tethi-i-thi E-shi-que-chi, Ugly Face. The boy is her grandson." Star Blanket paused, then continued to translate. "There are two braves in this wigwam, but they are away hunting. That's why the boy shot his arrow at you. Now he hangs his head in shame. He did a foolish thing to attack an armed

man without reason. We are welcome to share their food."
She looked at Adam expectantly. "It will be an insult if we
refuse."

The boy ducked his head to enter the small dwelling,
letting the skin flap fall behind him. With hand motions and
rapid speech, the grandmother repeated her invitation.

"How do we know it's safe?" Adam ventured.

Star Blanket laughed. "You are not afraid of one old
woman and a small boy, English-*manake?* Is safe." She
motioned toward the cornfield. "These people farmers, not
warriors. If you do not take her food, the old woman will be
afraid of you." She looked into his eyes guilelessly. "I tell
them I am your wife."

"My wife? Tied to a horse?"

"I say I am bad wife." She covered a giggle with the
palm of her hand. "Come, A-dam, you say you are hungry.
Let us eat while the corn cakes are hot."

Cautiously, Adam dismounted and walked toward the
wigwam. He pushed aside the skin flap with the barrel of
his musket and peered inside the dim interior. "Tell the old
woman we mean no harm," he said. He blinked, letting his
eyes become accustomed to the faint light.

There was no movement in the hut. The walls were hung
with bundles of animal hides and strips of dried pumpkin
and squash; a large pottery bowl full of beans was propped
in the center of the round dwelling, directly under the
smoke hole. On the far side of the cold fire pit the boy
huddled, his eyes clenched shut.

Adam sniffed, noting the unfamiliar but not unpleasant
odors. Herbs and tobacco mingled with the musky scent of
a bearskin and the sweet smell of freshly peeled willow
wands.

Rebecca had been telling the truth. There was nothing
here to fear. He turned to the two women and smiled. "Tell
her thank you. We would be honored to eat with her," he
said formally. "Tell her that her grandson has no need to be
ashamed. He showed courage. I am not angry with him."

Star Blanket translated as Adam untied her ankles and lifted her down from the horse.

A wide grin covered the old woman's face. Unconsciously, she straightened her back as she motioned them toward the fire. For an instant, Adam saw her not as she was, leathery faced with snow white hair, but young and graceful. The old eyes twinkled and met his in perfect understanding. Then the high voice shouted an order to the boy. Shyly, he joined her, and they began to serve their guests.

It was nearly an hour before Star Blanket and Adam remounted. Adam was pleasantly full for the first time since leaving Sheffield, stuffed with the delicious corn cakes, grilled trout, and a hearty venison stew. A hind-quarter of venison was strapped to the back of the packhorse. Sometime during the meal, Star Blanket had talked their hosts out of enough supplies to keep them well fed for several days.

"What do they want in return?" Adam asked suspiciously.

Star Blanket shook her head vigorously. "No, you no understand, Adam. Is not a trade, is a gift. Now…" A suspicious glimmer appeared in her green eyes. "Now you must make a worthy gift."

Adam took Rebecca firmly about the waist and lifted her into the saddle of the black horse. "Such as?" Something told him she had already decided on a worthy gift.

"The two horses we took from the dead Germans," she replied softly. "One for the boy and one for the *cocum tha*—the grandmother. It is a noble gift, worthy of a warrior such as Adam Rourke." Her slim hands reached for the reins. "You cannot eat their food and insult them, English-*manake.*"

Adam arched one thick brow dubiously. "And you think it shows good manners to return their hospitality with stolen horses? What happens if Steiner comes after the horses and hangs the both of them? Is that what you call fair?" He set a foot in the stirrup of his own mount.

"I promise the horses," Star Blanket said stubbornly. "I tell Ugly Face that you kill the bad men and take their horses. I tell her that you would leave them for the wolves." An undisguised note of satisfaction crept into her voice. "I say you are very brave for English-*manake* and not a baby killer."

"You told them?" Adam dropped into the saddle and stared at her. "You told them we killed the Germans?"

Star Blanket threw him a look of disgust. "They are Wolf Clan of the Lenni Lenape, Adam Rourke. They will not tell. Not if Steiner cut off their fingers one by one and throw them into the cooking fire. Not if—"

"You've made your point." Adam glanced from Rebecca to the old woman, who was grinning broadly and mumbling something to the boy.

The child dashed off into the bushes and returned a few minutes later leading a slim-legged bay mare with a white star on her forehead. Proudly, he handed the lead rope to Rebecca.

"Ugly Face gives us this fine mare," Rebecca proclaimed. "It is her gift. We cannot refuse."

"You traded those two stolen horses for the bay!"

"I did not!" Star Blanket protested.

"Damn it, woman! I will not be manipulated! You've put these people in danger."

"I have not," she replied hotly. "The *cocumtha* will trade our horses to the Susquehannock. He will trade to English-*manake*, who will trade to Dutch farmer, there." She pointed northeast. "Your head is like wood, Adam Rourke. Germans dead, wolf bait. They do not need their horses. You do not want the horses. The *cocumtha* does." She paused for breath. "We have a good mare. We have food for journey. Old woman and boy are happy. I am happy. Horses are not wolf bait. Only you are not happy." She shrugged. "Maybe English-*manake* too stupid to be happy."

Adam gritted his teeth and dug his heels into his horse, guiding the animal onto the rough track and away from the

Indian camp at a trot. At that moment, he didn't care if Rebecca followed or not.

They rode in silence for a long time. The trail widened and became a rutted road, wide enough in most spots for a cart or small wagon to pass. Twice, they forded small creeks, one deep enough so that the water came up to the animals' chests.

On the far side, they dismounted and let the animals eat some of the thick grass on the stream bank while they shared the remainder of the corn cakes.

"You are still angry," Star Blanket ventured, as she knelt beside the fast-running water and cupped her hands to drink.

"Yes," he admitted, "I am." Adam carried the musket in the crook of his arm. Even though they had not seen a trace of another living soul, he was unwilling to let down his guard. The memory of the boy's arrow was too fresh in his mind.

"I think so." She drank deeply, splashing the cool water on her face and rinsing her hands free of crumbs. "If I tell you first, you say no. No give horses." She shrugged. "So I not tell until it is too late." She offered him a shy smile. You do have a head of wood, she thought. Anyone could see that trading the stolen horses made sense. Still, she must placate him. If he was angry with her, it would be harder to make her escape.

And it must be soon. Tonight at the latest. She must win her freedom before they came too close to the settlements along the Chesapeake. Here, in the forests, she could find her way. She would use the path of the sun by day and the stars by night. They would blaze a trail for her, a trail that any Shawnee child could follow, a trail that would lead home to the Ohio country and her people.

When she was free, she would travel so fast on the fine English horses that no man could catch her. She could ride for many days and nights without sleep—she had done it before in times of war. She would bring home the horses and the little pistol. She would be a rich woman, rich enough to win the attention of any man she desired.

Star Blanket mounted again and rode docilely behind Adam. Her hands guided the horse, her eyes watched the trail, and her lips answered when Adam spoke to her. But her mind was far away. Clearer than the soft brown mane beneath her fingers was the image of a Shawnee warrior, a warrior with a scar over his right eye. Meshepeshe, the Panther. Meshepeshe with his laughing eyes. Meshepeshe who had offered her his blanket at the last Corn Dance, then chose another when she refused him.

A smile curved her full bottom lip. Meshepeshe had danced with She Who Whispers, wrapping her in his French trade blanket of scarlet wool. Later, they had slipped away in the moonlight as many couples did during the Corn Dance. He had hoped to make Star Blanket jealous. She sighed, wondering even now why she hadn't been.

She Who Whispers was free with her favors—too free, the old women said, even for a widow. Her body was soft and full, and she had a pleasing face. Yet Meshepeshe's eyes had followed Star Blanket as his feet had followed the steps of the Corn Dance. His arms had held She Who Whispers, while his heart had longed for another.

Star Blanket's smile grew into a throaty chuckle. A widow could do as she pleased among the Shawnee. A wife must remain faithful and a maiden pure, but a widow made her own choices without blame. She herself had been widowed two...no—how fast the moons flew by—she had been a widow for nearly three years as the white men counted. So long. There were times when she could not even remember the gentle boy who had been her husband. A little shiver passed through her. How could she forget him so easily?

He who had been her husband, the one whose name she could not speak, had been her friend since the first day she had come to live with the Shawnee. Inu-msi-ila-fe-wanu, the Great Female Spirit, had seen fit to have this child born with a crooked foot. Never had the boy been able to run, or even to walk, without limping. Only in the water had he been free of his handicap. Give him a creek or river to swim in and he became an otter! He won the prizes for swimming even against full-grown warriors.

And in fairness, because the Great Spirit had held back something at his birth, he had been gifted with a wonderful skill. His hands knew the secrets of stone and copper. Arrowheads and spearpoints, axes and amulets, came as if by magic from shapeless rocks at his hearth. He was a poor hunter, having little strength to track game or to bring it home once it had been slain, but his arrowheads had brought down more animals than there were stars in the sky.

And, wonder of wonders, he had been a spinner of stories. Marvelous tales! Tales of how the earth was formed and how the People came to be spilled from its lips. Star Blanket had sat by the hour listening to his stories when they were children. And later, when they had passed from childhood into man and maiden, they had joined in marriage.

Star Blanket swallowed a lump in her throat and blinked away the moisture in her eyes. She would not forget him! His spirit had been stronger than his body, and she would not let that spirit fade away.

A tear slipped down her tanned cheek, and she wiped it ruthlessly away. He had told her not to cry for him. He had made her promise.

They had married in the time of the young corn. His withered body had been laid in the earth before the first snowflake fell in winter. So short a time...

Star Blanket sighed. She had returned to her father's house, a widow before she had really become a wife. That first winter had passed in sorrow. Spring, with its first green shoots of life, had brought back her laughter, and by summer she could think of him and remember his wonderful stories. By the time the geese flew south in the time of turning leaves, she had ceased to hate the white men who had brought the sickness to her people, and she had learned the name of her husband's murderer—measles. That winter had brought healing to her troubled soul, and in the greening time, her parents had begun to suggest that she think of marrying again.

Star Blanket dug her heels into her horse's side and guided it close to Adam. Many men had boasted before her father's wigwam, and Meshepeshe had even tied his horse there for two days and two nights. But she had not fed it or even offered the animal water. She was not ready to choose another. Sometimes she wondered if she ever would be.

"Adam! Adam!" she called.

He turned his head to look down at her. "What is it? What's wrong?"

"Nothing." She laughed. "Nothing is wrong, English-*manake*. I only think of something funny. I think you are right. You wanted to give the fine horses of the Germans to the wolves." Her emerald eyes twinkled mischievously. "I argued with you, Adam. But..." She shrugged. "The wolves got them anyway, didn't they?" She waited expectantly for him to join her in shared laughter. "The horses," she repeated. "It was meant to be."

Adam's brow creased in puzzlement. "What? I don't understand. The wolves didn't get them. You traded them to those Delaware."

Giggling, Star Blanket covered her mouth with her hand. "You not see?" she gasped between spurts of laughter. "You not see, Adam? The Delaware are the wolves! They are Wolf Clan."

Feeling foolish, Adam ran a hand through his hair and forced smile. "I guess you're right," he admitted weakly. "In a manner of speaking, the wolves did get the horses."

"Wooden head," she taunted. "You English, you cannot laugh. Is funny." Shaking her head at the unfathomable reasoning of the whites, Star Blanket let the black horse fall back into line. *No wonder we cannot understand each other. The whites are just not very intelligent.* Still, it was hard to think of Adam Rourke as stupid. *There must be some other explanation for his lack of humor,* she decided. *It does not matter. After tonight, I will never see him again.* She wondered why the thought gave her little satisfaction.

CHAPTER 6

To Star Blanket's dismay, the opportunity to escape did not come that night or even the following night. Before dark, they came upon a settler's cabin nestled in the fold of a hill. Starved for news of the outer world, the isolated family would hear of nothing but that the two eat supper and sleep under a solid roof.

The family consisted of a man and his wife, three sons, a daughter, and the man's grown brother. Star Blanket didn't think she'd ever seen so many bodies packed into one house.

After a supper of salty corn mush and mutton stew, the group gathered around Adam and listened to his tales of the Chesapeake Bay country. Despite their genuine attempts at courtesy, Star Blanket felt uncomfortable. She was certain everyone was staring at her, probably thinking she was not quite human.

Sleep was almost impossible on the thin cornhusk mattress laid out on the hard-packed dirt floor. The door and window were shut and barred, and the air soon became close and stuffy. Coughs, groans, and snores filled her ears; she covered them with her hands to try and keep out the offensive sounds. The fire burning on the hearth made the room even hotter. The unfamiliar smells and unmistakable sensation of crawling vermin kept her scratching and rolling on the sour bedding.

Adam lay between her and the door; she would have to crawl over him to reach the latch. Angrily, she rolled onto her back and stared up at the dark rafters overhead. Flickering light from the fire showed cobwebs and soot-blackened walls and ceiling. Was this what Maryland would be like? She didn't remember anything like this. What she did remember of her English home was clean and soft and happy. What if all the English were dirty? She knew she could not bear it!

A flea bit viciously at her ankle; she caught it and cracked it between her fingernails, swearing under her breath in broken English. There were no swear words in Shawnee; nothing but English would do to express the rage she felt at such foul treatment.

Star Blanket's anger was still fresh as they rode away from the cabin in the faint purple light of early dawn. She inhaled great gulps of fresh air, noting with no little satisfaction that Adam's eyes were red from lack of sleep. His distaste for the accommodations had been as genuine as her own, and he said so in no uncertain terms.

"I not choose to sleep there!" Star Blanket flung at his back. "The Shawnee do not sleep with bugs!"

Adam tore off his hat and scratched violently at his hair. "I'm sorry. I didn't want to hurt their feelings. They don't see many strangers, and they wanted to hear the news from England."

"We ate with the Delaware and did not come away smelling like half-cured skunk hides."

"I said I was sorry!"

Star Blanket had hoped a lack of sleep would make Adam careless; it seemed to have the opposite effect. He did not permit her to wander more than an arm's length away when they stopped to bathe. They built a fire with green wood, and she showed him how to hold his clothes over the smoke to kill the vermin. He insisted that she cover her body with a blanket while they rid themselves of the biting pests, and he did the same.

"I not know why you are ashamed of your body," she repeated after they were mounted and riding southeast once more. "It make no sense."

"You're a woman and I'm a man. It's proper." He sighed, the back of his neck turning a dark red. "It's not proper for us to be together like this at all, but there was no way around it. Because we are alone, we have to be even more careful not to break the rules."

Star Blanket thought about that for a few moments, then ventured an opinion. "You mean, Adam Rourke, if other English-*manake* riding with us, it would be all right to take off my clothes?"

"No! It would never be right." He swung his body around and glared fiercely. "You don't take off your clothes in front of a man, any man. Not unless he's your husband and then only if you are alone."

"I can take them off in front of English woman?"

"No. Not in front of a woman, not unless she's your maid."

Star Blanket moistened her lips with the tip of a pink tongue. "What is this maid, Adam Rourke? And why do I take off clothes in front of her? Does she like to see another woman's body?" She shook her head until the heavy braid swung to and fro. "I not take off my clothes in front of that kind of woman. Not Shawnee custom." She wrinkled her nose. "I think I keep my own ways. English ways bad."

"You don't understand," he explained patiently. "A maid is a woman or a girl who is paid to wash your clothes and help you dress. She'll do up your hair and keep your bedchamber clean. It's all right to dress in front of her, but..." Adam searched for the right words. "She doesn't *like* to watch you. It isn't like that. She is paid to do things for you. It's her job, her way of making a living."

"Maid not want to watch me, I not want to be watched by strange English woman. Star Blanket can braid own hair. Is foolish. Why can't English woman wash own clothes? Too lazy?"

"It's got nothing to do with being lazy. It's the custom, Rebecca." Adam was sorry he'd ever gotten into the conversation to begin with. "Your grandfather is a very important man. People expect him to have many servants. As his granddaughter and his heir, you have to have servants-maids. It's a matter of…of honor."

"Grandfather's honor, Grandfather's maid. Let him take off clothes in front of crazy English maid. Star Blanket does not," she said stubbornly.

"Fine. Do as you like. Just be sure you keep your clothes on in front of men until you're married."

"I will do what I wish. I am Shawnee. I am a free woman." Silently, she added, You will go back to your crazy English alone.

Every mile the horses carried them from the Ohio country was another mile she would have to retrace alone. Star Blanket began to feel uneasy deep within herself. It was farther than she thought to the Chesapeake. Perhaps she should ride straight west toward the setting sun. Eventually, she would come to the Ohio River. Then it would be a simple matter to follow it north to the land of the Shawnee. That way, she would not have to backtrack through this land. It might be faster and safer. That way, if Adam did try to hunt her down, she would lose him easily. She would have to decide soon.

That night they camped beside a shallow creek, and Adam tied her wrist to his as he had when they slept in the rock overhang. It was a bitter disappointment, but she took care not to let it show. She must convince him she had given up the idea of escaping. Like the fox, she would be crafty. She would ask questions about the grandfather's home and pretend interest in Adam's answers.

Both of them were exhausted, and sleep came quickly. Star Blanket did not stir until Adam shook her gently awake the next morning. Startled, she sat bolt upright and rubbed at her eyes with her free hand.

"The sun's well up," he said. "It's time we were in the saddle. We'll cross the Susquehanna today."

Star Blanket watched unspeaking as he untied her wrist. Adam had been cold to her the night before, taking care not to touch her. She lowered her eyes so he couldn't read the wisdom there. He wanted to touch her. She knew it, and Adam knew it. He could pretend otherwise, but he couldn't outfox a Shawnee fox.

She offered him a shy smile. Perhaps today would be the day. If Adam let down his guard for even a moment, she would be gone.

They ate in silence, drank from the creek, then saddled the horses and rode south.

In early afternoon they passed a white man riding in the opposite direction on a mule. He and Adam exchanged curt greetings, and the man passed on.

"We'll be coming to the Susquehanna before nightfall," Adam said. "He says it's in flood."

"I have ears."

"It was calm enough when I crossed before. This isn't the time of year for flooding." Worry furrowed his brow. "The Susquehanna can be dangerous, but we've got to ford it. It's too far to ride around. It would take us days out of our way."

"Perhaps there has been rain in the mountains, Adam." She took care not to let him see her rising excitement.! A delay could only aid her escape plans. "I do not know your Susquehanna, but I know the Ohio. Rain far away can turn the river into place of great danger."

"That's probably it. Damn it." He took off his tricorn hat and wiped his brow. "It's wide but not too deep at the crossing, though there are deep holes and rocks that can trap the horses' legs." Adam straightened his shoulders and shifted the reins in his broad hands. "We'll find a way across, or we'll just wait until the water goes down," he said, more to himself than to her. "I know the trail on the far side of the river."

Mentally, he counted the days until they could expect to reach the Chesapeake. Rebecca had taken the journey far more easily than he would have believed possible. They would push the horses even harder and make more miles per day. He had to deliver her safely to her grandfather, and the sooner the better. The nights alone with her were torture. Once they reached Sheffield, his mission would be accomplished. It wouldn't be soon enough to suit him!

"Adam, you have wife?"

The question startled him out of his reverie. "I beg your pardon?"

"Do you have wife?" she persisted. "Children?"

"No. No wife, no children." He fixed his gaze on the trail ahead.

"Why?" She tilted her head to look up at him. "You are old enough to have sons, Adam Rourke. Do you like women?"

His lips tightened, compressed to a thin slash across his face. If he ignored her, perhaps she would be still.

Digging a heel into her horse's side, she brought the animal up next to Adam's and tapped his arm. "You think I do not hear. *You* do not hear. Are you a man who likes other men?"

A single muscle twitched in his taut jawline. "No! I like women." He glared at her. "Why would you ask such a thing?"

"You do not like me. Maybe you do not like any woman. Maybe you like man. I do not know you, Adam Rourke. I only ask. Is wrong to ask?"

"Yes." He fought for patience. "It's wrong to ask personal questions. And asking *that* particular question is an insult. I like women well enough. I've just never met any I wanted to marry."

It was a half-truth. No need to attempt to explain to Rebecca that he had been educated to take his place in English society, that his birth had led him to expect he would be received in the finer houses. If his father had not lost the family fortune, he would have been married by now to a woman of his own station in life. Adam sighed. All that was impossible now. As a bondman, he could not marry without his master's permission. And the women he could have chosen seemed like peasants, with their rough manners and uneducated speech.

Even now, now that he had earned his freedom and was considered to be the heir to Sheffield, there was a stain on his name. What plantation owner would want his daughter to marry a former bondservant?

Adam remembered that he was no longer the heir to Sheffield and laughed wryly. Good luck to his stepfather in finding a husband for Rebecca! It would be next to impossible. *She* was impossible. He could imagine her at a hunt ball, turning to her dance partner and asking if he liked women or only men. The laugh became a broad grin. He'd give his best coat to see it.

"I have husband, and I am not so old as you."

Adam's head snapped around. Incredulously, he stared at her. "You're married? To an Indian?"

Star Blanket recoiled from the shock of his reaction. "Of course my husband is Shawnee! Do you think I would marry with English-*manake*?" she scoffed.

Adam's heart lurched, and he felt a tremendous loss of something he couldn't describe. Married to a Shawnee. It had been a possibility too delicate to put into words. Considering Rebecca's age, Thomas Bradford had known it could have happened, but he hadn't wanted to think about it. Adam realized he'd felt much the same way. "Where is your husband?" he asked huskily. Was he trailing them with a war party?

"He is dead," she answered softly. "His bones are dust."

"How old were you when you married?" The word felt strange on his lips. Married. And he'd been thinking of her as a child...an innocent. He swallowed hard as the image of Rebecca in the arms of a copper-skinned savage formed in his brain. "Did you—"

Star Blanket's eyes narrowed dangerously. "You tell me is not right to ask *personal* questions. Always you English say one thing and do another! I think you make up customs as it please you."

She reined in her mount and allowed the animal to drop into line behind the packhorse, feeling even more perplexed than before. She must return to the Shawnee. She could never, never understand the English, not if she lived to be as old as a grandfather cedar tree. They were a people without logic, and more important, a people without heart.

They heard the river long before they saw it, a grinding, rushing sound that seemed to come from the bowels of the earth. They dismounted and led the animals up a final steep grade, then paused to stare in wonder at the splendor of the Susquehanna on a rampage.

A wide expanse of chocolate brown water tumbled southward between the low hills that formed the riverbanks. The churning surface of the water was broken here and there by massive boulders jutting into the torrent and forming barriers for the floating logs and debris swept along by the flood.

Star Blanket saw the carcass of a great stag, a deer that two men might struggle to lift, tossed and swirled by the current as easily as though it were made of birchbark.

"We cannot cross this," she murmured, her words nearly drowned in the rush of water.

Her horse nickered and shifted nervously. Automatically, her hand ran down the arched neck, and she whispered to him in Shawnee, soothing words of comfort.

Adam sighed and shook his head. "Damn it!" He pointed upriver to a rocky outcrop on the far side. "I crossed there on the way out. Except for a deep spot in the middle, the horses waded across. We'll just have to camp here until the river goes down. Another day, maybe two, might make the difference."

Star Blanket smiled with her eyes. If Adam believed he could cross this river in two days, he was crazier than she thought.

They set up camp beside a spring and waited. The two days stretched into three and then four. Despite her vigilance, there seemed no opportunity to escape during the wait.

At noon on the fourth day, Adam gave the order to saddle up. "We can still make ten miles before dark if we go now," he said. "Stay close to me and do exactly as I tell you."

Much of the flooding had subsided, but the muddy current still raced along much faster than normal for that time of year. The banks were littered with piles of branches and matted foliage, and a great many more rocks showed above the surface of the river.

"The bottom's uneven," Adam warned. "Let your horse have his head. He can swim when he must. I don't want any broken legs."

"I cross rivers before," she answered sharply. She'd had quite enough of Adam's bad temper. He'd done nothing but snap at her since they'd left the Delaware camp.

Adam had given her the chestnut gelding, the quietest of the horses. She led the bay mare with the white star by a lead line. He rode astride the black, leading the bay gelding.

Cautiously, Adam led the way down the muddy bank and urged the black horse into the murky water. The animal tossed his head but went gallantly forward, the bay gelding following on a lead line. "The bottom feels firm enough," Adam called back. "I think it's gravel here. Watch for deep holes."

Star Blanket dug her heels into the side of the chestnut gelding and entered the water. Her hands were firm and steady on the reins as the water covered her feet and rose to midthigh. Her eyes were firmly fixed on Adam's back.

Halfway across the river, her prayers were answered. The black horse slipped and fell sideways, scrambling with his hind legs for solid footing.

The bay gelding pulled loose from Adam's grasp and began swimming with the current. Adam shouted a warning and fought to keep control of the struggling black.

Star Blanket didn't hesitate. With a cry, she pulled hard on the left rein and drove the chestnut into deeper water. The bay mare followed, and the two animals began swimming. Muddy water swirled around her as she lay low over the horse's neck and fixed her eyes on the shoreline she had just left. Swimming with the flow instead of against it, the horses were swept along faster than she would have believed possible.

The chestnut passed dangerously close to a half-submerged boulder. Helplessly, Star Blanket watched as they were flung toward the unyielding stone, then whirled past in a tumble of white water. Somewhere, she had lost the line to the mare. She could not think about that, or about the shouts coming from behind her. Desperately, she clung to the chestnut's mane and willed him to struggle a little longer.

A floating branch gouged her knee, and she winced with pain. She caught sight of the bay mare as the horse's head went under. Then the chestnut's hooves found solid footing, and he heaved himself into the shallows. Star Blanket slid from his back and pulled him up onto the bank. He stood there, head down, sides quivering, in total exhaustion. She paused only long enough to loop the reins over a branch, then scrambled along the bank arid waded out to catch the bay mare. To her dismay, the animal was limping.

As she reached safety with the mare, she turned to scan the far shoreline for Adam and the other two horses. After careful searching, she caught sight of the bay gelding standing in an eddy downriver on the far side. There was no sign of the black horse or of Adam.

A chill ran through her body. He couldn't have drowned! Not a man his size. Surely he could swim like a fish. Even if the horse had broken a leg on the rocks, Adam should have been able to swim free. Anxiously, she climbed up on a rock and stared at the rushing water. She concentrated on the area downriver; if they hadn't made the crossing here, the current would have swept them in that direction.

She glanced back at the horses and decided they would stay where they were, at least for a few moments. She ran down the riverbank, wading around piles of waterlogged branches and scrambling over rocks. "Stupid Englishman," she muttered under her breath. "Wooden head. Even a child could cross a river without—"

The black horse! Star Blanket's breath caught in her throat. Adam's black horse was standing in the shallows just ahead. The saddle hung crazily to one side, and there was no sign of Adam.

Star Blanket splashed through the water and grabbed the horse's bridle. "Where is Adam?" she demanded. "A-dam! A-dam Rourke!" Her only answer was the sound of the swiftly flowing Susquehanna and the heavy breathing of the black gelding.

Cold terror seized her body, and she shivered violently. They had been more than halfway across. Why had the black horse come ashore here? Quickly, she tightened the cinch and vaulted onto the animal's back, straining to see some trace of Adam on the river of brown mud. The reflection of the sun off the water hurt her eyes; she blinked, then stiffened as she caught sight of something white in the middle of the river.

A logjam had formed in the depression between two boulders. There, in the tangle of twisted branches and debris, was something that just might be a man in a white shirt.

Stripping off her riding dress, Star Blanket flung it across the saddle. If she was to swim the river, she needed no heavy skirts to pull her down. She ran back a hundred feet and waded out, gauging the force of the current and the distance to the logjam downriver. When the water was waist deep, she pushed off with her bare feet and began to swim.

The sheer power of the current shocked her. She had known it was possessed by a mighty spirit, but one could not realize the strength of that spirit until one was caught in her arms. Objects bumped into Star Blanket, and once she struck her injured knee against something rock solid.

Ahead and to her right she caught sight of the boulders. She would have to swim harder if she didn't want the current to carry her past the logjam.

Taking a deep breath, she put all her heart and mind into an effort to reach that spot. The water was cold; her muscles ached, and her eyes smarted. Then, suddenly, she was within reach of a jutting branch She grabbed it and held on, working her way up the branch to the trunk and back toward the center of the pile of debris.

Adam lay half out of the water, his face against the trunk of a splintered pine. His face was as pale as his linen shirt, and Star Blanket could detect no sign of life.

"A-dam!" By swimming and pulling she finally reached his side. Her fingers found his throat; not as cold as the merciless river, it was still warm and alive. "A-dam," she repeated. His eyes were shut, his arms clamped around the log in a death grip.

"A-dam!" She beat on his shoulder with her fist. They must not remain here. At any second, the logjam might shift, crushing them in a tangle of powerful logs or trapping them beneath the surface of the river.

"A-dam!"

He groaned, and an eyelid flickered. The leather tie binding his hair had come loose, and his brown locks floated on the water. Star Blanket pushed aside a foolish urge to press them against her cheek. His helplessness tugged at her heart.

Her own weariness swept over her. Why not leave him here and let the spirit of the river decide his fate? Was he not her enemy? Even a Shawnee could not be expected to throw away her life uselessly for the life of an Englishman…for an enemy.

But Adam was not an enemy. She could lie with her lips but not with her heart. They had fought side by side; they had broken bread and shared fresh water. He had protected her and treated her with honor. She could do no less for him now…if it cost her life, she must try to save him.

As fierce as the current was, she doubted she could hold his head above water for long, and the sides of the boulders were too steep for her to pull him up. She must get him back to shore and a fire. But how?

The log that he clung to was too big. The roots were hopelessly entangled in the piles of refuse, and another log lay across the branches. Still, it gave her hope. If she could find a smaller log, anything floating that would hold up his weight, she might be able to get him to shore.

At that moment, another log slammed into the pile. Wood creaked and moaned, and a large section of the logjam broke free and was swept away by the current.

"Adam!" Rebecca screamed. She smacked his face hard and was rewarded by another groan and a half-uttered curse. "Adam! Listen to me! You must wake up. You must help me get you to the shore."

"Rebecca," he said raggedly. He opened bloodshot eyes and tried to focus on her face. "Where are we?"

"We in the middle of your damned Susquehanna!" She pulled at his arm. "It is not safe here. You must let go of that log. We must—"

The sound of snapping timber turned her blood to ice. There was an awful sucking noise and the pine log quivered, then slowly began to wrench loose from the pile and swing into the river. As it moved, it rolled, throwing Adam backward into the river. She grabbed for him, but to her horror, he slid away, down into the muddy depths of the Susquehanna. Without thinking, she followed, only half aware of the logs that closed over her head as she dove into the Stygian blackness.

CHAPTER 7

The water was a nightmare, a terrifying, clutching entity that would return to haunt Star Blanket's dreams in the dark hours of the night. Mud and branches swirled around her; when she opened her eyes, it was as though she was blind. Desperately, her hands reached and scrabbled, feeling for the yielding solidity of human flesh.

Her head began to pound, and her chest ached for air. Something struck the back of her head and scraped along her shoulder. Her foot touched bottom, sand and gravel, and then something soft and repugnant. A silent scream rose in her throat, and she fought the panic that she knew would bring her death.

Adam. She must find Adam. She let herself go with the current, let herself be tumbled across the rock-strewn riverbed. Then, just before the final blackness enveloped her, Rebecca's fingers closed around a man's hand. Joy shot through her as she pulled herself against him and felt her way up his arm to the contours of his face. He struggled weakly against her, but even that feeble battle was proof that he lived. Triumphantly, she seized a handful of hair and pushed upward toward the surface.

After what seemed an eternity, her face broke the surface and she gulped in lungfuls of life-giving air. That she couldn't see didn't register on her oxygen-starved brain until she had pulled the man up to choke and gasp beside her. Then it hit. Why was it so dark? It had been midafternoon when they entered the river. Where was the light?

Fear turned her bones to water, and Star Blanket began to shake. Magic! The River Spirit had held her trapped for hours in her grasp. Or…her mouth tasted of copper…or…had she been made blind for daring to take back a man the spirit had claimed for her own?

Star Blanket took another deep breath and reason trickled back. Her free hand reached and closed on the rough surface of a log. She would have laughed at her own foolishness if she hadn't been so frightened. Of course— they were in an air space under the logjam.

Adam moaned and choked again. She could barely make out his face in the dim light. Water ran from the corner of his mouth.

"Listen," she commanded hoarsely. "We are under the logs. We must swim down and out from under. Do you understand?"

He didn't answer, and she tugged sharply on his hair.

"Ouggh."

"Listen to me," she repeated firmly. "Take a breath and hold it. Now!"

Filling her own lungs with air, she dove, pulling Adam after her; down, down, under the tangled branches, down where the current ran free. The fingers of her left hand were wrapped tightly in his long hair. She used her right hand to push away objects and guide herself and Adam through the murky water. Silently she counted, trying to decide when it would be safe to swim to the surface. They would have only one chance. Her strength was fast dissolving; blackness nibbled at the corners of her mind.

Then they were up, and the sparkling surface of the river surrounded them. Rebecca's heartbeat quickened. Never had the sun looked more beautiful or the breeze caressed her more lovingly.

Holding Adam's head above water seemed almost easy as she let the Susquehanna carry them on its breast. The muscles in her arms and legs ached, and her head was light. Time seemed to stand still.

Rebecca's knees struck something solid, and she realized with a shock that it was hard ground. Staggering to her feet, she dragged Adam into a quiet pool of water and then, inch by inch, up onto the grassy bank.

She rolled him onto his stomach and threw her weight against his back. "Adam!" she cried. "Wake up! Adam!" When he didn't answer, she pushed his head to one side, smoothing back the thick mane of brown hair and running her hand down the rugged jawline.

"Adam?" She began to tremble, not from the chill of the river but from the fear that he was beyond the call of her voice. "Adam?" Tears welled up in her eyes, and she beat against his shoulders with her fists. "Stupid Englishman!" she wailed. "You cannot die so easily." In her desperation she lapsed into Shawnee, sobbing as she pounded at his muscular arms and shoulders. "*Atchmoloh! H'tow-wa-cai,* Adam!"

She leaned over him and took his ashen face in her hands. "Adam," she pleaded hoarsely. She pressed her warm lips against his cold ones, willing life into his body…willing his soul to return.

A spasm of choking wracked his body. With a cry of triumph, Star Blanket held his head as water spewed from his mouth. "*Lenawawe,*" she whispered. "Live." She slapped his back again, hard, and watched with satisfaction as he choked and coughed and a healthy tint replaced the ivory cast of his skin.

Adam raised himself to his knees and vomited great volumes of muddy river water. Then he fell forward into a half faint and lay without moving for nearly an hour.

Exhausted, Star Blanket lay in the hot sun beside him, letting the soothing rays ease the pain in her muscles. Night would be soon enough for a fire, she decided. It was warm here and sheltered from the breeze. Later, she would worry about the horses and their gear. For now, it was enough to feel the earth beneath her back and listen to the bittersweet song of a mockingbird.

Gradually, Adam's breathing became more regular. Star Blanket watched over him, pleased when he slept and alert to his first movements when he woke.

She moistened her lips with a hesitant tongue, remembering the touch of her mouth to his, savoring the strange sensations that had coursed through her body. Would he remember? Would he understand? She brushed her bottom lip lightly with her finger. How could he understand when she didn't understand herself why she had kissed him?

He groaned loudly and pushed himself up on his forearms. "Rebecca?" He blinked stupidly. "Rebecca?" He sat up and rubbed his eyes. "I feel as if I've been kicked to death by a horse. Are you all—My God, girl! Where are your clothes?"

Star Blanket laughed, clapping her hands together in glee like a mischievous child. "Crazy Englishman!" She covered her mouth with her hands and giggled. "You almost drown in river. We *both* almost drown in river, and all you can say is, 'Where are your clothes!'"

Adam frowned and rose unsteadily to his feet, almost driven back to his knees by the blinding pain in his head. "My horse slipped into a hole and then—Where are the horses? Did we lose the horses?" Without the horses, without his gun, how would he ever get them safely home to Sheffield? He blinked to try and clear the dizziness. "I remember..." His voice cracked, then he continued huskily: "We were caught in some kind of pileup in the river." His voice dropped to a bare whisper. "You saved my life, didn't you?"

Star Blanket's eyes glowed. She smiled and nodded. "I did, Englishman. You would be food for the turtles if it not for me."

Adam tore his eyes away and stared at the ground. Damn it! Why was she standing there as bold as brass without a stitch on? She was an Aphrodite hewn of living marble. His pulse quickened as he imagined what that satin skin would feel like pressed against his. Angrily he ripped at his shirt and, tearing the ties, yanked it over his head and threw it at her. "Here, put this on!" he ordered.

She fingered the damp linen, her eyes clouded with puzzlement. "I have done something wrong, Adam?" she ventured.

"Put the shirt on!" His voice was as cold as December frost.

"No!" She threw the balled garment to the grass and kicked it with a bare foot. "I will not! I will wear nothing of yours, Adam Rourke. If my body is so ugly, I will find my own clothes, but I will not wear yours!" She whirled and stalked off down the river bank. "Damn woodenhead," she muttered. "Stupid English. *Matethi-i-thi,* stupid woodenhead."

"Where are you going? Rebecca! Come back here!"

She broke into a run, not looking back but knowing that he was following her. She wasn't sure how far downriver they had been swept, and she hoped the horses were where she had left them, but it made no difference. She was going home! With or without the horses, with or without the English dress, she was going back to her people. She had saved Adam's life, and he owed her a great debt. His honor demanded that he release her and send her on her way with all his wealth. Even a stupid woodenhead must understand that. She would go home, and she would forget him. She would never think of him again, not if she lived for a hundred summers!

Adam was hard pressed to keep up with Rebecca as she scrambled over fallen logs and waded and climbed in and out of the river. He was even harder pressed to keep his eyes from lingering on the delightfully feminine buttocks or the flash of a firm, upthrust breast. God, but she was beautiful! Her hair hung in thick, dark waves nearly to her waist. Her shoulders, her long shapely legs, and the grace of her movements all fired his imagination. A desire he couldn't ignore kindled in his brain and loins as he followed her. His breathing quickened, and the tightness in his groin reminded him with every step that he had never seen a woman so gloriously sensual in all his life.

The black horse was grazing near the spot Star Blanket had last seen him; her discarded riding habit lay on the ground nearby. Still angry, she pulled it over her head and turned to scream at Adam. "Now I have dress! Now I am fit to look at, Englishman. Here is your horse. Do you have happy?"

Adam fought for control of himself. God, it would be so easy to take her in his arms...to kiss that beckoning mouth, to bury his face between those soft breasts. He knelt beside the horse, running his hands up and down the slim legs, searching for injuries. He couldn't trust himself to speak to her, not yet. He swallowed hard. Even now, knowing what lay beneath the cloth, knowing every curve and hollow of her luscious body, he couldn't bear to look at her. A faint sheen of perspiration broke out on his forehead as he stood up and checked the girth. "He seems fit enough," he said harshly. "I didn't think he'd be on this side of the river."

"I leave the other two ahead," Star Blanket answered coldly. "Only the bay is on far side."

Adam slipped the musket from its case and stroked it gratefully. The powder was bound to be wet, but it would dry. They'd been lucky, damned lucky. His gaze slid to her face, and he felt the blood rise up his neck and face. "I didn't thank you for saving my life," he said. "It was a brave thing you did."

"I am Shawnee," she shot back boldly. "Shawnee do not let companions die so easily, not even Englishmen."

"Shawnee or not, most men would have stayed safely on the bank," Adam continued. "Thank you, Rebecca. I'll never forget what you did."

"I will help you find your other animals, and then I will go." She waited for him to offer the musket. It was his most valuable possession, and therefore the finest gift he could give.

A sick feeling grew in the pit of Adam's stomach as he stared at her. *She thinks I'm going to let her go.* He moved toward her and caught her wrist, speaking with a forced harshness. "Nothing's changed between us, Rebecca," he said. "Nothing. I'm still taking you home to Maryland, to your grandfather." His muscles tensed for the struggle he knew would come, but he was unprepared for the clouding of her sea green eyes as their expression changed from bewilderment to cold fury and then to scorching hatred.

She trembled in his grasp, not fighting his grip but shrinking from it. "You will not let me go?" she whispered. "I save you from the river, and you will not give me my freedom?"

"I can't."

"Then we are enemies," she said softly. "And I will take your life if I can, for you have no honor and are less than a mad dog. Until I cease to draw breath, Adam Rourke, I will hate you and curse your name."

Her eyes filled with tears, but she made no protest when he set her on the black and tied her wrists together. His own anger rose within him and he wanted to hit out, to slap her, to hurt her as she had hurt him with her words. Instead, he walked ahead in silence and led the black gelding along the river, wishing he were a thousand miles away and had never heard of Rebecca Bradford.

The wish echoed in his ears, silently damning him in the days and nights to come. The second crossing of the Susquehanna was almost child's play, and they found the bay gelding on the far side waiting for them. The weather turned gentle, losing the oppressive heat of August during the day, yet staying warm enough at night so that they didn't need a fire except for cooking. It seemed Adam's luck had turned, so why did he feel so miserable now that success was in sight?

He kept Rebecca tied day and night, never letting down his guard for an instant. She had threatened to kill him. He didn't doubt she would try if she got the chance.

Traveling with her after they crossed the river was like riding with a ghost. She didn't speak; she hardly looked at him. Her green eyes were open without seeming to see. She had shut him out of her world once more.

"You've got to try and understand," Adam repeated as he lifted her into the saddle once again and tied her ankles under the horse's belly. "You've been away so long that you're mixed up. You don't know where you belong. Once you've been home for a while, you'll thank me."

He might have been speaking to stone for all the reaction he received. She was like a wooden doll. She ate and drank, and slept when he ordered her to, but the teasing sprite was gone as though she had never existed.

Wryly, Adam thought that this was what he had expected when he had accepted the mission. Rebecca Bradford would be frightened, quiet…perhaps even crazy.

Adam urged the bay into a trot. It wasn't possible to lie to himself. He missed the snarling little savage almost as much as he missed her fey sense of humor. Even at night she gave him no peace; his dreams were disturbed by images of her unclad form and his own unfulfilled lust.

Each day's ride brought them closer to civilization. They left the wilderness behind and entered an area of scattered farms and tilled fields. The game trail they had followed became a hard-packed path and then a wagon road.

Adam's spirits lifted as they passed familiar landmarks. Had there been enough rain to keep the tobacco crop from wilting on Sheffield while he'd been gone? It was time to start cutting. The empty tobacco sheds would soon be full to bursting.

He loved the smell of curing tobacco. He should have let someone else come after Rebecca; he was needed at home. There were a thousand things to do, and servants, no matter how responsible, couldn't be expected to run the plantation alone.

He glanced back at Rebecca, wondering if she would find happiness at Sheffield or if she would remain caught between two worlds. He decided to remove the bindings. It would only shame her to be carried home like a prisoner of war.

"You can't get away," he warned. "No one will know what happened between us if you don't tell them. Your grandfather loves you very much. You must give him a chance."

Star Blanket watched through hooded eyes as Adam unfastened her wrists. Her anger burned as fiercely now as it had the moment she had cursed him on the Susquehanna, but she was no fool. She had not spoken to him because she knew her silence hurt him more than any words could have. Escape from this place wouldn't be easy. She would have to wait and watch. She would have to learn this land and these people, and she could not learn if she let them know how she felt inside.

Why would she hate the grandfather who had gone to so much trouble and paid such a price to bring her back? Among the Shawnee, old people were respected. She would give him the respect he was due. Only Adam Rourke would she hate with all her mind and all her soul—only Adam, who had betrayed her.

Not far down the road, they were met by a farm wagon. The driver, a white man, called out a greeting to Adam. Adam shouted back and broke into a grin.

"It's John Brown and his wife Molly," Adam explained to Rebecca. "They work on the plantation." He urged his horse forward. "John! It's good to see you! Molly."

Adam talked excitedly with the two people for a few minutes, then returned to Rebecca's side and lifted her down from the horse. "They've brought us clean clothes. That rider we met yesterday carried a message home to Sheffield. They're all expecting us."

Rebecca's gaze met that of the woman. Slowly, she smiled and saw the fear leave the servant's face. "You are Molly?"

The dark-haired woman found her tongue. "Yes, ma'am." She scrambled down from the wagon seat and bobbed a curtsy. "Welcome home, Mistress Rebecca."

For an instant, Star Blanket wondered about this custom of bouncing up and down. Was she supposed to do the same? Adam's brown eyes flickered a warning. Servants…what had he told her about servants? Did it have something to do with her grandfather's honor? Oh, yes. She smiled and nodded gracefully. The woman gave a half smile in return. But she was waiting for something. "Thank you, Molly," Star Blanket said softly. The servant's smile widened, and Adam looked pleased.

Star Blanket's heart beat a little faster. Why should she care what these crazy English thought of her? Still, it gave her satisfaction to know she had passed some kind of test. Adam had been surprised. She pursed her lips and concealed her eyes beneath her lashes. Did he expect her to give a war whoop?

She allowed the Molly woman to help her into the wagon. If this was the English maid who liked to watch women take off their clothes, she would soon learn to play a different game.

"We've brought fresh things, Mistress Rebecca," said Molly. "There's a place a few miles back where you can change. I'll do your hair, if you like. I know you want to look nice for your homecoming." She opened a trunk and held up a peach-colored gown. "I think this will fit, ma'am. It was your mother's. It's a little old-fashioned but still beautiful, don't you think?"

Molly talked so fast, with such a heavy accent, that Star Blanket could hardly understand what she was saying. She fingered the heavy English dress absently as one word lodged in her consciousness—mother. Her mother. Her English mother. She had not thought of her in many years, but long ago they had walked together in dreams.

She had died in the day of blood. Rebecca winced as a ribbon of pain wound around her heart. She blinked to keep back tears; her chest felt strangely tight, as though she could not breathe. Images of her mother's death flashed across her brain. So long ago…so long and yet so clear. She drew in a ragged breath and straightened her back.

"I will ride," she announced. "I ride this far, I will ride the rest of the way to…to Sheffield." She glanced at Adam; he caught the black horse's reins and walked over to the wagon.

"If you wish," he said. "We'll make faster time that way. John and Molly can follow in the wagon, with the extra horses."

Rebecca met his dark eyes stubbornly. "I wish."

He lifted her down from the wagon and helped her back into the saddle, and they set off at a brisk trot along the dirt road. Rebecca kept her eyes on the trail ahead, unwilling to let Adam see the fear that was creeping over her. What would the grandfather think of her? Would he be ashamed? Would the English laugh at her? She sneaked a look at Adam. He was her enemy, yet in some twisted way he was her only friend in this foreign land.

Would she remember anything of the home of her childhood? Faces? Sounds? Or would it all be strange and terrifying?

The fear grew within her with every thud of the horse's hooves. Could Adam smell it? Star Blanket gripped the leather reins tighter to quell the trembling of her hands. She would not give him the satisfaction of seeing her fear. She was Shawnee! The English could do nothing to break her spirit if she did not let them. If they imprisoned her, she would escape. If they scorned her, she would scorn them. She would never forget who and what she was.

Adam turned in the saddle and smiled reassuringly at her. "It will be all right, Rebecca. I promise."

Her laughter was low and bitter. "Your promises, English-*manake,* are like autumn leaves in the wind. I put no trust in them or in you."

CHAPTER 8

S heffield seemed to grow out of the land as though it had stood on the banks of Chesapeake Bay for five hundred rather than only fifty years. Built of stone carried in the holds of sailing ships as ballast and of brick fired of Maryland sand and clay, Sheffield was a blending of England and this brash new world…a blending that had produced a graceful manor house as lovely as anything Adam had ever seen.

Sheltered by towering oaks, surrounded on three sides by water, the house dominated the landscape. The solid stone center structure was flanked by graceful twin additions. By English standards, Sheffield was a modest country estate. In the colonies, it was a home fit for the lord governor himself. And in wealth and breeding, Thomas Bradford was a match for any powdered lordling. Sheffield was a kingdom unto itself, and Rebecca Bradford would be the crown princess. Did she remember? Adam reined in his horse and gazed at her.

Her face was a study in porcelain; her hands trembled so that her horse sensed her distress and began to toss his head and dance nervously.

"Rebecca? Are you all right?" Adam guided his mount beside hers. "Rebecca?"

His voice came to her faintly, fading in and out as though a great distance separated them. Waves of memories swept over her; her head spun, and she felt empty inside, as though her soul had seeped out of her body.

The smells of Sheffield…it was the smells that tantalized and frightened her. Fresh-cut honeysuckle…bread baking on a dozen hearths…the earthy scent of stables mingling with the odors of ducks and geese, pigs and cattle. A brisk wind from the bay carried the smell of salt and seaweed and the faint, unmistakable scent of wood and canvas. And with it pine and cedar, late summer roses, and crushed mint from the herb garden all forced their memories on Rebecca at once.

Pictures whirled in her head, and she swayed in the saddle. From far away, she heard her little brother's lisping voice as shadowy children played hide-and-seek in the boxwood maze….

"Rebecca!" Adam caught her as she fell. "Rebecca, for God's sake! Are you…" His voice cracked and trailed off as her arms tightened around his neck and she clung to him, pressing her warm body against his. Shaken, he dismounted, still holding her, unable to thrust her away from him. "Rebecca," he repeated hoarsely, "are you all right?" His mouth went dry as he tried to ignore the sensations that raced through his flesh and bones.

A cloud of dark hair brushed his lips and chin; he could feel her warm breath against his chest. Her breasts were pressed against him; as he had swung down out of the saddle, his hand had grasped a softly rounded bottom. "Rebecca." Reason told him to push her away. In another minute, he would be unable to keep himself from tipping up her chin and tasting that beguiling mouth. "Rebecca?" he begged.

She stirred against him, staring up with eyes so green that a man could lose his soul in them. Her lips formed his name soundlessly, and her soot black lashes wavered.

She held fast to him, unwilling to let go of the only solid reality in her existence. Adam was like a rock that grew from the heart of mother earth. She could feel his strength flowing into her blood and sinew, pushing back the weakness and uncertainty, pushing back the icy shards of fear that numbed her brain and shattered her hard outer shell. Her body was seized with cold trembling, and she sensed the empty shadow of death brush against her. Feeling herself slipping away, she knew that this time there would be no return. And in utter desperation, she tightened her arms around her enemy's neck and strained upward to meet his lips with her own.

For half a heartbeat, Adam gave no response. Then he groaned deep in his throat and crushed her against him. His mouth was tender against hers, almost questioning, but the iron-thewed arms molded her body to his until she could hear the beat of his heart and feel the heat of his throbbing loins.

Her lips parted of their own volition, welcoming the touch of his tongue against hers. The fear washed away, replaced by a shining wonder and an inescapable knowledge that she had known from the beginning it would be like this.

That he was her enemy meant nothing. The force that drew them together could not be denied by mortal flesh. Surely the gods were laughing at her. Even as her body thrilled to Adam's kiss, her mind accepted that they had known each other in another lifetime, not once but many times. They had been lovers, perhaps even man and wife. She knew it as surely as she knew the sun would rise in the morning.

Their kiss deepened as a rush of heat enveloped her, and she tasted the sweet recesses of his mouth and felt his soul touch hers. She was no callow maiden; she had known the embrace of men. She had been a wife. Yet Adam's kiss was a thing apart, as unlike the kiss of other men as honey is from pine sap.

"A-dam" she whispered in the old way. "A-dam." And their lips met again, drinking love as the earth soaks up rain after a summer drought. "A-dam."

His fingers caressed her cheek and tangled in her hair; soft moans of joy rose in his throat and were met with muffled cries from Rebecca.

Then, abruptly, the echo of hoofbeats and a man's shot shattered their embrace. "Adam! Damn your eyes! You did it!"

Adam broke away from Rebecca, grabbing her when she would have fallen. Half dazed, he shook his head to clear away the madness. For an instant her gaze met his, and he could have sworn he saw amusement in those enigmatic depths.

"Adam!" the man called again.

"Can you stand?" Adam demanded. She nodded, and he let her go. Reason flooded his brain as he turned to mee the horseman. "Jock! I wish you'd come along. I could have used you." In more ways than one, Adam thought. "This is Mistress Rebecca Bradford."

Rebecca leaned against Adam's horse as the Strange weakness drained away. Her lips still tingled from his kiss; would the stranger notice they were swollen? If he had not come…if they had been alone…She shrugged imperceptibly. It made no difference. Adam could deny his desire for her; he could pretend it did not exist. But if they were meant to join as man and woman, his struggle would be in vain.

"Mistress Bradford." The rider pulled off a Scottish bonnet to reveal a square, freckled face and carrot red hair. "Thank God yer safe at home." He grinned broadly and dismounted. "'Tis an honor to meet ye, lady. The old laird has spoke o' little else fer weeks." Jock offered a courtly bow, graceful in spite of the tanned, muscular legs showing beneath his tartan kilt. "Ay be foreman at Cedar Grovi Plantation," he explained.

"Jock McMann is a good friend," Adam said.

Rebecca offered him a shy smile. "I am happy to meet with you, Jook Mak-man. You smile much for an English-*manake.*"

"What has he been fillin' yer ears wi'?" Jock twisted the bonnet in his hands. "Ay'm nay English, but Scottish to the bone."

Adam ventured a glance at Rebecca's face, only to be transfixed by a smoldering gaze. Damn her! What was she thinking? Instantly, he was seized by an overwhelming shame. The fault was not hers but his. She was bound to be confused, bewildered by the sudden changes in her life. He'd taken advantage of that disorientation. God! Another minute and I'd have had her here on the ground in broad daylight! "Master Bradford has no doubt heard of our arrival and is waiting to see Mistress Rebecca," he said stiffly. Had Jock noticed his unmistakable signs of arousal? If he had, he'd never let Adam hear the end of it.

"Master Adam! Master Adam!"

Excited cries filled the air as the servants recognized Adam and passed the word to others. A crowd of well-wishers formed around them, whispering among themselves and calling out. Rebecca took a deep breath and tried to conceal her fear.

So many people! Some were as fair of skin as Jook Makman; others were as black as a moonless night. Adam, her protector, had returned. Carefully he guided her through the gathering and across the hard-packed yard toward the house. His arm around her shoulders was brotherly now, but she could not forget the scorching touch of his lips.

Her determination grew with every step. Let them stare at her with their fishlike blue eyes. She had seen prisoners run the gauntlet in the Shawnee camps. Could she show less courage before the English? She nodded regally to Jock as he mounted his horse and waved to her. He had seen; the evidence was as plain in his eyes as a fresh trail. Jock had seen their embrace but he had not boasted of it. That was good; that was the Shawnee way. She raised a hand to wave back. Perhaps he would be a friend if she were here long enough to need one.

The distance to the house seemed very long; memories tugged at her heart, but she did not falter. The time of her weakness was over. She must meet this grandfather, this Thomas. If he was truly her father's father, he must be made to understand that her heart was now Shawnee, that he could not keep her here against her will.

Her feelings for the big English-*manake* had nothing to do with her desire to return to the People. What would be, would be. If a fire burned within her blood for this white man, then it must be stilled in the way of male and female. He remained her enemy. A faint smile lifted the corners of her mouth as she glanced at Adam from under her long lashes. He was a formidable enemy indeed. One to respect.

The way into the house was vaguely familiar; the smells of the great entranceway filled her brain, and she remembered a rainy day when she played with a doll on the staircase.

"Rebecca." A voice called her English name, and she looked up to see a gray-haired man standing in the doorway. "Rebecca?" He opened his arms, and her eyes filled with tears.

"Grandfather!" Somehow she was in his arms and sobbing against his chest. Her heart sang even as tears clouded her eyes and choked her voice. She remembered! This was no strange English-*manake* but her beloved grandfather, the companion of her dreams.

Thomas Bradford was smaller than she had thought he would be, and older. But it made no difference. Her fingers traced the lines of his jaw as she stared into eyes as green as the depths of the Ohio River.

Adam murmured something about leaving them alone, and then he was gone. The grandfather sank into a chair, and the serving woman closed the door, leaving them together. Rebecca dropped to her knees before him and laid her head in his lap.

"They said you were dead, child," he said softly, touching the soft waves of her dark hair. "I knew you weren't. You're all I have left of my own blood. I'd have known if you were dead." He took her chin between his gnarled fingers and tilted it up to look her full in the face.

"Did any man lay hand on you to do you harm since you left the Shawnee?"

Rebecca's heart warmed to the veiled threat. Thomas Bradford might be old, but he was still a man of power, one who carried *mesawmi,* the power of the soul bestowed on a chosen few by the Great Spirit. She had but to mention a name and that man's days would be short. The knowledge that he held her honor dear was satisfying, and she felt a flood of emotion that threatened to bring on a storm of weeping.

It was not worthy of a daughter of the Shawnee or of this house to behave so childishly. She took a deep breath and forced herself to smile. "I was well treated, Grandfather," she lied, "except for two Germans who try to kill us. Adam said they wanted the fine horses."

Thomas winced as pain shot down his arm and left him breathless. He could not have borne it if anything had happened to Rebecca on her way home. His fingers closed over her slim ones. "What happened?" he demanded.

"They walk the trail of shadows." She rose from the floor and traversed the room. If her grandfather was smaller than she remembered, the great hall was bigger. Never had she seen such fabrics, such polished wood. Light streamed through the windows and lay in pools on the shining floor. She spun about and smiled with her eyes. "I not remember Sheffield is so beautiful."

"Not half so beautiful as you, child. You're very like your grandmother, except for the eyes. You have the Bradford eyes. Your father had them too." A lump rose in his throat at the thought of his only son, struck down in his prime and buried in a lonely grave far away. "Do you remember him at all?"

"A little, I think. And my mother. She was quiet, not like Shawnee mother." Rebecca's tone grew serious. "Adam says you think Shawnee attack the white farm and kill my English mother and father."

"And your little brother."

"It was not!" Her eyes narrowed. "It was Iroquois. The Shawnee do not kill women and children. The Shawnee do not kill without reason."

"You were a child then yourself, and it was a long time ago," Thomas said soothingly. "You couldn't be expected to remember."

"I do not forget. I never forget...never. Iroquois, Grandfather. Iroquois. A Shawnee warrior saved my life. He took me to his people and made me one of them. You must understand." Her eyes pleaded. "I am Shawnee now. I am not English."

"Well, English or Indian, you're home now and that's what matters," the old man said. "Someone cared for you all these years, and if it was the Shawnee, I owe them my undying gratitude."

The pain dulled in his arm, and he breathed a little easier. The spells came more frequently now, sometimes every day. He didn't need a physician to tell him that his condition was serious. Thomas cleared his throat noisily. He wanted to ask about the attack by the Germans, but he was afraid of upsetting Rebecca even further. In time, he would have the whole story from Adam. "All this will be yours when I die, you know. And not just the plantation. I have ships and businesses, more wealth than you could ever spend."

"I want nothing from you, Grandfather. Only—"

The door opened and a middle-aged woman entered the room. Rebecca knew by the proud way she carried herself that this was no servant. Rebecca glanced toward her grandfather expectantly, trying not to show her apprehension under the woman's obvious scrutiny.

"So this is Rebecca?" A frown creased the woman's brow, and her mouth tightened. "Are you certain, Thomas? There can be no mistake?" She took a few steps forward and sniffed loudly. "She doesn't look much like Mary."

Thomas laughed and rose to his feet. "She is Mary's daughter, Isabel." He caught Rebecca's hand. "This is your great-aunt, child, Mistress Isabel Sinclair. She has come to stay with us so you won't be quite alone in a household of men."

The two women faced one another warily across the room. "Welcome home, Rebecca," Isabel said tersely. "God has answered your grandfather's prayers and delivered you from the hands of the heathen."

Rebecca decided that this was one relative she could do without. From the top of her starched white linen cap to the spotless embroidered slippers, the woman radiated disapproval. There was no softness in the plump figure or in the round gray eyes that matched the severely styled gray hair.

Rebecca's docile tone hid the mischief in her lowered eyes. "I know aunt, Grandfather, but why is the English-*equiwa* called the great aunt? I have seen much fatter women among the Shawnee, and they were not called so."

Isabel let out a small bleat of indignation. The gray eyes darkened to icy slate. "It is obvious that your years among the savages have done nothing for your manners. I can see that I shall have my hands full!"

Thomas coughed, covering a throaty chuckle with the back of his hand. "Isabel was your mother's aunt, child. She raised your mother from an infant when your mother's mother died in childbed." He cleared his throat. "Your mother's aunt is your great aunt. You may address her as Aunt Isabel." He paused and his thin voice took on a note of authority. "Isabel has made great sacrifices to come and care for you. I would have you show her the proper respect and affection she deserves."

"I believe I know my duty, Thomas," Isabel said coldly. "I told you what to expect. Time and prayer may mold her into the granddaughter you would like to have. My sacrifices are made out of Christian charity. I'm doing it for poor Mary and for the girl's own good."

Rebecca struggled to conceal the anger that rose in her breast. How dare this woman speak as though she were not even in the room, or worse, as though she were of little wit! The word "savage" echoed in her brain, and she wondered if this aunt would not feel perfectly at home around the torture fires of the Iroquois. Of a certainty it would give Rebecca great pleasure to turn this sour one over to them as a captive!

"My Shawnee mother teach me to give respect to all those who deserve," she said softly. "Know that I do not forget her teaching." Green Bradford eyes met gray in challenge, and Rebecca had the satisfaction of seeing the older woman flush with anger.

Thomas reached for a bell cord, and a faint ringing sounded from outside the room. "Rebecca must be exhausted. She needs a hot bath, something to eat, and rest. Tomorrow will be time enough for questions and getting to know each other." He turned his gaze on his granddaughter. "You'll never know," he said, blinking away the moisture that threatened to blur his vision. "You'll never know how I've waited for this day."

"My heart is glad that we meet again, Grandfather," Rebecca said sincerely. She swallowed hard. It would not be easy to explain to this magnificent old man that she could not stay at Sheffield, that she must return to her own people. In a day or two perhaps they could talk more easily.

A serving girl came to show her the way to her place of sleeping. As they crossed the hall and began the climb up the wide staircase, Rebecca could hear the low, angry murmur of words from the room behind them. The great-aunt did not like her. Well enough. She did not like the great-aunt! She was glad she would not be here long enough for the woman to make her life unhappy.

Cautiously, Rebecca gripped the rail as she ascended the steps. Her heart was pounding as her eyes took in the magnificence of her grandfather's house. It was so strange. Her mind seemed to play tricks on her. She remembered this shining wood…the tall-case clock at the landing…the way the light poured through the many-paned window next to the clock…and yet she didn't remember. It was not her memory but the memory of an English girl long dead. She was a Shawnee woman now; her name was Star Blanket, and her home was on the wild Ohio River. She must keep those thoughts fixed in her head.

Rebecca's gaze met a pair of high black boots, at the top of the stairs. Slowly, her gaze traveled upward over muscular calves encased in white stockings, lingering for a heartbeat on tan buckskin breeches, then rising to take in the fine linen shirt open halfway to reveal a broad masculine chest covered with a curling mat of golden-brown hair.

"Master Adam." The servant girl nodded and stepped aside to make room for him on the stairs. "Glad to see you home, sir."

"Emma," he said, acknowledging the greeting. He didn't move, forcing Rebecca's gaze higher to meet his own. Then he addressed Rebecca. "You've talked with him? And with your Aunt Isabel?"

"I do not like her."

"Don't judge her too quickly; she has a good heart."

"And you A-dam? Do you have a good heart?" He was quick to cover the flash of emotion in his eyes but not quick enough. Rebecca arched one dark eyebrow wickedly. "I think you have no heart at all, English-*manake.*"

"Emma will show you to your room, Rebecca. Your grandfather's expecting me," he said stiffly. He stepped around her and hurried down the steps.

Rebecca watched, noting the black velvet tie that held Adam's hair at the base of his neck. For days she had seen him brush and fasten his hair with a plain leather thong. She wondered if he would cast her away as easily as he had the sweat-soaked leather.

"Mistress?" The girl was staring at her.

Rebecca nodded and followed the one called Emma down a long hall with many doors. They paused before one, and the servant opened it awkwardly.

"This be yer room, Miss Rebecca." She bobbed in that ridiculous way and then scurried away, saying as she went, "Be ye want anything, just pull the bell cord, mistress."

Cautiously, Rebecca entered the room. It was large and airy with windows on two sides. A poster bed with magnificent hangings filled one corner of the room. Rebecca went to it and fingered the wonderful cloth, remembering how she had needed a stool to reach the bed when she was a child.

Her fingers traced the strange beasts and long-tailed birds that were woven into the bed hangings, her mind drinking in the rich colors—blue and red and green. A man…her English father…had sat beside her on this bed and told fabulous stories about the land where the cloud-cloth was made. She had never believed any of them, of course, but he had not expected her to. They had laughed together and whispered secrets and planned exciting things that they would do together in the morning.

Without realizing it, Rebecca crawled up onto the soft center of the bed, her eyes seeking a special place, a place where the blue—her mind searched for the word—dragon had been almost worn away by childish fingers. Her English father had said dragons were for wishing on and that a girl who rubbed the back of one hard enough would get her wish.

Her fingertips found a rough spot in the silk, and disappointment caused her eyes to blink away a film of moisture. Someone had mended the dragon! But the stitches were not so fine, nor the thread the same vivid blue. It was not the same. Rebecca's throat felt scratchy, and she rose from the bed, pushing away the childish fantasies. Why did she seek the old memories? They were gone, just as the English father with his teasing laughter was gone. His scalp hung in an Iroquois lodge, and she was a woman grown, too old for stories and bright blue dragons.

Restlessly she moved about the room, noting the large fireplace with its finely carved mantel and the heavy dark furnishings. In one corner a rush chair held a battered doll, and beside the doll lay a large, leather-covered object. Tenderly Rebecca opened the scarlet cover and began to turn the leaves that she remembered were called pages. It was a book, with stories and wonderful pictures. Her lips moved silently as she began to sound out the words. Her grandfather had boasted of her ability to read in English and in...in French, but it had been so many years since she had tried to decipher the strange markings.

Engrossed, she sank to the floor and took the book on her lap. Her favorite story had been one of a great boat and many animals. She found it and began painfully to read the words, one by one.

Long shadows sprawled across the room, making the pages difficult to see before Rebecca finally put the book away and crossed to the window. To her delight, she could see a vast expanse of water. She had known the water would be there, visible from the front window, but she had been reluctant to look. Suppose that, too, had lost some of its wonder?

She breathed deeply of the salt air, wrapping her arms around her waist and chuckling to herself. The water was there as it had been in her dreams, gold and silver in the sunset, looking like nothing else in the world.

Below the window, gardens stretched toward the shoreline, with tall green hedges and white oyster-shell paths, and in the center of the garden stood a stone deer with great antlers. She had not believed there was really such a thing, but there he stood, as large as life, frozen in flight with one perfect hoof in midair.

A knock on the door startled her, and she whirled around. The maid's round face appeared in the doorway. "Would you care to come down for supper, Mistress Rebecca? It's early this evening, but Master Thomas is not feeling well and wants to be in bed early. I'm to help you dress."

Rebecca shook her head. "No, I am not hungry." She could not face them again so soon. The morning would be time enough. She needed to be alone to sort out her thoughts. "I will sleep now," she said firmly. "Tell my grandfather I will talk with him tomorrow."

"Yes, Miss Rebecca. I'll tell him, but I don't know if he'll like it. Him and Master Adam—"

"Go!" Rebecca's eyes hardened, and the girl fled. A smile softened Rebecca's lips as she closed the door and slipped the bolt. These English were like rabbits. You had only to glare at them, and they vanished.

The chuckle turned into a yawn, and Rebecca realized she was tired. Slowly she pulled off the English garments and, taking a blanket from the bed, curled up on a rug beside the window. In the morning she would convince the grandfather to let her go home. She closed her eyes and stretched, trying not to think of Adam as she had seen him last, trying to push back the thoughts of their time together and the kisses they had shared. Ruthlessly she cleared her mind of him, remembering instead the sound of the Ohio at first light and the music of raindrops on her mother's wigwam.

But her dreams betrayed her; instead of Indian faces and the soft whispers of the Shawnee tongue, she saw the craggy outline of a plain white face arid heard Adam Rourke's voice calling her English name.

CHAPTER 9

Moonlight spilled through the open windows of Adam's bedchamber as he twisted and turned on the soft feather mattress. Outside, an owl sat on a branch of the nearest oak tree and hooted mournfully into the still September night.

Adam cursed softly and buried his face in the linen sheet. His body ached with weariness; he had spent the evening beside the field workers, stripped to the waist, cutting tobacco and loading it onto wagons.

His stepfather had been ill, and much that should have been done at Sheffield while Adam was gone had not been completed. The acting foreman had been unwilling or unable to give the necessary orders and see that they were carried out. His ears were probably still ringing from the reprimand Adam had given him. There would be extra work for everyone until they were caught up.

Still, Adam did not deceive himself into thinking that the uncut tobacco was the cause of his sleeplessness. He knew better. It was Rebecca's green eyes that troubled him...her eyes and the way her soft body had fit against his when he kissed her.

Why in God's name had he done it? And since he had kissed her, why practically on Sheffield's doorstoop? She must have bewitched him with her pagan Indian ways. The knowledge that he'd betrayed Thomas Bradford's trust cut into his innards like a barbed arrowhead. The fault was his, not Rebecca's, and trying to put the blame on her made him even more foul.

All at once he sensed rather than heard an alien presence in his bedchamber. He held his breath and listened, trying to catch some sound that would identify the intruder. There was nothing. He strained his eyes, staring into the darkest corners of the room, seeking a faint movement. Nothing.

"Who is it?" His voice sounded strained and unnatural in his ears.

A breath of air brushed his cheek, and Adam realized that the door was partially open. He knew it had been closed. Instinctively his hand moved toward the pistol he kept on the candlestand beside his bed.

"A-dam."

He froze. "Rebecca?" He sat bolt upright and fumbled for the sheet to cover his nakedness. "Rebecca!" he exclaimed. "What in hell are you doing here?"

Her low chuckle was followed almost instantly by a weight on the far side of Adam's mattress. Moonlight illuminated a shapely thigh and one bare shoulder.

"What are you doing here?" he repeated stupidly.

"I cannot sleep. I must talk with someone, and you are only one I know." She sighed, dropping onto one elbow and coming dangerously close. "I know we are enemies, but you bring me here. You are responsible." She curled her feet up under her. "Also, I save your life. To keep your honor, you must help me."

"To keep my honor, I must get you out of my bed!" he whispered urgently. "You'll have me hung."

"A-dam, you worry. Never do I know a man who worry as much as you. I told you, I must speak with someone."

"Not here." As the last traces of sleep drained away, he realized that she was naked. "It's wrong for you to be here," he protested. "It's against the custom."

"Not against Shawnee custom."

"You're not an Indian! I'm not an Indian!" Sweat broke out on his forehead. In any other place, at any other time in his life, and with almost *any* other woman, he would have been delighted to have such an apparition appear in his bed. But this was crazy! "Out!"

"I will not. Not until you talk to me."

With a strangled curse, Adam rose from the bed, dragging the sheet with him, and stalked across the room to shut and bar the door. "Keep your voice down. You'll wake the house," he warned. Grabbing his breeches, he moved into a dark corner to pull them on.

"You make no sense at all, A-dam. You tell me to go. Then you lock door. Why you do this?" Rebecca made no effort to hide the mischief in her voice. "Why you are afraid that I see you without clothes? Are you missing a warrior's parts?"

"You know damn well I'm not." He crossed the room and threw her a clean shirt. "Put this on."

Rebecca giggled as he turned his back and folded his arms across his chest. Obediently she slid from the poster bed and donned the soft white shirt. "This is foolish custom," she insisted. "I do not understand why the English have shame of their bodies."

"You don't have to understand. You just have to do it."

Rebecca noted the strained tone of Adam's voice. "Like you lock the door so I will go?"

"Damn you, woman," he said, exasperated. "Say what you have to say and get back to your own room. How did you know where to find me anyway?"

"Is easy. I open doors and smell. You are third door. This room smells of you. Room just beyond is empty. No one sleep there for long time."

"Are you decent?" He turned to face her.

She stood not five feet away from him in a pool of moonlight. Adam's heart skipped a beat, and he swallowed hard. Rebecca had put on the shirt as he had ordered, but she had merely tied it around her waist to form a skirt open on one side from hip to ankle. Above the makeshift garment she wore nothing but waves of dark hair. They cascaded over her perfectly formed shoulders and framed the taut, proud breasts and narrow waist. Moonlight turned her flawless skin to ivory-hued satin, a living satin that begged to be caressed.

Adam's breath came in ragged gasps, and he felt the heat rise in his blood. "What do you want of me, Rebecca?" By sheer force of will, he held himself in check when every fiber of his being wanted to take this teasing nymph in his arms and bury his face in those tempting ivory breasts. Would her skin taste of salt, or would it be sweet like stolen honey? Trembling, he raised a hand. Whether it was to touch her or to keep her from coming closer he did not know.

Rebecca's lips curved in a knowing smile; she could smell the man-heat of him. Shawnee or English, some things were the same. Adam desired her body. And, as a delicious warmth flowed up through her veins, she was forced to realize that she desired him, too.

"I do not understand, A-dam," she said softly. "You are my enemy. I have sworn to take revenge against you, yet..." Her voice trailed off into nothing. The words were meaningless, even to herself. Was she becoming English, that she could hide behind words that were dry leaves in the wind?

She had not come to Adam's room to share pleasures of the mat with him; she wanted him to tell her the English words that would make the grandfather understand that she was not the woman he believed she was. For the sake of what they had been to one another, Rebecca could not bring pain to Thomas Bradford, but he must realize who and what she was. Adam, her enemy, knew her as no one in this strange country did. He had seen her spill the blood of the German; he had faced her anger when she would have killed him that first day at the stream in the forest.

She was not heartless; she knew her decision to return to the Shawnee would hurt the grandfather. It would hurt her, too. Never again would she know the happiness of the days before the Germans attacked her village. She would leave a part of her here on the shores of the Chesapeake.

But Adam knew that she could never become the English woman her grandfather so desired. She had seen the realization grow in Adam's eyes. She had lived among the People far longer than she had among the English; even her English speech was that of a child, not that of a woman. An English woman would know what to say to Adam now, would know how to tell him that it would do no harm if they took comfort in each other's bodies. She knew what to say in Shawnee. The soft words formed on her lips as delicious sensations caused a familiar aching in her breasts.

She took another step toward Adam. "*Ki-te-hi*," she whispered. Unconsciously she arched her back to ease the heavy-limbed languor that was making her feel an unnatural light-headedness. Her knees felt weak, and she became aware of an intensely pleasurable, almost painful, throbbing in her erect, swollen nipples. "A-dam?" Her hand rose to touch his, and the shock of that touch caused her to tremble with yearning. "A-dam," she repeated huskily, "you make a burning in my blood."

Adam groaned deep in his throat and lifted his hand to stroke her cheek with one calloused finger. She shuddered and captured his hand with her own, pulling it against her to cup a creamy breast.

His arms encircled her, crushing her against his hard, muscular body. Their mouths joined in an exquisitely provocative kiss that sent Rebecca's heart pounding as she stared up into his dark eyes, fierce and glowing in the moonlight. Adam's hot, wet tongue plundered her mouth, and she welcomed it, clinging to his massive head and pulling him ever closer. Their limbs entwined, and the burning that had driven her into her enemy's arms raged higher, driving every thought but Adam from her brain.

His fingers stroked her breasts, tantalizing the tumescent peaks and sending feverish chills of desire through her body. He murmured her name over and over, and the sound of his voice caused a singing in her heart. His mouth seared a scorching trail down her throat and breasts, then gently closed on a love-swollen nipple. She moaned with pleasure as the tip of Adam's tongue flicked against the bud, causing a warm moistness in her secret woman's place.

"Rebecca…Rebecca…darling."

Her arms tightened around his neck as he picked her up and carried her to the bed. "You are so beautiful." He ran his hand across her silken belly and caressed the hollow of a curving hip. "I've wanted to touch you…to feel your skin against mine…to do this…and this…."

She inhaled deeply, reveling in the strong male scent that was Adam's alone, a clean odor of tobacco and spice and something more, something she could not name. Her tongue followed a shaggy eyebrow and flicked against his eyelid. Even his hair was clean, softer than a Shawnee's and as thick as a beaver pelt. She ran her fingers through it as her body writhed beneath his touch.

He joined her on the bed, molding his virile body to hers. The knot came loose, and the shirt fell away, leaving her thighs and legs free for his exploring touch. His big hands were gentle as they slowly stroked her legs and buttocks, lingering to trace sensual circles on her bare skin.

Soft cries of joy rose in her throat as Adam's fingers tangled in the damp curls between her thighs, and she fastened sharp white teeth on a male nipple, biting down just hard enough to drive him mad with longing. He groaned, and she felt his hot breath against her breast as she dug her nails into his back and shoulders.

He moved astride her, and instinctively she opened to receive his love. The heat of his throbbing male member pressed against the inside of her thigh as their lips met again.

"A-dam," she murmured. "*Dah-quel-e-mah*…loved one. Make of me a woman."

With a cry of pain, he tore his mouth from hers and rose on one elbow. "This is wrong," he said, panting. His face was stark in the moonlight, and she felt the anguish of his soul.

"How can it be wrong?" she asked, bewildered. Tears gathered in her heavy-lidded green eyes, and one spilled down her cheek. "Why is wrong, A-dam? Do you not want me?"

In one motion, he rolled free and rose to his feet, backing away from the bed. His fingers rubbed at his lips, lips that had been one with hers only seconds before. "It's not right," he said hoarsely. "I want you. God only knows how I want you. But I can't. I can't use you like a tavern wench." He turned his back on her and crossed to the fireplace, leaning against the mantel as if for support. "Get you back to your room, Rebecca, and never come here again!"

"Aghqueloge!" Bitter words rose to her tongue as she fought back tears. Shame flooded her. She had offered herself freely, and Adam had refused the greatest gift a woman could give. *"Matchele ne tha-tha.* You are truly my enemy, Adam Rourke. I was fool to forget it, but I will not forget again. Other men would welcome what you have cast away!"

"Hold your tongue!" he flung back. "You sound like a dockside slut."

Her eyes darkened with fury. She did not know the word slut, but his tone was clear. He believed her to be without honor! Ruthlessly, she wiped at the hateful tears with the back of her hand. "English custom is bad if it makes what is between a man and a woman without honor. I will have none of your English customs." Catlike, she leaped from the bed and walked proudly to the door. "I will not keep you from sleep again, English *-manake.* Do not fear." Her fingers found the bolt and shot it back. Before he could reply, she had ducked into the shadowy hall and was gone.

Adam closed the door and leaned against it, feeling sick. His body still yearned for release, but worse, he had hurt Rebecca terribly, and she didn't even know why. What was this power she had over him? He'd had his share of women, but none like this; she was beyond his comprehension.

Shaken, he lowered himself into a chair and buried his face in his hands.

Safe in her own bedchamber, Rebecca let the tears flow. She was truly alone in this place; it had been a mistake to ask Adam's help, and more of a mistake to let her desire for his body cloud her thinking. She had shamed herself. If she were to hold her head high again, she must find a way to redeem her lost honor.

A woman's scream, followed by the murmur of angry female voices, brought Adam upright in his bed. It was full morning and hours past his normal time of rising.

There was no mistaking Rebecca's voice as a door banged and a flood of irate Shawnee filled the air. Adam yanked on enough clothing to avoid indecency and stepped out into the hall.

"Amatha e'shi-que-chi!" Rebecca spat as she threw a woman's corset at the retreating back of an equally incensed Isabel Sinclair. "Take your torture weapon and put it on a pig!" Rebecca pushed a lock of wet hair from her face and fired a parting volley. "Iroquois!"

Adam swallowed the chuckle rising in his throat and glared at the short Welsh maid standing a few feet from his door. "What are you gaping at, wench?" he demanded.

With a frightened squeak, she turned and fled down the back staircase. Adam took a deep breath and stepped between the warring factions.

"What's amiss here?"

Isabel's beet red face loomed in front of him. "If you can communicate with this…this *savage,* I suggest you do so immediately!"

"Hahhah! She calls *me* savage! Look, Adam! See what she would tie my body in." Rebecca gave the garment a kick with a slender foot.

Adam tried to ignore the fact that Rebecca was clad only in a thin lawn shift and that she had been in a bath only minutes before, obviously without properly drying her body afterward. Damp hair clung to her face and neck, and bright spots of color tinted her cheeks.

"You're as bad as she is," Isabel exclaimed. "Staring at her nakedness. Have you no shame, Adam!"

Rebecca flung herself at the older woman. Adam stepped into her path and caught her in his arms, shielding his face from the blows she rained upon it. With an unconcealed oath, he picked her up, carried her back to her room, and dropped her into a chair.

Before the angry Shawnee could change to English, Adam closed the door and leaned against it, his arms folded over his chest. "Now calm down and tell me what this is all about."

Rebecca sprang from the chair and paced the floor like a caged animal, muttering furiously under her breath.

"Do you want them all to laugh at you?" His soft words hit home, and she turned to face him, her wide eyes meeting his. The amusement she saw in his face shocked her; it hit her like a blow, and she whitened.

She chewed on her full lower lip like a child. "They must not laugh at me," she protested. "Is not fair. She is not fair! First she has English maid woman bring water for me to take bath. I tell her I will bathe in the Chesapeake, but she will not listen. I remember I am guest here, so I wash in iron pot." She gestured wildly toward the tin bathtub set in the corner of the chamber. "Then the Isabel woman say I cannot wash my hair proper. I must have English maid who like to watch naked women wash my hair. I say no. Isabel woman say yes—is proper. I give in." She paused for breath. "Do not laugh. I hate you, Adam Rourke. I do not want you laugh at me."

The lazy grin vanished, and Adam's face paled beneath the tan. "I'm not your enemy." He hesitated, groping for words that did not come easily. "I've come to care for you a great deal."

Rebecca exhaled sharply. Adam Rourke was speaking the truth. Lips might lie, but eyes were the openings of the soul. She could read plainly that he believed what he said, and her pulse quickened as memories of the night before washed over her.

She had felt with Adam as she had felt with no man before. Even now she shivered with inner joy as her heart remembered. He had opened his arms to her with more than lust; his touch had been tender and giving—the caress of a lover.

And yet he had shamed her. He had turned her away. Rebecca's voice dropped to a whisper. "If you care for me, why you drive me from your bed?" Heat rose to stain her cheeks with the red marks of her shame, but she could not retreat. Trembling, she took a step in Adam's direction and held out a hand. "Why, Adam? I must know why you shame me."

Her heart was beating so fast that it made her lightheaded. What was this strange magic that drew them together? Unconsciously, she moistened her lips with the tip of her tongue. He was not even handsome, this big Englishman. His skin held none of the dusky copper that she had come to admire in a man; his hair was beaver brown instead of crow-wing black. He was too tall and too broad. And worse, he did not have sense enough to know that he owed her her freedom for saving his life at the river.

The intensity of her gaze shattered the last of his amusement. Cold realization flooded Adam's brain. Whatever this fey creature was, she was not a child. And right or wrong, it was clear that she had formed an attachment to him. To hurt her with a careless word would be cruel and unjust.

He had wanted her in the night, wanted her as he had never wanted another woman. He wanted her now.

"I didn't make love to you because we aren't married," he said gently. "Not because I didn't want to. You're a beautiful, desirable woman. And…" He ran his fingers through his hair as he remembered the insults he had flung at her. "I'm sorry for what I said. I was angry with myself, Rebecca, and I blamed you."

"It was a bad name you called me, that 'slut,'" she said. "When I say it to the great aunt, it make her very mad."

"You called Isabel a slut?"

"Only one time." A sly smile spread across Rebecca's face. "I call her worse in Shawnee, but she does not understand." Her eyes narrowed. "You say you are sorry you speak to me with an evil tongue."

"I was wrong, very wrong. But it was wrong for me to kiss you…to touch you in…in that way." Adam clenched his hands into tight fists at his sides. Why did everything he said sound so damn stilted and pious? He had to make her understand. "You are my stepfather's granddaughter. It is forbidden for us to…" God! He could still smell her sweet, wild scent. His fingers ached to push aside those damp strands of hair and cup her face between them. He wanted to crush her mouth with his and feel the length of her warm body against his own. "It's against the law."

She laughed. "Against law to share pleasures of the mat?" Her green eyes clouded with suspicion. "I do not believe you, Adam. You speak false." She shook her head knowingly. "We share no drop of blood, English or Shawnee. And the English know not the way of clans. You are bad liar, Adam. There is no such law against us joining as man and woman."

"Not a written law, perhaps," he hedged, "but it would not be honorable. Your grandfather put his trust in me. I can't betray him."

She shrugged. "I see only that you have honor in dealing with the grandfather but not with me," she said stubbornly. "You are the one who does not understand. My body does not belong to Thomas Bradford. It is mine. I am a free woman; I am a widow. I can share pleasures of the mat with any man I choose, when and where I choose. I do not accept your English law."

Voices outside the door brought Adam back to reality. "Some things you'll have to accept," he declared, loudly enough to be heard in the hallway. "Such as proper clothing and respect for Isabel." He pointed to the dimity gown that lay crumpled on the floor. "You really should put that on. You can't go down to breakfast in your shift; it would cause a scandal among the servants. They'd laugh behind their hands at you." He picked the dress up and smoothed out the wrinkles. "It's a pretty gown, Rebecca. Peach is a becoming color. It will look beautiful on you."

She jerked the gown from his hands. "I said I will wear dress. I will not wear that lacing thing. It pinches me here." She indicated her breasts, and Adam swallowed a chuckle. "Shawnee women do not wear such things! I could not breathe in it. How would I ride a horse or run or fight if I had to? I know I could not climb a tree in such a thing." She grimaced and pursed her lips.

"No, I guess they're not much for tree climbing," he agreed solemnly.

"English women must be very stupid."

A lazy grin spread across Adam's face, making his rugged features warm and alive. "Some are," he admitted. "Are you going to tell me there are no stupid Indian women?"

"No." The sparks faded from her eyes, replaced with a gleam of mischief. "Do not these laces make it hard to share pleasures?"

"Sometimes. But what goes on can come off."

"Too much trouble. I will leave it off."

"But you will wear the dress over the shift to breakfast."

Rebecca nodded reluctantly. "But no laces."

"Agreed." Adam put his hand on the doorknob. "And you will apologize to Isabel for calling her a slut."

"I will not. I am a savage." She grinned. "If I do not take her scalp in the night, she will have happy!"

"Just so long as you don't lift mine."

"Do not sleep too sound, Adam Rourke," Rebecca threatened softly.

CHAPTER 10

Three weeks had passed by English reckoning since that first breakfast with her grandfather. In those days and nights, Rebecca had come to care for the old man deeply. Together they had ridden over the broad fields of Sheffield, their horses so close they could have touched hands. They had sat together in the peaceful twilight of the thick hardwood forest and walked along the shoreline of the plantation in early morning.

Slowly, word by word, her grandfather had brought back memories of her family and childhood; and bit by bit, they had created new memories together.

"You are a Bradford," he insisted. "The last of my line. All I possess will go to you and to your heirs, save whatever I leave to Adam. I don't have long to live, and you must prepare yourself for the responsibility."

"When I am with you," Rebecca replied, "I feel I belong here. But in the night I dream of home and my people."

"You were born English, a Marylander—not an Indian. Your place is here."

"But I am not like these people. I do not think like them; I do not act as they do." She sighed, bent to pick up a shell from the damp sand, and tossed it back into the bay. "Your food is strange to me and your religion even stranger."

In the weeks since she had arrived at Sheffield, her English had returned. She was even beginning to think in English, and it frightened her.

Thomas leaned on his cane and stared thoughtfully into his granddaughter's sea green eyes, eyes so familiar they brought a tightness to his throat. Damn, but she was a beauty, even in her outlandish attire.

She had demanded and gotten a gown of the softest doeskin, cut and stitched in the English fashion but scandalously short and slit up the sides above her knees. She had embroidered the V neckline with a design of wild strawberries, cunningly stitched in red and green silk against the cream-colored leather. The dress was sleeveless, with fringe where the sleeves should have been, and it was loose about the waist instead of tightly laced.

Thomas had to admit that she walked and ran as gracefully as a doe in her high moccasins. They rose to her knees, covering what would have been bare legs. She had made them herself, working all one day and night with the shoemaker's tools. The resulting footwear was undeniably Indian, but the terrible blisters on her feet from proper leather shoes had been reason enough to allow the substitution.

"Time will make the difference, child," Thomas said, easing himself down on a log. He propped his silver-headed cane beside him and breathed deeply of the salt air.

Sea birds wheeled overhead in a flawless azure sky. Their cries blended with the soft slap of water against the narrow shoreline, giving the old man the peace he had always found there.

Slowly he rubbed his left foot back and forth in the sand. "I thought I would die of grief when they were all murdered. What did I have to live for? You, your brother, my only son and his wife—all murdered. I came down here and sat right on this point and thought about taking my own life."

Rebecca knelt at his feet, her eyes wide with compassion. One thick braid fell over her shoulder, its end secured with red silk and decorated with a tiny silver bell. "The Shawnee say it is a terrible thing to take your own life. You must face the judgment of Wishemenetoo in the dream world, and if he finds you did it for a selfish reason, or because of cowardice, the punishment will be harsh." She shook her head as she spoke, and the other braid slid forward.

Thomas caught the braid between his fingers and rubbed the dark, shining strands. "I wanted to die, but I got to thinking about you. What if you were out there, waiting? Waiting for me to find you. What if someone brought you home and there wasn't anyone here to take care of you?" He looked down at the sand. "Adam and his mother gave me a reason to go on. The two of them, and the hope that you were alive. It took years, but gradually I built a new life. In time, you'll adapt. You'll forget the Indian ways and come to love ours."

"But I don't want to adapt, Grandfather." She lay her smooth, tanned hand over his gnarled one. "I like me the way I am. I don't want to be English. Time won't change that."

"It will if you let it, if you don't fight it." He cleared his throat. "What do you think of Adam?"

"I don't think of Adam." A lump formed deep inside her, constricting her heart. I spoke a lie. I am becoming English. "No," she admitted, "that is not true. I have...I am angry with Adam. He does not speak to me unless he must. He treats me like a stray dog."

Thomas's forehead wrinkled in concern. "Adam's rude to you? When? I'll not have it! Why didn't you say something to me before?"

"No, Grandfather, I did not mean that he was rude. He is always very polite, a gentleman. But he looks through me, not at me. I do not think he wants to be with me at all."

"I had hoped you two would become...would become friends. Adam's been like a son to me. He's hardworking, fair, and as honest as a saint. His blood's good, despite the fact that he was a bondservant. Did you know that Adam sold himself to pay his dead father's debts?"

"No. But he is an honorable man; he would do such a thing." Rebecca sat back on the sand and raised her knees, wrapping her arms tightly around them. She did not wish to talk of Adam Rourke, or even to think of him. Such thoughts disturbed her. She stared out across the gray-blue waters of the bay, unable to keep certain scenes from playing across her mind.

What kind of man was Adam? He was so different, so unlike the dusky warrior who waited for her on the Ohio, that she couldn't decide if she loved him or hated him.

There was no doubt in her mind that they had been together in other lives. The Shawnee held such belief strongly. A man did not die, the old people said, but was reborn into a new child's body. And, sometimes, when the spirits were kind, a soul remembered the old life and the ones he or she had loved or hated.

Isabel had been shocked when Rebecca had hinted at such a thing.

"Blasphemy!" the older woman had shrieked. "Devil's notions! Never let me hear you say such filthy words again. You'll be burned as a witch."

Rebecca had asked the grandfather about this burning. "It is true that the English tie women to the stake and burn the flesh from their bodies?"

He had nodded sadly. "For witchcraft and sometimes, I fear, for treason against the Crown. In the old country and up in the north." Thomas waved his hand in that direction. "In New England. They're a hot-headed, psalm-singing bunch up north. But not in Maryland. At least not for witchcraft. Why ever do you ask, child? You're surely not wishing to have dealings with a witch."

"No, Grandfather. I promise not to."

That conversation, too, Rebecca had held in her heart and made a vow to choose her words more carefully from then on. Any talk of spirits or dreams seemed forbidden. It only added weight to her feelings of being alien to these people. Shawnee men and women prided themselves on being able to speak their mind. Even a great chief had no power over what a man said. Truly, the English knew little of real freedom.

"Adam will make a good husband for some woman." Thomas's words broke through Rebecca's reverie.

"What? I'm sorry. What did you say about Adam?"

"I said he will make a good husband. He's well educated and respected by the community. He has the head of a much older man. Most of these youngsters don't have sense enough to come in out of the rain."

Rebecca nodded politely. What was it to her that Adam would make a marriage with some English woman? She would probably have cold blue eyes and skin like tallow. She would wear tight dresses and feet-pinching shoes and never bathe except on Sundays, if then.

After the bath the great aunt had forced her to take in the iron pot, Rebecca had been surprised to learn that the English people were not as clean as the Shawnee. A Shawnee bathed every day, even in winter. It was a habit Rebecca did not intend to break.

Every morning she rose before dawn and went down to the river to swim. The river was not far from the manor house and easier to reach without being seen than the bay.

She had been greatly tempted to steal a horse and just keep going. Escape would not be difficult. She could head due west to the mountains and then north to her own land. But her conscience would not permit her to steal away like a thief in the night. She must convince her grandfather to send her back with his blessings, or…

The thought returned to haunt her. Or she must stay until he died. It might well be that it was Inu-msi-ila-fe-wanu's wish that she remain here as long as the old man lived. If this was true, she would never be free again if she didn't fulfill her obligation. It was a difficult decision to make and a hard one to live with.

"No one will give you a horse without my permission," Thomas said.

Rebecca jumped. Had he read her mind? She stared at him in disbelief. "How did you know what I was thinking?"

"Because you're a Bradford, damn it. You've got the Bradford mind and stubbornness. When you get that far-off look in your eyes, I know you're thinking about those Godforsaken Indians!"

"We are not God-forsaken," she protested. "I worry for my Shawnee parents. I don't know if they're dead or alive."

"Perhaps I can make inquiries, send some messages north to the forts."

Rebecca scoffed. "You think I'm a child to believe such tales? What would a white soldier know or care about Shawnee? There will never be word. Or, if you paid enough coin, there would be. But it would be a lie, no matter what was said."

Thomas eased himself forward and put his weight on his cane. "I can see, Rebecca, that it's time you and I made a bargain."

She raised one dark eyebrow quizzically. "What kind of bargain?"

"If you will remain here at Sheffield and continue your instruction and your duties for a reasonable time, I will help you to return to your Indians if you're still not happy here."

"You mean that? I can go home if I wish?" Her face lit with excitement, then grew serious again. "What is a reasonable time? Until the first snowfall?"

Thomas laughed. "This is October. You give poor exchange." He rubbed at his chin thoughtfully. "How many years were you with the Shawnee? Eleven? Well, then, it's only fair I have a full year to win you back. You must stay until the snow flies next year, and then, if you insist on going back, I'll send you to them a wealthy woman. I'll load you down with blankets and muskets and shiny beads, and whatever else those heathen fancy. What say you, Rebecca? Do we have a deal?" He offered his hand.

Rebecca felt empty inside. A year? So many things could happen in a year. Would she wither and die in this foreign place away from the sweet, soft sound of the Shawnee tongue and the warm laughter of shared stories around a flickering campfire? She would miss the fun of maple-sap gathering and the breakup of the ice on the Ohio.

In a year's time new babies would be born and old people would die. She might even be counted among those dead. The vise around her heart tightened. Not even her name would remain with her people; if they believed her dead, none would speak it.

A tear gathered in the corner of her eyes, and she wiped it away with the back of her hand. The grandfather was waiting. She must give him an answer.

High above them, an osprey wheeled; his piercing cry echoed in her mind. She looked up. Was it an omen? As if in answer, a single feather drifted earthward, swirling in slow circles toward the damp sand. Rebecca nodded silently and took her grandfather's hand; the wishes of Inumsi-ila-fe-wanu, the Great Spirit, were clear. She must obey the command.

"I will stay until the snow flies next year," she said solemnly. "And I will try to learn your ways."

"Good." The old man gripped her hand tightly. "And you can start by being on time for your lessons. Your tutor tells me you are a difficult student." The twinkle in his eyes softened the censure. "Master Byrd is very expensive. You should try not to upset him."

"I do not need a tutor like a child!" she retorted. "And I don't want to sit indoors when the wind whispers to me to come. He is a fool." Rebecca puckered her lips in imitation of the pompous schoolmaster. "I know I must learn English and to speak the French and even the dancing. But why must I learn the tongue of dead men...this Latin?"

"The Bradfords have always prided themselves on their education, the women as well as the men. It is expected that you be fluent in the classics. Later, I will see that you have music lessons as well."

Rebecca grimaced. "Byrd smells, and I think there are creatures in his great powdered wig. If I took him into the woods, he would starve to death in a week."

"Try and restrain yourself. I won't have him frightened away as you did the other one."

"He called me a savage!"

"You *are* a savage." Thomas grinned. "But a lovely one. Run along now, child. You will be late." His arm ached from the now-familiar pain; he wanted nothing so much as to lie down. He wondered how much longer his heart would hold up, and prayed to God that it would last until he saw Rebecca safely situated.

"Go," he insisted. "I wish to sit here a bit longer. And remember to address him as Master Byrd."

Rebecca's answer was lost in the brisk breeze as she hurried down the beach toward the manor house. Thomas chuckled. Even with her promise, his granddaughter would be a trial to the poor tutor. Her temper was becoming legendary in the household.

If Adam did take her to wife, he would have his hands full. It was obvious that Rebecca would never become entirely civilized. Still, her coming had brought new life to Sheffield, and Thomas was sorry he wouldn't live long enough to see the changes she would make in the future.

Slowly, he got to his feet, trying to ignore the pain in his chest. Today was a bad day; sometimes he could get through the whole afternoon without it.

"Just a few more months," he muttered under his breath. "Long enough to set things right." He leaned heavily on his cane and began the long walk back to the house.

"Drink up, sir! There's plenty more where that came from!" The barmaid winked saucily at Adam and wiggled through the crowded public room of the Merry Widow.

Adam leaned back against the high wooden bench and drained the last of his rum. Damn Rebecca Bradford. He'd done all he could to avoid her, working long hours and even spending nights away from the house. Still she plagued him day and night. Now the men were complaining about his evil disposition.

"What ye need is a night in Annapolis," his friend Jock had suggested. "In the warm arms of a wee lass at the Widow."

"You're a fine one to be giving advice," Adam had replied good-naturedly.

"When ye start snappin' at yer bondmen lak they be cur dogs, I ken ye have been too long wi'oot the warm arms of a sweet lassie. How long ha' it been?"

"None of your damn business!"

They'd laughed off the conversation, but after his business had been completed at the custom house, Adam had stayed on for supper at the Annapolis Inn and then had made his way down to the harbor.

The Merry Widow had a reputation for providing rough but honest entertainment. A mixed bag of townspeople and sailors filled the smoky room; you had no need to fear you would have your throat slit if you took a bit too much to drink, and there was no danger from the press gangs that usually frequented such waterfront taverns.

Big Kate ran an honest place that was known from Boston to Port Royal. It was said that no high sheriff had ever entered the low doorway and none ever needed to. Killings were few and fights almost as scarce. Big Kate's bondservant, Ivan, stood guard beside the entrance, a Norseman's axe leaning on the wainscoting beside him. The blade of the terrible weapon bore a single chip—damaged, men said, when Ivan drove a British press gang from the Merry Widow and missed slicing the head from one man by inches.

The tobacco was cut and hanging; Adam should have felt well satisfied. Instead, he was restless as he hadn't been in years.

Once, in England, there had been another woman who had caught his fancy—Mary Sutcliffe. Her brother had been a fellow clerk with him at the Inns of Court, and Adam had visited their country house. Lord Sutcliffe had given every indication that his suit was not unwelcome. God, but Mary had been a beauty, a tiny little thing with a waist he could span with his hands. Her eyes were Dresden blue and her cheeks like roses.

The serving wench filled his mug again, and he absently tossed her a coin. Mary. He hadn't thought of her in years. Mary's hair had been like spun gold; once, he'd caught a lock and twisted it around his finger when they were playing blindman's bluff. She'd squealed and turned right into his waiting arms. Mary Sutcliffe had been as soft as…Adam cursed under his breath. Doubtless Mary was long since wed and the mother of a half dozen wailing children.

He sighed and lifted the mug to his lips. Lord Sutcliffe had been kind but firm after Adam's father's suicide. There could be no question of him courting Mary. Third daughter or not, the family did not wish to be involved in scandal. No mention had been made of the debts Adam's father had incurred, although Adam had learned later that Lord Sutcliffe had paid the remainder of Adam's overdue apprentice fees.

He had lost Mary at the same time he'd lost his home, his father, and almost everything else he'd held dear. But all that was long past, only memories now.

He'd been content enough here in the Maryland colony—more than content. He'd found a purpose and a way of life he cared more for than the study of law. Now Rebecca Bradford had complicated everything!

"Lonely, m'lord?" Big Kate sat down beside him on the bench.

Adam regarded her through bleary eyes and murmured something unintelligible. She laughed, and he smiled crookedly. Big Kate was tall, six feet in her stockings if she stood an inch, but that six feet of woman was well formed. And if her blond hair held streaks of gray, what gentleman would mention it? "You're a sight for sore eyes, Katy," Adam said gallantly.

"I heard you were out hunting Indians, Adam. Is it true Bradford's granddaughter is as wild as an Indian herself?"

Adam nodded. "Just about." He frowned. "Mean…she's mean." He straightened up and blinked. "Don't call me m'lord. You know better than that, Katy. Save it for the...for the *oronookoes.*"

"You're as fine a gentleman as any with a tide, Adam Rourke," she said soothingly. "A man like you..." Big Kate laid her hand on his and traced circles on his wrist. "A man like you needs a lot of woman."

"That's right," he said, his words slurred. The room was growing unbearably warm. "I think I need another drink."

"Come up to my room. I've got just what you need up there."

Grinning, Adam rose to his feet and followed her through the room and up a flight of narrow stairs, to the obvious delight of half the people in the tavern.

"Take good care of him, Big Kate!"

"I been tryin' to get up them stairs wi' Big Kate fer three years," another man roared.

Adam turned, gripping the handrail for security, and nodded to the onlookers. "And a pleasant night to you too, gentlemen."

"What good would it do me if I let you come up?" Big Kate shouted back. Laughter rocked the room as the two reached the door at the top of the steps and closed it behind them.

Big Kate's private quarters were larger and more tastefully furnished than Adam had expected. He sank into a large chair beside the fireplace and looked around the bedchamber.

"Well, what do you think?" Kate began to slice wedges from a golden round of cheese.

"It's nice," Adam admitted. "Verra...very nice." The four-poster bed had satin hangings that matched the curtains. A cherry table stood beneath the window, adorned with an elegant white bowl full of red apples. The table looked Italian, a costly addition to a tavern keeper's home. The rest of the room was furnished simply but with good taste. It was a room in which a man like Adam could instantly feel at home.

Adam rubbed his eyes. "Your pardon, Katy. I'm not feeling my best. It's not what I expected at all."

She laughed heartily and handed him a pewter plate of bread and cheese. "I wasn't born a whore, Adam Rourke." She knelt down beside him and began to pull off his tall boots.

"You're no whore." He grinned. "I've seen you knock a man cold for suggesting such a thing."

"Aye, that's true." She regarded him shrewdly. "I do pick my friends carefully. A helpless widow can't be too careful."

"You're about as helpless as a hungry wolf," he said. She was massaging the calf of his leg, and it felt good.

"I try not to mix business and pleasure, but sometimes I break my own rules." She moved closer and began to rub the other leg. "Would you like a hot bath?" she added huskily. "The water's hot, and the soap's as soft as a baby's bottom."

Adam's eyes twinkled. "A bath with you might be just what I need, Katy." He caught her hand and pulled her easily into his lap. "I may be drunk, but I'm not so drunk I don't know an irresistible offer when I hear one."

CHAPTER 11

First light was just beginning to break in the eastern sky as Adam neared the river. A soft mist rose off the water, enveloping the forest trail in an eerie haze.

The only sounds were the soft footfalls of his horse and the creak of saddle leather, interspersed with the *rat-a-tat-tat* of a far-off woodpecker. There was no breeze at all, and the falling leaves drifted quickly to earth, adding to the dreamlike quality of the morning.

Adam cursed under his breath, flushing once more as he relived his attempts to satisfy himself and Kate. He had failed. Failed utterly and miserably. It was the first time such a thing had ever happened since he was fifteen, and he fervently hoped it would be the last.

What worried him most was that he knew it wasn't the rum that had kept him from performing. He had been far drunker on past occasions and still managed admirably. Kate had been clean and warm and more than willing. The fault all had been his.

He reined in the horse and pulled a flask from his saddlebag. The bite of the strong rum filled his brain without dulling his distress. Big Kate had handled the situation well. "I owe you one," she'd teased. Adam knew she would keep what had happened private, but that assurance didn't assuage his shame.

He had enjoyed the kissing and the feel of her soft body curled around his. He had equally enjoyed the sweet woman smell and the shared laughter. But his mind and body had refused to cooperate. Damn Rebecca Bradford! It was *her* face he had seen in his mind, *her* body he was embracing. Despite his pent-up desire, Kate was no substitute for the woman he really wanted. It was a sobering thought.

Adam carefully dismounted and led the animal toward the river. He had circled around the house, hoping to reach the plantation without seeing or being seen by anyone. It was a Sunday morning, and once safely in his room, he would not be expected to appear until later in the day. He put each foot down deliberately, conscious of the weakness in his knees.

How much had he drunk? He'd lost count. With a groan, he contemplated the pain of a monumental hangover. Normally he wasn't a drinking man, and when he did indulge, it took a lot to make him drunk. Unfortunately, this was one of those rare times and he was paying dearly for it.

Adam leaned heavily against the horse's withers as the animal dropped his head to drink from the river. Suddenly Adam jerked back in surprise and nearly lost his balance as the water swirled not two yards from the bank. A vision rose from the depths to taunt him.

"Adam? What are you doing here?"

He blinked, not certain if what he was seeing was real or the product of strong Haitian rum. "Rebecca?"

She laughed and wiped streaming water from her face. "Not Rebecca but Alagwa Aquewa, Star Blanket. Have you come to bathe in the river this morning?"

The desire that had eluded him the night before with Kate was now in strong evidence. Adam's breath caught in his throat as he stared at her, clad only in a glorious mane of dark hair and the faint morning light. She stood hip deep in the river; little drops of water rolled off her upthrust breasts and sparkled in the nest of ebony curls below her taut belly.

He dropped the reins and took a step toward the water. "You're the second woman to ask me to bathe with her, and I'm inclined to take you up on it."

Rebecca didn't miss the soft slur of his words; she offered a hand gracefully. "You have had too much to drink, English-*manake*. Perhaps the cold water will cure your sickness."

"They say water's a cure for fever." Adam drew in a shuddering breath as he fumbled with his clothing.

Rebecca stood like a statue, watching as he stripped away his shirt and breeches, revealing the hard male body with it's strange covering of beaver brown hair. Her pulse quickened as she savored the delicious sensations that spread through her body. She felt her nipples harden, the spreading ache of her suddenly heavy breasts, and a surprising lightheadedness. What enchantment was this that she felt so? She had seen Adam's beautiful body before.

A shiver of fear passed through her, and she turned and dove beneath the water in a single motion. Eyes open, she swam with sure, even strokes toward the far side of the river. She was halfway across when Adam's arms closed around her.

They rose to the surface as one. Rebecca stared at him; the familiar brown eyes were glazed and heavy lidded with passion. "Adam?" she whispered. His mouth covered hers.

Her senses reeled at the provocative power of his kiss. One muscular arm supported her back; the other caressed her breasts and stomach and tangled in the ringlets above her woman's mound. "Rebecca," he murmured hoarsely. "Rebecca."

She met his kiss with equal fervor, wrapping her legs around his waist and pressing her body against his. Her mouth opened to receive his seeking tongue, and she felt the flame of his ardent kisses ignite the banked fires of her soul. She pulled his head down to hers, no longer aware of the cold current of the river, knowing only that her own fever must be quenched.

The taste of rum on his breath was sharp but not unpleasant. The curling pelt on his body felt wildly exciting as he kissed her again. Her mind and body welcomed the searing kisses as they welcomed the tumescent pressure against her clinging thighs.

An all-encompassing languor spread through her, shutting out everything but this man, this moment. She scarcely felt Adam carry her into shallower water. "You'll drown us both," he whispered.

He took the bud of one love-swollen nipple between his lips and tenderly sucked, licking it until she moaned with joy for the hot, tingling desire that coursed through her veins. "I've wanted to do this for so long," he murmured. "And this…and this."

He was still not certain that she was real, that this was not a dream. "You do taste of honey," he said. "Honey and pine and salt." A red haze filled his brain; he couldn't get enough of her. "God, I've wanted to hold you like this, to kiss you here…and here…"

Rebecca chuckled deep in her throat and traced the curve of his shoulders with the tip of her tongue, dipping down to flick at the hard nubs of his aroused male nipples. He writhed against her, and she caught his flesh between her teeth and bit with just enough pressure to send his passions soaring.

"I want you," he uttered raggedly. "God help me, I want all of you."

"And I want you, Adam Rourke."

They kissed again, and Adam's touch was tender, filled with a lifetime of longing. Joyfully, Rebecca opened her body to him. *"Ki-te-hi,"* she whispered against his mouth. *"Ki-te-hi.* "The pain of his entry was quick, replaced almost at once with a driving need for something, something she could not fathom. She rose to meet him, welcoming the powerful thrusts that lifted them out of this world and into another. And when she thought she would die of the wanting, their world exploded in sweet, glowing rapture. For what seemed forever, she drifted, not wanting to open her eyes and see the earth that had become solid once more, not wanting to feel the cold water about her waist.

"Rebecca."

The steel in the voice shattered her magic circle. Her eyes flying open, she looked full into Adam's brown gaze. Sparks of fury darted from those dark orbs. Rebecca pulled back and would have fallen if it weren't for his arms, like bands of iron, that held her to him.

"You lied to me." Adam was suddenly cold as the enormity of what they had done washed over him. "You said you were a widow! But you lied, damn you. I was the first, wasn't I? The first man ever to make love to you."

She stiffened, and her eyes narrowed in anger. "I did not lie. I had a husband." She struggled to break away, but it was like trying to free herself from solid rock. Adam was so close that she could feel his warm breath on her face. "Let me go," she demanded.

"You were a virgin! Look at you." He lifted her half out of the water, and stains of pink ran down her inner legs and were washed clean by the river. "Why? Why, Rebecca? Why did you lie to me?"

It was impossible to miss the agony in his voice. Adam was not drunk now; he was cold sober. Somehow she had done a terrible thing. "I didn't lie," she repeated. Tears welled in her eyes. "I..." The words would not come; she turned her face away.

"You were a virgin maid, and I dishonored you and Thomas." Adam exhaled loudly. "We'll have to be married. As soon as decently possible."

The thought of telling Thomas what he had done sickened him. The way Rebecca had talked, the provocative way she'd acted—he'd never dreamed she was an innocent. "I'm not a fit match for you, but we'll have to make the most of it."

Rebecca found her voice. "I'd sooner marry an Iroquois!" Her flying hand stung his cheek and left a white imprint there. "Sharing pleasures did not dishonor me, but you dishonor me now. I am not a liar! And I will not marry you! I want no stupid Englishman, and if I did, you, Adam Rourke, would be the last man I would choose. Now, let me go before I scream for help and bring half of Sheffield running."

Stunned, he let her drop back into the water. "You made love with me in broad daylight, but you won't marry me?"

Tears rolled down Rebecca's cheeks. "The lovemaking was a gift for what we had and what we might have had. You refuse my gift, so be it." The beautiful face hardened into a mask; the tears might have been crystalline. She surged out of the water onto the bank; Adam followed. There she shook the heavy mane of wet hair away from her face with the dignity of a queen and regarded him coldly through narrowed eyes. "Marry you? Phaaa! I was married to a Shawnee, and if I marry again, it will be to a man of my own choosing, a great warrior. Not to an Englishman who has yet to prove his manhood."

"I didn't hear any complaints in the river!" Adam lashed back.

"To make love is not *dah-quel-e-mah,* that which binds two people together for all time. And that which hangs between your legs does not make you a warrior. You are still a boy, Adam Rourke. And I am sorry for you, for I thought you more."

"You refuse my offer of marriage?"

"I have said it!"

"Damn you, Rebecca," Adam muttered between clenched teeth. His hands were knotted so tightly into fists at his sides that the veins stood out on his forehead. Waves of angry confusion washed over him. "You don't understand. This will hurt your grandfather. It will shame him. We must become man and wife to salvage his honor."

Rebecca sniffed disdainfully. "If it will hurt him, then don't tell him. No one knows but you and me. Will your horse carry tales?"

"You might have a child. Do you realize that?"

"If we have made a life, it has nothing to do with you. It is mine and I will care for it and give it all that it needs. Among the Shawnee there are no bastards. A child takes his mother's clan name, and every child knows his mother."

"Rebecca...please." Adam's voice cracked with emotion. "Listen to me. I've made a mess of this. I care for you. No, don't turn away! It's true. But there are things here you can't be expected to understand." He reached out to touch her, but she backed away. "I'm in no position to take a wife. I have nothing to offer you. Even my clothes over there"—he motioned to the pile on the ground—"were bought with Thomas's money."

"What has money to do with you and me?"

"You are a great heiress. If I wed you..." The words caught in his throat. "If we married, it would be said that I married you to get Sheffield. Men would taunt me with it, and..." Adam swallowed hard.

"Maybe they speak the truth." Rebecca's eyes spat cold fire. "The whites hold money above all things. Most men marry for land or for the fat purses of their wives."

"I'm not most men, Rebecca."

"And I am not an English woman!" Quick as a cat, she dashed across the grass, caught up the reins of Adam's horse, and threw herself into the saddle. With a cry, she brought the ends of the leather thongs down across the animal's rump and urged him into the river.

"Rebecca!" Adam lunged for the horse and was knocked aside by the force of the bay's charge. Horse and rider plunged into the water. Cursing, Adam hurried to his clothing and began to dress hastily. There was no question of catching her on foot. He'd have to find another mount.

Rebecca paused on the far side of the river long enough to retrieve her own dress and pull it over her head. After donning her moccasins, she remounted Adam's horse and turned him toward the bay. She had no intention of running away; she had given her word, and a Shawnee woman could not break a promise. She wanted only time to be alone and to sort out her thoughts.

Becoming a woman was an important thing; it should have been a time of happiness. Indeed, she could remember the wonderous feelings Adam had caused. Why couldn't she savor those feelings instead of tasting salt tears of sorrow?

She loved Adam. It was not just the call of flesh to flesh. He was as dear and familiar to her as her own right hand. She wanted to be near him, to hear his voice. Even in anger, the sound of his voice was a joy.

The bay slowed to a walk as they reached the shore, and she turned his head south, away from the manor house. She couldn't face Adam until she had tamed her own wild emotions.

He had said he cared for her, but what did that mean? How strong was the love of this Englishman if he valued what other men said more than he valued her feelings? Tears welled again in her eyes, and she dashed them away. She was not a weeping woman; she had never been. What was it about this man that made her own spirit betray her?

Memories of their lovemaking swirled about her, bringing a warm tingle to her skin. The brief pain had been as nothing compared with the glory that had followed. Adam was a dear and loving man, a man who had doubtlessly pleasured many women. Rebecca raised a finger to her swollen lips, unable to suppress a faint smile. The heat of their joining had shut out the cold of the river. The smile became a chuckle. She doubted if any of Adam's former lovers had lured him into such an unlikely spot.

The wind off the bay was cool, and Rebecca shivered. She reined in the horse and slid off. Walking would warm her until her hair and damp clothes dried.

Overhead, a pair of wild ducks winged their way southward. She noted their passing just as she took in the details of every living thing around her. Winter would soon lock the tidewater land in an icy embrace. She sighed softly, unable to remember the time of snow here on Sheffield and wondering if it was a time of hunger as it was for the Shawnee.

The reins trailed limply through her fingers. Adam. She could not understand him. He frightened and fascinated her at the same time.

They had absolutely nothing in common, were of two different worlds. She knew the ways of birds of prey and four-legged hunters, but this man with the fair skin and knowing eyes was beyond her. Surely there could be no happiness in the joining of earth and fire. They did not even pray to the same gods. It was impossible.

Adam had accused her of lying, and she was certain he did not even realize what a terrible thing that was. The English wrote down their thoughts; they crammed them into books and placed them on walls for all to see. But the Shawnee had no such sign writing. A thing must be held in the mind of a man or woman. A person was without worth if he did not speak the truth.

The Shawnee considered the spoken word to be sacred. Were not all the deeds and legends of the past repeated to each generation of children? If a lie was allowed, would not all the history of the Shawnee be in danger?

And if he believed that she would lie to him about being a widow, how could he ever trust her in the simplest matter? Rebecca kicked a piece of driftwood. It was so unfair!

She had been fifteen when she exchanged vows with—. Her breath caught in her throat. Among the Shawnee one did not speak the name of the dead. Even to think of him by name was unnerving. How could she explain him to Adam if she couldn't even say his name? Rebecca dropped the reins and sat down, folding her legs under her. If Adam were Shawnee, it would be so much easier!

Her husband had been her friend from her first day among the People. He had offered her his hand and his protection, patiently teaching her the language as only another child can. Otter. There, she had said the word in her mind! It was his childhood name and not the name of the man. Surely there could be little harm in using that.

"Otter." Hesitantly, Rebecca repeated the word out loud. Adam's horse flicked his ears. "Otter." The marsh grass bent in the wind, and a red-winged blackbird loudly defended his territory from an intruder. Nothing else happened. The sky didn't fall. "Otter!" she shouted, and the name became laughter.

How many stories had he told her? How many games had they shared? He had taught her how to make fishhooks by wrapping slivers of bone together and how to catch trout with your bare hand by tickling their bellies. He had taught her…"Oh, Otter, how I've missed you!"

She couldn't remember when she'd realized that Otter was not like the other boys. Oh, his twisted leg was there for all the world to see, but that wasn't what made him different. His crooked body was only a shell. Inside was a marvelous mixture of tricks and stories and magic—real magic, not just the quick hand of a conjurer. He knew the secrets of plants, and he could foretell the coming of a storm long before anyone else. Otter could even read her mind—at least he could until he had shown her how to keep anyone from doing it.

She had loved Otter, and when his father had asked for her hand in marriage, there had been no question of her refusing. They were kindred souls. Otter had insisted that they had been twin brother and sister in another lifetime. She had gone willingly into the marriage, knowing the life she was choosing, knowing that she would never bear a child or live the life of other women because of Otter's handicaps. And they had been happy together.

Their joining had been of the mind, not of the flesh. And nothing, nothing under the sun, had prepared her for a man like Adam Rourke. She had not known that a man's touch could sear her skin like a living flame or that his kiss could make her forget who and what she was…could make her desire him above even her life.

Otter's caresses had been gentle, the kiss of a brother to a sister. Her strong arm had supported him when he walked. They had lain together in the night as innocently as children.

The horse nudged Rebecca's shoulder with a velvety nose and blew softly through his lips. She lay her cheek against the broad head and sighed: "Why? Why now?"

There was another man who waited for her among the Shawnee, a warrior in his prime. He had declared his intention of making her his woman, and she had not refused him. With such a man she would know what to do. They would think alike—each would know what to expect from the other. Such a man would make a far better mate than Adam.

The weight of her promise to the grandfather rested heavily on her shoulders. She had given her word to stay until snow flew the following year. There was no question of avoiding Adam for that length of time, not when she yearned for his touch, not when desire flamed within her at the very thought of him. She rubbed at her throat thoughtfully. There could be no wrong in lying with him to quench that fire. Loving Adam and sharing pleasures with him did not commit her to him forever. She would take the joy with open arms, and when the time came for her to return to her people and to another man, she would take the bittersweet pain of parting.

"I will love Adam, but I will love him today without thought of tomorrow," she whispered to the horse. Low rumblings from the animal's throat seemed to give assent. "I will not forget who I am, or what he is," Rebecca vowed.

Her brow smoothed as she gathered the reins and remounted. Her world shifted back into place. "I am Alagwa Aquewa," she cried to the cloudless tidewater sky. The echoes of her voice were lost in the vastness of the land as she turned the horse firmly back toward Sheffield. Her lips silently formed Adam's name as she urged the bay into a canter along the sand, and she savored the sweetness of its unspoken sound.

CHAPTER 12

Fair weather held into November, and the only indication of the passing season was the endless lines of waterfowl that flew over Sheffield. Ducks and geese by the thousands lent their mournful cries to the lapping of bay tides against the sandy beach and the ever-present melody of the salt breeze. Rebecca delighted in the softness of the land, knowing that at the headwaters of the Ohio ice was already forming in the early hours before dawn.

The chill on the tidewater was a more subtle thing but just as real. There had been no reconciliation with Adam; he might have been a stranger for all the attention he paid to her. He never mentioned their joining or his desire to make her his wife. Rebecca found his detached attitude maddening.

In truth, she hardly ever saw him. He rose before dawn and was in the saddle for fourteen hours at a stretch, rarely appearing at the manor house for meals. And when he did join Rebecca, Isabel, and Thomas for dinner, he barely looked up from his plate except to murmur polite responses to direct questions.

Coupled with Rebecca's anger was her concern. Adam was working far too hard. With her grandfather's deteriorating health, the full weight of the responsibility of running Sheffield fell on Adam's broad shoulders.

Besides the harvesting of the last of the crops and the culling of animals for slaughter, work at the prize house went on day and night. There tobacco, Sheffield's main cash crop, was packed into five-hundred-pound casks for shipment to England. It would then be sold and the money returned to Sheffield in the form of goods available only in England. The bondmen and free men and women who worked on Sheffield were well trained, but there were a dozen emergencies a day that required the authority and decision-making ability that only Adam possessed.

Rebecca understood all this, but it wasn't enough. Adam could not have forgotten what had happened between them. His strange sense of honor, so foreign to her, could not be so easily cast aside. He had been deadly serious when he'd insisted that they would have to be married. Now it was as if that morning in the river had never existed.

How could a man's behavior change so completely? Had she injured his pride when she refused his offer of marriage? It was a puzzle that kept her awake many nights.

She and Isabel had reached a guarded truce. Rebecca listened to the endless instructions on proper dress and etiquette for an English lady. Fortunately, Isabel had to say a thing only once for her to remember it. Her command of English had returned in full, along with memories of her English mother's lessons in behavior. But learning the rituals did not make them any easier to comprehend.

The hated fan was a prime example. Isabel had talked about the use of a fan, demonstrated it, and then related endless stories about English women she knew and their skill with a fan until Rebecca had wanted to seize the object and stamp it underfoot.

"A lady holds her fan thusly," Isabel said, inclining her head slightly. "Notice the finger grip—firm but not clutching. A fan has its own language. This"—the older woman pursed her lips, narrowed her eyes, and touched the corner of her mouth with the closed fan—"indicates pique. And this"—she opened the fan and covered the lower part of her face with it—"shows interest, but not vulgar—"

"Enough!" Rebecca cried in exasperation. "Let English women hide their faces behind folded paper. It is a ridiculous custom, and I will not do it." The hem of her rose chiné gown caught on the leg of a chair, and she jerked it free. "I don't like your fan, and I don't like your dresses with these absurd skirts!"

"'Absurd.'" Isabel chuckled. "Your vocabulary is improving daily, but your accent, I fear, is hopeless." She picked up the edge of Rebecca's dress and examined the precious material for tears. "A lady does not concern herself with what is and what is not absurd in fashion. You should have seen the shoes I was forced to wear at my wedding to Edward." She shrugged. "Your place is to follow the dictates of mode. As a Bradford, you are expected to set an example for Annapolis society, even for the colony. You simply cannot dress and behave like a painted savage."

With great effort, Rebecca held back the sharp retort forming on her tongue. Isabel's rigid posture and shrewish nature hid a genuine concern for her charge. It was not until Grandfather had explained Isabel's personal reasons for coming to Sheffield that Rebecca had begun to soften her attitude toward the woman and look for something positive within.

Isabel Sinclair was a widow, and her only son, named Edward after his father, had died of fever two summers before. Isabel had continued to make her home with her daughter-in-law and granddaughter until her daughter-in-law remarried. Now there was a new master in residence, and Isabel's daughter-in-law was pregnant with her new husband's child. Even though the law guaranteed Isabel a home and support for her lifetime, it was obvious that there was little welcome in the house for her. Without money to maintain her own separate household, she had welcomed as a miracle Thomas Bradford's offer that she come and care for his granddaughter.

Rebecca had known widows without children among the Shawnee and had often felt sorry for them. Unless such a woman could remarry or had a family to provide for her, her life was often one of sorrow and bitterness. Such women sometimes adopted captive white boys or the orphaned children of others to keep from being alone, without the protection of a hunter in the lodge.

"Isabel is a proud woman," Rebecca's grandfather had said quietly. "It's important that she feel needed at Sheffield."

Rebecca had nodded; she could understand pride and the suggestion that perhaps Isabel's forbidding exterior was a defense. At times she felt that way herself.

Rebecca tried to summon up her sympathy for Aunt Isabel that morning, but it was useless. She had already spent two hours with Master Byrd and another with the seamstress. Her patience was at an end.

"I wish to go riding," Rebecca said. "Now."

"Impossible. Tomorrow we go to Annapolis to watch the tobacco fleet sail. As your grandfather has told you, we are to be the honored guests of the high sheriff. There will be a party and a ball afterward, and you simply aren't ready to be presented to society. We must continue with the lessons all afternoon."

"Enough!" Rebecca's green eyes glittered dangerously. "If I am not ready to be presented to Annapolis society yet, then it is better that I remain hidden at home." She crossed to the doorway and put her hand on the brass knob. "Tell my grandfather not to wait on me for dinner."

Isabel's indignant protests were easily ignored as Rebecca closed the door behind her and hurried up the steps to change into her deerskin dress. She felt that if she didn't breathe fresh air soon, she would go mad!

The stable was quiet, with only the familiar sound of horses shifting in their stalls and munching hay. A calico kitten rubbed against Rebecca's ankle as she reached for a bridle. She bent and gathered the kitten in her arms, cuddling it against her cheek and whispering a few words in Shawnee.

She looked around the shadowy barn with satisfaction; it was one of her favorite places on Sheffield. Even as a child she'd loved to come here and hide in the hayloft. The stable was spotless as always; the horses stood knee-deep in clean straw, and the hard-packed floor was raked clean. The rich smell of grain and hay mingled with the pleasant odor of the horses and the spicy scent of drying tobacco.

The bay mare nickered a greeting as Rebecca entered her stall and slipped the bridle over her head. There was no need for a saddle; today she would ride bareback. "Good girl," Rebecca murmured. "You'd like to get out of here for a run down the beach as much as I would, wouldn't you?" She easily vaulted up onto the mare's back and guided her out of the barn.

A stableboy looked up from his raking and waved as they passed. Rebecca grinned and waved back, digging her heels into the animal's sides and sending her cantering out of the farmyard.

It was late afternoon when Adam spied the mare grazing beneath a huge tree a few miles from the manor house. He reined in his own mount and looked around for the rider. "Rebecca? Where are you?" The mare raised her head and stared at him. "Rebecca?"

"What do you want, Adam?"

The voice came from over his head. "Rebecca, where—?" He peered up through the branches and caught sight of her sitting on a limb. "What in God's name are you doing in that tree? I've been looking for you for an hour. Come down here!"

Something struck him on the head, and he threw up a hand to protect himself from a rain of chestnuts. One struck the black's hindquarter, and the animal shied. "Whoa! Whoa, boy!" Rebecca's laughter brought a flush to his neck and face as he struggled to keep his seat. "Damn it, girl!"

Rebecca leaned away from the trunk and took careful aim with her last bit of ammunition. The chestnut flew as straight as an arrow, smacking Adam sharply on the ear. The resulting roar of rage brought a self-satisfied chuckle from her lips. He can't pretend he doesn't see me now! she thought. "What's wrong, Adam?" she teased. "Having trouble with your horse?"

"Come down out of there!"

"I like it up here." It was true. She could see for miles across the water. The air was cool and fresh, and she was completely alone except for the wind and the birds and an occasional saucy squirrel.

"Come down out of there before you break your neck."

"Why don't you come up, Adam? You can see all of Sheffield from here. There's a schooner going north toward Annapolis, a big one."

"I don't have time to climb trees, and I don't have time to run after you. Now get down here!"

"Maybe you should take the time to climb trees, Adam Rourke. You work too hard. A little play is good for the spirit." Rebecca swung down to a lower limb, the better to see his face. "I told Isabel I would not be back for dinner. Why are you following me?"

"We have guests. The high sheriff and his wife have arrived. Your grandfather wants you there to meet them." Adam tried to keep his voice stern as he watched her move agilely down the tree. She was still more than thirty feet from the ground; one slip could mean disaster. Lord, she had magnificent legs. The fringed dress left little to the imagination.

In the days and nights since they had made love in the river, he had thought of little else. Twice he had almost gone to Thomas and confessed what he had done; both times he'd lost his nerve and been unable to tell Thomas the extent of his betrayal. If he and Rebecca were married, he would have a right to what he'd taken, a right to those lush curves and laughing mouth. Adam felt a painful tightness in his loins as he remembered her satin skin next to his.

"Be careful," he warned.

Rebecca's answer was cut short by a sharp crack as the branch beneath her foot snapped. Frantically she tried to catch herself, gasping as the rough bark scraped her hands. Lights exploded inside her head as she slammed against a limb. Then she was in the air and tumbling toward the hard-packed earth below.

Adam broke her fall, and the two of them went sprawling. Rebecca rolled free and sat up groggily. "Are you all right?" he demanded.

Numbly she nodded, breathing too hard to speak. Gingerly she touched the back of her head where a knot was already rising. She started to get up, but Adam stopped her.

"No, wait until your head stops spinning. You're sure nothing's broken?"

She shook her head. The tenderness in Adam's voice was impossible to miss. He cared. Rebecca looked down at her smarting palms; they were skinned and bleeding, and one hand had a piece of wood lodged in the flesh. Childlike, she held it up to Adam. "Can you get it out?" She felt sick and foolishly happy at the same time. Adam cared, really cared about her.

"I told you you'd break your neck in that damn tree," he said, his tone belying the scolding words. "You would have if I hadn't been here to catch you." He cradled her hand in his wide palms and deftly pulled the splinter free. Blood welled up in the gash. Adam gently pressed his lips to the wound and sucked it clean, turning away to spit out the blood. "My mother always says this is the only way to clean a puncture."

His lips brushed her palm again, sending waves of delicious sensation through Rebecca's body. Adam's words were brusque, but she could feel the tenseness of his muscles. *I was in his arms; why did I move away?* she asked herself. It was where she wanted to be, where she *had* to be.

Deliberately she gave a low moan and went limp. Adam caught her head before it hit the ground.

"Rebecca!" He gathered her into his lap, cradling her against his chest. Fear paralyzed his brain, and his mouth felt dry as dust. His fingers touched the swelling at the back of her head. "Rebecca," he whispered.

Her dark lashes lay motionless, her lovely features so still they might have been carved of wax. A purplish bruise was rising on one cheekbone. The rose-tinted lips were slightly parted, and her breath was so shallow he could hardly hear it. "Rebecca," he repeated urgently.

In one fluid motion, she slipped both arms around Adam's brawny neck and pulled his head down to meet her kiss. His shock lasted no more than a heartbeat, and then he was kissing her in return, kissing her with all the pent-up passion of a lifetime. Rebecca moaned and strained against him as hot, tingling desire washed through her. Her mouth opened to receive his deepening kiss, welcoming the intimacy of his tender exploration; her fingers tangled in his hair. "Adam," she murmured in return. "My beautiful Adam."

She met his gaze and held it, noting instantly the flicker of doubt that crossed the sea of brown. Abruptly, he pushed her away and rose to his feet.

"You tricked me!" The flushed face darkened with anger. "I thought you were hurt!"

She raised herself on one elbow and lazily let her gaze travel over him, from the muscular calves rising above the sturdy black leather boots to the muscle-corded neck and broad, sinewy shoulders.

He stood as solid as the chestnut tree, his legs firmly planted, his arms akimbo and his face as impassive as that of an Iroquois. Rebecca's giggle caught in her throat as a trace of fear sent a shiver through her. How big he is. How wonderful that his bigness no longer seemed strange but right. The sheer maleness of his stance and aura bade her be cautious.

"I'm sorry as to that," she said, "but not sorry we kissed. I think I love you, Adam. I don't know why you act so coldly to me."

His eyes narrowed. "You've decided to become my wife, then?" His voice was deceptively light, as if the words didn't matter.

Rebecca sighed and got to her feet, taking a step toward him. "Marriage has nothing to do with love, Adam. We are too different to be happy together for a lifetime. We are of different worlds. We do not want the same things. I love you, but..." Her voice dropped to a whisper. "But I cannot marry you. It would be a lie."

Adam's big hands curled into fists at his waist. "You would have me dally with you, but you will not be my wife." He shook his head. "No, you can't have it that way. I want you, but I won't betray Thomas again. Your price is too high, Rebecca. Choose another man to torment."

She took another step. "I don't want to hurt you." Tears welled up in the sea green Bradford eyes. "I feel hurt as well."

"A marriage between us would work if it wasn't for your damned stubbornness."

"Would it, Adam? And what happens next year when I want to go back to my people?" It took every scrap of her self-control to keep from flinging herself into his arms. Her fingers ached to smooth the lines from his brow, to trace his stiff upper lip and roam through the dark mat of hair on his chest. "Can't we just share a little happiness while we're together?"

"No, we can't. I'm not an Indian, Rebecca. If I make you my wife, I'll never let you go. I'll hold you close and protect you." He ran a hand through his hair, and his voice cracked with emotion. "I want my wife to give me children and to lie beside me in the darkness and listen to the wind on a stormy night. I want to be able to trust her completely with all my worldly goods...and with my life, if need be."

He took a deep breath. "If you marry me, Rebecca, you give up all thought of going back. You must take your rightful place as the mistress of Sheffield and as a highborn Englishwoman. "

"You are the one who wishes to marry!" she cried in exasperation. "I only wished to share pleasures with you." Liar, her heart cried. Her back stiffened, and she forced her tone to frosty aloofness. "If we cannot share that together without fighting, how could we share anything more?"

"Then we have nothing more to discuss, have we?" Adam caught the reins of her mare. "They're waiting for you back at the house. Can you ride?"

In answer she vaulted onto the bay mare's back and jerked the reins from his hands. "Let them wait," she cried. "I'd be no fit company for the high sheriff and his lady wife. Tell them they can wait until tomorrow to see the Shawnee squaw. Maybe I'll shock them all and come to the celebration in paint and feathers."

Adam grabbed for her arm, but she wheeled the mare in a tight circle, then dug her heels into the horse's sides and galloped away.

"You can't run away from who you are!" he called after her, but his only answer was the cry of a swooping hawk. In tight-lipped fury, Adam swung into the saddle of his own mount and rode back toward the manor house.

Rebecca stared in awe at the huge gathering of people in the market square. Never had she seen so many human beings gathered in one place. Men, women, and children, black faces and white, and even a few of copper hue, mingled and pushed their way good-naturedly through the streets of Annapolis.

They had all come, rich and poor, free and indentured, to witness the sailing of the tobacco fleet, Grandfather had explained. "This is a general holiday. Only the stingiest of masters would expect any work from his people today." He pointed to the harbor, filled with boats of all shapes and sizes. "Our fortunes all rest in the holds of those vessels."

Rebecca couldn't suppress a gasp of wonder. The ships seemed like great white spirit birds, with their sails billowing as they skimmed over the sparkling surface of Chesapeake Bay. Tiny dugouts and rowboats bobbed amongst the larger anchored vessels, carrying last-minute passengers and letters. The flawless blue of the tidewater sky made a perfect backdrop for the colorful panorama; it was a sight that Rebecca knew she would never forget. Even the seagulls swooping down for bits of food seemed louder and brighter on this crisp morning.

The smell of freshly baked gingerbread wafting on the breeze drew her attention back to the market square. Wedged among the wagons and carts and stalls were pie sellers and gingerbread women and vendors of all manner of food and drink. There were dogs and horses and even a stray pig, squealing and rooting amid the crowd.

The sound was deafening; everyone seemed to be shouting at once. Babies were crying and oxen bawling. So loud was the din that the military band practicing at the top of the hill could hardly be heard.

The family of Thomas Bradford had no need to compete for a clear view of the festivities. As honored guests of the ranking government official, they had been ushered to chairs in a roped-off section of the dock beside the high sheriff and his party. From the safety of their privileged position, they could see and be seen without the annoyance of rubbing elbows with the common people.

At first Rebecca had been ill at ease, unsure of herself in the midst of hundreds of staring eyes, loud music, and booming cannons. She felt strange and uncomfortable in the rose gown and many petticoats. The hateful lacing pinched her waist and cut off her breath until she thought she might truly faint. She would have gladly given the matching rose slippers to any tavern maid had she been offered a pair of worn moccasins. Adam, she was delighted to note, looked every bit as ridiculous, in his curled wig and square-toed shoes with the red heels, as she did.

Last night she had deliberately stayed away from Sheffield until she had seen the strange carriage roll down the rutted lane toward Annapolis. She'd been in no mood to be exhibited like a prize cow, not even by her grandfather. And when she did finally return the bay mare to her stall and slip into the house, it was well after the hour of the evening meal. She had snatched a bit of bread and cheese from the kitchen and gone straight to her room.

It had been a sleepless night. For hours she'd sat by the window watching the slow procession of the full moon across a cloudless sky. She had thought about Adam, but she was no closer to an answer today than she had been yesterday when they'd parted so bitterly.

He had not spoken to her at breakfast, and the words they had exchanged on the sloop that took them to Annapolis might have been between polite strangers. He had placed his hands around her waist to help her ashore at the dock, but his touch had been cold and emotionless. The pain had run deep. She would rather have had sharp words than cool acceptance.

At the moment, Adam was devoting all his attention to the daughter of one of the ship's captains, Mistress Jane Trimbull. The young woman was reed thin, with an upturned nose and barely a hint of a chin. Her hair was the color of straw and so sparse that she had to hide it under a wig. Rebecca had seen her hair when a passing child had given the wig a swift tug as Mistress Jane was joining the sheriff's party.

Rebecca stifled an urge to wiggle in her seat as she watched Adam and the Trimbull woman out of the corner of her eye. Adam looked so smug she wanted to smack him. How could he sit there and pretend to be interested in what that stupid Englishwoman was saying?

"...the very latest mode. Father brought it on his last voyage from home. I do miss the shops and tradespeople. One is so limited here, don't you think, Master Rourke?" The china blue eyes blinked rapidly, and she continued her endless chatter. "Father says..."

Adam squirmed and tried to look interested. His wig itched, and somehow a damned pebble had worked its way into his left shoe. And damn, Rebecca was beautiful. The rose-colored gown was a perfect foil for her tanned skin, and her cheeks sparkled with natural color beneath the emerald green eyes. Her dark hair hung loose, secured only with a bit of rose ribbon. A single strand had worked its way free, and he wanted to tuck it back behind her ear so badly that his arm ached from his locking it in place.

There were stares aplenty, from the gentry as well as the common folk, but Rebecca sat there like a queen on her throne, accepting their tribute as her rightful due. He'd been mad to suggest they marry, Adam thought bitterly; she could have a title for the asking. He had nothing to offer her except his bare hands and an out-of-date honor that she had scorned. Damn, but the girl was maddening. If she'd been anyone but Thomas's granddaughter...

"I *said*"—Mistress Jane cleared her throat loudly—"I said you must miss home as much as I do."

Adam blinked. What had she said? Something about home? "Sheffield?"

"No, not Sheffield, your real home in England." She tapped him sharply on the knee with her fan. "You weren't listening, Master Rourke."

Lord, why wasn't he sitting next to the sheriff's wife? The woman weighed seventeen stone, but at least she had some sense in her head. This wench was a goose. "Sheffield is my home," he answered smoothly. A warm feeling of satisfaction washed through him as he realized it was true. Home had been where his mother's laughter had brightened the shadows of dark stone hallways. She'd brought the love with her to make a home of the tiny servant's cabin they had shared in their first days at Sheffield. And later, when they had gone to live in the manor house, her laughter had spread through the rooms and stairways to make them familiar.

Adam's gaze fell on Thomas Bradford. The old man held himself erect with a rigid pride that would not permit the frailty of his health to infringe on his dignity. If the lines of pain around his lips were evident to those who loved him, they were balanced by the snapping vitality of his eyes. An aging falcon, but still fierce and proud. A trace of a smile curved Adam's lips. Disloyal to his own father or not, he could not deny the truth. *I love Thomas Bradford as well as any son ever loved a father.* A sharp twinge of guilt twisted his heart. Thomas had raised him up from servant to heir, had taught him all he knew about being a planter and had made a man of a foolish boy. *And how do I repay this gift? By seducing the woman who means more to him than any other living person.*

"Adam!" The fan clipped his knuckles. "You aren't paying the least bit of attention to me, are you?"

Rebecca caught sight of the flush spreading up Adam's neck and cheeks and she giggled. For just an instant, their eyes met, and he felt the full sting of her mocking amusement. His fingers closed over the fan, and the wood and paper snapped effortlessly. "My apologies, Mistress Jane," he said with glib insincerity. "I shall see that your fan is replaced, since this one seems defective."

Mistress Jane's indignant gasp became a strangled choke as Adam turned away from her to rise and bowed gallantly to a towering blond woman in a starched white cap.

"Mistress Kate," Adam called. "Are you well?"

Big Kate's laughter matched her frame. "Well enough, Adam." Her eyes danced merrily as she approached the sheriff's party. "I see you've got a prime spot from which to watch the goings-on!"

"That we have. Would you care to join us?" Adam offered a hand. "I can have another chair brought."

Big Kate put her hand on her hip, threw back her head and roared. "I believe you would at that," she managed to sputter when she could finally speak. "But I'll decline your offer today. There's so much business at the Merry Widow, I've no time to dally." She dipped a graceful curtsy. "Good day to ye all, lords and ladies, and God speed our ships." With a wink, she turned and strode purposefully away.

Jane Trimbull's voice was a squeak. "That woman! I know her. She's...she's..." Jane's face was beet red, and her eyes seemed close to popping. One hand clutched her throat, the other the remains of the broken fan. "I can't believe you..."

"Mistress Kate is an old friend," Adam said, easing back into his chair. "She's a sensible woman, Mistress Jane. One you would do well to emulate."

Rebecca made no effort to hide her own low, throaty chuckle. She didn't know who the big woman was, but anyone who could upset Mistress Jane merely by stopping to speak to their party had her sympathies.

Thomas Bradford paused in his conversation with the sheriff and covered Rebecca's hand with his. "There are many young gentlemen here who are anxiously waiting to dance with you tonight at the ball. Adam and I will have to keep a sharp watch lest one of them sweep you away."

Rebecca hid her uneasiness under demure lashes and murmured something in reply. She wasn't looking forward to the evening at Kentwood. Aunt Isabel had told her that the cream of Maryland society would be there and that they would all be watching her, waiting for her to do something strange and uncivilized. She would be expected to dance and to talk about foolish things, things that meant nothing to her. She would have preferred to explore Annapolis or to watch the ships. She would have preferred anything to being stared at.

When Rebecca looked back at Adam, she saw that Mistress Jane was gone. A slow, lazy grin spread over Adam's face. Was he watching to see if she would do anything wrong too? Would he abandon her to strangers tonight at Kentwood?

A unit of soldiers in bright uniforms moved up the street before them, stepping precisely to the beat of the military drums. All eyes turned toward them, and Rebecca pushed back her fears to take in the colorful performance. She could not stop the night from coming, but she would face it only when the time came. For now she would savor the unexpected pleasures of the day. It was a strength she had learned from the Shawnee, and one that would serve her well for the rest of her life.

CHAPTER 13

Rebecca's hand rested lightly on her grandfather's as he led her down the grand staircase to the splendid hall of Kentwood Manor. Her head was held high, her eyes were wide and sparkling in the light of a hundred candles, and her movements were as graceful as any dancer's. No one watching could have guessed she was so terrified that her breath came in shallow whispers and her skin felt cold and clammy.

"Steady, child," Thomas murmured proudly. "No other woman here can touch you for wealth or beauty." He smiled, nodding to this acquaintance and that as he escorted her through the swirling mass of aristocracy to greet her host and hostess.

The people. There were so many people. Rebecca swallowed hard, smiling woodenly. It took every ounce of courage she could muster to keep from turning and fleeing this house and those staring English eyes.

Her Shawnee father had told her tales of running an Iroquois gauntlet. His arms had been bound and he had been forced to run between two lines of enraged, screaming Iroquois. Men and women had beat him with clubs, tripped and stabbed him, and sliced at his arms and back with steel knives. Rebecca thought now she would rather run such an enemy gauntlet than walk through the crowd of these hard-eyed English.

Large as the rooms were, the walls and ceilings seemed to close in around her. Hundreds of candles glittered from chandeliers and wall sconces, their radiating heat adding to the body heat of the guests. The odor of so many people mingled with the scents of perfume and rum and polished leather. The English voices seemed harsh and overly loud, so unpleasantly different from the soft lisp of the Shawnee tongue. Even the rustle of starched petticoats and the squeak of leather against leather were overpowering as bewigged, powdered faces and staring eyes combined to deepen her panic.

People were talking to her, touching her dress, invading her body space. Why would they not leave her alone? In the stables, with the horses and dogs, she would have felt at ease. In the forest she knew what to do, how to survive. But here? Her tongue felt as though it were made of clay. Her mouth was dry and numb. Every muscle in her body was poised for flight, even as her will forced them to be still.

Her brain had ceased to function. Even the simplest English words seemed foreign. She could not remember how to address the high sheriff. Was it "your honor"? "Your grace"? Instead, she nodded dumbly like an ox.

As Thomas led Rebecca into the room, Adam turned from his conversation with a friend to gape at her as crudely as any peasant. He had believed the rose gown she had worn earlier was the prettiest he had ever seen; this fragile-looking thing of silk and lace far surpassed it. The color was a soft peach that shimmered with every step she took. He'd seen that same shade in a sunrise over the bay, all misty and glowing. The neckline was cut straight across, edged with that filmy lace, and dipped so low it made his heart skip a beat. Her hair was pulled back away from her face and held with some kind of glittery combs so that the mass of her rich, dark tresses fell in curls across her shoulders and back. Lord, how he wanted to pick her up and carry her out of this place! Away from all these people! Someplace where there would only be the two of them.

She carried herself like a queen, and her flawless skin needed no powder or patches. Her brows were like perfect wings above the sparkling green eyes with their thick, dark lashes. Even that stubborn chin seemed made to fit in a man's hand. Adam sucked in his breath. He wanted her. Badly. She'd bewitched him with her Indian sorcery, with the ancient mystery that lurked behind those ever-changing Bradford eyes. His hand tightened on the pewter cup in his hand until the metal bent and punch spilled over his hand.

"By our lady, Adam! Watch what yer doin'!"

Adam jumped, spilling the rest of the punch and cursing under his breath. The laughter of his friend Lee Mathews brought a flush to the roots Adam's hair.

"She's exceedingly fair, but I'd have thought you'd had your fill of her beauty. I heard from Mistress Jane that the two of you don't exactly see eye to eye," Mathews said.

Adam glared a warning and turned to shove the ruined punch cup at a servant. "I'd say Mistress Jane was green with jealousy." He dried his hand on an offered towel. "There can't be above four eligible young ladies within a day's ride of Annapolis, but I'll wager Mistress Jane and the others will lack admirers until Rebecca chooses a husband." He motioned toward the door. "Let's go into the library. They're serving something stronger than punch in there."

"And leave Mistress Bradford free to dance with all these gallants?" Laughing, Mathews followed Adam from the room.

Rebecca watched with bitter disappointment as Adam's broad back disappeared through the crowd. She had thought he would at least dance with her. She automatically followed the intricate steps of the dance, smiling mechanically at the sheriff and nodding the same way in reply to his conversation. She tried not to let the strange music interfere with her thoughts. Why was Adam avoiding her tonight of all nights? Didn't he realize how much she needed him?

That dance ended, and her grandfather claimed her for the next one. He smiled warmly at her and whispered, "I'm so proud of you, Rebecca."

She felt a cold shiver pass through her body as she looked up into his loving eyes. The shadow of death lingered there. The dance was a slow one, but it drained a great deal of strength from the tired, sick old man. "Please," she murmured. "May I have something to drink? I'm thirsty."

Thomas led her away from the dancers toward the punch table. He was breathing hard, and she felt fear numbing her throat. What will I do when he's gone? And then the immediate answer came: I'll go home. A flicker of doubt taunted her. But what of Adam? She pushed the question away. She could not let herself think of him.

A stranger came to ask her grandfather for the privilege of a dance with Rebecca, and she went without protest after Grandfather found a chair and sat down. The man had offered his name, but she paid little attention to it. What difference did it make? They were all alike, these Englishmen, tall and pale with blue eyes and powdered wigs. She pretended to listen to him, wondering why she hadn't stayed home at Sheffield. At least at Sheffield Adam wasn't quite so much of a stranger.

She had enjoyed seeing the ships and the excitement in the market square. The Shawnee would never believe half her stories about Annapolis. She wished she could have seen more of the town instead of coming here and being put on exhibit.

The music ended, and the gentleman took her hand to lead her back to her grandfather.

Suddenly the close press of bodies, the overloud laughter, and Adam's betrayal became too much. She could not let herself become one of these overdressed fashion puppets. She stopped, pulled her hand free of her partner's, and smiled sweetly at him. "I must go upstairs for a little while. I have the faint head," Rebecca murmured. Or was it the headhurt that Aunt Isabel had said? "If you will excuse me, sir."

"Certainly, Mistress Bradford. Is there anything I can do?" The blue eyes looked ridiculous beneath the oversized white wig, as though the man were wearing a cloud on his head. "Should I call your grandfather?"

"No. Do not trouble him for such a small thing as a lady's headhurt," she replied softly. "I'm certain I will feel much better in a few minutes."

That at least was true! She would rid herself of this crashing garment and the silly slippers, and then...A smile danced behind the sweeping dark lashes. "Thank you"— she hesitated, and then his name came back to her—"Lord Michael, for the...for the care."

With a feeling of relief she hurried up the wide staircase. If she didn't get out of this house, she'd go mad! As she paused on the landing to look back over her shoulder, a feeling of uncertainty passed through her. This is Adam's world. There's no place in it for me. Even if she wished to try to fit into it, which she didn't, it would never do!

Her mouth set in a stubborn line as she nodded to a passing matron and continued on her way to the elegant chamber she was sharing with Aunt Isabel. They might force her body into their strange English ways, but never her spirit! She would spend her evening as she pleased, not as an object to be passed from man to man to drag about a crowded dance floor. What was it the maid at Sheffield always said? To hell of them!

"If anyone asks for me, tell them you don't know where I've gone," Rebecca said to a black manservant. She closed the bedroom door and slid the bolt; it would buy her a little time.

She would need money, and she knew that Aunt Isabel carried a leather pouch of coppers for the servants. That would have to do. Quickly Rebecca retrieved the sack from Isabel's red leather chest and dumped the contents into her palm. In return, she left a single silver filigree earring. The great aunt would know by that who had taken her money and that it was only a loan. Rebecca didn't want any servants beaten for her mischief.

Even in the wide peach gown with its cumbersome petticoats, it was easy for her to open a window, make her way along the narrow ledge, and drop onto a sloping porch roof. The slippers were impossible on the slick wooden shakes; she pulled them off and ran along the peak of the roof in her stocking feet.

It was a glorious night. Stars beyond counting were strewn across the heavens, and the full moon made the plantation yard and stables as bright as day. A bonfire glowed in the distance, and muffled voices and laughter told her that the servants not engaged inside were holding their own celebration.

The porch led to an enclosed well house with a catslide roof, one that sloped almost to the ground. Getting down was child's play. Rebecca paused in the shadows of the building long enough to put the slippers back on and then to locate the nearest saddled horse. Boldly, she crossed the cobblestones and untied its reins from the hitching ring. Had it not been for the gown, she could have stolen a dozen horses and probably a few carriages without being noticed. With luck, she would borrow the horse, explore Annapolis, and have the animal back before his owner even called for him.

By the time she was halfway back to Annapolis, she had decided that the gown had to go. She would be marked as a member of the aristocracy on sight, and people would begin to ask questions—questions for which there were no proper answers. The first dwelling she came to provided a solution. A clothesline behind the house offered several homespun gowns and caps.

Rebecca tied the horse to a tree, made a quick circle of the farmhouse to make certain no one was about, then stripped off the constricting ball gown and petticoat and donned a well-worn dress and apron. She considered the caps for a long moment. They looked silly, but a hat might add to her disguise. She pulled one down over her hair, then traded it for another when the first proved far too big. It took only a second to pin her gown to the line in place of the blue homespun. She hoped the woman of the house would be pleasantly surprised. In any case, it would serve her right for being too lazy to take her clothes in at night.

Humming a rather risqué Shawnee song about a maiden and an aging warrior, Rebecca swung up into the saddle and again turned the horse's head toward Annapolis.

Thomas Bradford joined a circle of men gathered in the library and accepted a brandy from a uniformed servant. Carefully he eased himself into a comfortable chair and sipped at the amber liquid with obvious relish.

Adam caught his eye. "You look out of breath, sir. Don't tell me you've been dancing?"

Thomas nodded to Mathews. "Evening, Lee. Your tobacco safe aboard the *Regina?*"

"It's aboard. Whether it reaches England without being washed overboard by storm or stolen by pirates is in God's hands. Adam's been telling me you had the best crop ever this year."

Thomas motioned for a pipe, then waited until the servant had filled it and offered a coal from the fireplace to light it with. Thomas took a few slow puffs, inhaled, and let out a sigh of contentment. "This is where I belong, not out there with the youngsters. Damn right I was dancing, Adam. As you should be." He smiled at Lee. "A good crop and a good man to see to it. Adam deserves the credit. I'm of little use around Sheffield anymore." Thomas fixed Adam with an intense gaze. "Lord Michael has just asked me for Rebecca's hand."

Adam choked on his rum. "Lord Michael? That popinjay!" He wiped at his chin and shirtfront with an offered towel. "Good God! He's a fifth son. His brothers sent him over here to get rid of him. Rumor has it he's run up a fortune in unpaid gambling debts. You wouldn't consider him for Rebecca, would you?"

Thomas shrugged and took another puff on the long-stemmed clay pipe. "She's rich enough that she can wed whom she chooses. If they get on..." His voice trailed off, and he coughed to cover a chuckle. That was the fire of jealousy he saw in Adam's eyes or he was more senile han he thought he was. "I'm not going to be around long, and I want Rebecca to be happy. Michael may be a little foolish, but he's got good blood in him. He'll not mistreat her."

Adam took another cup of rum and downed it in a single gulp. Lord Michael! To think that that fop had the nerve to ask for her! "She could do a hell of a lot better," he said aloud.

"I'd gladly swap her for my Evelyn," Lee said. "But Evey's with child. I couldn't give away my son and heir."

Thomas laughed. Lee's infatuation with his plump young wife was well known. Evelyn Landover had come from Bristol, the only daughter of a wealthy ship builder. Their betrothal and marriage by proxy had been made without either party setting eyes on the other.

It was Thomas's belief that the system worked as well as any. Certainly an older family member was better able to choose a husband for a young woman than the chit herself. Despite his lip service to the contrary, he had every intention of picking a husband for Rebecca and seeing her safely wed as soon as possible. "Rebecca's upbringing may prevent offers from the best families. She's not every mother-in-law's dream."

"Sheffield's broad fields will overcome those obstacles," Lee said. "With her face and the Bradford gold there'll be no problem in finding her a dozen husbands, perhaps even a few with genuine titles."

Adam's face darkened as he reached for another cup. He was not normally a drinking man, but the thought of a boy such as Lord Michael claiming Rebecca was enough to drive him to it. "The boy has good blood," Thomas had said. Lord Michael's father had died in his bed and been buried with the full blessings of church and community. He had not been disgraced and committed suicide. Good blood. What then, as the son of a suicide, the son of a man without honor, was his own blood? Thomas would scorn his offer for Rebecca's hand. He would be marked as a fortune hunter, no better than Michael.

Damn it to hell! Damn her! His life had been orderly before she'd come back to knock it from its axis. He'd had hope then of...

Angrily, he pushed the thoughts away. Thomas was right. He didn't belong here with the graybeards. He'd join the party, or better yet...Better yet, he'd leave this grand affair and see if he could find Jock and some of his friends at the Merry Widow. If Rebecca was to be offered to the highest bidder like some blooded mare, at least he needn't stay and be a witness.

"I believe I'll take my leave, sir," Adam said to Thomas. "I've some friends in Annapolis with whom I'd like to spend a few hours. I'll be here to escort you home in the morning."

"No need to worry about me. God knows there are enough servants to see to that, and enough stout fellows to sail the sloop. Meet us at the dock or at home, it makes no difference. You've been working hard. You deserve a little fun." He paused. "Of course, Rebecca will be put out if you don't dance with her at least once. She's been practicing with Byrd." Thomas pretended interest in the bowl of his pipe. "You might ask around and see if you note anyone of interest who catches her eye. There won't be another gathering this big until next summer. It's too good an opportunity to miss."

Adam mumbled a half-civil reply as he strode from the room. It was unlike Thomas to be so unfeeling where his granddaughter was concerned. Could he be serious about finding her a husband so quickly? Adam was certain Rebecca would fight tooth and claw against the idea of marriage to anyone Thomas picked for her. She'd made plain what she thought of his own offer.

As he strode down the passageway, he glanced briefly toward the great hall. Men and women were forming a circle for a country dance. He didn't see Rebecca; doubtless she was surrounded by admirers. He stepped out into the warm November night and tossed a coin to a young boy. "Fetch my horse. I'm Adam Rourke of Sheffield."

"I know who ye are. Thank ye, sir." The boy grinned widely, exposing a missing front tooth, and caught the copper in midair. "It's the bay in the second stall." He darted off across the yard, dodging an arriving carriage and two men on horseback.

Adam pulled off his coat and tossed it to a footman, then did the same with the vest and wig. He had no need of such finery where he was going. In fact, they'd be likely to earn him a black eye in the streets. The common folk in Maryland were scarcely in awe of the upper classes; they would think nothing of tossing a powdered lordling into the nearest ditch if he offended their sensitive pride.

The carnival atmosphere continued through the streets of Annapolis. The market square near the water was still as closely packed with horses and vendors of food and drink as it had been in the afternoon. Though mothers with young children were no longer visible, their places had been filled by saucy young indentured maids and boys too young to shave.

In one corner of the market, a one-legged sailor was playing a hornpipe while his trained monkey hopped back and forth from one hind foot to the other in time to the music. A crowd had gathered to cheer on his antics and to occasionally toss a small coin into the sailor's hat.

Adam dismounted and led his horse through the square, unwilling to chance mayhem if a boy should dash under his mount's hooves. A red-cheeked country girl stepped from the crowd and offered him a foaming tankard of ale. He grinned his thanks, took a long swallow, and handed it back.

It always amazed him how much at home he felt among these people. In England, it had been different. Class lines still existed here in the colonies, but they were less clearly defined. A butcher might never hope to become a gentleman, but he could drink with one if he had the coin and share laughter and tall tales. There was something exciting about Annapolis, something too elusive to put a name to, almost as if the salt wind off Chesapeake Bay and the rich soil had combined to create something never seen before.

Laughter poured from the open windows of the Merry Widow. Adam dismounted and tossed the reins to a waiting boy. "Stable him," he ordered. "I'll be here awhile." Sidestepping an embracing couple on the porch, Adam bade a good evening to the bondservant Ivan and looked around the public room for someone he knew.

Big Kate looked up from the side of roast beef she was carving and called a greeting. "Have a seat, Adam. I'll fetch you a cup as soon as I finish wi' this."

The Merry Widow was packed; Adam couldn't remember seeing so many strangers in the place since he had first come to Annapolis. Spying an empty seat near the fireplace, he picked his way carefully among the good-natured drinkers. He'd been seated only a minute or two before a young woman approached with a full tray.

"What's yer poison, sir?"

"Evening, Maude." He grinned at her. "Just bring me a bottle of that Haitian Kate keeps in her locked cabinet." He eased back in the chair and propped his feet up on a low stool. There was no sign of Jock McMann, but sooner or later he was bound to turn up.

Outside in the square, Rebecca clapped her hands with excitement as the monkey danced faster and faster to the hornpipe. She'd read about wonderful monkeys in her books, but this was the first time she had ever seen a live one. She gladly tossed one of her coppers into the hat when the performance ended; then she asked the sailor if she could share the gingerbread she had bought earlier with the little animal.

"Sure enough, Jill, but he'd druther 'ave ah pint."

"Ale?" The sailor nodded, and Rebecca dodged through the onlookers to buy a mug of ale. When the ale woman protested that she couldn't allow her customers to take the cup away with them, Rebecca seized her hand and dragged her back to the sailor and his monkey.

"Yer not givin' my good cup to thet beasty," the woman cried.

"'E ain't got nothin' you ain't," the sailor retorted, to the delight of the monkey's admirers.

Rebecca offered the wooden mug to the animal and laughed as much as anyone when the monkey sneezed at the foam and handed the cup to his master. With a wink, the sailor downed the ale without stopping for breath. "Son'ah'betcth loves 'is pint, 'e does!"

Then nothing would do but that each onlooker in turn must buy a mug from the ale woman. Rebecca drank hers with the rest. She had already had a cup of dandelion wine and a sip of something an old man called moonshine. It had made a warm glow in her middle, which the ale seemed to increase.

She felt light-headed. How strange, since she had eaten dinner at the manor. Usually she felt this way only when she'd gone for days without eating. She knew she wasn't sick; nothing hurt. It was a puzzlement.

With a final wave to the monkey, she walked on toward the edge of the water. The ships were clearly visible in the harbor. Most had their sails lowered, but small boats still moved between them and shore, and lights and voices still drifted over the water. The Shawnee had boats, of course, but nothing like these. The huge ships fascinated her.

She was glad she had sent the horse back to Kentwood Manor. Someone might have stolen it from her here in the town. She had given the animal to a freckle-faced girl and told her she would get a reward for returning it to Kentwood.

Rebecca leaned against a post and licked the last of the gingerbread from her fingers. When she got back to Sheffield, she would demand that gingerbread be prepared for her every day. She would store some to see if it would keep, and if it did, she would take an armful of it home to the Ohio country for the children. They would love it!

She dug in the pocket of her gown to see how much money was left. She had plenty for more gingerbread if she wanted it, probably even enough for gingerbread and more of that moonshine. Money was so confusing. Grandfather had told her how much things cost, but here in the street it was always more. She wiggled her toes, glad of the comfort of the thick leather moccasins. She'd been afraid she was taking advantage of that woman when she'd traded the foolish dancing slippers for the moccasins, but the woman had seemed well pleased, especially when Rebecca had added two coppers to the bargain.

"Rebecca? Rebecca Bradford? Be that ye, lass?"

Rebecca looked up and caught sight of a familiar mop of carrot red hair. Jock McMann! Jock's path was blocked by a pack train of ponies, and he turned to go around them.

"Rebecca! Wait!" he called.

Jock was Adam's friend. If he caught her, he'd return her to Kentwood Manor and her grandfather's care. She wasn't ready to go back yet. As Jock came around behind the last pony, Rebecca scrambled under the hooves of the first and wiggled her way into the crowd.

"Rebecca? Where the hell are ye?"

With a low chuckle, she slipped between two arguing old women and headed toward the moonshine seller. It would take a better tracker than Jock McMann to catch her when she didn't want to be caught.

CHAPTER 14

J̲ock crossed the market square for the third time and cursed under his breath. Where in hell do the lass think she's goin'? She'd vanished like a will-o'-the-wisp! "Damn it!" None of his plans for the evenin' included chasin' down Bradford's half-wild granddaughter. He liked the lass well enough, but free nights in Annapolis were few and far between for an overseer. He'd looked forward to sliding between the sheets with a soft young thing.

With a scowl, Jock turned down an alley toward the stable where he'd left his horse. Adam was out at Kentwood Manor with the gently; he'd have to ride out and tell him. He'd bet a month's wages none of them knew the puir wee thing was gone. Heaven only knew what she had in that head of hers to make her want to roam the streets of Annapolis on such a night. Living with the savages like she'd been doing, she was an innocent. A wee bairn would be better prepared than she for the dangers that an unescorted lass might meet.

Oh, Adam had raved on and on about Rebecca being some kind of an Amazon, but Adam was something of an innocent himself. He was fair smitten with the lass, the more so because it was bloody unlikely that old Thomas Bradford would even consider him a fit match for Rebecca.

Adam had a lot to learn about life if he thought love and marriage went together. Love was for bards and unwed maidens; Jock had given up on it long ago.

Rebecca waited for several minutes in the shadow of the ship chandler's warehouse after she had seen Jock disappear down the dark alley. He'd been more persistent than she'd expected, even stopping people to ask if they'd seen a dark-haired lass "aboot so high" in a blue dress. She wondered if he would make the effort to hunt down Adam or her grandfather at Kentwood. Probably he would. But it would take time, and she could do a lot of interesting things in that time.

Around the corner, she'd seen a witch telling fortunes. A girl had said the woman was a Gypsy, but she looked like a witch. Otter had been able to see into the future by staring into a pool of water or sometimes by joining his mind with that of the spirit of fire. He had even foretold his own death.

What was it Otter had told her about a bird? "I see you under the folded wing of a great bird," he had said one starlit night. "There is danger, but a warrior will come and win you free. There will be blackness and then light."

Rebecca had laughed it off. "It would have to be a great bird to tuck me under his wing." Still, the words had made her uneasy, as had his prediction that she would be the mother of many sons. How could that be when he was not capable of fathering a child? It was then that he had told her gently of his own death.

"With the first snowfall," Otter had murmured, "I will breathe no more, and the north wind will carry my spirit across the river of no return."

He had been right. Rebecca shivered in the warm November night. She didn't want to think about such things now. Only foolish English men and women would pay a witch to tell them of troubles yet to come. Trouble would find you soon enough; there was no need to part the clouds of tomorrow to see it far off.

"Good evening, pretty thing." A man's hand closed on Rebecca's shoulder. "Oh, I beg your pardon, mistress."

He swept off his hat. "I mistook you for a friend."

Rebecca stepped back and eyed the dapper young man warily. "I don't know you," she said. His uniform was unfamiliar but of costly material. She wondered if he was a soldier. "I am called..." She hesitated. Should she give her name? "Rebecca."

"And I am Roger. Roger...uh...Roger Smith, at your service, mistress." His broad smile was disarming. "I was about to hunt out an inn and quench my thirst. Will you join me in a cup?"

"Are you a soldier?" Rebecca was not unaware of the effect his dashing figure and smooth manner was having on her lighthearted mood. "I'm not sure I have enough coins left," she admitted.

Roger chuckled warmly. "I was asking you to be my guest," he assured her. "My ship sails tomorrow, and I know no one here in Annapolis. That's why I was so excited when I thought you were someone I knew from home."

"Your ship? You have a ship?"

Roger gauged the wide green eyes and took a chance. "Yes, the *Constant,* anchored just beyond that ship. I'm the youngest captain in the fleet," he lied blithely. He had seen her earlier looking out at the ships, and he'd planned to use her interest as an opening. His friend Will would never believe the wench's stupidity, mistaking a training cadet for a captain. Boldly he took her arm.

"There's a refined place just a short distance away where we can share a few drinks and a little conversation. The bridge is a lonely place. I couldn't bear the thought of spending this evening alone too. It will be many weeks before we sight land again."

Rebecca allowed herself to be led along the street. The English captain seemed harmless enough, and he had promised to share his money with her. Perhaps he would tell her more about the great ships and the distant shores they visited. She wondered if it would be rude to ask for wine. Ale she found too bitter for her taste, and the moonshine was doing strange things to her head and middle. "Is your family in England?"

"I've none left but a sister just about your age," Roger replied, ruthlessly cutting from his family tree his parents, four older brothers, and a bevy of sisters. "She lives in Lincolnshire, and I see her only infrequently." He moistened his lips with the tip of his tongue. Simpleminded or not, the wench was an armful, with a face like an angel. She'd make a tasty morsel, something to think about on the endless voyage ahead.

The lack of women was the worst thing about a life at sea, and women were very important to him. Damn the luck that had made him a fifth son of a tight-fisted baron! He would have preferred almost anything else. At least at the end of his two years of sea duty he would be eligible to become a first officer and eventually a captain, if his luck didn't suddenly change and his brothers all be wiped out by the plague. As captain, at least, he would have a measure of freedom.

The wooden sign of King William's tavern loomed ahead and Roger escorted the young woman inside and safely to a corner table. "What will you have?" he asked. "Rum for me," he told the serving girl.

"Wine," Rebecca answered. "Red wine, if you please."

A faint doubt nagged at Roger. The wench was too well spoken for a serving girl; her manners were more those of a lady. Doubtless she was some colonial lady's maid putting on airs. It made no difference to him anyway. Lady or maid, if they were old enough and willing—or could be made willing—the results were the same.

"Bring us each a bottle," he ordered. "And a pewter goblet for the lady."

The barmaid grimaced, bobbed a curtsy, and hurried to fill the order. "Men! They're all the same," she mumbled to no one in particular as she threaded her way through the crowded public room. Like as not the girl wouldn't even have sense enough to get paid for it!

Rebecca curled her feet up under her and listened to the fables the captain was telling about a tribe of Indians that rode on elephants. He had sworn he was telling truth and that he had ridden the elephants himself, but Rebecca knew a tall tale when she heard one. She knew that the land stretched to the west so far that a man could ride a horse through all the seasons of the year before he came to the other great salt ocean beyond the Sky Mountains. But no tribe that she had ever heard of had elephants. Horses and buffalo, but no elephants. Besides, he talked of cities and towers and jungles. He must believe she was stupid to swallow his stories so easily.

The girl returned with the bottles and poured them each a glassful. Rebecca smiled at the barmaid and got only a frown in return. English! She would never understand them. Hesitantly, she tasted the red wine; it was like nothing she'd ever had before, and it intrigued her.

"You're the prettiest thing I've laid eyes on in years," Roger was saying as he sipped his own drink. "If it wasn't so late and we didn't have to sail in the morning, I'd take you out to my ship and show you around."

Rebecca's eyes widened with interest. "You would do that?" She hadn't finished her wine yet, but he filled the goblet to the brim. "I could see your ship? I could climb the"—she searched for the right English word—"the mask. My grandfather said he would take me to see one of the ships, but he couldn't. The sheriff wouldn't let him."

Roger choked on a mouthful of rum, then went into a coughing spasm. Rebecca jumped up to slap him on the back, then sat down quickly. "It's all right," he gasped. "I'm all right."

Rebecca blinked and rubbed her eyes. It was suddenly very warm in the room, and her stomach felt as if she had eaten green cherries. She blinked again, trying to focus on the captain, who looked for an instant as though he had four eyes. "I think I have had enough wine," she said weakly.

"I think perhaps you have." He dropped a few coins on the rough wooden table, tucked the bottle of rum under one arm, and caught her by the other. "If we hurry, we might have time to see the ship. There's something in my cabin

I'd like you to see. It's a monster we caught off the Cape of Good Hope. It's got two heads and a dozen arms and teeth the size of eggs."

Rebecca swayed slightly on her feet and giggled. More lies. English children must have minds like rabbits to believe such tales. "But I want to climb the mask," she reminded him.

A pale-faced man wearing a uniform much like Roger's came across the room and called to him. Roger frowned and shook his head. "Not now, Will." He motioned toward Rebecca.

The blond man grinned. "What are friends for? We've shared before, and that looks like enough to go around." He gave a mock bow in Rebecca's direction. "Will Rodale, esquire, mistress. And what might your name be?"

"Forget it, Will." Roger's face hardened. "Not this one. I'm taking her out to see the ship. Go down to the captain's skiff and see that the men are ready to row us there."

Will arched an eyebrow. "You're not serious!"

Rebecca looked suspiciously from one to another. "I think I will see the ship another time."

"And miss seeing the monster?" Roger grinned at her. "I'll have you out and back before your mistress even knows you're gone." His dark eyes narrowed. "Quickly now, Will, before I lose my temper. I'm too soft on you for friendship's sake, I know."

Will folded his arms over his chest and shook his head slowly. "Not without something for me. It's too big a risk."

"Give me an hour then." Roger's arm went around Rebecca. "Come, mistress. I'll show you something you'll want to tell your friends about; the tale will keep them spellbound."

The blond man nodded, turned on his heel, and hurried from the room.

"I don't believe your story of the monster," Rebecca murmured, "but I will come to see the ship. Will you raise the sail for me?"

"Anything your heart desires, sweet. I'm the captain, aren't I?"

Outside the great hall at Kentwood Manor, Isabel Sinclair descended on Jock with the rapacity of a barracuda. "Where are they?" she demanded.

Jock stepped back into the shadows of the overhanging porch roof. "Ay don't know what yer talkin' aboot, Mistress Sinclair. Ay've come to find Adam, that's all."

"He's not here, and neither is Rebecca!"

Jock exhaled loudly. "Ay saw the wee lass, but she was alone. Adam was nae wi' her. Ay thought he was here."

"He was here. They both were," Isabel hissed. "And now both are conveniently gone. Can you imagine what this will do to Rebecca's reputation? To her chances of a good marriage?"

"Aye, mistress. Ay think ay can." Jock shifted uneasily from one foot to another. The lassie had truly ruined his night! If Adam wasn't here at the manor with the gentry, he had to be at the Merry Widow. He himself had wasted nearly an hour riding out here when it seemed that all he had had to do was step across the market square and seek Adam out. Damn the luck!

"I've lied to her grandfather and told him the girl is ill. If she's not here in the morning, the shock will kill him. You find Adam Rourke and tell him to bring Rebecca back here at once. He must bring her into the house secretly. God alone knows how he got her out without being seen." Isabel gave Jock a withering stare. "And if I hear you've mentioned a word of this, I'll see you end up herding pigs in Boston."

"Ay don't need ye to tell me to hold me tongue, Mistress Sinclair," he answered stiffly. "Ay came here to Kentwood only because I saw the lass in Annapolis and knew she wa' in danger, runnin' aboot by herself." Jock put his hat back on and yanked it into place. "Ay'll find Adam and tell him. If anyone can fetch her back, it be Adam."

"If you saw her, you should have had sense enough to bring her back yourself," Isabel said sharply. "If anything happens to her, it will be on your head."

"No doot." Disgusted, Jock mounted his horse and rode off into the night. He hoped that Adam was at Big Kate's; if not, he, Jock, would have the thankless task of looking for the lass alone!

Rebecca's heart was pounding as the little skiff moved across the water toward the larger vessels anchored in the harbor. A burly seaman sat on the bench in front of her, rowing. He used two paddles instead of one as the Indians did. Another man was rowing behind her, and the "captain" shared her bench, his arm around her waist to keep her from falling into the water.

"I'm a good swimmer," she protested. "I can manage a canoe almost this big by myself. You needn't worry about me falling in and drowning."

"You couldn't swim in this harbor," Roger lied smoothly. "There's a swift undertow and there are whirlpools beneath the surface." He pulled her a little closer to him. "As it is, I'm breaking the rules in bringing you out here. If there should be an accident, think how it would look."

One of the sailors muttered something under his breath, and Rebecca looked back over her shoulder at him. The man was large and red faced; his single pigtail was soaked in tar and hung like a club down his back. She wrinkled her nose. He smelled like rotten fish. It never ceased to amaze her that white men referred to Indians as stinking savages when it was the white men who seldom bathed.

The captain, at least, was clean smelling. Rebecca pushed his hand away; she didn't like being touched by strangers. Among the Shawnee, it was considered very poor manners.

Lights flickered and voices called out from the ships as they passed. Close up, the sailing ships were even larger than Rebecca had imagined. They smelled of dampness and moss and tar. She let her hand trail in the dark water, still amazed at how warm it was for November.

"Will winter come at all this year, do you suppose?" she asked Roger. "At home we would have had snow by now."

He shrugged. "I've never known it to be this warm. It was spring the last time we anchored in the Chesapeake. When it does get cold here, you'll probably have snow up to your a—" He cleared his throat. "To your neck. I heard that the bay froze from bank to bank one year, hard enough to walk across."

"There she be, sir." The man in the front of the boat rested his oars, and pointed at the ship directly ahead. "Hello, the *Constant!*"

A torch bobbed, and a face appeared at the rail. "Who—?"

"'Tis I, Falk. Hold your tongue and drop the ladder," Roger called. "I'm coming aboard."

"Aye, sir." A rope ladder tumbled over the side.

"Don't be frightened," Roger said to Rebecca. "I'll be right behind you. I won't let you fall."

The men held the small boat close to the side of the ship as Rebecca scrambled up the rope ladder. A big man glared at her as she climbed over the gunnel and dropped to the deck. Roger followed.

"Be about your business, Falk. The wench is my affair."

"She'll be your affair if Mister Durban sees 'er," the man grumbled.

"And where, may I ask, is our Mister Durban?" Roger's tone was full of sarcasm.

"It ain't for the likes o' me t' say."

Rebecca watched the huge sailor from under her lashes; she didn't like him one bit. He made her nervous, staring at her with his bulging eyes. She wished she hadn't come. Not even having the opportunity to see the wonderful ship was worth the price of being insulted by these English scum. "I think I will go back now," she said to Roger.

"Drunk again, is Mister Durban? I thought as much," Roger said to the man Falk as he took Rebecca's arm. To her he said, "Not yet, sweet. There's much I promised to show you." His voice hardened. "A wise man would see nothing, Falk, if he preferred to keep his hide on his back."

With a grunt, the man turned and walked away. Roger guided Rebecca along the deck, pointing out items of interest. Her uneasiness grew. The ship seemed almost deserted; its shadowy masts and unfamiliar sounds gave her a sense of foreboding.

"The *Constant's* a two-hundred-and-eighty-tonner. She's square rigged and carries eight cannon." Roger paused before a low door and glanced around the empty deck. "She's faster than she looks. Of course, we'll be slowed by the fleet, but last time, we crossed the Atlantic in thirty-one days." He opened the door and stepped back to let her pass. "Go on in, Rebecca. This is my cabin. The creature I told you about is in here."

"You go first."

Roger chuckled as he stepped around her into the darkness. In a minute there was a flicker of light and then the glow of a whale-oil lamp. Its light revealed a spacious cabin.

"There's nothing to be afraid of." Roger laughed as he took her hand. "Come. Sit down and we'll have a sip of brandy." He slid the bolt on the cabin door behind her.

"I want nothing more to drink. I have had enough." It was true. The boat ride had cleared her head a little, but she still felt strange. "Show me your monster and then take me back to shore." Her grandfather would be very angry if she didn't get back to the house before anyone realized she was missing. It was late, and Aunt Isabel would be returning to her room by now.

Hesitantly, Rebecca followed Roger to the center of the low-ceilinged room, her eyes taking in the exotic Turkish carpets and rich furnishings. The desk, the bed, everything but the chairs seemed to be built into the ship. She let a finger slide across the polished surface of the desk; the wood was beautiful and unfamiliar. The lamp gave off a strong smell that blended with the odors of tobacco and spice. Maps lay scattered on the desk beside a tray with crystal glasses and a matching brandy decanter; a pewter plate with a single crust of cheese and a wicked-looking ivory-handled knife rested on the maps.

It was a gentleman's room, and judging from the books and beautiful objects, one that belonged to a man of taste and wisdom. Rebecca was surprised that so young a captain as Roger would appreciate such fine things. "What is this wood?" she asked, touching the desk again. "It does not come from our forests."

"It's called teak." His grip tightened on her fingers, and he pulled her closer. "But let's talk about something nicer, Rebecca. Let's talk about you and me." He put his other arm around her and kissed her suddenly on the mouth.

"No!" She jerked back and wiped at her lips with the back of her hand. "I do not wish to kiss you. I want to go back. Now!"

Roger's face creased in a scowl. "Did you think I bought you drinks and carried you out here to take you back without so much as a kiss?" His fingers bit into her wrist; she gasped at the pain and brought her knee up to strike him in the groin.

"None of that, my girl!" he said, sidestepping the attack. He yanked her arm down and twisted it behind her back, striking her twice across the face with his free hand. "Behave yourself," he threatened, "and we'll have a good time."

Stunned, Rebecca stared wide eyed as realization flooded her brain. Red-hot anger rose to dull the smart of her swelling cheek.

"Don't make me play rough, little colonial," Roger murmured huskily. "I like a woman with fire, but not too much of it." He applied a hint of pressure to her wrist and began to fumble with the ties of her gown. "Let's see what you've got hidden in there."

With a whimper, Rebecca closed her eyes and let her muscles go limp. Instinctively, Roger released her wrist and caught her falling body. Her teeth closed on his arm and bit until he screamed with pain. He threw his hands up to protect his face from her slashing nails, and agony washed over him as her foot connected with his knee. He fell backward with her on top of him, his head striking the corner of the desk. Rebecca rolled free and came to her feet, breathing heavily.

"I think you do not know what means to play rough, English-*manake*," she whispered.

"You bitch." Roger's hand went to the back of his head and came away wet and warm with blood. "I'll kill you for this."

"Matchele ne tha-tha." Rebecca's eyes glittered in the lamplight. "Come, little captain, and we will see who kills who." Sweeping aside the crystal glasses, her hand closed on the ivory-handled knife. "Your scalp will hang from a Shawnee lance," she promised softly. "And I will feed your bones to the earth."

CHAPTER 15

"Jock!" Adam crossed the market square for a third time and waved to the Scotsman. They'd searched the streets and taverns of Annapolis for over an hour without success. It was as though Rebecca had vanished; no one remembered seeing her. "Damn it to hell, Jock. Where can she be?" Adam's face showed the strain of his concern. "Are you certain it was she you saw?"

Jock grimaced. "How many times do ye intend to ask me that? Ye must take me for a bigger fool than ay am to think ay'd spend me free evenin' huntin' fer a lass what wasna' lost. She saw me, all right, saw me and lost me, quick as ye can wink an eye. She's a sly one. No wonder we're chasing our tails in a circle. It's like huntin' a shadow."

"Or an Indian." Adam pushed back an unruly lock of brown hair. "It's late, too late even for Rebecca's devilment. Something's happened to her; I know it."

Jock scanned the fast-emptying streets. Most of the merrymakers were gone; only a few knots of men remained. The stalls were closed and shuttered, the vendors with their trays of hot food and drink noticeably absent. The market was strangely quiet, with only an occasional burst of drunken laughter or a loud word to break the silence. The only woman in sight was a gray-haired farm wife attempting to settle her rather tipsy husband on the saddle of a patient mule.

"Ye don't suppose she took off bock to the savages, do ye?" Jock arched a sandy eyebrow. "Could be we're hunting for the lass here, and she's off to the wilderness."

"No." Adam shook his head. "She wouldn't do that, not without letting me or her grandfather know. She gave her word to stay until next winter, and I don't think she'd break it."

"Want to try the taverns again? There's a new one on the hill we didna' try."

"No, she'd know it's the first place we'd look." He kicked at a broken flask. "Maybe we should go back to Kentwood and see if she's there."

"And if she's noot?" Jock leaned against a mooring post at the edge of the water. "She's already gained a few hours on us. If she be in trooble, as ye think, she may not have another one t' spare. The trouble is, ye been thinkin' like Adam Rourke. Me grandsir always said that if ye want to catch a fox, ye got to think like a fox. Now, what do ye suppose yer vixen would want to see or do in Annapolis on Fleet Night?"

"Damn it, Jock, how in hell would I know? There's no logic to her. She thinks like a Shawnee squaw."

"Then *ye* got to think like an Indian squaw. Dinna' they all go for bright beads and—" A grin spread across Jock's freckled face. "Ay know who we havena' asked."

Puzzled, Adam followed Jock back across the market square to the front of a brick building where a one-legged man was slumped against the doorstep, snoring loudly. Curled up next to him was a small animal. "The monkey man?" Adam said skeptically. "What's he going to—"

"We willna' know until we ask, will we?" Jock grabbed the sailor's shoulder and shook it roughly. He moaned and threw up an arm, dislodging the monkey from his warm nest and sending the little creature into a chattering rage. Teeth bared, the monkey threw himself the length of his chain and delivered a volley of shrieking simian insults.

The sailor opened his eyes, belched loudly, and peered at them suspiciously.

"What do ya want, ya rascals? If yer thieves, ye've come to the wrong man. Me and the monk 'ave drunk ever drop 'is coin would give us. There's nothin' ta steal and nothin' ta beg, lessen' yer after me oak leg. Be off wi' ye and let an honest man sleep off 'is pint, afore I call the watch!"

Adam grabbed him by the shirtfront and lifted him off the ground. "Hold your tongue, sailor, until you've something worthwhile to say. We've no wish to steal from you. We're looking for a woman. We know she was here in the market tonight. If you've seen her, we want to know it."

"A woman, is it? Why didn't ya say so?" the man sputtered. "Put me down afore I have the monk rip yer leg off. 'E's a vicious beast when 'roused." Cautiously, Adam lowered the sailor until his good foot hit solid earth. "Wenches aplenty I seen. Why should I give a cook's biscuit about yours? There's nice ones to be found at the Merry Widda, so I hear. Go get one o' them and leave an old salt to 'is sleep."

"It's not just any lass we be lookin' for," Jock said. "It's me wife. The darlin's been steppin' out on me, and ay mean to catch her at her sport. There's coin in it for ye if ye tell us true. If you know nothin'"—Jock shrugged—"then it's sorry I be for troublin' yer sleep. You can have the copper just the same. But if ye did see her, and I'd guess a man like yerself would have good eyes fer what's happenin' around him, then I'd take it as a personal favor if ye'd tell me." He dug into his pocket and held up a coin.

The monkey scrambled up the man's wooden leg and began to pull at his pigtail. "Belay that, ya heathen beasty!" the sailor cried and swatted at it. "Been wi' me so long, 'e takes 'vantage, 'e does." He sniffed loudly and wiped at his bleary eyes. "Well? I ain't got the sight. What do yer wench look like?"

The sailor listened while Jock gave a description of Rebecca and what she'd been wearing when he'd last seen her. "She be ah saucy one," Jock added. "And green as bilge-water. She's led a country life and could be hoodwinked by a canny tongue or a handsome face."

The sailor paused a long moment, then spat into the dust. "Aye, the saucy one. I seen 'er. She come to see the monk dance. Paid too." He rubbed at a scraggly chin. "Most don't, ya know. Most watches the monk, then slips away like grease. Oh, I seen 'er all right, more'n once I seen 'er."

"And last?" Adam said impatiently. "Where did you see her last?"

The man cackled. "Green as bilgewater, eh? If I'd'a knowed that, maybe me and the monk woulda' tried to buy 'er a pint." Adam took a step forward menacingly, and the sailor hurriedly continued. "Saw her last right there." He pointed. "At the dock. Fer a green one, she didn't do bad for herself. Had herself a ship's officer in tow."

Jock flipped him the coin. "Which ship? Do ye know?" His spirits sank. If Rebecca had boarded one of the ships, he knew full well what her fate had to be. God willing, they could get her off alive.

"Aye. I know right enough," the sailor answered. "But it'll cost the two of ya another copper to find out."

"You bastard," Adam said.

Jock stepped in front of him and slipped the sailor another coin. "Me friend has a short temper. Ye'd best tell what ye know before he wrings yer monkey's neck and throws ye to the fishes."

The man shoved the money deep inside his clothing and chuckled. "'Tis the *Constant,* anchored off there. Carried her out in the captain's own skiff, they did. But they've a long voyage ahead. You'll not get 'er back till ever' man, boy, an' sailmaker 'as 'ad 'is turn." He called after them as Jock and Adam turned toward the harbor. "Ya'd be better t' do as I said and get yerself a fresh 'un from the Widda's stock. Yer wench is gonna be too wore out t' please you or yer friend."

Drunken laughter echoed in their ears as they searched along the dock for a boat. "Why in God's name would she go with a sailor?" Adam's voice was harsh with worry.

"She coulda' been forced or drunk," Jock offered, almost as concerned about Adam as he was for the girl. Adam was near the breaking point; if he lost his temper, he was capable of almost anything. Jock had seen it happen only once before in all the years he'd known him, but once was enough for a lifetime. "It might be better if we notified the high sheriff. Ye don't think it's a bit much fer the two of us to take on a whole ship's crew?"

"Stay here, if you're afraid." Adam climbed down a ladder and began to untie the lines on a small skiff. "I can't wait that long, Jock. I'd like to have you at my back, but do as you think right."

"Ye'll see the both of us in hell, and where will that get yer lass?" the Scotsman grumbled as he joined Adam in the boat. "Ay've nothing but me wee dirk, an' ay'll wager yer not armed a'tall."

"Just row."

The sound of the water lapping against the bow of the tiny skiff echoed off the hulls of the larger vessels as they passed between them. The black water was as smooth as glass, and not a breeze stirred. Other than the creaking of wood and sail and the steady scrape of the oarlocks, Adam heard nothing but the rasp of his own breathing.

The moon shone round and golden, a merciless eye; the gleaming light illuminated the harbor and ships and cast dark shadows on the water. Adam saw the captain's skiff nestled beside the *Constant* as clearly as if it were full day. He motioned silently to Jock, and they altered course, putting the *Constant* between them and the skiff with the sailors in it. They brought their own boat close to the side of the large merchant vessel.

Jock looked at Adam expectantly. "Now what, laddie? Ay doot they'll invite us aboard for tea an' crumpets."

Adam ignored the sarcasm, straining his ears for any sound of a woman's screams. There was only silence; not even a human voice broke the gentle rhythm of the tide. Was she already dead? Lying at the bottom of the river? Pain knifed through Adam, a pain so intense and real that tears welled in his eyes. She can't be dead. The lump grew in his throat as the image of Rebecca descending the great staircase at Kentwood formed in his mind. No wonder she had dazzled the eyes and hearts of every man in the room. Her bewitching allure had been more than physical beauty; her provocative aura had a timeless quality that seemed as ageless as Eve.

"Adam." Jock nudged him. "If ye've any brilliant ideas, let's hear 'em noo."

Adam blinked, taking a deep breath to clear his head. The numbing fear must not keep him from thinking rationally. She's alive. I know it. She must be!

"Damn your eyes, Adam!" Jock whispered. "What are we to do?"

"How many are in the skiff?" Adam stared as water droplets dripped from the end of his raised oar. He would believe she was alive until he saw her body. And any man who had harmed her would think hell a mercy when he was done with him. "I saw two." Jock nodded. "Two, then," Adam murmured, half to himself. "We'll have to get past them before we board the ship. Try not to kill any of them. I don't want a charge of murder against us...not yet, at least."

Jock's hands tightened on his oar as they pushed off from the side of the *Constant* and let the tide carry them toward the stern. As they rounded the ship and began to row toward the spot where they had seen the skiff, he cursed under his breath. The skiff was gone, and the ladder hung in place. He grinned at Adam and rowed hard for the ladder. There didn't seem to be a living soul in sight. "The luck o' fools," he said in disbelief. "Where's the watch?"

"Do we care?"

"It's been me experience that a mon's luck holds just so far."

Adam's feet had just touched the deck and Jock was coming over the rail when they were seen. "Who goes there?" The man Falk stepped from the shadows. "Avast!"

Adam faced him squarely, fully aware of the belaying pin clutched in Falk's massive hand. "Where's the girl?"

"Arrrg!" The seaman lunged toward Adam swinging the weapon in a deadly arc. Adam sidestepped him and drove a fist against his jaw. The blow rocked the sailor, but he recovered and brought the belaying pin up sharply to jab at Adam's middle. Jock circled behind the sailor and dove at his legs.

A second sailor ran toward them, shouting for help; Jock blocked his path. "We want the lass!" he cried. "Hand her over or there'll be hell to pay!" The blade of a cutlass glinted in the moonlight, and Jock cursed under his breath as he drew his knife from its scabbard. Warily he backed away until he felt the solid bulk of the mast behind him. "Yer makin' a mistake," Jock warned the sailor, as his foot lashed out, catching the man in the groin. The sailor doubled over, and Jock struck him once with his fist and took his cutlass, leaving the man rolling on the deck.

Adam winced as the belaying pin struck his shoulder. Pain shot down his arm, numbing the fingers of his left hand as he seized the club with his right. Falk struck at his face, and they went down together, rolling across the deck. Falk's teeth closed on Adam's wrist. Adam slammed him against the deck, yanking the belaying pin from his grasp and knocking him senseless just as two more sailors leaped at him.

Adam rose to one knee, barely avoiding a vicious kick from the closest man. Jock suddenly appeared and brought the second crashing to the deck with the flat of the cutlass across his head. The remaining sailor backed away, turned, and ran toward the stern of the ship calling out an alarm.

"Thanks." Adam wiped at the trickle of blood running down from the cut over his eye.

"I'd venture we have aboot two minutes before we're faced wi' more angry laddies than we'll know what to do wi'," Jock said.

"I'm not leaving here without her."

"Then find her and let's get the hell off this ship! Ay've nay wish to swing for piracy." Jock gripped the cutlass tighter. "Ay'll hold the deck as long as ay can wi' this. The master's cabin's behind us. Try that, and fer God's sake be quick aboot it."

Rebecca's heart skipped a beat as the latch rose and the hatch to the captain's cabin rattled. The bolt held as someone applied force from the other side.

"Rebecca? Are you in there?" an urgent voice called. "It's Adam!"

"Adam?" She dashed toward the hatch, then threw herself sideways as wood splintered and Adam crashed into the cabin.

"Rebecca? Are you all—?" Slowly he got to his feet and gazed around the room. "What the—" He stopped in mid-sentence, stunned by the sight of a man suspended upside down, dangling from a rope tied to an overhead beam and wearing only his breeches.

"Help me, for God's sake," the man moaned. "She's crazy."

"Rebecca, what—?"

"I'm very happy to see you, Adam," Rebecca said. "I did not know how I would get off this boat and back to the land. There are many sailors out there." She motioned to the door.

"Get me down! Please," Roger begged.

"Silence, English-*manake,*" she ordered. "I tell you, if you make noise, you die quickly." Rebecca jabbed at his chest with the handle of the knife she had snatched from the desk, spinning him slowly about and exposing the back of his head.

Adam stared. The hair on the back of his head had been sawed off close to the skin, leaving ragged patches and bald spots. The officer's face was ashen, his pupils dilated with fear, his cheeks wet from crying. "What have you done?" Adam demanded.

"I have done nothing yet," she answered hotly. Only lifted his scalp. "Not yet..." Her voice trailed off menacingly. "He tricked me. I was a fool to trust an Englishman. I will not do so again. He said he would show me his boat, and he wanted only to share pleasures of the mat." She made a low sound of disgust. "I do not believe he is even captain of this boat."

The echo of steel against steel rang through the cabin, and Adam grabbed Rebecca's hand. "We don't have time to stand here and argue. Come with me!" They ran out on the deck to find Jock holding off two more sailors, both with cutlasses.

"I've got her," Adam cried. Keeping Rebecca behind him, he circled away from the fighting and moved quickly toward the ship's rail. "Climb down the rope ladder," he ordered Rebecca. "There's a small boat below." The sailor swung at his knees and he sidestepped the blow. A boy ran across the deck shouting for reinforcements. Rebecca hesitated. "I said go!" Adam shouted. "Jock! Come on!" He picked Rebecca up in his arms and tossed her over the side, then dove after her. Jock followed them seconds later, feet first.

Rebecca came up spitting water; Adam was already climbing into the skiff. He untied the line and pushed off from the ship, ignoring the shouts and curses from the crew as he helped Rebecca and Jock into the boat.

Shivering, Rebecca curled into a ball as the two men rowed for shore. Adam was very angry; she could tell by the way he looked at her, by the way he did not even speak to her. His hands had not been gentle when he picked her up, and he had pulled at her roughly as he was getting her out of the water.

She realized that coming to the ship had been a terrible mistake. She had put Adam's life in danger and also that of his friend Jock. Shame seeped through her, and tears welled up in her eyes. "I am sorry," she whispered. "I did not mean to cause trouble for you."

"When do you ever do anything else?" The shouting had caused alarm on the other ships, and lanterns were bobbing on their decks.

"Save yer energy and row," Jock warned. "Ay want to be away from the dock afore the high sheriff arrives. Ye two can fight later."

Neither man spoke until the bow of the skiff nosed against the port side of the Bradford plantation sloop. "It might be best if I leave ye and the lass here," Jock suggested. "Ay can draw off the hounds by playing the fox a bit. There's nowhere ye can take her and not be noticed, all dripping wet like ye are."

Adam grunted assent, pulled in his oars, and lay them in the bottom of the boat before shaking Rebecca's shoulder. "Come along. We'll dry you off and try to figure out how to get you back to Kentwood without being seen."

Rebecca allowed him to help her quickly onto the sloop. He sounded tired. She did not believe his anger had faded; it was only lying in wait for something to trigger another flare-up. She watched silently as Jock rowed the skiff slowly away into the darkness.

"Go below."

"I said I was sorry."

The sound of angry voices drifted across the water, and a bobbing light came from the direction of the *Constant*. Rebecca tried to keep her teeth from chattering with cold. One moccasin had been lost in the water, and the other was squishy wet. She pulled it off and tossed it into the water; it sank without a sound.

"I said go below. Do you want your grandfather's name dragged into this mess?" Adam gave her a push toward the open hatch. "It's a wonder there's no hue and cry for you on the streets already."

The sloop's small cabin was intended as a shelter from Chesapeake Bay storms rather than to provide luxurious comfort. Rebecca turned her back to Adam in the darkness and began to strip off her wet clothes. "I said I was sorry. What more do you want? How was I to know he was lying?"

"He said he wanted to show me his boat, and I wanted to see it. I have never been on a great ship." The gown caught, and she yanked it over her head, sending a button flying. Adam's silence was worse than his yelling. "I did not *really* hurt him. He was a coward, and there is no honor in besting a weak enemy."

Adam's voice, when it came, was harsh. "You expect me to believe that you went out there not knowing what he wanted? Even you aren't that naive." He threw down his shirt and began to dry himself with a woolen blanket. "It wouldn't have been just the one, Rebecca. When he finished with you, there would have been another and then another. They'd have killed you. My God, woman! Don't you have any common sense at all?"

"No! I didn't," she sobbed angrily. "Among the Shawnee, a man asks."

"A man just walks up to a perfectly strange woman and says, 'Do you want to sleep with me?' Now you take *me* for a fool!"

"It's true." She turned toward him. The moonlight spilling through the porthole spread a liquid trail of glittering magic across the rough cabin. "Sometimes." Her voice dropped to a whisper. "And sometimes a woman goes to a man and says, 'Will you share joy with me?'" She took one step toward Adam and then another. "*Ki-te-hi*. I did not wish to share pleasures with that Englishman. I do not know your games. My moccasins know only my own path." She lay a trembling hand on his bare chest. "Adam, will you share joy with me? I want no man but you."

"Rebecca, don't," he pleaded. "What do you think I'm made of?"

"You are flesh, Adam, as I am." Her fingers moved up his chest and locked behind his neck, pulling his head down so close that he could feel her breath against his lips. "Adam," she murmured. "I love you."

A moan died in his throat as he met her lips with his own, and his arms went around her, crushing her against him. One hand intertwined in her damp hair as the other arm swept her off her feet.

Hot desire surged through Rebecca as Adam placed her gently down across the narrow bunk. His body pressed against her; the corded muscles tensed as their kiss deepened.

His hands moved over her skin, adding to the fire that raged in her blood. Each breath she drew seemed to bring him closer. His mouth left hers to caress the corners of her lips and then to tantalize the softness of her throat and shoulders. Her name on his lips brought exquisite shudders of delight that intensified as his warm, seeking tongue found her nipples and licked them until they swelled with excitement. The rough scratch of his stubble blended with the velvet smoothness of his tongue against her breast to produce a magic surge of sensation in her loins. Her limbs grew weak as a wonderful feeling possessed her body. Again and again, she whispered his name as she traced hot circles of moisture on his chest with her tongue, then sought out the hard nub of his male nipples to tease and caress. Her nails dug into his broad shoulders, and he shuddered with pleasure as his own desire quickened.

This is wrong, Adam's conscience cried, even as his hand moved to savor the feel of Rebecca's silken belly. I swore I wouldn't let it happen again, but I can't help it. He had no right to love her, no right to claim possession of the soft, sweet flesh of her inner thighs and taste the faint salt flavor of her skin. No right, and yet every right. She was his! He would have killed to get her back, and he would kill any man who tried to claim her!

A low, sensual cry escaped Rebecca's lips, and she wrapped her legs around his and felt the proof of his aroused passion press against her burning skin. Adam's hands were trembling as he pulled away the last of her wet undergarments.

"I want to touch you," he said with a moan. "Please, my darling, let me touch you."

Joyfully, she opened to his gentle touch, welcoming his lips on hers, feeling the overpowering need to join with him body and soul as they had joined before. "I want to touch you, too," she whispered. "I want to give you pleasure as you give me." In answer, his powerful hand closed over hers and guided her to stroke and squeeze the source of his own male ardor.

"I'll never let you go," Adam said breathlessly. "Never! You're a fever in my blood, Rebecca."

It was true. She wasn't the woman he would have picked if he'd had a choice. She was too wild, too unpredictable. But he had no choice; she had become his life, and without her he would have nothing.

And you in mine, English-*manake,* she thought. But nothing is forever. She could not promise forever. His world was not hers. "We have tonight," she murmured. "This moment."

The ringing of a bell came loudly from the dock. "Fire!" a voice shouted. "Fire in the market!"

"Adam." Rebecca struggled to sit upright, but he pinned her with his body.

"Hush, girl, it's all right. It's only Jock. He promised to cause a distraction. He'll do no great harm. Lie still and let me love you." His lips on hers quieted her halfhearted protest. "Shhh." They clung together in the darkness of the cabin as Adam whispered outrageous nonsense, in her ear and ran his hands over the curve of her buttocks.

"They will find us," she whispered.

"They won't look for us," he countered. "They'll be too busy keeping the fire from spreading to the town." He rose on one elbow and bent to take a rosy nipple between his lips and suck gently at it, creating ripples of excitement that washed through her body like sweet waves of warm honey.

He rolled onto his back and pulled her on top of him. "I like to look at you." His voice was thick with desire. "You're so beautiful, Rebecca...so very beautiful." He kissed the hollow of her neck, marveling at the faint throb of her pulse and the fresh woman scent of her silken skin.

"I've never met a woman like you," he murmured, winding a strand of her dark hair around his finger and tasting it with the tip of his tongue. "I think about you day and night." He placed a feather-light kiss below her ear, and then another and another. "I want you," he breathed heavily. "I want you...."

Their lips met again, joined in an urgent kiss of soul searing passion. Rebecca clung to him, pressing her body ever closer, wanting to be part of him. "Now," she pleaded. "Now…" Eagerly she received him, meeting the powerful thrusts with equal fervor, letting the wild glory of the wanting and giving carry her far above the earth. And then, when the glory exploded into a firestorm of falling stars, wrapped tightly in each other's arms they drifted slowly back to earth and kissed again, a slow, sweet kiss of exquisite fulfillment.

"Never leave me, darling," Adam whispered hoarsely. "Never."

Rebecca drew a long, shuddering breath and laid her head on his chest, listening to the cadence of his heartbeat. I love this man. I do. But even now, lying in this Englishman's arms, satiated with his love, her spirit was troubled. He wanted her. But he did not want Alagwa Aquewa, Star Blanket; he wanted Rebecca Bradford, the English woman. He wanted something she could not give. If she surrendered and gave up the dream of returning to her people for this man, she would have only him. What if Adam tired of her?

She had her grandfather, but he was old. She had read death in his eyes. When he was gone, there would be no one but Adam Rourke, and she would be a stranger in a strange land.

"I want to tell you about Otter, my first husband," she whispered.

"No." Adam's voice was rough. "I don't want to—"

"Shhh." Her fingers touched his lips. "It is not as you think. I did not lie to you, A-dam. No man but you has ever shared pleasures with me, but I was married. Let me tell you about the Otter. He was a good man, and I think you would have liked each other."

"You're still in love with him," Adam said accusingly.

Her laughter was soft in the darkness. "I am, and I will always love Otter, but not as you understand." Rebecca pulled her legs under her and sat up. "Now you must listen.

It is not good manners to interrupt a storyteller."

Adam swallowed hard. Rebecca's hair fell over her naked breasts like a dark wave, and he was overcome with the desire to possess her again. Moonlight touched her cheekbones and bare shoulders, lending mystery to her lilting voice and soft, regular breathing. Trembling, Adam reached out to cup a full, rounded breast and then to kiss the swollen bud. "No stories," he whispered. "Later I'll listen…not now."

Her arms closed around his neck, and she buried her face in the thick beaver brown hair, chuckling as she moved seductively against him. "But you said this was wrong," she teased. "Would you lead a helpless woman into wrongdoing?" Somehow she slid into his lap, giggling louder as she felt his rising manhood. "I think it is very late," she murmured. "Shouldn't we go back to Kentwood?"

"Witch."

"But Adam…"

"Later, woman."

"A-dam!"

Laughing, they came together in a joyful joining of mind and body, a joining that lasted until the first pale light of dawn began to spread across the waters of the Chesapeake. It was a dawn Rebecca knew she would remember as long as she drew breath.

CHAPTER 16

A s he entered the library at Sheffield, Adam flinched inwardly at the cold fury in the old man's eyes. Thomas was seated rigidly in a high-backed chair beside the fireplace, his faded green eyes as fierce as those of a threatened osprey, and equally unforgiving.

"Why?" The single word dropped like a stone in the silent room.

There was no stopping the shameful flush that spread up Adam's neck and cheeks. His eyes misted as the full magnitude of what he had done to this grand old gentleman sank in. "I'm sorry," he stammered. He felt sick, as sick as he had been the day he was called into the headmaster's office for leaving cow pies in the chancery when he was ten years old. He'd been severely beaten for that, and he wished a beating would clear his conscience of this transgression as easily as the other had done.

"You're sorry?" The Bradford eyes narrowed in contempt. "You've dishonored my granddaughter and Sheffield, and all you have to say is that you're sorry?" The gnarled hands gripped the edge of the chair. "I trusted you, Adam. I've loved you as much as any man loves a son, and you do this to me and expect to get away with it? By God!"

Thomas rose to his feet. "If I were ten years younger, I'd call you out!"

Adam took a deep breath. "She's not to blame, sir. It's all my doing. I take full responsibility."

"You're damned right you do. And you'll take full responsibility for the child, if she has one. You'll do no less than marry the girl, or I'll see you dead and in your grave." He crossed the room to Adam and seized his arms. "You'll be wed at once."

"Marry her?"

"Of course marry her, you young fool! What did you expect? It's only by God's grace that you managed to slip her back into Kentwood without being caught this morning, but it changes nothing. Her disappearance from the ball followed by your own will cause talk. I won't have her reputation sullied further. They already talk of her as though she were a woman of easy virtue."

"But I *want* to marry Rebecca," Adam said. "I love her. I didn't think you'd consider—"

"Wouldn't consider Martha's son a fit match for Rebecca? A man I've trained myself?" Thomas sniffed loudly and returned to his chair, where he poured himself a glass of brandy from a crystal decanter that stood on the small table alongside. "You do take me for a senile old man." He sipped the brandy slowly, then looked full into Adam's face. "I meant her for you all the time. I was only giving the two of you time to get to know each other. It's better that way. Rebecca's grandmother, God rest her soul, my first wife...she and I were wed after meeting only once, a family alliance. It took us years to come to terms. She had her eyes on another, and I..." He chuckled. "Well, that was long ago. I didn't want the same for you and Rebecca." He took another drink. "You would have saved me many a night's sleep if you'd told me you wanted her."

"But why?" Adam ran a hand through his hair. "Why me? You could have your pick of men, men with wealth and—"

"Damn their wealth! I've enough for both of you. The money means nothing. It's Sheffield I care about! Sheffield and that child's happiness." He smiled faintly. "You'll not mock her for her strange ways or value her less for the years she spent with the savages. I've taught you all I know, and I can die knowing that what I've started here will continue. It's time the Bradfords had some strong new blood. You've got that strength in you, more than my own son had, if the truth be known." Thomas drained the last of the brandy. "I want no early great-grandsons. You'll marry now, today if the parson can be found. I'll not risk leaving Sheffield open for the taking."

"I would have looked after her, no matter what," Adam said. "You should have known that."

"Ha!" Thomas grimaced. "And when the high sheriff came with orders from the court to name a guardian, what would you have done then? Your rights to Sheffield mean nothing in court without Rebecca. They would find a way, mark my words. She would be married off to some favorite, then packed off to England to live out her life in seclusion. An heiress as innocent as Rebecca? What does she know of managing her wealth? What does she know of deceit? What has the law done to protect Isabel's rights? Would it do more for Rebecca?"

"And if we marry?" Adam savored the word: marry. Was it possible she could be his honestly? Without shame? His to care for and cherish?

"Then all of Sheffield is yours by law through her. No man can take it from you, Adam. It will be yours and your children's. Lock, stock, and barrel."

Another doubt rose to dampen Adam's joy. "But will she agree to it? I've asked her to be my wife, and she refused. You said she could—"

"Could go back to the Indians?" Thomas laughed. "Adam, Adam, you are too trusting. Did you think I meant to let her return to—"

"*I* did!"

Adam turned to see Rebecca standing in the half-open doorway. "Rebecca," he called. "How long have you been there?"

"Long enough to hear the two of you deciding my fate without consulting me." Head held high, she entered the room and closed the door behind her. There was no need to let the servants know that Adam and her grandfather regarded her as a mindless child.

Her eyes were large in her pale face, her skin almost translucent against the ivory satin dressing gown. She'd been half asleep when she'd heard her grandfather's angry voice echo up the stairs and had wrapped herself in the gown and come down to see what the trouble was. "If you want the land, Adam," she said evenly, "you have only to ask. I do not want it. I told you that, Grandfather. I want only to return to the Shawnee." She threw an accusing look at the old man. "You deceived me. You promised I could go home if I wished, and all along you were planning to marry me off." Unconsciously her body stiffened and her chin went up. "Am I a slave to be treated so?"

"If you were listening at the door," Adam snapped, "then you heard me say that I love you, that I asked for your hand in marriage before and you refused me."

"No." Rebecca shook her head. "No, I did not hear that. I heard you say that I refused you, but I heard no words of love—only of money. Sheffield is what matters to you both! Take it and be damned to your Christian hell. Only let me go!"

"Rebecca." Steel rang in the old man's soft voice. "It is decided. You *will* marry Adam. If you are angry and hurt now, in time you will understand that I mean only your best. He will be good to you and to your children." He held out his hand to her.

"No," she repeated stubbornly. "I will not have him."

"You should have thought of that before you gave him what should have been saved for your lawful husband," Thomas said.

"Will you tie me hand and foot and drag me to the altar?"

Adam laid a soothing hand on her arm, but she brushed it away.

"If need be."

"No, don't make me do this," she protested.

Thomas's face hardened. "I know you are not of a loose and immoral nature. You aren't to blame for your lack of Christian training, but it is better if you are safely married. Your hotheaded ways will bring you only unhappiness and ruin. Adam loves you, and I know you care for him. If it is not love you feel, then in time it will become love. Whom should a woman love if not the husband provided for her by a loving family? Willy-nilly, walking or carried, miss, you shall wed, and you shall wed Adam. Get you upstairs to your room until you can control your tongue. I'll send Isabel to help you pick a bridal gown and such. That should keep you busy until the parson arrives." He waved to Adam. "See she goes up, and set two men to guard her door and another to watch the window. We'll have no more games of in and out the window."

Rebecca turned toward Adam. "You will not go through with this?"

He sighed. "I would have you willing, Rebecca, but even unwilling, I will have you any way I can get you." It was true. To let her go back and live out her life among the savages now was unthinkable. Surely, when she thought about it, she would agree. She was angry and hurt, but she had said she loved him.

"Would you rather see her go to a bridegroom of the sheriff's choice?" Thomas asked harshly. "She is a woman, Adam. You must begin as you would go. I have been too soft on her, or we would not have this rebellion on our hands." He rose in his place. "You are excused, Rebecca. I will see you at your nuptials."

Adam frowned. "Surely not today, sir. The banns have not even been read. There are rules which must be—"

"There are no rules that cannot be bent with silver coin. Prepare yourself. You will be a husband by sunrise tomorrow, or I will be in my grave."

Rebecca looked from one strained face to the other, then turned and ran from the room and up the stairs. A lump closed her throat and a tight band pressed around her chest until she could hardly breathe. The shock of Adam's betrayal was as great as that of her grandfather's. Thomas Bradford's words were as empty as those of any English man. From the first he had meant to keep her here. Am now, now they would force her to marry a man against he will.

Dry eyed, she flung shut the door to her chamber and threw herself across the bed. Her anguished mind gave no solution. She was a prisoner in the house she was to possess. No, not her; *Adam* would possess Sheffield. Had not her grandfather said that everything would be Adam's through her? Englishmen treated their women like chattels. Among the Shawnee, none would think to force a woman into marriage! The English were barbarians.

The Shawnee woman was regarded as an equal when it came to choosing a mate. When she chose a man, the suitor offered gifts to her family for the privilege of joining with them. The house and all the household goods would belong to her. The children would belong to her clan, and if she wished a divorce from her husband, she could get one merely by placing his moccasins and weapons outside the wigwam.

Her thoughts were interrupted by a light tap at the door. "Rebecca?" It was Aunt Isabel's voice, sounding surprisingly gentle.

Rebecca sat up. "Come in." She didn't know what to think of the older woman. When Adam had brought her back to Kentwood, Isabel had hugged her tightly and told her how frightened she had been before launching into a tirade against Rebecca's outrageous behavior. Her concern had seemed sincere.

Isabel entered the room and crossed to the bed. "Thomas just told me."

"Did he tell you I refused?"

"He said you were being difficult."

"That's not the same thing. I don't want to marry Adam. They can't force me. I will refuse to answer the English godman. They will have to chain me like an animal! I won't do it!"

"Rebecca, listen to me. I know you don't hate Adam, and he's a good man in spite of his background. It's truly the best thing for all of you." Isabel sat on the edge of the bed and took Rebecca's hand. "I have seemed harsh to you at times, I know. Here at Sheffield, I am only an added burden. I am a proud woman." She sighed. "I would much prefer to have my own house and my own servants to order about. But it was not to be." She turned Rebecca's palm up and brushed the skin lightly. "You are young and without the knowledge you need to survive. Take Adam for your husband and thank God for the chance. There are much worse men and much worse fates. A generation ago, you would have been put into a religious house, and that would have been the end of you."

Rebecca pulled her hand back and wrapped her arms around herself. "It's so unfair. No one should be able to put you out of your own house. Among the Indians, possessions belong to the woman."

"Not here," Isabel said bitterly. "And what would women do with them if they had them, all silly chits like yourself? No." She shook her head firmly. "We must take what security we can find."

"I am not an English woman. I do not need to take what I can get. I will go back to my people."

Isabel exhaled sharply. "I did not want to tell you this, but you leave me no choice. There is a more important reason why you must wed Adam, and quickly. Thomas is dying."

"Dying? No," Rebecca protested. "I know that his years are not long, but I do not think—"

"Then argue with his physician. Thomas saw him again in Annapolis. It is his heart; he could go at any moment. He is to have no upset of any kind. The physician has forbidden him to ride or even to walk more than a short distance."

"And if I refuse to go through with the wedding..." Rebecca's voice trailed off.

"Then you may cause his death." Isabel went to the carved chest at the foot of the bed. "Which gown will you choose?"

Rebecca flung herself face down on the bed. She would not cry, despite the crushing sensation of walls closing in around her. The angry words, the wails of utter frustration, died in her throat. She was trapped. She knew it as surely as if a noose lay around her neck.

She closed her eyes and willed her breathing to come more regularly. What was the Shawnee way? She was not an animal to throw herself against a trap until she had broken her own spirit. She would not destroy part of herself to escape. She had a mind, and she would use it.

How to escape the trap and not cause the death of her grandfather? Even if she hadn't loved him, she couldn't do such a thing. For a Shawnee to kill a member of the family, even indirectly, was an unthinkable crime, one that would haunt a soul for lifetimes to come. No, there must be a way to salvage her freedom and still do no harm to her grandfather.

When she had cleared her mind of anger, the answer came, so clear and simple that she laughed out loud. Isabel ceased digging through the clothes chest and turned to see why Rebecca was laughing.

"Have you taken leave of your senses, Rebecca?" she demanded.

"No, Aunt Isabel, I have not." Slowly, almost catlike, Rebecca opened her eyes and rolled onto her back. "I will do as you bid me. I will marry Adam."

"Naturally. Now come and help me pick out something so sweet and dainty that it will make them forget what a scene you caused. It will do you no good to begin your married life as a shrew. Adam will have complete control over you once you are his wife. It is better to please him in little ways so that you may have your own way in the larger ones."

"You choose," Rebecca answered softly.

Why was I so concerned? she asked herself. I don't care about the plantation, only about grandfather. A small voice reminded her that she also had strong feelings for Adam, but she pushed the thought ruthlessly away. She would marry as they ordered her, and she would be the wife Adam wanted. But only for a little while…As soon as her grandfather died, she would turn her back on the Chesapeake and return home to the Shawnee. The ceremony they would force her into would be an English one. It had no meaning for her. Besides, if her conscience troubled her, she would divorce Adam in the Indian way when she left. And if her grandfather saw from the spirit world what was happening, perhaps he would then have the wisdom to understand why.

"I know you." Isabel's chiding voice broke into her thoughts. "You're plotting something." The older woman's brow wrinkled with suspicion. "You must rid yourself of these heathen ideas. Soon you will be a wife and mother. No one will permit you to behave as you have in the past." She shook a plump finger admonishingly. "If you behave decently, people will forget your past and accept you as the mistress of Sheffield. You can help your husband rise in society. You must think now of your children."

"I am, Aunt," Rebecca answered smoothly. "I know I must do what is best for them. I have been foolish." She lowered her thick lashes and tried to look contrite. How easily the English customs of deceit came to her now. "I know that Adam Rourke is a good man, even if there is a stain on his family name." She swallowed a giggle. She could easily repeat their senseless phrases. "My grandfather wants only what is best for me, and he is wise."

"Humph," Isabel grunted, still unconvinced. "There is a servant outside the window and another in the hall. You will go nowhere, my girl, so you may as well make yourself presentable. I'll send up Massie to do your hair. She has a way with it. We'll have no beads or braids tonight. You will look the part of a Bradford woman, whether you feel like one or not."

"As you wish, Aunt." Rebecca offered a faint smile. "And if I am to be truly mistress of Sheffield, you must never question your place here again. This is your home and always will be. I do not have the skill to direct the servants or the knowing to order supplies for the winter or..." She scrambled off the bed and threw herself at Isabel, embracing her with genuine emotion. "I am wise enough to know what I do not know," she admitted. "You must be the real mistress of Sheffield. Promise me."

For an instant, Isabel caught Rebecca to her; then she pushed her away. "And where would I go?" Her voice cracked. "I suppose I owe you something for your mother's sake. I did my duty by her, and I shall do so by you, though God knows why." She wiped at what she tried to convince herself was a bit of dust in her eye. "Enough of this nonsense now. Next you will be weeping like a kitchen maid and have your eyes as red as a barn kitten's."

Rebecca laughed. "No, I shall not. I shall go down and talk with my grandfather again."

"They will not let you through the door," Isabel warned.

"Won't they?"

Thomas looked up from writing entries in his journal as Rebecca burst into the library. "What are you doing here?" he demanded. "I said—"

"I have not come to fight with you, Grandfather," Rebecca said meekly. "I am sorry that I behaved so...so badly. I will do as you say." She bowed her head and looked up at him shyly. "I will marry the man you choose," she murmured softly. "You know what is best for me." She came to the edge of the desk. "Please, do not be angry with me."

"If you do as I bid, we will have no quarrel," Thomas said crisply. "I have only your good at heart. It is not your fault that you don't know your place. Adam and I have both spoiled you." His eyes softened. "You are lucky he'll have you. Another man would beat you black and blue for such tricks."

And I would have his scalp in the highest tree, she thought, or I would have his life. "Adam is a good man."

"Too good at times. It is his only fault," Thomas grumbled. "But that will change with time. A man must be hard if he will hold what is his in these times." He lay down the quill pen. "I have sent the sloop for the minister. There will be no tricks. You two will be wed as soon as he arrives."

"Yes, Grandfather." She moved around the desk. "But there is something I think has not been done. Is it not the custom to have a marriage…a marriage contract between man and wife, to protect my…" She sighed. "I do not remember the words, but you must know what I mean."

He chuckled deep in his throat. "I think you know the words well enough when it suits you, girl. It has already been done. I would not marry you off without such a contract. My solicitor has already drawn one up, and Adam signed it earlier. You may sign now, if you like."

Rebecca's eyes widened in astonishment. "What if I had not agreed, or if Adam hadn't?"

"Another man's name could have been inserted." Thomas pulled a handful of papers from the desk drawer. "It needs only your name and that of a witness. I will call Isabel or one of the manservants. A man who cannot write can still make his mark."

"There is something I want added to your contract," Rebecca said firmly. Her lips hardened in a perfect imitation of her grandfather's expression. "About Aunt Isabel."

"Isabel? What of her?"

"I want it written down on your English paper that she is to have a place here as long as she lives. And she is to have money of her own, money Adam must pay every season."

"Isabel? Did she put you up to this?" Thomas pushed himself back from the desk in disgust. "What place has Isabel's affairs in your marriage contract? She has a home here as long as she wants it. What does she need with her own income?"

"She did not put me up to it, as you say it," Rebecca replied sharply. "It is my own thought. And it is my thought that Adam may not always want her here, and that I do not know all that I should to be the woman of Sheffield. What do I know of entertaining or buying cloth or buying house slaves or bondmaids? I know nothing of these things, and I do not have time to learn. Isabel does all these things very good. She belongs here. Show her you know this is true by giving her honor. The English value silver above all things. If you promise her silver, she will know. All men will know. Besides"—her voice softened— "she will make a better mistress for Sheffield than I will. True?"

"True," Thomas admitted with a chuckle. "Damn you, girl, you do have a bit of sense. Adam will have to agree; he's already signed the contract once, but it can be added to." Thomas rubbed his chin thoughtfully. "Are you certain you want this? In time to come the old woman may become more difficult. She won't mellow with time, you know."

"I am certain, Grandfather," Rebecca said. Adam will have her to deal with, not me. She lowered her eyes to hide the twinkle in them. "She will not bother me. It will ease my heart to know I need not worry over these things." That, at least, was true. Her grandfather cared about Sheffield, and Isabel would be certain that things were done exactly as they had always been done on the estate—properly.

"Good enough." He dipped the quill into the ink. "There's room on this last sheet to add it. To be paid every season, eh? And how much should I give her?"

Rebecca smiled sweetly. "That I leave to you, Grandfather. You are wise in all things. You know that the amount you set will prove her worth, and the more you give, the happier she will be. Does it not follow that if Aunt Isabel is happy, things will go happy at Sheffield?"

* * *

It was close to midnight when the minister arrived by sloop from Annapolis. His protests at the irregularity of the hasty marriage had been soothed by a large donation in silver and the excuse that Thomas Bradford was near death. As proof of this last, the parson was escorted upstairs to the master bedroom where Thomas lay propped up in his bed.

"It grieves my heart to see you like this," the good parson said. "You looked so hearty at the sailing-day celebration."

"God's will be done," Thomas murmured. "The important thing is to secure my granddaughter's future. I had already given my approval to the union: we would have had a Christmas wedding anyway. Adam was my first choice for her; I've trained him myself, you know."

The minister began to thumb through his Bible for an appropriate prayer. "It's a pity we could not have held the ceremony in Annapolis this morning," he commented. "The sheriff himself would have stood as witness."

"I've summoned my neighbors," Thomas said weakly. "And there is my own household. I'm certain no one will question your authority, sir."

"I should think not—not after a lifetime of serving the Lord," the man said, bristling. "Indeed not. It's just an unfortunate circumstance." He sniffed loudly. "I should hope I could perform a lawful ceremony in this colony."

The bedchamber was crowded with guests and servants when Adam entered and made his way nervously to the curtained four-poster bed. He murmured something to the minister and signed the parchment the man offered. He would have signed anything they thrust at him. He was still in shock, unable to believe that Thomas was actually having the wedding performed.

Isabel had told Adam Rebecca had agreed to the marriage. Her acceptance had taken away none of the hurt of her earlier refusal. What should have been the happiest day of his life was ruined. She was being forced into the union, and he knew she would never forgive him for it.

He had dressed carefully in his finest clothing, a pale blue coat and breeches and a ruffled shirt of the finest lawn. His hair was drawn back and fastened with a black velvet tie, and his square-toed leather shoes boasted silver buckles. He looked every inch a gentleman, yet he felt like an imposter. In a few minutes he would be a wealthy man, and his mouth tasted of ashes. His stomach turned over, and he swallowed hard. Was he a bigger fool going through with the wedding or worrying about his good fortune?

He wanted Rebecca; he wanted her so badly he could almost taste her. If he didn't stop thinking about her, about the soft silk of her skin, about the lush curves of her body, he would shame himself in front of the guests and the minister. She was young and beautiful and passionate. She was rich. Any man in the colony would give his right arm to take Adam's place and receive Sheffield and Rebecca in one fell swoop. So why did he feel so damned dishonest, as though he had stolen something precious? As though he had betrayed the woman he loved?

Rebecca. Adam straightened. He had to think of her best interests. Despite the charade he'd put on for the parson's benefit, Thomas really was close to death, and the inescapable fact was that Rebecca might be carrying a child. She would be helpless without a protector. And if Adam's best interests and Rebecca's were the same, why then all the anguish he was feeling? He would care for her with all his heart and soul, as he would this plantation. Could anything more be asked of a man? A stir at the door jarred him from his reverie.

The group of whispering servants parted to let Isabel and the bride pass. There was no sound but the rustle of petticoats as Rebecca crossed the room to stand beside Adam. Isabel had chosen the rose gown for Rebecca and had woven a crown of pearls into her dark, flowing hair.

"Proceed," Thomas ordered, a bit sharply for a dying man. "All are here who are coming."

Isabel stepped back to stand beside Thomas, and the minister began to address the couple in loud, dramatic tones. Shyly, Adam reached out to take Rebecca's hand in his and gave it a reassuring squeeze.

The look she flashed him was anything but compliant, and he flinched inwardly. Protests rose in his throat but went unuttered. There was still time to put an end to this. He had only to tell the minister that the bride was being forced into marriage against her will. The parson hesitated, then repeated his last utterance.

"Do you, Adam Rourke—"

"I will...I mean, I do," Adam said, too loudly. He gripped Rebecca's cold hand, wondering what he would do if she refused to answer or if she fainted again or tried to run from the room.

But she gave her answers in perfect English and without hesitation. So quickly did the ceremony pass that it was over and the minister was shaking his hand in congratulation before he realized it.

"You may kiss the bride," the parson prompted.

Adam bent and brushed her lips with his. He might as well have been kissing a steel blade for all the human warmth he received. Her eyes were closed and there was no resistance to his kiss, but neither was there a response.

The other people in the room stepped forward to offer their good wishes, anxious to gloss over the awkward moment, and Adam welcomed the diversion. There would be hell to pay for this forced marriage, but better in private than in front of witnesses. He forced a wooden smile and murmured appropriate replies.

Rebecca allowed herself to be kissed and patted, then offered her cheek for her grandfather's kiss of peace. "Grandfather," she said softly, "I have done as you asked."

"Good enough." Thomas raised his voice. "It's late, past time for all of us to be in bed. The servants have prepared rooms for all of you. In the morning we will feast the happy couple. Let us allow them to go to their marriage bed and us to our own beds." He clapped his hands. "God willing, I will be down to share the festivities with you all tomorrow."

Plainly dismissed, the guests and servants began to file out of the chamber. Adam gripped the old man's hand, too full of emotion to speak.

"I've entrusted you with that which I value above my immortal soul," Thomas said. "Don't fail me."

"I won't, sir," Adam managed to say.

Rebecca executed a graceful curtsy. "A good sleep to you, Grandfather, and you, sir." She smiled faintly at the minister. "Husband, let us leave them to their prayers. Morning will come early, and there are guests to see to." She offered Adam her hand and blushed prettily. "Will you come to my room, sir, or I to yours? I believe we must complete this ceremony, must we not?"

Adam flushed to the roots of his hair, caught her around the waist, and hurried her from the room, but not before he heard the minister's gasp of horror and Thomas's hearty chuckle. "Your room," Adam said, pulling her along the hall. "It was hardly the question to bring up in front of them."

"And why not, husband?" she replied. "Have not all your English customs been satisfied? I belong to you, do I not?"

Adam caught a flash of green fire in her eyes as he turned the knob of her chamber door. "God only knows," he said with a sigh. "But I am certain I shall soon find out."

CHAPTER 17

"Before you say anything, let me try to explain," Adam said, closing the bedroom door and sliding home the iron bolt. "I know you're angry, but…" Rebecca's back was to him, and she had bent to take off her slippers. Something was wrong. He had expected to face the full fury of her wrath, yet there was nothing in the set of her shoulders or her graceful movements to indicate rage. "Rebecca," he called softly, "you must listen to me. This is not how I wished it to be between us."

She glanced at him over her shoulder. Her face was expressionless, the green eyes devoid of emotion. "I must listen," she answered meekly. "You are my lord and master by English law." She sat on the edge of the bed and began to fumble with the ties at the back of her gown. "As my husband, it is your duty to tell me when I do something wrong." She pulled the gown off one shoulder, then began to worry at the laces again. "Will you beat me if I disobey you, A-dam?" The faintest hint of a challenge lurked behind her soft tones.

"Damn it, Rebecca, stop this," he snapped. "You know better than that. Have I ever hurt you? Why would I start now?" He yanked at his coat and threw it over a chair. "You must understand." He took a deep breath. "I love you, and I think you love me. We have a chance to begin a whole new life together. I want to start as friends."

A silken tie gave under pressure, and Rebecca wiggled out of the dress, letting it crumple to the floor in a shapeless heap. Without answering, she began to undo the laces on the bodice of her undergown. "I do not understand English friends. I was raised by savages. The Shawnee do not hold their friends prisoner, or force them into marriages against their will. You must be patient with me. In time, I will learn all these things—how friends lie to each other and marry for land and silver."

The undergown followed the rose satin along with a cloud of cream petticoats and then a wisp of silk that Adam could have crumpled in one hand. A final garment was flung aside, and Adam had a glimpse of dark curls as Rebecca scooted up onto the bed and under the spread. She sat up, drawing the cover around her waist, and leaned back against the pillows, seemingly oblivious to his reaction to her bare breasts and tumbled hair.

"Don't behave this way," Adam begged. "I don't want to fight with you on our wedding night." His hands were trembling slightly as he unfastened the buttons of his shirt. "I would not have forced you into marriage, Rebecca. If I'd had my way, I would have wooed you as sweetly as any court gentleman. Besides"—his eyes narrowed in a frown—"I love Sheffield as you love your woods and Ohio River country. I've worked it and sweated over it. I'll build us a future here, I swear it." He came to the side of the bed wearing only his breeches and stockings. "I'll force you into nothing, least of all into my arms. I want you, but I take no woman by force, not even my wife." He sat on the bed and began to strip off his stockings. "We are wed, Rebecca, for better or worse." He sighed. "I would have it for better. Will you?" His glance was beseeching. "Can we have peace between us?"

Damn her for what she was doing to him, he thought. Was she deliberately teasing him with her body, waiting to lash out if he should reach for her? The room felt hot, almost stifling. There was no sound but the faint patter of rain against the windows. When had it begun to rain? Adam wondered. "Are you tired?" He blew out the last candle next to the bed, and darkness settled over the room.

He had not expected her to sulk. Was it possible that she had accepted the situation and was awaiting his embrace? He didn't think so. Rebecca wasn't about to make the situation easy for him. Quickly, he removed his breeches and hung them over a chair, then slid between the sheets.

When he'd moved to blow out the candle, Rebecca had turned her back and pulled the linen sheet up around her shoulders. She lay still, listening to his breathing. Only a few inches separated them, inches and worlds.

What did he expect? That she should come willingly into his arms and offer her body for his pleasure? Her husband. Adam was her husband. No, that was not right—he was her English husband, a man forced upon her. She sighed and curled into a ball. It was difficult to lie so close to Adam and not think of the pleasures he had given her in their lovemaking. His bare chest with the curling hair was pleasing to look upon, as were the rippling muscles that even silk and satin could not hide. She wondered what he would look like in the leather loincloth of a Shawnee warrior and giggled silently at the thought. His skin would be too fair. His legs were pale below the waist. Englishmen hid their thighs and calves; perhaps their women did not appreciate the beauty of a man's body as Shawnee women did.

Adam had powerful thighs. Rebecca's lips curved upward in a secret smile. Would it please him to know she was lying there thinking of his thighs? Adam's size was no longer disturbing. As long as she did not drive him into an uncontrollable rage, she need not fear him. In some ways he was like a bear, peaceable as long as one remembered what he was capable of if aroused.

Her pulse quickened as she remembered the feel of his furry chest against her breasts. Now that he was her husband, they would share a bed every night as long as she remained at Sheffield. Sleeping with Adam would not be painful. In truth, she had to admit that it would hurt her as much as it would him to deny him the pleasures of man and wife. A growing warmth in her loins tempted her to reach out to him. There would be no need to admit defeat. Her lips on his would say all that was needed.

The rhythm of the raindrops soothed her wounded spirit. Their predicament was not really Adam's fault; he had a strong sense of honor, even if it was a twisted English honor. He had not grabbed her or tried to force her into coupling with him, even though he believed he had that right as her husband. What would be gained by refusing his offer of peace between them?

With a little murmur, Rebecca rolled onto her back, letting the toes of her foot brush against his bare leg. "Adam."

He drew his leg away from her touch. "What is it?"

"I do not think we can be friends. I wished to be your friend before, and you didn't want that of me."

"I've always wanted you." His voice was distorted with tension. "I want you now." His hand closed on her wrist, and he moved instantly to pin her against the bed, catching her free hand and imprisoning it in his own. He brought his face down so close to hers that she could feel his warm breath.

"No! Let me go!" she cried. "I won't—" Her protests were cut off by Adam's hard, demanding mouth. In vain she struggled beneath him, fighting the ripples of excitement produced by his searing kiss.

Then, as quickly as he had seized her he released her, and she was sucking in ragged breaths of air. She rolled free of the sheets and retreated to the farthest corner of the bed. "Why?" she whispered hoarsely. "Why did you do that?"

"To prove to you that you can't play your games, Rebecca," he said, his voice raspy. "If you don't want me to touch you, you'd damn well better keep yourself covered up!" He turned his back to her and lay back on the bed. "I'll not ask you to be a wife in bed if you don't wish it, but I won't sleep on the floor either."

Rebecca bit her lower lip until she tasted the salt of her own blood. Her wrist tingled where he had held her, but the ache was nothing compared to the pain she felt within.

She had been helpless. Worse, she was not certain she could have fought him if he had wanted to take his pleasure with her.

"I will remember," she said softly. There was no reply except Adam's steady breathing. I will remember, she repeated silently. She had misjudged this bear of a man who claimed her as wife. She would not do so again.

Adam was already gone when Rebecca opened her eyes in the morning. The rain had stopped, and sunshine streamed through the glass panes in rainbows. Slowly, she walked to the window and stared out at the broad fields of Sheffield. Even with the brown hues of autumn they were beautiful, making her aware of a haunting, familiar tug at her heart that she did not understand.

Her strangely pensive mood lasted while the maid assisted her in dressing and then arranged her hair in a festive style befitting a new bride. "Tell my grandfather I'll be down shortly," she told the girl, dismissing her with a wave. There were guests to face...and Adam. A little shiver passed through her. She must play the part of the happy bride no matter how she felt inside. She could not shame either of the men she loved.

Rebecca sank into a chair and let her thoughts drift back to her first marriage. Otter had been as much a man as Adam was, but he had been a man more of the spirit than of the flesh. Even before their wedding day he had explained that they would join only their souls, never as men and woman do with their bodies.

"It is better this way," he had assured her. "For I will take you where no other living man can."

She had believed him, for the radiant glow about him was of the spirit world. She had put her hand in his and pledged her trust. Rebecca clasped her arms around her middle. How could she ever hope to explain Otter and her marriage to Adam when she did not fully understand them herself?

At the time, she had not thought theirs a strange marriage. A woman who has not known the physical love of a man does not miss it. Otter had been her husband; they had lived together, eaten together, and played together, yet part of him had always remained a mystery.

"The Wise Ones have given me a great gift," Otter had explained, "and for everything of great value, there is a price." The price for Otter had been the loss of the desires and pleasures of an ordinary man. If he regretted the cost of his magic, he had never told her so.

"I loved you, Otter," Rebecca whispered into the empty room. "I'll always love you…but it is a different love than I feel for Adam. You were of the spirit, and I am very much"—she smiled—"very much of the flesh."

And then she remembered. The memory of her dream washed over her like a warm summer shower. Suddenly, she could see it all as clearly—no, more clearly—than her hand before her face.

She had dreamed of her wedding, not here in this grand house but in the forest of her people. In the dream, Adam had worn the clothes of her people and his face had been painted as a Shawnee warrior's. She had run to him joyously amid the happy cries of her people. Her Indian mother had been there and…and Otter. Otter had been a guest at her wedding to Adam, and his eyes had told her of his happiness for her and his approval.

"Rebecca!" Isabel's voice cut through the memories, and Rebecca opened her eyes to see her great-aunt standing impatiently in the doorway. "You must come down at once. People are asking about you."

"I had a dream last night," Rebecca murmured. "Adam and I were to be married."

"It was no dream," Isabel chided. "Your marriage is a fact. I declare! Your head is as full of cobwebs as that of any silly maid. I would not have believed it of you. Downstairs with you, and act the proper hostess of Sheffield. None of your nonsense today. I won't have it.

You'll have years to dream of Adam." Isabel arched an eyebrow. "But if you're wise, you'll keep your dreams to yourself. Men have little patience with such talk."

"But this was different," Rebecca protested. "It was…" Realizing the futility of trying to explain, she clamped her lips shut and followed obediently.

Her grandfather was in the great hall chatting amiably with a neighbor about a new tobacco strain he was planning to try next year. He looked surprisingly hale for a man who only the day before had been on his deathbed, she thought. Had they lied to her about that, too? No, she decided; she had known that his illness was mortal before Isabel told her. She had just convinced herself that he had longer to live than he actually did. If he had died while she was still with the Shawnee, it would have meant nothing to her. Now it would be a great loss.

Adam saw her and smiled, waving her to his side. If he was still angry at her behavior the night before, he gave no indication of it. Together they welcomed the guests and accepted congratulations and gifts. Because the wedding had been so hasty, there were more promises than actual presents. Still, the genuine expressions of good will touched Rebecca, and she felt more at ease with these planters and their families than she ever had before.

Adam's gift to her was a trained sparrow hawk complete with tiny leather hood, jess—the short leather strap attached to the bird's leg—and gauntlet for her hand. "The glove will be too big," he said apologetically, "but I can have Jenkins make another for you. I thought you might like the hawk. Her name is Reine; it means queen in French."

"She is beautiful, Adam. But I have nothing for you in return." Gently, Rebecca stroked the hawk's wing. "I like this gift very much. I have never had a hawk for a pet. I had a crow once when I was a child, but it flew away. Thank you." Reluctantly, she allowed a manservant to carry the bird away. "Take good care of him," she called. Excitement stained her cheeks red and brought a sparkle to her eyes. "I will hunt with her tomorrow," she said to Adam. "Or…" Rebecca moistened her upper lip with the tip of her tongue. "Or am I still not allowed to leave the house?"

"Hush," he warned, smiling at a neighbor. "Someone will hear you. Of course you're allowed to go out. You're not a prisoner; you are my wife."

"It is difficult to know the difference," she replied smoothly as she turned to accept a kiss on the cheek from a stout matron and give a polite answer to the woman's question. She permitted Adam to take her arm and escort her from room to room; later she allowed him to fill a plate of food for her from the groaning tables.

"So much food," she murmured. "The servants must have been busy all night preparing it." There were hams and rounds of beef, oysters on the half shell, crab cakes, and fried fish as well as eggs and biscuits and all manner of pies and sweets. Women who Rebecca knew usually worked in the washhouse or weaving sheds were dressed in starched white aprons and caps and had been pressed into service as maids.

"Yes, Miss Rebecca," the manservant John agreed. "Not only here but at Cedar Grove, too. The master said we were to see that no one had cause to complain of a lack of hospitality at Sheffield fer your and Master's Adam's wedding."

"Thank you, John. And tell them in the kitchen how nice everything looks," Adam said. "We couldn't be more pleased."

Couldn't we? Rebecca thought. Wondering if Adam would be hurt when she left Sheffield, Rebecca looked sideways at him from under her lashes. He was playing the part of a happy bridegroom better than she would have believed. She sighed and nibbled at a biscuit. She didn't feel married, and she certainly didn't feel married to Adam. Someone had called her Mistress Rourke. English women changed their names when they took a husband; she knew that, but no one had told her why. It seemed a foolish custom. Why did a woman give up her own name? Nothing the English did made any sense.

Her grandfather called out to her, and she forced a smile. It would not do to let him know how she really felt. She must play out the game for as long as he lived. There was no need to let him know what went on in private between her and Adam, no need to hurt him at all. She had followed his wishes in the matter of the marriage. Now she must live with it gracefully. She would wait and bide her time until the gods willed otherwise.

Then she remembered the hawk, and her smile became genuine. The hawk would help to pass the days. If she was truly free to come and go as she liked, it might not be so bad. At least she could put an end to the tiresome lessons with Master Byrd. As a married woman, she had no need to go to school like a child. The tutor could make someone else's life miserable.

Except that she and Adam now shared a bedroom, life was little different at Sheffield after Rebecca's marriage. Isabel continued to act as mistress of the house, and Adam was still busy from early morning until dark with plantation matters. Released from the hated schoolroom, Rebecca spent her days on horseback, exploring the fields and woods and waterways with the little hawk firmly ensconced on her wrist.

As the days passed, the weather gradually grew cooler, but it was still warm enough for Rebecca to ride out in her deerskin dress without a cape. If the air was nippy in the early morning, it would soon become more comfortable with the full rising of the sun. The grass was still thick and green, and many birds, which had usually traveled south by this time, still chirped and squabbled and filled the trees of the plantation. Even the ducks and geese, coming down from the north to winter along Chesapeake Bay, had not reached their normal numbers. Instead, the flocks of migrating waterfowl were thin and scattered.

Rebecca wondered if the warm autumn had affected the Ohio River country. Usually, the fur-bearing animals such as beaver, fox, and bear would have grown thick coats by now. Her people trapped them, both for trade and to use the warm skins for winter clothing and blankets. It was a good time to hunt bear; they were fat from a summer and fall of stuffing themselves and had not yet found caves in which to hibernate for the winter.

The Shawnee would be hunting ducks and geese and smoking and salting them for the winter. If she were home, Rebecca would be hunting a bee tree or running rabbit snares. She had hunted deer, but the creatures were so lovely that she had often let them live once she had found them. It was better to let her father bring home a prime doe. Once an animal was killed, it didn't bother her to help with the skinning and preparation of the meat: without such food stores, her people could not live through the long, hard winters.

In the Shawnee villages there would be pumpkins and squash to dry, fish to salt, and cornmeal to grind and mix with berries and dried meat. Often, her people would trade with Indians to the north for wild rice and maple sugar. Such treats were especially appreciated when a blanket of white covered the land and the north wind howled around the wigwams.

She would not miss the cold if she stayed the winter on the Chesapeake. Getting used to the bitter winters was one of the hardest things she'd had to do as a child. Often her fingers and toes had been stiff with cold, and she and her family had shivered beside a wavering fire. Rebecca smiled, remembering those frigid winter nights.

Her father had told wonderful stories around those fires. She would be wrapped in a blanket and pressed close to her Shawnee mother's side while she listened to tales of magic, demons, ghosts, and heroes. Sometimes she would fall asleep before the end of a story, and the next day she would have to ask Otter what had happened. Otter knew all the stories by heart, even the magic ones that were not usually told to children. Rebecca always asked how he knew them, but he would only laugh and look mysterious.

Now, as she rode through a patch of woods she had never explored before, she thought she would like to share some of those stories with Adam, but she was afraid he would laugh—not with her but at her. It was strange to think of Adam as her husband when he wasn't even her friend. The thought of him sobered her, and Rebecca reined in her horse and dismounted, carefully transferring the sparrow hawk to a nearby tree branch. The bird fussed and she laughed, adjusting the tiny leather hood to make it more comfortable on the bird's neck. "Be patient, Reine. I will find you game to hunt in a little while."

She had to be careful with the creature. Once, the little hawk had tried to take a duck much larger than she was. The duck had escaped, but the hawk had lost several feathers and had just missed being badly hurt. "You know you have more courage than brains," she added in a soothing voice. "Like Adam."

Why did everything always come back to Adam? Thinking of him made her feel empty inside. Night after night, he lay beside her and made no move to take her in his arms or make love to her. It was what she wanted, and yet…She didn't know what she wanted.

Loving Adam was painful. He was so different from the men she had known. He expected her to be someone she wasn't, someone English. Once she left Sheffield, she would never lay eyes on him again. In time, he would find an English woman and bring her here to Sheffield. They would make strong sons and daughters to hold this Chesapeake land. She was not part of it. Her destiny lay elsewhere.

So why did it hurt that he did not seek her out? The physical pleasure they could give each other would be nice. Pleasure always brought joy and then sound sleep. She had certainly enjoyed the lovemaking they had shared before they were married. But the hurt went deeper than the lack of pleasure. She had a feeling that Adam would rise in her thoughts for the rest of her days. And every man she looked at she would silently measure against the big Englishman.

"Damn!" She cursed him with a strong English oath and felt better. Even when she escaped from Adam, she would not really escape. She would remember his touch and the sound of his voice when he was angry, or the contented moan he gave when she was pleasing him.

Rebecca tied the horse to a tree and walked down a deer path to the bank of the creek. Tall river reeds grew close to shore, and she was glad it was too late in the year for mosquitoes. She found a dry spot where a deer had slept the night and sat down in the flattened circle of grass. The reeds and cattails formed a thick barrier around her, and she lay on her back and stared up at the blue sky.

The sounds of the living creek drifted on the breeze—a red-winged blackbird's call, the croak of a frog, and the occasional splash of a fish. It was a good place to think; she might have been the first woman ever to set foot on this spot. It was a place to ease her wounded spirit and regain her will.

To her surprise, she yawned. Her eyelids were heavy and her breathing slow and regular. She drifted into sleep, unconscious of the time or place.

The sound of gunfire brought her upright. Her heart beat fast, and her mouth turned dry. It took a moment to realize the gun was not close and she was not in danger. She rubbed her eyes, stretched, and sat up. From the position of the sun she determined it was late afternoon—a strange time to be hunting. How long had she slept? It must have been several hours.

Her first thoughts were for the hawk and her horse; she hurried back to where she had left them. To her relief, both were still there, seemingly unruffled by the long wait. A shot came again, and curiosity tugged at Rebecca. Who was hunting on Sheffield land in the afternoon? It was a workday, and the bondservants should have been at their chores.

Leaving the horse and hawk, Rebecca crossed a short section of woods, then a meadow, and circled beyond the section of creek from which the shots seemed to be coming. Cautiously, she made her way down to the water's edge, pushing through the reeds as silently as a shadow and then dropping to her stomach.

At the bend of the creek lay a fallen cedar tree. Cornstalks and branches had been used to form a crude blind, and just beyond it, swimming in the water, were several live decoys. A few moments' scrutiny assured Rebecca they were semitame mallards that were used to lure wild birds close enough to shoot. The decoys were secured by a cord around their legs, which was in turn attached to a weight on the creek bottom.

Seeing the ducks answered all her questions but one. Who was hunting? She waited, not letting her steady gaze falter. Minutes passed. She knew someone was in the blind; she could hear the rustle of leaves and see an occasional faint movement of branches.

Then a pair of black ducks circled the area, warily eyeing the decoys. They dipped low to investigate, and Rebecca recognized Adam as he stood to get off a shot. He fired before the ducks were close enough and missed. The pair soared upward and winged their way to safety. Rebecca chuckled at the easy escape, and a gleam of mischief sparkled in her eyes.

CHAPTER 18

Adam cursed his impatience and began to reload his musket. All he'd done so far was waste powder and shot; he'd never had such a rotten day of shooting. Early morning or dusk was best for shooting waterfowl, and a clear afternoon was probably the worst. But Thomas had asked him to try and get a few ducks for the evening meal, and he'd willingly left the dry account books for a few hours' sport.

Even the decoys seemed to be working against him. They'd gotten their lines tangled twice, and one had bitten him when he'd taken it out of the bag. In a few minutes, he'd give up on the ducks and tell the cook to chop the heads off a few chickens instead.

Thomas had asked him how he and Rebecca had been getting on, which had given him even more reason to get out of the house quickly. He didn't want to lie to his stepfather, and the truth would only hurt the old man. It was certainly hurting Adam enough—physically as well as mentally.

Lying beside Rebecca night after night without touching her was pure agony. Every nerve in his body, every muscle, screamed to take her into his arms and make passionate love to her.

The scent of her was maddening...the sweet, clean woman smell that clung to the sheets and covers and filled the bedchamber. If he accidently brushed against her skin, he felt as if he'd been scalded. It amazed him that the sound of his pounding blood didn't wake her out of a sound sleep.

He thought about her day and night; he dreamed about her in his sleep. Last night, he had lain awake for hours, afraid to close his eyes lest he seize her in his sleep and ravage her body. His head hurt, and his nerves were ragged. That morning, he'd shouted at one of the maids for no good reason and had sent two of his best workers to clean out the stables when he'd caught them ogling one of the bondwomen.

He'd been married only two weeks, but if something didn't happen soon between him and that hellcat he now called a wife, he knew he'd have to visit the Merry Widow for some relief. The thought of betraying his marriage vows shocked him, but the thought of begging Rebecca for what should have been his by right was even more unthinkable.

Was he a fool for not taking her by force? If he grabbed her and threw her across the bed, would she fight him? A man had a right to make love with his lawful wife, when and where he wished, didn't he? Did she think him weak for not pressing that right? She'd been raised among the savages. Would a Shawnee brave allow her to indulge in such intolerable behavior?

He knew that she was angry, and with good reason. She felt betrayed, and she probably believed he had married her to get his hands on Sheffield. And who was to say that hadn't been part of it? He didn't know...he didn't know anything anymore.

Adam rubbed the calf of his left leg; it had gone to sleep on him. Wincing, he wiggled it, resting the stock of the musket against the ground. One of the female mallards began to quack, and he peered cautiously through the cornstalks at the front of the blind. Instantly he was alert. Several wild ducks were swimming downstream toward the decoys. He hadn't seen them light; they must have just

come around the bend. Moistening his lips with the tip of
his tongue, he rose to his feet and eased the musket up. This
time he would wait until he couldn't miss. It was his last
chance to have duck for supper.

Slowly, tantalizingly, the wild mallards swam toward the
tame decoys, pausing now and then to bob in the water for
food or to fluff up their feathers. There were two males and
three females in the flock, all close enough now for Adam
to see the males' iridescent green heads. Ordinarily, he
wouldn't shoot birds on the water, but when he was
hunting for food, anything was permissible.

He had only one shot, and the surviving ducks would be
up and gone before he could load a second time. He had to
line up the birds by eye so that he could kill two or three
with the single shot and still not ruin the meat. It meant he
couldn't let them get too close to him. The first duck he had
ever shot had produced only a handful of feathers and
mangled bones. How Thomas had laughed over that.

"You can't call yourself a gentleman if you can't hunt,"
his stepfather had said. Except that Thomas Bradford
hadn't been his stepfather then; he'd been his master. "And
you can't call yourself a gentleman if you kill for the sake
of killing. Every bird, fish, and animal on the tidewater has
a better right to be here than we do. If you kill for food,
that's one thing. But if I ever see you shoot something and
waste it, I'll stripe your back with a horse whip."

It had been good advice, and Adam had never forgotten
it. He'd learned more about being a gentleman from
Thomas Bradford than he had in his father's house or from
the titled "gentlemen" he'd known in English society. He'd
carry on Thomas's beliefs; it was part of the responsibility
that went along with possessing Sheffield.

The decoys had seen the other ducks now and were
becoming excited, swimming in circles and calling to them.
Adam steadied the musket. Just a few more feet and he'd
have them in range. If they stayed bunched up like that, he
was sure of getting two. His finger tightened on the trigger,
and he held his breath. "Closer, just a little closer," he

whispered. "Come on…" He sighted down the barrel at the green, shining head of the lead male. "Now."

Adam gasped. Before he could get off the shot, the duck vanished. It hadn't dived; something had pulled it underwater so smoothly the other ducks weren't even alarmed. "What the hell?" Shaken, he moved the barrel to aim at a large female. To his utter astonishment, that duck, too, went under. The single flap of its wing and the jerk of its foot frightened the rest, and they rose in a flurry. Adam fired and missed by an arm's length. Cursing, he slammed the gun down and burst out of the blind to untangle the agitated decoys before they injured themselves.

He waded into the water, trying not to let it rise over the tops of his old boots, and reached down to catch the nearest drake. "I ought to ring your neck and let Cook serve you up for supper," he threatened, half seriously. He still couldn't believe something had snatched those ducks right out from under his eyes. Snapping turtles took ducklings all the time, but what was big enough to pull a grown mallard under without a fight?

In answer to his unasked question, the water swirled a few feet from where he stood, and Rebecca surfaced. Paddling in place, she shook the water from her eyes and held up the missing birds. "You want ducks, A-dam?" she taunted. Her green eyes danced with mischief, and her merry laughter brought a rise of blood to his neck and cheeks. "I think that if you cannot hit anything with your musket, you should learn to swim after ducks like Shawnee children."

"Damn you, Rebecca," he sputtered. "You might have been killed! I might have shot you." Cold fear hit him. His musket ball would have snuffed out her life, and she would have sunk to the bottom of the cheek. If they hadn't found her body, she would have simply vanished. That chill realization numbed his brain. He might have killed her. It would have been an accident, and no one, not even Thomas, would have believed a word of it.

"How could you hit me with your English gun when you couldn't even hit a flock of ducks on the water?" Rebecca found bottom with her feet and began to wade ashore.

Adam's oath caught in his throat. She was stark naked. Her dark hair fell over her breasts almost to her waist, and the skin beneath her hair glistened with water droplets like an ethereal mermaid's. Adam's breathing quickened as he felt the heat rise in his loins; he stared at her, his brown eyes heavy lidded with passion. "Rebecca," he said thickly. "Rebecca…"

She held out a hand to him. "If you want ducks," she teased, "you may have mine. I cannot eat both of them." She paused to push a strand of damp hair from her cheek and smiled at him. "I think there is much you can learn from me about duck hunting."

Their eyes met, and the laughter died in her throat. She began to shiver, not from the cool air but from an inner tension. She caught a whiff of his scent, and ripples of excitement washed through her body. The hand holding the ducks dropped to her waist, and she took another step toward him. What was it about this man that called to her? A heavy ache in her breasts brought a flush to her skin, and her lips silently formed his name.

"You're cold," he said hoarsely, stripping off his shirt and wrapping it around her.

How could she be cold when his touch seared her skin like glowing coals? Her limbs were suddenly heavy; she stood ankle deep in the running water and leaned against him as the shivering became a trembling.

"Rebecca?" He wiped a single crystalline tear from her cheek with a calloused thumb. His dark eyes begged for what his lips refused to ask.

The flame of her own desire ignited, and she pressed against him, drawing his head down to join her mouth with his in a scorching kiss that left her senses reeling. Adam groaned deep in his throat and pulled her after him to the riverbank. The ducks fell to the ground unheeded as she buried her face in the warm mat of his chest and let her blood feel the beat of his.

"I want you," he murmured into her hair. It took all his strength to push her away. "Not here...we have to find a proper place." She was so beautiful! "Lord, woman."

His voice was ragged with raw passion. "You'll be the death of me."

Her nostrils flared delicately, and the green Bradford eyes grew dark with unconcealed sensuality. "I know a place," she whispered. Her voice sounded strange in her ears, as though it came from far away. She raised a hand to caress his throat, letting her fingers slide down his bare shoulder, reveling in the hard muscle beneath the tanned, sleek skin. "I want you, my husband," she admitted, knowing that she had lied to herself when she denied their union. He was her husband. It mattered not that the words had been said by an English minister. He was hers...a part of her, as much a part as an arm or an eye. "I have been a fool." She bent toward him and flicked at the hard nub of his erect male nipple with the tip of her tongue. "I have denied us both," she murmured throatily. "Come...there is a place I would have you see."

Gracefully, she led the way to where she had abandoned her dress and moccasins. "It is not far," she assured him as she pulled the deerskin garment over her head. "Through the woods. We will take your horse."

He swung up into the saddle, then held out a hand to pull her up before him so that she sat sidesaddle. Rebecca's arms went around his neck, and they kissed again, savoring the delicious sensation of love-swollen lips and velvet-soft tongues. "It had better not be far," Adam said with a groan.

Laughing, Rebecca dropped her hand and lightly stroked the source of his pain and desire. "Not far," she whispered.

"Witch," he breathed.

When the woods became too thick to ride through, they dismounted and tied the horse to a tree. Rebecca moved to what appeared to be an impenetrable wall of greenbriers and pushed them aside to reveal a game trail. "Sometimes I need to be alone," she confided, catching his big hand in her small one. "This place is mine. Now it is ours."

Adam followed her through the tunnel of briers, bending low to keep his head from being caught. The path went only a few feet before ending in a grove of cedar trees. "Where are you taking me?" he asked.

She laughed. "You will see, A-dam."

Rebecca pulled at a cedar bough and ducked through a hole in the greenery with Adam right behind her. Inside was a clearing about twenty feet across, and in the middle was a low, bark-covered structure. "This is my wigwam," she said. "Just a very small one, but big enough for two." Deftly, she lifted the deerskin door covering. "Here we will be alone, you and I. Do you like it, A-dam?"

He bent to enter the hut; inside, there was barely room for him to stand in the middle. He blinked his eyes, letting them adjust to the dim interior. The wigwam smelled of pine boughs and fresh herbs. Half the space was taken up by a low sleeping platform heaped with furs. There was a firepit, but it was cold.

"What do you think of it?" Rebecca asked, as eager for approval as any child. "Do you like it?" Carefully, she slipped off her moccasins and placed them by the door. "I did not steal the skins. I traded for them. They are all beaver, except there is one wolf pelt. I got that from your friend Jock. A wolf pelt is warm in winter; it sheds water almost as well as beaver."

"Come here, woman."

She laughed and threw herself across the bed. "You come here," she parried.

Adam grinned, his fingers already fumbling with the ties at the waist of his breeches. "No more running away," he murmured.

"I have brought you to my wigwam, husband," she said, holding out her arms to him. "Where would I run?"

The pine boughs gave beneath his weight as he knelt on the bed and took her in his arms. Eagerly, they sought each other's embrace, crying out in joy at the touch of warm flesh against flesh. Somehow Rebecca's dress was off and pushed aside, and she lay naked and trembling in his arms.

"If you knew how much I've wanted you..." he said. "So much, my darling..."

"And I have wanted you," she whispered, meeting kiss with kiss and tangling her fingers in his thick, dark hair. Their limbs entwined, and she pressed her aching breasts against him. "A-dam," she breathed. "Husband."

Adam's fingers moved across her skin, fanning the fires of her rising pleasure. Gently, he cupped a breast and lowered his head to take the swollen nipple between his lips and suck.

Rebecca's nails dug into the knotted muscles of his upper arms as she writhed beneath him. The heat in her loins grew as she felt a familiar moistness spread through the dark tangle of her woman's core. "Now," she begged. "Adam...I want you inside me...I need you."

"Not yet, sweet," he answered hoarsely. "Not yet." He moved to tease and tantalize the other breast and then to trail a burning path of kisses down her flat stomach and onto the softness of her inner thighs. The bittersweet agony of his kisses and the rough sensation of his whiskers combined to make the throbbing need within her almost more than she could bear. His fingers brushed her most intimate flesh, and she strained against him, opening to his touch as her hips undulated in invitation to the age-old dance of love.

Slowly he entered her body, thrusting deep and melding with her in a joyous rhythm of unchecked passion. Rebecca clung to him, meeting his soul and body in a glorious merging of two people into one. Together, they rose to the stars and beyond, even to the shores of the spirit world...that place of wonder and mystery from which few mortals return. And in the stillness of their joined rapture, they were no longer English and Shawnee, male and female; they were only one....

The shadows of the afternoon had turned to dusk when Adam's feather-light kiss on her lips awakened Rebecca.

"It's time to go," he whispered. "They'll have a search party out for us." He lay propped on one elbow, half above her, and she blushed at the intensity of his gaze.

"Let them look; they will never find us. We can hide here forever, until the rivers cease to run and the sun sets in the east." She caught his hand and brought it to her lips, nibbling at the knuckles of his first two fingers. "You are different when we are alone, Adam, and I like it."

Her face lay in shadows, and her dark hair blended with the rich texture of the furs. Adam moistened his lips; she seemed different, too, vulnerable and utterly female. He wondered how he had ever lived without her. "We must go, darling. But..." He smiled wickedly. "We can come back another day."

"Every day," she said, stretching and sitting up. "Oh! My hawk. I forgot her." She scrambled out of his arms and reached for her dress. "Unless you wish me to cook those ducks here for you?"

"The ducks are for Sheffield's table." He watched as she pulled the soft doeskin over her head and let it drop around her hips. "Don't you ever wear anything under that?" Adam asked, teasingly. "It must be cold." He'd glimpsed a flash of dark curls before the folds of the dress hid them from view. "Or scratchy when you ride horseback."

"Of course I do." Chuckling, Rebecca picked up a length of soft hide and twisted it about her loins after hiking up the dress. "It is nicer than the things Aunt Isabel makes me wear, especially when I ride a horse."

"I don't think we'll ever make a respectable tidewater lady of you," he murmured and then smiled with his eyes. "Maybe I wouldn't really want to."

"The old ones say it is best if a man does not wish for what he cannot have." She tugged on the moccasins. "I am me and I will always be me, Adam. I cannot be an English woman."

"Then I guess I'll have to love you the way you are," he answered softly.

For an instant the happiness was more than she could stand, and moisture rose to cloud her eyes. She turned away so Adam would not see and called to him to follow her back to the outside world they both must share. Can you love me the way I am? she wondered. Truly? She would not think of that now. She would only seize the joy in both hands and hold it tightly, savoring each heartbeat of contentment.

Winter came at last to the Chesapeake country, borne on the wings of a northwest storm. Snow and bitter cold grasped the tidewater in an iron grip, covering the creeks and rivers with a thin coating of ice and driving people and animals alike to shelter. Many a planter, lulled by the unusually warm fall, suffered from the storm, but Sheffield was well prepared.

Hay and grain filled the barns and sheds; wood had been cut and stacked beneath stout roofs. There were stalls enough for horse and oxen alike, and warm pens for the poultry, sheep, and swine. The cabins and cottages of the slaves and indentured workers were weathertight and stocked with food and winter clothing. No man or woman lacked for good leather shoes or a wool cloak or blanket.

The storm was a gift to Adam and Rebecca, allowing them precious hours together they might not otherwise have had. They slept late in the mornings and then made love in the four-poster bed before a crackling fire. The warmth and comfort of Sheffield were a delight to Rebecca. Always before, she had dreaded the onslaught of winter. Icy winds had whipped through the thin walls of the wigwams, and rain had run down the inside. Water had had to be carried from frozen streams or made by heating snow over the cook fire. At Sheffield, there were servants to bring hot water for baths and to heat bricks that warmed cold beds. Rebecca knew she was being spoiled, but she loved it.

Day by day the friendship between Adam and Rebecca grew. She followed him to the stables and to the prize house, where the tobacco was pressed into casks. She grew to know the many servants and their families, learning the names and habits of each. And gradually, through these simple people, she began to realize that she had unfairly judged all Englishmen by the actions of a few.

As she grew more familiar with the English language and more at ease in her position as mistress of Sheffield, she found she could laugh and joke as easily here as she could in the Shawnee village. She came to appreciate the English way of doing things and was not so quick to make comparisons between Indian and white customs. It was not that she forgot the Shawnee way; rather, she came to realize there was much she could learn from the people of her blood.

Most of all, she came to appreciate the man to whom she was married. Hour by hour, she and Adam grew closer, until she almost knew what he was thinking or what he was doing when they were apart. By necessity, much of their time was spent with Aunt Isabel and Rebecca's grandfather and, naturally, the house servants. But they still found time to be alone—time to talk. It was during these private interludes that Adam told Rebecca about his childhood and his early days at Sheffield. She was touched by the sincerity and depth of the emotion he revealed when he spoke of Thomas Bradford and the plantation.

"I did not know it meant so much to you," Rebecca whispered, gazing into Adam's brown eyes. They were lying on her sleeping platform in the hidden wigwam, snug in their closeness, while snowflakes drifted down to coat the forest in a fairyland of frost.

Adam tucked the wolf skin around Rebecca's bare shoulders and leaned across to toss another log on the fire. "It was all I had until you came along," he admitted. "I'd be a fool and a liar if I didn't admit that the money Sheffield represents is important. I've seen what a lack of money can do to a family. My own mother had to give up everything she held dear and sell herself into slavery because of it. She was a good woman, and she deserved better."

"But she found happiness with my grandfather, did she not?"

"Finally, yes. But she was never accepted by the other planters and their wives. They never let her forget she had been a field worker and then a housekeeper. She was a proud woman and uncomplaining." He snuggled down beside Rebecca and nibbled on her right earlobe. "You have the nicest ears," he teased, blowing gently.

Rebecca giggled. "You are too big to say such silly things. You are too big for a wigwam. Your mother must have fed you magic herbs when you were a child. If we make a baby, I will not let it grow so big." She tangled a finger in the queue at the back of his neck and unfastened it, letting Adam's rich beaver brown hair fall over his shoulders. "Now you look like a proper Shawnee, or you would if your hair was black instead of brown."

"I thought all Shawnee shaved their heads except for a rooster crest on the top." Adam's mouth moved up her cheek to kiss the corner of her lips and then to take her lower lip between his teeth and tug at it. "Mmm," he moaned.

Rebecca pulled free and buried her face in his neck, giggling. "Foolish English-*manake*. All men do not wear their hair so, and they don't shave it. They pull it out, strand by strand, with a clamshell."

"Ouch!" he cried in mock pain. "That proves they're crazy."

"All men are crazy, Shawnee and English alike," she agreed. "And you, A-dam, are the craziest of all." A shiver of delight passed through her as he laid his hand on her bare breast and began to tease her nipple with the tip of his finger. "You are crazy," she repeated huskily, "but it is a good crazy." The familiar warmth began to grow in her loins and she pulled him down on top of her, eager for his love once more.

It was long past dark when they finally arrived back at Sheffield, but even Aunt Isabel held her sharp tongue when she noted the contented look on their faces.

"I can tell what those two have been up to," she confided to Thomas. "They've been behaving just like rabbits."

The old man laughed heartily. "And did we never do the same when we were young and full of ginger? I'll wager you did your share of fluttering when you were newly married, eh?"

Isabel's face turned a dark crimson. "Certainly not!" she snapped. "I was properly raised. In those days, *that* was for procreation and nothing more, at least not between decent people."

"Well, I guess I didn't know any decent people, because I'm older than you, and I know what I thought about day and night." Thomas chuckled and held out his brandy glass for a refill. "Just a bit more to keep away the night chill."

"You've had more than enough. You know what the doctor said about your condition."

"My condition, as you term it, is called dying. You know it and I know it. And if a little brandy will warm these bones on the way out, so much the better. It's not as though I have a lot of bodily pleasures these days. Although I suppose I could take to bedding the maids."

"Humph!" Isabel poured the brandy, careful to hide the amusement in her eyes. "An Irish girl in your bed would be all you'd need to push you through the pearly gates. You've enough sins to answer for without adding attempted fornication to the list." Isabel handed Thomas the snifter and poured a second portion for herself. "I'm not altogether disappointed in this marriage, you know. It seems to have cured Rebecca of most of her fey notions. At least we've heard no more of her returning to the savages."

"That was my intention. Now, if Adam will do his duty and get her with child at once, an heir will be assured for Sheffield. I'd like to live long enough to set eyes on him and to include him in my will."

"Him! Him!" Isabel fussed. "Half the children born in this world are female, in case you haven't noticed. Rebecca and Adam may well breed a dozen girls and not a manchild in the bunch."

"Girls or boys, they'd be heirs. When you get to be my age, Isabel, you worry about continuing the line. The Bradfords almost died out."

"They have died out. When you go, it's the end. Rebecca's children will be Rourkes," Isabel said firmly.

"That they will not! Rebecca took Adam's name with the marriage, but all the sons must carry the name Rourke-Bradford. It's in the contract. There'll be Bradfords here—I've made sure of it!"

CHAPTER 19

Rebecca leaned from the open bedroom window and inhaled the fresh spring air. How could she have slept so late on such a wonderful morning? Not ten feet from the window ledge a mockingbird trilled saucily, as if daring her to intrude upon his domain.

Rebecca laughed. "Your nest is safe enough, noisy one. My hawk is fastened to her stand. I won't let her hunt in your territory." She leaned even farther out and strained her eyes to discern the tiny figures of men and horses plowing in the south fields. The man on horseback was surely Adam. He would tease her for lying abed when he was already at work.

How glorious the spring was in this Chesapeake country! Rebecca closed the window and began to dress hastily, choosing an English riding habit for the morning. She would saddle up and ride out to the fields to watch the big horses and sweating men carve long furrows in the eager earth.

Isabel had said something about teaching her to order supplies for the kitchen, but that would have to wait until later. Rebecca had no intention of remaining indoors today! Her skills in mathematics were atrocious, and she would not subject herself to the struggle with smeared ink and badly formed numbers when she could be as free as the wind.

Rebecca paused to transfer the sparrow hawk from its stand in the corner of the bedroom to her wrist, then moved swiftly down the grand staircase and out through the front doors. Isabel would be looking for her in the kitchen, or at least expecting her to come down the servants' stairway. Rebecca's stomach felt hollow, but she could always beg some bread from one of the workers' wives or do without. Freedom was worth being hungry.

She had nearly reached the safety of the barn when a scream came from the house. Rebecca stopped in her tracks as the wailing of another woman was added to the first. She grabbed the arm of a stable boy and pulled him around.

"Here, take my hawk and put her in her cage in the stable. Treat her gently. I must see what is wrong." She passed the bird to the boy and ran back to the house, entering by the kitchen.

The cook looked up from the table, her dark face lined with sorrow. "It's the master," she said slowly. "Master Thomas."

Rebecca dashed up the back stairway and pushed her way past weeping servants. Her grandfather lay in his four-poster bed as if he were asleep; only his waxen color and the absence of movement showed that he had passed from this world to the next; Isabel, standing by the bed, turned to look sadly at Rebecca.

"He's gone, child. At least he was in no pain," Isabel said gently.

Rebecca came closer and sat on the edge of the bed, catching up her grandfather's lifeless hand. How small he looked in death! His expression was serene, his eyes closed. "Adam," she whispered. "Adam must know."

"I've sent a boy to fetch him." Isabel turned to the maids and Thomas's manservant. "Out! All of you! Leave your master some dignity. There's plenty to do. The house must be cleaned from top to bottom, and we must be prepared to feed all those who come to the funeral. Well, what are you waiting for?" She clapped her hands sharply, and the servants fled. "They'll take any excuse to avoid work," Isabel said to Rebecca. "You must be firm with them." Her crisp words did not quite cover the quaver in her voice. She sighed heavily. "He's gone to a better place and left us to carry on. You must be strong, Rebecca. I know you can be."

"May I be alone with him for a few minutes?" A lump in her throat made it difficult for her to breathe. She had not believed it would hurt this much when the old man died. "Please?"

Isabel nodded and left the room, closing the door softly behind her. Rebecca lowered her head to rest it on her grandfather's still hand. She felt such a sense of emptiness, of words left unsaid. No tears filled her eyes; the ache was too deep. With Thomas Bradford's passing, she had lost the last link to her English heritage. She had Adam, but it was not the same. Her grandfather had been of her blood; sometimes he had understood her when no one else could. And he had loved her in spite of all their differences.

Rebecca had no fear of death. Her Shawnee mother had taught her that death was part of life. Always, for every living thing, be it tree or stalk of corn or bird or human, there was a never-ending circle of birth and death and rebirth. Thomas Bradford had been old; he had been sick and weak. Once he had been a strong and virile man. In time he would be born again into the body of a babe and would have a new life to live. It was the way of all things.

Still, the way was hard for those left behind. Rebecca could only hope that someday she would look into the eyes of a child and see her grandfather's indomitable spirit staring back at her. She would offer prayers that she and Adam might have a baby and that their son might be the one chosen to carry her grandfather's soul.

Soon others would come and begin the rites for English burial. Her grandfather would belong to her no longer. She must hurry to the kitchen for cornmeal and water. She would send him on his journey with all the tenderness due a

Shawnee warrior, and should the English godman not be powerful enough, Shawnee prayers would see him safely to the spirit land. There was only one God, no matter what men called him. Surely, Wishemenetoo would welcome Thomas Bradford and keep him safe until the time of his rebirth.

"Swift journey, Grandfather," Rebecca whispered in the Shawnee tongue. *"Dah-quel-e-ntah."*

People came from Annapolis and the Eastern Shore and from plantations up and down the bay for the funeral of Thomas Bradford. He had been a wealthy and powerful man, well liked and honest, and not one of those who came could claim an unpaid debt.

Thomas was to be buried in the family graveyard on Sheffield. An open grave waited beside the marble stone carved with the name and dates of birth and death of Martha Rourke Bradford. The graveyard was a peaceful place, with tall chestnut trees and carefully tended boxwood; the whole was enclosed by a low brick wall. Rebecca approved of the spot. It was a good place for her grandfather to rest; someday, perhaps, her own bones would lie nearby.

Isabel had been a rock in this time of confusion. She had given orders as regally as any queen, meeting the distinguished guests and seeing that everyone, high sheriff and lowly farmer alike, was offered refreshment and attention.

Adam never left Rebecca's side, pointing out the various officials and introducing her to the colonial governor, John Seymour, who had taken time from his busy schedule to pay his respects to the Bradford family.

Rebecca had hardly had a minute alone with her husband since her grandfather's death. Even at night, they had fallen into bed exhausted, too tired to do more than sleep in each other's arms.

Adam had been deeply shaken by the old man's death, and he had shed private tears. Rebecca knew that he wondered why her eyes were dry, but their relationship was still too new for her to try and explain to him. She had performed the ritual of the soul's departure, using the fresh water and cornmeal in the ancient manner, a custom going back among the Shawnee people to the dawn of time. She had done this alone, with no one to watch or scorn her heathen ways. She knew instinctively that Adam would disapprove, and so she had not told him of it.

She had done all she could do for her grandfather until the English had finished with their burial ceremonies. She did not want to embarrass Adam or Isabel, or to bring disgrace to the Bradford name. But the rituals must be completed. She must do what she must do. Until then, she would wait and try to act as they wished her to.

Playing the part of the stricken mistress of Sheffield was not difficult. People did not expect her to talk; she could hide her face behind a handkerchief and keep her eyes lowered. If she let Adam speak for her, no one thought it strange. Rebecca Bradford Rourke was regarded as somewhat backward anyway. And if there were sly glances and whispers, it made no difference to her.

The service at the graveside was long, as behooved the ceremony for a man of Thomas Bradford's position. The minister spoke of his good qualities, of his long life of hard work and sacrifice, and of the loss the colony had suffered in his passing. Rebecca waited patiently, her arm linked in Adam's. She did not listen to the godman's words; they meant nothing to her. If the high sheriff died tomorrow, the godman would give an equally impassioned sermon.

When the talking was finished, everyone returned to the house to eat and drink and to talk again. Faces and voices swirled until Rebecca wanted to run and hide. She could eat nothing, drink nothing, until the rituals were carried out. If she were at home on the Ohio, she would have slashed her arms and face in sorrow and rubbed ashes in her hair. She would have wailed with the other women without loss of dignity. Here, she could only stand silently and murmur foolish nothings. She had never felt like such an outsider.

At last the guests were gone. One by one the carriages and wagons rolled away down the dusty lane, and the sloops pushed off from the dock. Men and women on horseback and on foot made their way homeward, and Rebecca and Adam and Isabel were left alone with the people of Sheffield.

"You haven't eaten a thing all day," Isabel fussed. "You're white as a sheet. You'd best go up to bed. I'll have one of the girls bring you some broth and bread."

Rebecca looked toward Adam questioningly. "Go along," he said. "I've got some things that have yet to be done. Jock's waiting for me down by the prize house."

Nodding, Rebecca ascended the stairs. She would not lie down, but it suited her purpose that they should think she had. She had little time; the sun was already sinking in the west. The sky was a canvas of pinks and oranges and vivid rose, each shimmering shade blending into the next over the edge of the world and into infinity.

The ancient chestnut trees were casting long shadows by the time Rebecca reached the brick-walled cemetery. She paused by the iron gate, listening to the chorus of spring peepers and the regular breathing of the horse she was leading. A robin hopped across the new grass almost at her feet, a fat worm dangling from his beak. She took it as a good sign; the red-breasted bird was a messenger of the coming season of growth, as were the tiny frogs. It was good for a soul to leave the earth in the midst of new life. It would hasten that soul's return.

The stallion next to her pawed the ground restlessly and shook his proud head. Even the herbs Rebecca had fed him could not quench the fiery spirit of this noble animal. His hide was as white as snow, his tail hung in rippling glory, and Rebecca had braided his mane with eagle and hawk feathers and bright red beads. On his glossy rump shone mystical symbols drawn in her own blood. Her mind reached out to join with that of the horse, praising him for his beauty and assuring him that there was nothing to fear.

Adam would be furious when he learned she had taken the animal. Caesar was the pride of Sheffield's breeding stable. He had sired riding horses that were now prized animals in stables as far away as Philadelphia and Williamsburg, and many of his colts and fillies showed the speed that had won the stallion a reputation as a racehorse to be reckoned with.

Caesar was in his sixteenth year, too old to be risked any longer in racing but not too old to carry Thomas Bradford as long and as far as he had to go. Adam had bred Caesar to a dozen Sheffield mares, and men were still bringing strange mares to be mated with him before the season passed. Rebecca had asked Adam what the value of such a stallion was. He had replied that Caesar had no price.

Yes, Adam would be very angry. He would not understand, but that did not matter now. The ritual must be carried out at the last moment before the sun vanished. It must be done in the time between day and night, when the door to the spirit world stood open.

The gate squeaked as she pushed it open and led the stallion inside the graveyard. The earth was trampled beneath their feet, a reminder of the many people who had stood there that morning for the burial of Thomas Bradford. Rebecca sniffed the air. It smelled of salt and newly turned earth. The mound over Thomas's grave was raw despite the partial covering of evergreen boughs and early spring flowers. She slipped off her moccasins and began to chant, letting her spirit seek the soul of her grandfather, which must be close by.

The singing began as a whisper and slowly grew louder as every part of her body became entranced. She was no longer Rebecca but Star Blanket, the Shawnee, and she became part of the song, indistinguishable from the rhythm and words, an instrument for the spinning of a web of magic that would guide and protect the soul of Thomas Bradford on its journey from this life to the next.

Slowly, gracefully, she began to unfasten the polished saddle that lay across the stallion's back. Her movements were as stylized as a long-forgotten dance as she knelt to place the saddle beside her prized pistol on the mounded earth. Smiling, swaying to the music in her head, she added the leather bags of tobacco and cornmeal, the stone knife she had patiently chipped out herself, and Thomas's finest musket. From a basket, she took freshly shaved cedar kindling and dried hardwood. Flint and steel made fire, and the spark leaped to catch the waiting wood. The air was filled with the stench of burning leather and oil.

In that instant, when the last salmon ray of light spilled across the newly plowed fields of Sheffield, Rebecca grasped the stallion's halter rope and drew a razor-sharp steel blade across the great vein in the horse's throat. The great animal gasped and fell forward across the burning grave goods, his life's blood running down across the raw earth and mingling with her prayers for the safe passage for her grandfather.

The scent of blood filled the air, and the flames scorched the sleek hide of the animal, sending up a column of black smoke into the trees overhead.

"For the love of God!"

Rebecca turned slowly, still caught in the spell of the sacrifice, and saw Adam and Jock standing just inside the cemetery gate.

"What have you done?" Adam thundered.

"Ach, lassie," Jock added. "It's an evil thing."

Rebecca shook her head to clear away the fog. The English words meant nothing to her. What were they saying? She looked down at the knife in her hand, which ran red with the blood of the horse; her arms and dress were soaked in it.

"Kesathwa," she murmured. The sun. Did they not realize the sun had set? There should be no talking now, nothing to hold the soul of the departed loved one to the earth. The gateway was open. Her grandfather could ride his horse into the spirit world as proudly as any chieftain. He could swim the bottomless river. *"Kotha,"* she said to Adam. *"Kotha, lenawawe."* Your father lives. He had been

released from his box in *Ake,* the earth. It was a time for joy, not anger. Why was Adam's face a thundercloud? Why was Jock staring at her as though she were a mad woman?

"Rebecca." Adam's voice was accusing.

Puzzled, she took a step toward him; then a blackness began in the back of her brain and spread to encompass everything in a crackling lightning bolt of sizzling energy.

Rebecca was aware of the earth falling away, but she didn't know it when Jock caught her unconscious body.

"How could you?" Adam ranted. "Do you have any idea what that animal was worth? To be slaughtered for some pagan rite! My God, woman! Are you a mindless savage?"

A night and half the following day had passed since Jock had carried Rebecca up to the bedchamber she shared with Adam. Now, the sun was high in the heavens. She had passed from fainting into a deep sleep, a sleep that had lasted until only minutes ago. And when she opened her eyes, Adam had been staring at her.

At first he had spoken calmly to her, almost too calmly, as though she were a backward child. He had asked her if she was in pain or if she was ill. And when she had denied both and began to dress, his anger had spilled over like water from a cracking beaver dam.

"Do not speak of what you do not know," Rebecca answered softly. She did not want to fight with Adam. There was no need for his anger. What was done was done. Could all his fury bring back the horse or make him understand why she had done it?

"I want an answer out of you! Why did you do such a thing?" His eyes were black with unconcealed wrath. "I've put up with a hell of a lot from you, more than any other man would, and now this! Damn it, Rebecca! I think you truly *are* crazy. These Indian practices have gone far enough. Do you have any idea what you looked like covered in Caesar's blood? It sickened me." He doubled his fist and plunged it into the other hand. "What am I going to do with you? What will the servants say? There's no way to hide a dead horse roasted in the family graveyard. We'll be lucky if they don't accuse you of witchcraft."

Rebecca sat on the edge of the bed and bent to slip on a moccasin; her hair hung over her face in dark waves, hiding the expression in her eyes. "I am not a witch. That is a foolish thing to say. You know better, Adam." She parted a lock of hair and peered up at him. "Besides, they do not try witches in the Maryland colony. Master Byrd told me so."

"That doesn't change anything. You killed a magnificent horse without reason. Caesar would have given us another ten years of colts and fillies, if we were lucky. He was one of a kind. How could you do it?"

"Would you have my grandfather *walk* into the spirit land? Would you have him trade a future life for passage across the bottomless river? Would you deny him the rank of which he was worthy?" She made a guttural sound in her throat. "It is you who sickens me, Adam. You care only for the worth of the horse, not for my grandfather! You said all of Sheffield was mine on his death. If all is mine, you should not begrudge me a single horse and a few flintlocks. The pistol was mine in any case."

"You know damn well we're not talking about the cost of the horse or the guns," Adam lashed back. "We're talking about you, about this delusion of yours that you're some kind of primitive savage. You're white, Rebecca, do you understand? White!"

To her horror, Adam caught her by the shoulders and shook her. "Unhand me," she cried coldly.

He let her go and stepped back, breathing heavily. His face was ashen, the lines around his mouth taut. "We've got to settle this, woman. Once and for all." He regarded her strangely. "How do I know that if we had a child you wouldn't take it into your head to drown it in the river to appease some heathen spirit?"

Rebecca put her hand to her mouth and gagged, turning away to the window. The room spun around her. By sheer willpower she regained control of her body, gripping the windowsill with both hands so tightly that her flesh turned numb from the wrists down. Adam's words echoed over and over in her head. She had suggested that she might kill their child. He had called her a savage, a heathen. His accusations had insulted her soul.

Her head rose proudly as she turned and fixed him with a gaze as far away as that of a hawk. "So you believe," she whispered. "I am sorry. There is nothing I can say that will change what is in your heart. I cannot deny such evil. To do so would be to admit that it could exist. I will not." She raised a hand and pointed at his chest. "You are English-*manake*. I am Shawnee. It was wrong that we tried to blend our worlds." Sorrow filled her voice. "It was not to be, A-dam Rourke. We are too different."

"There's no sense in this," he snapped. "You are my wife, and you will remain so. You'll live like the civilized woman you are if I have to lock you up and set a watch on you day and night to keep you from hurting yourself."

Rebecca's green eyes narrowed to smoky slits as she brought her other hand forward and made a slashing motion in the air, one palm above the other. "It is finished between us," she spat out. "I divorce you."

"It's not as easy as that," Adam said with a shake of his shaggy head. "We were married in the sight of God, once and for all time. I don't believe in divorce. Whatever is wrong between us will have to be fixed, or we'll have to learn to live with it. I married you for better or worse, and if worse means a mad wife, then…" He shrugged and turned toward the door. "There'll be no running away, Rebecca. I'll set men to watch you. I've told them your grandfather's death has unbalanced you." He sighed and looked back, his eyes an open wound. "I love you more than the hope of my immortal soul, woman. But I'll have an end to this craziness or know why."

She took a step toward him in disbelief. "You cannot believe me crazy. You know why I do these things. I am a free woman. I only follow the time-honored beliefs of my people."

"No, Rebecca, you're wrong. I don't know why you act as you do. I've tried to understand you, but I can't. I'm sorry, but I don't have time to argue with you anymore. I've a plantation to run. There's more work than hours to do it. Stay in your room today. Sleep. Perhaps you'll feel better in a few days. I won't bother you; I'm moving into another bedchamber."

"Where? Into my grandfather's room? Will you try and wear his coat next?" she demanded. "It won't fit! You aren't big enough," she said sarcastically.

Adam slammed the door behind him and stomped down the hall to the stairway and out of the house. Rebecca ran to the bedroom door and fired a parting volley. "You'll never be the man he was!"

A maid coming from the opposite room blushed and nearly dropped the armload of sheets she was carrying. Rebecca ran back to the bed and reached underneath for Adam's good leather boots. She carried them to the window, pushed it open wider, and threw the boots at Adam's retreating back. "I divorce you!" she yelled. He continued on down the brick walk and through the gate without looking back.

Rebecca returned to her bed and curled up in a miserable ball. Her mouth tasted like the floor of a henhouse, and her stomach still felt queasy. She had not believed that she could feel worse than when her grandfather had died, but she did. Not even the growing suspicion that she was with child could raise her crushed spirit.

She loved Adam. Leaving him would be like leaving part of herself, but her grandfather's death had freed her in more ways than one. She was no longer bound here by honor. She had a choice. She could remain and be what Adam wanted, or she could return to the Shawnee. After what had just passed between them, she no longer had a decision to make.

She had no intention of telling Adam about the baby. She was only late in her woman's time; it could mean nothing. Besides, a child belonged to its mother. If Adam knew, he would make it harder for her to leave. Perhaps he would not even want the child of a savage. He had said she sickened him! Would he always watch their child for evidence of her taint?

She had no doubt that she would be welcome among the Shawnee. In time, she might decide to choose another husband—probably not. Men complicated life. Some Shawnee men tried to dictate to their wives as the English did, and she would not have it. She would manage her own life and that of her child by herself.

The jingle of a tiny bell drew her attention to her hawk. The bird was hooded and tied on her perch in the corner of the room. "Ooh, poor Reine. You don't like all this loud talk, do you?" Rebecca pulled on the leather glove and took the hawk on her wrist. "It is *me-loh-cak-ne,* the season of spring," she crooned to the bird. "It is time you flew free to find your own destiny, to mate and build a nest…to raise young ones and teach them the art of hunting."

Gently, she carried the hawk to the window and removed the hood and tiny leather straps. "You are free," she said. "Fly well." Without hesitation, she cast the bird up and out, watching with pride as Reine beat her wings a few times and then soared up and over the trees toward the bay. You long to be free as I do, she thought. And she knew she would never keep another hawk.

In the days and weeks that followed, Rebecca put on a gentle face. She said nothing more about the Shawnee, and she even wore her English clothing. Although she and Adam did not share a bed, at least they did not fight. Once she even found a bouquet of spring flowers at her place at the dinner table.

Adam threw himself, body and soul, into the work of Sheffield. There were the new tobacco plants to be tended in the woodlots and fields to be prepared for the transplanting in late May. The corn and vegetables had been planted, and the work of clearing timber must go on continually. A new tobacco barn was being built near the prize house, and repairs had to be completed on the dock. There was little time for Adam and Rebecca to be together, even if they had wanted to.

By May, Rebecca was certain that she was carrying Adam's child. The time of sickness had passed, and she was always hungry. Her thoughts were often of home and her family. She wanted to see her mother's face, to feel the touch of her father's hand on her cheek. She wanted to go home. And if she lay awake at night and wept into her pillow for the loss of Adam's love, it was something that must be endured.

She had not forgotten Adam's threat to keep her a prisoner at Sheffield, and she was well aware of the servants who kept her always in sight, following her when she rode out. Let them watch! It was nothing to her; when she was ready to go, the English could not hold her.

Isabel found her more obedient, more willing to spend days learning to supervise the maids, discovering the secrets of spice, and being instructed in how to make cheese. The older woman accepted these changes as the natural order of things. She had known that time and marriage would settle the girl.

It was not until the third week of May that Rebecca found her opportunity. There was a discrepancy in the manifest of one of Sheffield's sloops, and Adam was called to Annapolis to clear up the matter and pay the additional tax if it was needed. He did not want to leave Rebecca alone, but Isabel had assured him that there was no need for worry.

"What happened after Thomas's death was unfortunate," Isabel stated flatly, "but that was weeks ago. Her behavior has been without fault since then. I think she's learned a lesson. Besides, she's been complaining of a headache and has taken to her bed. If you go at once and come back in the morning, I doubt she'll know you're even gone."

Adam's conscience nagged at him all the way to Annapolis. He'd been hard on her the day of Thomas's funeral. The shock of seeing her kill the horse had made him say things he hadn't meant, things he'd regretted as soon as they were out of his mouth. His anger had cooled in the past weeks, and he was sorry he'd moved out of her bedchamber. It had been a stupid thing to do. He missed having her beside him, and he didn't know how to move back in without making a fool of himself.

She didn't seem to be carrying a grudge, but it was hard to tell with Rebecca. Behind those enigmatic emerald eyes lay unfathomable thoughts; she was unlike any woman he had ever known. And she was as stubborn as he was. If there was to be a reconciliation, he would have to bring it about. He decided to buy her something special in Annapolis. Maybe a puppy. She seemed to miss Reine. Isabel had told him the hawk had flown away and hadn't come back. Perhaps a cuddly puppy would do the trick.

He had gone to say good-bye to Rebecca, but she'd been asleep. She'd turned a cheek for him to kiss and then snuggled down under the sheets. Adam moistened his lower lip. She'd looked so irresistible! If she hadn't been ill, he'd have climbed into bed with her then and there, and the high sheriff be damned.

Rebecca's conscience did not trouble her at all. She had waited for such a chance, having made her decision long ago. In her heart she had already said her good-byes to Sheffield and to Adam. The pattern had been broken; it was time to form a new one.

Patiently, she waited until the household was asleep. It was the time of the full moon, and the trails would be as bright as day. She would need the light; she wanted to ride hard and fast before morning. She would head west and south. They would hunt north for her, if they bothered to hunt at all. She would ride west until she reached the foothills of the mountains and then cut north until she found a pass. With luck, she would be in the Ohio country before the next full moon. If not...Rebecca shrugged. The weather was warm and growing warmer. She would be well mounted and well armed. She had no doubt that she would reach home safely.

To sneak a horse from the stable was child's play, to take three only a little harder. She used rags to muffle their hooves so no one would note their passing. She would have preferred to take more horses, but it was not possible. Three would be enough to handle, and she could switch mounts as each animal tired.

Silently, she led the animals from the farmyard, swinging up into the saddle only when they were far enough from the barn so that no one could hear them. She had enough supplies for several weeks, good English muskets and steel knives and powder. It was little enough to take as her portion. Adam could have everything else.

Blinking back bitter tears of regret, Rebecca turned the black gelding's head west. Adam and Sheffield were behind her; soon they would be only memories. With a cry, she kicked the horse into a gallop. She could shed tears tomorrow; now, she would only ride.

CHAPTER 20

Adam's anxiety grew as he approached home. Damn the sheriff and his prissy, self-important ways. The man had wanted to impress on him that he was an official of the Crown and that he knew Adam wasn't due the respect Thomas Bradford had been accorded. First, Adam had been kept waiting for nearly two hours; then, a matter that could have been rectified in ten minutes had taken all afternoon.

A black-and-white puppy squirmed and whined inside Adam's shirt. He hoped it wouldn't have an accident. All he needed was to arrive back at Sheffield smelling like stale dog. He'd passed a terrible night's sleep at the inn, thinking about Rebecca and what he would say to her. It was foolish for them to continue this stupid argument. What was done was done. They'd both said things that shouldn't have been said. It was time to pick up the pieces and go on with their marriage.

The stable boy who took his horse was strangely quiet. Adam arched a heavy eyebrow. "What is it? Is something wrong?"

"Ye'd best talk wi' the mistress, sir."

Adam left the puppy in the boy's care and hurried to the manor house. Isabel met him on the steps, her white face confirming his worst suspicion. "Where's Rebecca?" he demanded. "Is she hurt?"

Isabel suddenly looked old. "She's gone back to the Indians. She must have left in the night. I sent out a search party, but so far they haven't turned up a thing. It's as though she's vanished off the face of the earth."

"Perhaps she didn't run away," Adam protested. "Perhaps she's hurt or lost!"

"No." Isabel shook her head sadly. "She left a note. She said she doesn't want you to follow her." Isabel held out a wrinkled piece of parchment.

Adam read it twice, then crumbled it into a ball and threw it to the ground. Cursing, he wheeled and started back to the stable. "Saddle me a fresh horse," he yelled. "She can't be that far away yet. Someone must have seen her."

Shouting orders, Adam transferred the saddle from his tired horse to a fresh one. "I want every available hand," he insisted. The ache inside him was a raw, pulsing wound. Rebecca had left him! Despite all her threats, he'd never really believed she would do it. She was his! She belonged here on Sheffield—she belonged with him.

"Damn her soul to hell!" he swore. "When I find her, I'll..." Swinging up into the saddle, he dug his heels into the bay's side and galloped out of the barnyard.

For five days search parties combed the area west, north, and south of Annapolis. Men were recruited from neighboring plantations and from the capital to look for Rebecca. Soldiers and sailors joined in the effort, and a reward in gold was offered for her safe return. Most of that time, Adam remained in the saddle, taking little time to eat or sleep.

On the sixth day, the search was officially called off. It was time to transplant the fragile tobacco plants from the woodland lots into the fields. Each plant had to be gently dug up and hand carried to the new spot. A delay in the replanting could mean the loss of the tidewater's main cash crop. As concerned as the searchers were for Adam's missing wife, the tobacco had to come first. Apologetically, the planters and their servants returned to their own fields.

Jock brought Adam back to Sheffield so exhausted that he had to be lifted from the saddle and carried in to bed. He slept for twenty-four hours without waking. When he did come downstairs, Isabel was shocked by his appearance.

Adam's face was lined and his eyes were sunken in his head. Dark shadows underneath gave him a haunted look. As Isabel signaled the cook to put food on his plate, he seemed to be only partly conscious of what was going on around him.

"Eat," Isabel coaxed. "You need your strength." She had gotten precious little sleep herself since the chit had taken off. "You have responsibilities to Sheffield, Adam. I won't allow you to kill yourself by starvation." She watched as he brought a piece of buttered bread to his lips and began to chew woodenly. "Amos started to transport the tobacco to the fields, but I think he made pretty much of a mess of it. He had only the boys and women to help, and they stepped on as many plants as they got into the ground."

Adam eyed the plate dully, seeming not to hear, but he kept eating.

"Thomas will turn over in his grave if the tobacco seedlings are ruined. He used a special seed this year. He had such high hopes for it." Isabel waved for the maid to bring more bacon, which she pushed onto Adam's plate. "If you're bound and determined to look for Rebecca, at least wait until the tobacco is replanted. Besides, she may get sick of sulking and come home on her own."

Adam looked up slowly. "I guess I don't have much choice, do I?" His voice sounded older than his years. "She's halfway to the Ohio by now. It'll take a month or better to fetch her home."

Three months, at least, Isabel thought but held her tongue. She had no fear that the girl had come to harm. Rebecca was about as helpless as a poisonous snake. "If you wait until the crops are in the ground, and you write down everything that must be done, I can manage," she said. "I've never claimed to be a planter, but I can make the servants follow orders."

Adam sipped at the scalding hot tea that had been set down before him. The ache within him had become an emptiness; whether from loss or anger he didn't know. Why was he hitting his head against a stone wall? Rebecca didn't want him, and she'd never wanted Sheffield. It was all his now, his to run and his to profit from. He didn't need her.

Like hell he didn't! Without Rebecca, his life was nothing. He exhaled loudly and looked up at the older woman. Who would have thought that Isabel could be so strong in a crisis?

"You win, Aunt. I'll stay until the crops are in." A few more weeks wouldn't matter. The delay would only put off the need to decide what he would say and do to Rebecca when he did find her.

He'd have to go as far as the Ohio, he knew that. And he'd have to deal with the Shawnee when he got there. He swallowed the last of the tea and reached for another biscuit. It made no difference. Satan himself couldn't keep him from bringing Rebecca home to Sheffield, not as long as he lived and drew breath.

Adam got to his feet and wiped his mouth with a linen napkin. "I believe we've got tobacco to plant," he said, but his thoughts were far away, seeking a green-eyed witch on a fast-moving horse.

It was still spring in the foothills of the mountains of the Blue Ridge. Rebecca had seen no human being for days, not since she had swung wide around the smoke of a settler's cabin two nights from Sheffield. The horses were holding up well; her plan of switching animals as each one tired had proven to be a good one. It meant many hours of riding at breakneck speed for her, but then she could stop at night, tie the horses, and sleep for twelve hours at a time.

She made no fire, trusting to the keen sense of smell of the horses to tell her if there was danger. Once she heard the hunting cry of a pack of gray wolves at night, but it was spring and hunting for the wolves was good. She knew she had nothing to fear unless the animals were starving or mad.

Another time, the horses had shied and acted skittish as they passed through a thick forest. Rebecca had then seen the paw tracks of a huge cat. "*Meshepeshe*," she had murmured, a shiver passing through her. *Meshepeshe,* the great panther of the mountains. She had urged the horses even faster, not stopping until they were miles from the spot. *Meshepeshe* was not an enemy to the trifled with; the cat could leap from a tree and tear out the throat of a man or horse in the space of a heartbeat.

The dangers of the trail kept her mind alert and on the forest around her. In a way she was almost grateful to the mountain lion. By thinking about the stalking cat, she would not have the time to remember Adam and wonder if she had done wrong in leaving him.

Rebecca prayed for an answer, but her spirit guardians remained silent. They gave neither censure nor approval. There was nothing but emptiness.

The English life was behind her; now she was pure Shawnee once more. Why did she let her thoughts become troubled by the memory of a white man? He was no longer her husband; he would not even be the father of her child. Her own Shawnee father would fill that role, or perhaps another. Adam did not know the child existed. Was it not better that way?

In the beauty of the far-off Ohio country, she would raise her son or daughter to be a free person. Life would be harder than it was on the Chesapeake, but a hard life made a strong spirit. There no one would laugh at her for her strange ways or ridicule her when she spoke of spirit matters. It was better this way—much better for Adam and for her. Why, then, did she wonder if the child would have green eyes or brown, or whether it would carry the thick beaver brown hair of the Englishman?

Rebecca had brought enough supplies so that she had no need to hunt for meat. Her animals grazed at night, but her small supply of grain was running low. It had been important to travel fast for the first week. Now she could take her time. She knew she had pushed her strength to the limit, and she did not wish to endanger the child.

Though the Blue Ridge country was safe, or as safe as any wilderness could be, there was one ever-present danger. Down the spine of the mountains ran the war trail of the Iroquois. In spring and summer the warriors of these fierce tribes would move south to rob and pillage. If they saw her, her scalp would become a trophy of war and her horses would carry Iroquois braves. She knew they would take no captives so far from home. A scalp was lighter to carry and didn't eat.

The forest in the spring was as beautiful as any she had ever experienced. Huge hardwoods sprang from the loamy floor and formed a living roof of intertwined brown and green branches overhead. The ground was springy soft, padded with many years' accumulation of fallen leaves and dark green moss. There was little underbrush; the foliage shut out the light that would have meant life for small bushes and new growth.

The air resounded with the chirp of birdsong and the ever-present melody of the dancing breezes that wafted off the slopes of the ridges, caressed the trees, and mingled with the fast-running rocky streams. Frogs peeped, and small animals rustled through the leaves in the flurry of activity that occurred only in the time of mating and nest building.

It was impossible to be lonely in such a place. There were owls with their wide-eyed stares to laugh at and an occasional lumbering opossum mother with baby opossums clinging to her fur and tail. Once, Rebecca caught sight of a wobbly fawn, its spotted coat still damp, taking its first hesitant steps in the new world. A telltale crackle of twigs had assured her that the doe was nearby, and she passed the baby deer with only a smile.

Still, thoughts of Adam would not leave her mind, no matter how hard she tried to push them away. Was he following her trail? Would he try to bring her back? A Shawnee warrior would have done so. Rebecca was torn between being glad no one had tried to catch her and wondering why no one had. Was Adam glad to be nd of her? She had given him every reason to be. Perhaps he had seen the good sense of her decision and decided it was best for them both. She was haunted by the thought that her departure might have been what he had wanted all along.

All that day, she had crossed and recrossed a small stream. She had had the good fortune to catch a trout when she stopped to water the horses, grabbing it from a shallow pool between two rocks. She decided to stop early and risk a fire; she had no desire to eat the fish raw, although she had eaten uncooked fish in the past when there had been nothing else.

She made the fire as small as possible, caked the fish with mud, and buried it in the coals. She tied the horses, unpacked their saddlebags, and sat down to wait. The fire felt good; the day was overcast, with the threat of rain. Rebecca hoped the rain would hold off. She didn't want to take her time to build a rain-proof shelter, and her blanket would soak up water fast.

When the fish was done, she cracked open the mud casing and devoured the delicious baked meat inside. She even had a little salt to sprinkle on it. The fish and water from the stream made a filling meal. Rebecca rolled up in the blanket and shut her eyes; even though it was barely dusk, if she got a good night's sleep, she could rise early in the morning and ride north again.

The dream was so real that she woke in a panic, scrambling for her musket. It was pitch-black, without a sign of stars or the moon. She smelled the horses close by; from their steady breathing she could tell they were sleeping. Nothing was left of the fire but a few ruby coals. On her hands and knees, she crawled to it and pushed dirt over the glow.

She swallowed hard, trying to bring her mind back from he world of dreams. Adam had stood beside her. He had said nothing, only stared down at her sleeping body, but she had read his message as clearly as if he had shouted, "Danger!" The hair on the back of her neck stood up, and she vas trembling with fear. Something was terribly wrong. She must leave this place as quickly as she could.

Swiftly, she fumbled in the dark for her belongings, throwing the saddle on the brown gelding and cinching it tight. She couldn't see her hand in front of her face. The horses read her nervousness and began to nicker among themselves. Her hands were clumsy in the blackness, her throat thick with fear. Breathlessly, she flung herself into the saddle and rode out, leading the spare horses.

In the dark, she knew she must trust the animal's instinct. It was beginning to rain, a slow mist that coated the horse's hides and chilled her to the bone. They had not gone a quarter of a mile when she heard the unmistakable snarl of a mountain lion. The snarl rose to a scream, not unlike that of a woman's cry of terror, and then was replaced by utter silence. Even the night birds were still. Rebecca urge the horses on, heedless of her direction.

The big cat must have been hunting them, following for miles. She thought it had already killed, perhaps a deer. Once it ate its full, it might give up the chase, but it might follow still. A lion could travel faster than a horse in this terrain; Rebecca had to use whatever precious time she had even at the risk of breaking a horse's leg or her own neck in the darkness.

She dreamed of Adam no more, but perhaps his soul spirit rode before her, she decided, for she saw and heard no more sign of the cat, although she did pass the fresh tracks of an Iroquois war party.

She decided to risk no more fires and completed the trip to the Ohio country in as good a time as any Shawnee brave could do. She saw no human face, red or white, until she entered the camp of Alwe Ki-be-tar-leh, Lead Tooth. Alwe Ki-be-tar-leh was the chief of a band of mixed

264 Judith E. French

Delaware and Shawnee who hunted farther south than her own people, but Rebecca was well known here and was greeted joyously a one returning from the dead.

Her happiness at arriving safely among people she knew was tempered by the sadness of learning that her mother had died in the raid the summer before. All these months and she had not known; she had thought of her mother as going about her life, missing her daughter and worrying about what had happened to her. It seemed a betrayal to have fallen in love, married, and conceived a child when all the time her mother's bones were turning to dust.

Alwe Ki-be-tar-leh urged her to stay for a few days among his people to visit and rest from her long journey. He promised to send a runner to tell Rebecca's father that she was safe with them, but she wanted only to be home. A few more days in the saddle could not matter. When the old chief saw that she would not be persuaded, he sent his own sons to guide and protect her to the end of the trail.

Few words were spoken between Rebecca and Alwe Ki-be-tar-leh's sons. If the warriors wondered at her silence, they said nothing. Rebecca felt as though her spirit was already racing ahead of her body as she saw first one landmark and then another. Excitement bubbled in her breast until she could hardly contain it, and when a brave pointed to the rising smoke of campfires, she laughed aloud with happiness.

In the village, Rebecca's father, Cut-ta-ho-tha, dropped the bow he was stringing and walked toward the riders. Cries of welcome were already ringing from wigwam to wigwam. Tears clouded the old warrior's eyes, but he did not stop to wipe them away. A horse that carried a familiar figure broke from the group and galloped toward him across the ball field, the rider's black hair streaming behind her.

"Father!" Rebecca cried. "Father." She threw herself from the saddle and into his arms, hugging him tightly.

"Child, child," he sobbed, touching her face and hair. "Is it you or some ghost?"

"It is I." She laughed and cried at the same time and saw that he was crying too. "I'm home, Father. I've missed you so. Are you well? You look thin. Who has been cooking for you?"

"You sound like another one," he teased, then looked at her sharply to see if she understood. Their eyes met, and she nodded, hugging him wordlessly again.

He would not mention her mother's name; it was not the custom. But her face hung between them, and they could laugh in remembrance of her scolding tongue. "Do you sleep alone, Father?" Rebecca asked softly.

"Bird Woman keeps my fire. She was widowed, and I was not seemly that a chief should not be able to offer food to guests."

Rebecca knew that Bird Woman was elderly, an aunt to her mother's. If she was there, her father had not taken another wife. Lead Tooth had told her that her father had been elected chief in the month of running sap. It was a great honor, and one he well deserved.

"My heart sings with pride for you," she whispered. "You will make a mighty chief."

Cut-ta-ho-tha shook his head, and together they walked back through the village arm in arm. "It is a heavy burden," he said. "As you can see, this is a new campsite. There are more wigwams than before. He who was chief of the river people broke his leg and passed on to the spirit world. There was no suitable replacement, so they joined with our people. We lost so many in the raid last year we needed the young men to protect the women and children."

So, Stone Bull had died too. Rebecca wondered about her brother's child, the baby she had carried from the village. She didn't want to mention the baby's name lest it hadn't survived. No one had mentioned her brother either. Hesitantly she began, "There were others of my blood who faced danger in that raid. I do not know if..."

Cut-ta-ho-tha patted her arm reassuringly. "Your brother is alive and well. He has taken his winter's catch of furs north to trade with the Fox. A woman there has agreed to become his wife. His little son and the boy Amatha wait in our wigwam for his return. It will be good for them to have a mother again."

Rebecca laughed out loud for joy. She had thought her brother dead, and he was alive. The people were becoming whole once more; they would welcome the birth of her child. She squeezed her father's copper hand tightly. "I have much to tell you, Father, and not the least of which is that you may be emptying your lodge of two children, but another is coming to fill it."

"Hahhah! That is news that is dimmed only by the light of your coming. Welcome home, my daughter." The seasoned warrior grinned broadly. "Would that she were here to share this day."

On Sheffield, Adam supervised the workers from the first pale shades of dawn until it was too dark to see. The tobacco was transplanted, the late corn and vegetables put in the ground, and the lumber crew set to their tasks. He did all that was required; then he ordered a servant to pack all that he would need to travel to the Ohio. He had rejected Isabel's idea that he take armed men with him.

"I'm not going to war, and I'm not going to steal her away. I intend to make contact with the Shawnee and deal with them as equals." He had acquired maps from Annapolis that would give him a rough idea of where he was, but he knew that finding one woman in that wilderness would be like looking for the proverbial needle in a haystack.

"It's dangerous country. If the Indians don't take your scalp, you might be eaten by wolves or bears." Isabel pursed her lips. "You should take a dozen men with you, at least."

"I'd have to take an army, and then we might be ambushed. No, I'll be safer alone. I'll travel faster, and I won't be seen as a threat. Believe it or not, I've picked up a few words of Algonquian."

"You'll not last a week. You'll end up as dead as Thomas, and then where will I be?" she protested.

"You'll be in charge of Sheffield and a wealthy woman in your own right. You forget: other than Rebecca, I have no one." Adam grinned at her. "If you offer prayers, perhaps you should pray that the wolves do eat me."

Adam took four bullet molds from a leather sack and added them to the pile of steel knives and needles. Rebecca had told him that the Shawnee gave gifts to their guests and expected gifts in return. He would choose carefully, bringing useful items rather than gaudy trinkets. He had already packed powdered dyes, tobacco, and steel fishhooks. He couldn't afford to weigh himself down with heavy baggage, yet to appear before Rebecca's family as a pauper was unthinkable.

Rebecca's family. Adam chuckled; he was getting as bad as she was. He thought of her as Indian, as Shawnee…as having kin among the tribe. She had influenced him with her strange beliefs more than he knew.

"I'll worry about you, Adam," Isabel admitted. "No nonsense now! Just ride out there and bring our Rebecca back. It's likely she's had enough of playing at Indian by now anyway."

"I'll do the best I can, Aunt." He'd fallen into the custom of addressing her as Aunt in spite of himself. Isabel wouldn't let on, but Adam was certain she enjoyed it. "If you have any problems, call on one of the neighbors or ol' Jock. I've asked him to keep an eye on things while I'm gone."

"Humph," Isabel grumbled. "It's not likely that I'd need help from that skirt-wearing Scotsman. You be about your business; Sheffield will be here in one piece when you get back."

CHAPTER 21

Western Pennsylvania
June 17, 1704

Adam had followed the rutted path for most of the morning; it had turned due north at the river crossing. He'd seen smoke ahead, a single column, and had assumed that it came from a settler's cabin. Indians were usually too wary to have a fire in daylight, unless it was a camp, and then there would be smoke from more than one source. It was hard to gauge the distance. Everything in the clear air of these hills looked close until you tried to reach it.

Actually, he was looking forward to talking with someone other than the two horses. He had shot a yearling buck at dawn and had packed most of the meat. He'd be glad to trade fresh meat for human companionship and a few distractions. He didn't expect these settlers to know much about the whereabouts of the Shawnee; he was still too far east. In fact, he'd decided to say as little about his mission as possible. Feelings were high against the Indians on the frontier, and it wouldn't do to be labeled a squaw man. It would earn him a bullet in the back.

Adam considered stopping to switch horses; he'd been riding the sorrel since he'd shot the deer. But that would mean unloading the deer meat and transferring the trade sacks. He decided to go on for a few more miles. The sorrel seemed to be keeping up the pace without any trouble.

He was rewarded at the top of the next rise. Below him stretched a green valley intersected by a rocky stream. He could make out two log cabins, some outbuildings, and several cornfields. A log stockade held several oxen and one horse. The barking of a dog came from the area of the stockade, but he didn't see any people. He hesitated. Why aren't there men in the fields? Still, if there was trouble, the animals wouldn't be there. He decided to ride in closer and have a look.

The path was wide and the slope easy. Adam urged the sorrel into a trot, all the while keeping an eye out for the settlers. When he had approached to within a few hundred yards of the cabins without sighting anyone, he realized that his first instincts had been right. There was trouble here of some kind. He reined in and checked his musket. He fell uneasy but not in danger.

The lone horse in the pound trotted to the fence and whinnied at Adam's animals. Adam called out, "Hello? Anyone here?" Anxiously, he scanned the yard and fields for any movement. Where was everyone? They wouldn't have just walked off and left their animals and crops. "Hello, the house!" he shouted. "I'm a white man! I mean you no harm!"

The dog strained at the end of his rope, barking loudly Cautiously, Adam rode to within a few feet of the larger cabin and dismounted, keeping his musket ready. Smoke still trailed from the mud and log chimney; the heavy door stood ajar. "Is anybody here?" he repeated. With the barrel of the musket, he pushed open the door and peered into the semidarkness.

A wave of stench hit him, and he gagged. Something white moved against the far wall, a woman's arm. A faint voice rasped, "Help. Help us. For God's sake, help us." A baby's feeble whine came from beyond the woman, more like a cat's cry than a human's. "Help me," the woman begged. "My babies...my babies are all sick."

Adam leaned his musket against the doorjamb and ducked low to enter the cabin. The smell inside was stifling. A rush lamp lay on the table, and he carried it to the hearth and lit it, unnerved by the moans and renewed weeping.

How many people were there? The cabin was not more than twenty feet across. He lifted the lamp high and stepped over a still form on the floor wrapped in a blanket. If he didn't get some fresh air soon, he knew he'd be sick. It was worse than the open sewers of London!

Adam shuddered. The people of this homestead were deathly ill, and there was no one else to help. Setting his jaw, he bent and lifted the body by his foot. To his surprise, a skeleton hand moved. Quickly, he carried the frail creature outside into the sunlight. Kneeling, he gently unwrapped the threadbare quilt to reveal a little girl; she couldn't have been more than five years old. Her eyes were squeezed shut, her hair matted with vomit, and the bones were nearly coming through her skin.

"God in heaven," he murmured, blinking away tears and rocking the child against his chest. She began to whimper, and he stroked her hair. "It will be all right, baby. I promise. It will be all right."

Four times, Adam went back into that black hole and came out with dead and dying members of the family. Twice, he had to stop and be sick himself. The smell of feces and vomit stuck to their clothes and skin and penetrated his until he shook like a man with fever. One boy, about twelve, was beyond help; he had curled into a ball and weighed no more than two stone. Altogether, there were five living beings, including the woman and the baby, who seemed to be starving rather than suffering from the malady that had seized the rest.

It looked like cholera to Adam, but there was no way to be certain. People had died of it on the voyage from England, but his mother had carefully boiled every drop of water the two of them had drunk, and they hadn't caught it. If the well was infested, it would explain why the nursing infant hadn't gotten the disease. Adam himself would avoid the well water here in any case.

One by one, he laid them out in a row, carefully carrying the dead boy around the cabin out of sight. A grave would have to be dug and quickly; he'd already been dead for a while. But the living must come first.

The baby and a male child of about two seemed to be in the best shape. The two girls and the woman were very bad; he didn't know if he could do anything for them. Whatever he did attempt, it would be out here in the open. Venturing into that dark cabin was like descending into hell.

He decided to investigate the second, smaller cabin. To his relief, he found that, although it was musty smelling, everything was in order, and there were clean, dry blankets and some clothing hanging from pegs on the wall. He could light a fire there when night came and provide shelter for the stricken family. On second thought, he realized he would need a fire now to boil water. He could do nothing for them until they were clean and had something to drink.

When the fire was going, he took a leather bucket and mounted his horse to ride back to the stream. He'd take no chances with the shallow well water, even boiled. He tried to remember everything he'd ever heard about cholera. Some said it was brought by night fog and seeped through your skin when you slept. He doubted it. Cholera was mainly a disease of the poor who lived in dirty, crowded conditions. If it was carried on the wind, it would affect rich and poor alike.

It was almost evening before he had bathed and tended to everyone. He would bury the boy before nightfall, but he could work in semidarkness if he had to. He had milked the cow and dribbled milk spoonful by spoonful into the infant's mouth; the shrill mewing of hunger ceased. The baby was a boy, very wet and dirty. When the child had been fed, wrapped in a somewhat clean man's shirt, and tucked into the corner of a box bed in the smaller cabin, Adam felt that the infant's chances of survival were very good.

Once the baths were completed, he boiled water from the stream for drinking. Giving tiny sips to each patient in turn was a maddeningly slow process. Then he boiled the deer liver and a haunch to make a broth. He wasn't sure deer soup was right for sick people, but he didn't think they should have milk.

The woman had been lucid long enough to tell Adam that her husband and an older son had died first. The other family, her married daughter and husband, had gone east to visit the husband's family. The sickness had come quickly after they left. She said her name was Jane Clough, and she didn't know how many days it had been since they'd buried her husband.

The baby woke to eat every two hours through the night. It didn't matter; Adam was on his feet all that time tending the others. It became a nightmare of changing soiled blankets and boiling water. Sometime during the night one of the girls died. Adam wept for her, then carried the small body into the stable and returned to continue struggling to save the others.

The days and nights blended into one another…a week, two…Adam lost track of time. Twice, he thought the woman would die; she weighed no more than a child when he lifted her to change her clothing or just to move her from one spot to another. He couldn't begin to guess her age. Her dark hair was streaked with gray and many of her teeth were missing. She might have been thirty or fifty. It was evident that the family were of the lowest class, unlettered and rank of smell even in good health. But he could not abandon them; they were human beings, and they were in trouble.

He snatched sleep whenever he could, sitting up or lying on the dirt floor of the cabin. There was no time to shave or to keep his clothes clean. Never had he thought he would be reduced to playing nursemaid to a band of runny-nosed children. His hands cracked and bled from the harsh lye soap as he washed bucket after bucket of the rough cloths that acted as diapers for the baby, not to mention the soiled clothing and blankets of the others.

Sometimes he dreamed of Rebecca—disturbing dreams, dreams in which she was lost and wandering in a swamp or traveling on a storm-tossed ship at sea. But the dream that returned again and again was one that had no beginning and no end. He was standing over her, looking down into her sleeping face. There was mist all about, so thick that he couldn't see where he was. He tried to reach out and touch her, but he couldn't move. He tried to call her name, but he couldn't speak. He could see her, but she might have been behind a wall of glass. In the dream, he stood there for what seemed an eternity, straining every muscle until at last the glass was shattered by the scream of a mountain lion. He would wake then in a cold sweat, unable to forget the nightmare or to make any sense of it.

By now he had intended to be with her, even to be on their way back to Sheffield. What must she think? Did she believe he had forgotten her—that he had just let her go like that, without a word?

He avoided the thought that she might never have reached the Ohio and her precious Shawnee at all. A thousand dangers could befall a woman alone in the wilderness. She might have drowned crossing a river or been buried in a landslide. She might have been captured by white men or hostile Indians, or she might even have fallen from her horse and broken a leg. Thoughts of Rebecca starving to death or dying of thirst were not to be borne. She was tougher than that; she had to be. Right now, she was probably sitting in front of a Shawnee campfire, gnawing on a deer bone and cursing him for being a stupid English-*manake.*

Since the woman and children were too ill to provide companionship, and the baby was too young, Adam had a lot of time to think. He went over and over in his head the time he and Rebecca had had together.

He'd made mistakes with her; he knew that now. He'd expected too much too soon. What was the death of one horse compared to the life they could have had together? She had sacrificed that animal out of love for her grandfather, not out of savage bloodlust, as he had accused her.

Was her Shawnee ritual any more barbaric than stuffing a body into a pickle barrel and sending it back to England for burial four months later, as was commonly done in the military?

He found himself picturing the way she walked and the way she sat a horse. She had an inborn grace. When she moved, it was like water flowing over rocks, or like the movement of a doe. She made love with no holds barred, giving everything without shame or regret. He'd trade five years of his life to have her in his arms now.

He'd been a fool, a proud fool, but a fool nevertheless. Rebecca had brought him everything—land, wealth, loving companionship. She had placed happiness in his hands, and he had thrown it away because she wasn't the woman he'd always expected to marry. He'd been afraid she would shame him with her Indian ways. He'd always considered himself an honest man, but he'd been less than honest with the one woman who should have meant all the world to him.

If he found her—*when* he found her—he'd make her understand that he knew better now. And if she gave him another chance and came home, he'd spend the rest of his life trying to make it up to her.

The sound of oxen bellowing brought Adam from his sleep. He grabbed his musket and stumbled outside to see a wagon lumbering down the slope. He waved; a man and woman on the wagon seat called back a greeting. Adam rested the musket barrel across the crook of his arm and walked with long, even strides down the path to meet the wagon.

By the next day he was free to leave. The couple in the wagon were the married daughter and her husband. With relatives to care for the invalids, and the worst of the illness past, Adam could continue his journey. They sent him on his way with heartfelt thanks and directions to the next river crossing.

* * *

The Ohio August 1, 1704

Rebecca knelt in the flimsy birchbark canoe and paddled toward the sandy bank. In the bottom of her boat lay three fat fish, all taken with her spear. They would make a welcome change from the deer meat Bird Woman had been preparing all week. The fish would be delicious with corn cakes, especially once they'd been sweetened with honey. Rebecca chuckled to herself; since she was swelling with child, all she seemed to think of was her stomach.

She wondered if they would have a guest at the evening meal. The warrior Meshepeshe, the Panther, had been quick to renew his suit and had become a regular visitor to the wigwam, bringing fresh game and tobacco to her father as well as the container of dripping, sweet honeycombs.

Meshepeshe had married She Who Whispers at the time of first snow, but She Who Whispers had run away with a French trader in early spring. He had slept alone since then taking his food at a brother's fire. Meshepeshe was a handsome man by Shawnee standards, his dark, intense features enhanced by the scar over his right eye.

Rebecca's father had watched in amused silence as this respected warrior came again and again to his wigwam or one pretense or another. He would sit and talk for long hours, speaking to Rebecca only when absolutely necessary. He gave no hint that he might be the mysterious donor who left gifts nightly by the door—gifts that might catch the eye of a young and desirable woman, such as hawk bells of silver with loops to adorn the ears, or strings of red and blue beads. Even more precious was a woman's knife of good German steel secured in a white doeskin sheath worked with intricate patterns of porcupine quills.

Neither was there evidence to prove that Meshepeshe was the brave who came each night to wait in the forest and play an eagle-bone flute in the age-old custom of Shawnee courting. The clear, silvery trill of the flute spoke of feelings a warrior could not utter, and no woman, man, or child who heard the haunting plea was untouched by the magic of the melody.

Meshepeshe's brother's wife had asked Bird Woman if Rebecca had a husband in the Chesapeake country, and Bird Woman had passed on the news that she was divorced. No mention was made of the coming child; the evidence was clear for all the tribe to see. Still, to speak of the coming baby would be to raise Rebecca's value. A wife who came to a husband's wigwam already with child had proved she was capable of giving him sons and daugthers. And since every child would belong to the mother's clan, it made little difference who the biological father might be.

Rebecca gathered her things from the bottom of the canoe and stepped out into the shallow water. A boy ran to pull the boat up on the bank for her.

"Amatha! Thank you." Rebecca smiled at him. He was growing tall. His copper skin shone with health, and his large, bright eyes glowed with intelligence. He was a far cry from the frightened child she remembered the day of the raid. "Come later to the house. Bird Woman is making com cakes." No need to tell him there was honey; Amatha was all boy, and knew where sweets were to be found.

As she walked back toward the village, Rebecca felt the child stir within her. The thrill she felt each time the infant moved was tempered by a sense of loss for Adam. The weeks and months had not dimmed her ache for him. *Why haven't you come for me? Why, Adam?* Her brain knew that it was too far, that this was not the Englishman's world, but her heart cried out that he should have come. And once more, she wondered if she had made a mistake in leaving Sheffield.

Her father favored Meshepeshe's suit. He had not said so, but she knew. And why not? Meshepeshe was a respected warrior, a skillful hunter, and a man who would treat a wife with respect. It was common knowledge that he had not shamed the name of She Who Whispers, even though she had cheated on him with other men and had proved to be a bad wife.

Rebecca had tried to find fault with Meshepeshe; she had given away all the gifts that were left at her door, even the beautiful knife and case. It was not an insult. An insult would have been to return them to his wigwam. By giving away the precious things, she honored the unknown giver but remained neutral. A woman had a right to think about such a serious decision.

She did not love him; she knew that. Rebecca loved Adam. But Adam was gone; he was part of another life. A woman and child needed protection. She needed companionship, not just her father's but that of another man. She had begun to think of him in her mind as little Meshepeshe. He was not small by Indian standards; he was of average height and very muscular. The Panther was not too small—Adam was too big. When had she begun to accept bigness as a natural thing in a man?

There were other men she could have chosen if she were looking for a husband, here and in Lead Tooth's camp. She was strong and healthy and fair to look upon. She did not deceive herself that her father's new status as chief wasn't an added attraction. Of course a man's family would want to link themselves to a powerful clan. No one would force her to take a husband; she could remain single as long as she wished. Her father would not begrudge the food it took to fill her mouth and that of the child.

But if she refused Meshepeshe and he chose another woman, she might never get as good an offer. She liked Meshepeshe. He would be an able provider and a good father. She was not interested sexually in him, but she had no doubt that after the child came she would feel the old stirrings of her blood. She was a woman grown, with a woman's needs and desires.

The trouble was, she desired a man she could not have, an Englishman who did not want her enough to come after her when she ran away.

Rebecca knew that part of the trouble in her marriage had been her fault. She had been willful and stubborn. She had condemned Adam for not understanding her ways and had poked fun at his. The incident at the graveyard was unfortunate. She was not sorry she had provided a mount for her grandfather to ride to the hereafter, but she had done many other things that had rankled her husband. And many of those she had done just for that reason.

She thought often of the wigwam they had shared in the thicket. Whispered conversations and childish laughter came back to haunt her. She remembered his kindness in removing the splinter from her hand, and the magnificent hawk he had given her as a wedding gift. But most of all, she remembered his scent and the feel of his broad hands against her bare skin. "Adam," her heart cried, and she knew again the pain of parting.

What would it have been like for their child to grow up on Sheffield? Could they have given a son or daughter the best of two worlds? Might that small soul have grown to be an adult who could understand the heart of both Indian and English, and have helped to mend the ever-widening breach between their peoples?

It was useless to torture herself with such questions; she would never know the answer. Adam probably would have felt shamed by the idea of such a child. Perhaps he would have taken it from her and had it raised by tutors and English nursemaids.

"No," Rebecca whispered, "that is a lie." Adam would never do such a thing. He had the hot, quick temper of a man, but there was no cruelty in him. He would never have separated her from her child, not if she had smeared the infant with bear grease and paint and swung it from a cradleboard on the steps of the customhouse in Annapolis!

Her yearning for Adam did not solve her problem. No matter how much she wanted him, she couldn't go back. To return would mean a loss of honor. No runaway wife ever went back on her own. If a man came to seek her out among her family, she would protest a little for courtesy's sake and then return to him if it was what she really wanted to do. To go back to Sheffield without being asked would be unthinkable. Suppose Adam had taken another wife?

The way was long and dangerous; she could not risk her life and that of her baby for a lost cause.

Meshepeshe would not wait long. Everyone knew that he had courted her before and that she had refused him. He was a proud man. If he paid too much attention to her and was turned down again, people would remember and ridicule him for years to come. She must decide soon.

The memory of the panther that had followed her on her journey home returned to haunt her. Was it a real panther, or was it the spirit of Meshepeshe the warrior? Was it a sign from the spirits that she was to accept him? Was he to be her protector rather than her enemy? It was a terrible puzzle, and there was no one she could ask. If Otter were alive, she could talk to him about it.

Rebecca laughed as she dropped the fish onto the grass beside the scaling board. If Otter were alive, she would still be his wife and none of this would have happened. "But," a little voice whispered slyly, "if Otter were alive, you would not be carrying a child." And Rebecca knew, for the first time, that she was glad Otter was no longer of this earth.

Rebecca's days had fallen easily into the patterns of her people. Life with them had a rhythm the English did not seem to possess. The Shawnee were a part of nature, as much a part of the Ohio country as the river and the trees. They went about the tasks of food gathering and preparing for winter as their fathers and grandfathers had done before them. There was time for play and for laughter, and for the sharing of music and memories, but there was none of the vital throb of energy that Rebecca had noticed on the tidewater. But a tiny part of her missed the excitement of opening her eyes in the morning and not knowing what the day would bring. Perhaps she was more English than she was willing to admit.

She missed other people besides Adam and her grandfather. She had made friends among the workers and the house servants. She wondered if the cook had given birth to a boy or a girl and if her little hawk had found a mate. She even missed Isabel's scolding tongue. The older woman would have been highly indignant if she knew that Rebecca compared her to the widow Bird Woman, yet in another time and place the two would have been friends; Rebecca could picture them with their heads together trying to decide which spice was best to season the trout.

But if the days were soft, Rebecca's nights were not. She saw Adam in her dreams and heard his voice calling to her. Usually, the dreams were without substance…one faded into another, leaving her only faintly anxious. But she woke from one dream screaming, the nightmare of Adam's death more real than the bark sides and roof of the wigwam. Her father and Bird Woman tried to calm her and finally called the shaman to give her a sleeping potion. She surrendered to the drug at last and dropped into the soft darkness of a deep sleep. But the reality of the dream returned in the daylight to haunt her.

CHAPTER 22

August 23, 1704

A dam urged his horse through the pines and onto a game trail; he hoped he was still heading northwest. The sky had been overcast all day, and it was hard to keep a true direction even with the aid of his compass. He'd come upon signs of Indians early that morning, the moccasin tracks of several men on foot. He had a feeling that Rebecca could have studied the signs and known exactly how many men there were, what tribe they belonged to, and what they had eaten for dinner the night before.

After leaving the farm, he had passed only one white settlement, and that had been at the river crossing. The people there had warned him about bad Shawnee to the west and had advised him to turn back. He hadn't much cared for the looks of them; they had shown too much interest in his packhorse and the trade goods he was carrying.

Adam had refused an offer to spend the night there and had ridden out in a different direction than he meant to go. He hadn't slept at all that night, keeping the horses at a steady walk, even when the ground turned rocky.

He scratched his beard, tracking down a biting creature and cracking it between his fingernails. Another louse. He shuddered. He hadn't gotten cholera from the settlers, but they'd given him vermin to remember them by. No amount of scrubbing with river water or wet sand seemed to get all of them. He'd rubbed his hair and beard until he was sure both his face and his head would soon be bald, but after a few days the lice would begin to torment him again.

A few drops of rain hit his face, and he began to think about making camp for the night. If a real downpour came, he'd be soaked through. He decided to wait; there were rocky outcrops ahead, and he might be able to find a cave or a shallow overhang in which to take shelter. A rabbit hung across his saddle, but he had no intention of eating it raw. Somehow he would have to light a fire.

The horses were beginning to look a little straggly. They were used to being stabled at night, accustomed to plenty of rich pasture and grain in their feed boxes. Recently they'd had to make do with snatched mouthfuls of leaves and grass. Less vigorous animals would probably have had to be left by the wayside long ago.

Adam had lost weight himself., though he'd never felt better—except for the vermin. His face and arms were tanned as dark as an Indian's, and his mind was sharp and alert from first light until he fell asleep. He'd not come down with as much as a sniffle, although he did suffer some from hunger pains. Not that he was lacking in meat, but he yearned for bread and fresh vegetables and cheese. He'd tried to vary his diet with whatever berries he could find along the way, as well as a few plants such as lamb's quarter and wild onion that Rebecca had said were good to eat. But none of it made up for the lack of corn on the cob with butter and salt, or steamed bay crabs with hot seasoning.

Adam's mind was on the last crab feast he'd attended in Annapolis when the ground suddenly gave way under him, and he and the horse began sliding down a rock-strewn, muddy incline. Adam tried frantically to hold his seat, but the sorrel went down on its forelegs and tumbled headfirst over the edge of a six-foot drop. Adam hit the ground hard and rolled, and then a knifing pain seemed to slice his body in two. He grabbed for his leg to see if it was still there, and then blackness closed over him.

Something warm and soft brushed his face. Adam moaned and pushed it away. The sensation returned insistently, and he opened his eyes to see the sorrel standing over him, its saddle askew. The horse made a soft snuffling sound and mouthed Adam's chin again.

"All right, all right," Adam said hoarsely. "I'm awake."

It was raining, a soft, misty rain that coated his face like dew and felt as warm as bathwater. Adam rubbed his face—a few lumps, a little blood, nothing serious. He held out his arms and flexed his fingers. One elbow was oozing blood from a nasty scrape, but everything worked. Then he tried to sit up, and his world tilted and he screamed aloud in pain.

The horse jumped back in fright, ears flicking. Adam caught his hand between his teeth and bit down hard, trying to control the waves of agony that rolled through his body. "Whoa, boy," he said between clenched teeth. I'm hurt. Badly. If I lose the horse, I'm a dead man.

Nausea rose in his throat, and he fought it down. He tried to move the toes on his right leg. No problem. Then he ran his hand down his left leg, afraid to look; the leg was twisted under him at an impossible angle.

It took long minutes to retrieve the knife from his waist sheath and cut away the baggy breeches to see the damage, long minutes and more courage than Adam thought he possessed. The leg was broken above the knee; he could feel the lump of the bone.

"It's not broken through the skin," he told the horse. "Bones have a better chance of healing when they don't do that."

The horse looked sympathetic. From high above them came the plaintive nicker of the other horse; the sorrel whinnied back. Adam tried to pull himself into an upright position, wondering why the pack animal hadn't been pulled over the edge too.

How in God's name did I do anything so stupid? He hadn't seen the drop-off, hadn't even guessed he was so near the edge of the ridge. The earth around him looked raw and new. Mud slides must have eaten away at the slope right up to the trees. What good did it do to worry about how it had happened? Getting down the hill had been easy; getting back up would be more than a little tricky. And first he had to get up on the sorrel.

Adam knew he would relive the agony of those minutes for years to come. Somehow, he straightened the saddle, mounted the sorrel, and rode down to level ground and then up again to a spot a few hundred yards from the place where he had fallen. It was pitch-dark by the time he found the packhorse with his lead line caught on the stump of a tree.

The rain provided water and kept him conscious. He had lost the rabbit in the slide down the hill, but he was long past caring. He didn't know where he was going; only knew that if he got off the horse, he'd lie down and die. So he stayed in the saddle.

At noon the following day he rode completely by accident into the hunting camp of a band of Delaware Indians. A squaw looked up from the doe she was skinning and screamed. Men came running, armed with bows and muskets, but one glance was enough to convince even the small children that this white man was harmless. Two braves lifted him screaming from the saddle and lay him full length on the ground.

Adam gained reason long enough to murmur a few hoarse words in Algonquian. *"Calumet...*peace." Or was it peace pipe? His mind stumbled over the words, repeating them as awkwardly as a backward child. *"Jai-nai-nah,"* I am your brother. *"Keewa."* My wife. I'm looking for my wife. "I seek the Shawnee woman...*equiwa*...the *keewa."* Someone moistened his parched lips, and he nodded gratefully. *"Alagwa Aquewa..* Star Blanket, daughter of Cut..." Adam's brain seemed to be functioning in slow motion. What were the words? He had heard Rebecca say them often enough. "I am Alagwa Aquewa, daughter of Cut-ta-ho-tha of the Shawnee." Adam forced his eyelids open and stared into ebony black eyes. "Alagwa Aquewa, daughter of Cut-ta-ho-tha," he whispered. "My *keewa.*"

Adam's leg became a flame that would not burn out; it tortured him until the fever in his brain shut out the pain and left him in a lost world of confusion. He did not know when the Delaware woman bound his leg with splints or spooned willow tea between his dry lips. He did not know when they tied him to a litter and carried him for hours through the forest to another Delaware camp.

Few of the Delaware spoke English, but they remembered the words the bearded white stranger had muttered. "He seeks his wife, Alagwa Aquewa of the Shawnee, daughter of Cut-ta-ho-tha," the Delaware woman told her chief. "I have seen this woman, and I heard that she was taken far away to the east and returned to the Ohio in the season of wild strawberries. It could be that the English-*manake* is, indeed, her husband."

Smoke Rising, shaman of the tribe, agreed and suggested that a runner be sent to their cousins the Shawnee. Meanwhile, he would turn his skill to setting the man's leg and bringing down the fever that ravaged his body. Although feelings were bad between the English and the Delaware, this white man's claim to marriage with a Shawnee woman made him possible kin. As a medicine man and spiritual leader, Smoke Rising was compelled to use all his knowledge to heal the Englishman. It did not matter that the whites would leave an injured Delaware to die or would murder him without a second thought. The Delaware considered themselves beyond such savagery.

The leg was badly broken, and the bones had not been pulled back into place at once. Smoke Rising knew that healing the leg would not be easy, and he considered amputating it. If it began to turn bad, he would have no other choice, but he hoped it would not be necessary. A warrior was better off dead than crippled; without a leg, he could not ride or walk and would be a burden to others for the rest of his life.

First Smoke Rising prepared a strong potion that put Adam into a deep sleep and reduced his breathing to the slightest movement of his massive chest. Then he summoned women to bathe him and to cut away the beard that harbored vermin. His skin must be scrubbed clean and his hair combed and washed. A man could not enter the sweat lodge if he was unclean. There the fever and the evil demons could be driven from his body. Sometimes the demons were too strong, and the person died. Smoke Rising did not believe this white giant would die. Too much strength slept in those iron thighs and sinewy arms. The Englishman's neck was as thick and strong as a bull's, his shoulders bulged with muscle, and his stomach was flat and rock hard, as a warrior's should be. His hands were unnaturally large, but the square fingers and calloused palms were in perfect proportion to his size.

The women's giggles when they washed his loins assured the shaman that the Englishman was well endowed in his man's parts. "*Meshewa,*" one twittered—stallion. "*Ahquo-iteti chobeka.*" The others laughed and murmured praises of their own.

Smoke Rising pretended not to hear. It was beneath his dignity to notice the jests of women when he was preparing a healing. If he were a better shaman, perhaps he could draw off a little of the white man's virility for his own use. Smoke Rising had not noticed any complaint from his two wives, but it was no secret that the snow of winter was invading his crow-black braids.

They carried the white man into the sweat house as the moon rose over the trees. He wore nothing but a small loincloth and the splint of wood and leather on the injured leg. He did not stir; the drug had sent him deep into himself. Smoke Rising was pleased. The medicine went better when the patient did not cry out in pain. He himself wore nothing but paint—the sacred red of life; yellow, the color of the sun; and the blue of his calling. The shaman would stay beside the patient; he would chant and pray and reach out with all his powers to touch the soul of the Englishman and encourage it to fight the demons of fever.

A hush fell over the encampment as the first sounds of the muffled drum echoed through the wigwams. Mothers pulled their children close and dropped the skin coverings over the entrances of their houses. It was better to remain close to the fire in the time of magic. Even the dogs ceased their barking and crawled close to their masters. The air was thick with what had been and what would be. The wind dropped, and the moon hid behind a curtain of clouds. It was a time of waiting, for the scale could move either way. The white giant's soul could slip away to the land of hereafter, or it could return to his body with full force. All was in the hands of the Wishemenetoo, the Great Spirit, and their own shaman, Smoke Rising.

For two days and two nights, Adam stayed in the sweat lodge. Hot rocks were carried in time and time again, and water was thrown on them to send clouds of steam rolling through the structure. All that time, Smoke Rising prayed and chanted and shook the sacred turtleshell rattle and beat upon the drum to drive away the demons of Matchemenetto, the Bad Spirit, and to evoke the powers of light.

On the third day, when Smoke Rising came from the sweat house and bid the warriors carry forth his patient, the whole tribe gathered to watch in admiration. There was no doubt that the shaman had won; if the demons had snatched the white man, the drum would have told them so. It had been a terrible battle; even a child could see the strain on Smoke Rising's face. He staggered as he walked, and his skin was pale and drawn. But his eyes proclaimed victory, and the women began to dance, celebrating the triumph of life over death and sharing their pride in such a mighty shaman.

Adam knew nothing of this; he did not hear their cries of celebration or the change of the cadence of the drum. He did feel the cool air on his face and naked body; it soothed and comforted him, and he slept the sleep of the near dead. He felt no sign of the demons' retreat, not knowing or caring when the fever fled before the power of Wishemenetoo or even when the pain receded to something a man could bear and keep his sanity.

He knew nothing until a feather-soft hand touched his forehead and warm drops fell on his cheek.

"A-dam."

A familiar voice called across the chasm of time and space, a voice that would not be ignored. It came again, louder and more urgently.

"A-dam."

His eyelids flickered, and a shadowy face came into focus. Rebecca? His lips moved, but no sound came. Rebecca? It couldn't be! It was a trick of the fever; he was dead and gone to hell. This was only another torment. Adam's eyes filled with moisture, and he blinked.

"Ki-te-hi, my heart. I am here. It is Rebecca, Adam. Can you hear me? It's Rebecca."

An arm closed around her shoulders and pulled her down against him. A sound that might have been her name issued from his throat, and she felt a shudder go through his body.

"Don't try to talk, *ki-te-hi.* I am here, and everything will be all right." She tried to remember to speak only English, but what came out was a mixture of tongues. "You were hurt badly, but the Delaware shaman has set your leg and taken away the fever. You will be well and strong again, A-dam."

She kissed his lips and cheeks and eyelids, touching his face and hair as if to prove to herself that he was real. She was sobbing, her face wet with tears for all to see, but she didn't care. Adam had come for her after all; he had not cast her from his heart and mind. He had suffered greatly to find her, and she would make right all that was wrong between them.

"Sleep now," she said hoarsely. "I will take you home to my father's camp. You must rest and regain your strength, and then we will talk."

Adam wondered how merely opening his eyes could tire him so much. It didn't matter; the sight of Rebecca only inches from his face was like rain after a drought. He felt like crying and laughing at the same time. If it was a dream, he would pay the cost later. For now, he would soak up the joy of her nearness.

"I am here," she assured him. "I won't leave you, I promise. And when you are better, I will have a wonderful gift for you." Her eyes glowed with an inner light, reflecting the happiness that filled her being. She had not believed the message the Delaware brave had brought. She had questioned him closely, accepting it as true only when he spoke of Adam's size, the fine horses he rode, and the costly goods he carried.

Both horses and all his wealth were turned over to Rebecca intact, including the musket which the braves had retrieved after riding back to the scene of the accident. The Delaware did not rob their guests; it would have been unthinkable.

Rebecca presented the sorrel horse and one half of all Adam's belongings to the Delaware with her sincerest thanks. The goods were not payment but a token of her indebtedness. She kept the musket and the second horse, a bay gelding, so that Adam would not be shamed by his poverty among the Shawnee. And, as a special gift to the shaman, she offered a string of wampum, precious shell beads handed down in her mother's family for generations. For Adam's life she would have given everything she owned, but she could not shame the Delaware by giving too much. It would be as great an insult as giving nothing.

Once again, Adam was placed on a litter and carried by strong warriors through forests and open meadows. Rebecca rode beside him on the bay, giving him water and drugs to numb the pain and checking the splints to see that they held the leg straight. He woke and slept and woke again, lulled by the easy motion of the litter and the sight of her smiling face beside him.

* * *

September 20, 1704

Adam lay propped up on the elk-bone backrest and watched as Rebecca stirred fresh herbs into the savory-smelling stew. He never tired of watching her or of touching her rounded belly and feeling the movement of their child beneath her heart. He shifted a little, moving the leg to a more comfortable position, and took up the leather rope he was braiding.

"I told Amatha he could exercise the bay gelding today. That horse will grow fat and lazy eating grass all day and never being ridden." Rebecca pushed a strand of hair away from her eyes and smiled at Adam. "The boy is becoming a good rider. He has a light hand on the rein."

Adam nodded. "Do as you see fit." The coil of rope was growing, and it gave him comfort to do something useful. He meant to make a present of the rope to Rebecca's father when it was finished. God knew there was little enough he could do to fill the days. He rubbed at his leg absently; it hardly ached at all now, and the swelling had gone down in his toes. He hoped the leg would heal straight; it was hard to tell under all the wrappings.

"The men will hunt bear today," she said. "The animals are fat now after the summer's feasting. Bear fat has many uses." Rebecca stirred the pot with a wooden ladle. "The animals all have very thick fur this year. Father says it is a sign of a hard winter to come."

The doeskin dress strained over Rebecca's full breasts, providing Adam with pleasant fantasies. Her hair hung in two thick braids secured with a beaded headband. She looked all Indian, he thought, with the green eyes hidden from view; he didn't give a damn. She was his. If she wanted to be an Indian or a fortune-telling Gypsy, it was fine with him.

The long days of inactivity were hard to endure. The shaman of Rebecca's people had agreed with Rising Smoke. His leg had suffered a bad break, and it would take many moons to heal. If the white man put strain on the leg or moved it unnecessarily, it might break again or heal crookedly. Adam must be patient.

He was surprised by the ease with which the Shawnee had accepted him among them. The people might dislike whites and mistrust them, but they did not insult him or try to do him any harm. Some, such as the boy Amatha, actually cultivated his friendship, asking many questions about English life and shyly trying out one English word after another. Only a few of the young men, Meshepeshe the panther in particular, avoided him completely.

It had not taken Amatha long to tell Adam that the panther desired Rebecca for his own. "All the people know he wants to marry her," Amatha said. "And now that you have come, he hates you."

"She cannot marry. She is already married," Adam explained patiently.

"Star Blanket said she divorced you in the tidewater country. He is divorced, too. I would not trust him, English-*manake*. He has a terrible temper. Once he killed a great rattlesnake with only his bare hands. People will laugh at him if Star Blanket rejects him again."

"We are married. She is to have my child." Why was such a simple thing so difficult for these people to understand? "My people do not recognize divorce."

The boy shrugged. "English always do foolish things. I guess they think foolish too."

Adam's command of Shawnee was improving daily; he hardly ever had to ask Rebecca to translate something for him now. Not only did the two of them speak Shawnee together, but he also spent long evenings next to the fire talking with Cut-ta-ho-tha.

Adam developed a genuine respect for Rebecca's Indian father. The man was not what he had expected at all; in many ways he was not unlike Thomas Bradford. There was no doubt that he loved Rebecca and wanted her happiness. Adam had not yet gotten up the courage to tell the older man he had come to take her home, although both knew there could be no other reason for his presence.

Rebecca watched the two men together, secretly proud of Adam and grateful that her father would know the man she had chosen. They were very different, and yet they had much in common. Both were good men by nature, men who would give their lives to right a wrong.

"We will move again in the time of melting ice," Cut-ta-ho-tha said quietly. He puffed a long-stemmed trade pipe and offered it to Adam. Night had fallen, and the only light in the wigwam came from the glowing coals of the fire pit. "We will cross the Ohio, and we will not return. Twice we have moved in this many years." He gave the signal for ten. "The white man is greedy. He will eat the whole world and cut the mother into slices with his plows."

Adam was silent, recognizing truth in the older man's accusations and having no rebuttal. He had never thought of the Chesapeake country as being Indian land, but it had not been many years since the first white settlements had been built there. True, there had been little bloodshed, but only because the Indians had chosen to depart rather than fight for the land.

"We die by the white man's lead and steel. Our children swell with spots and burn up in our arms, and our young women die of filthy diseases. Why, Adam Rourke? We held this place for a thousand years." The slim fingers signaled time out of time. "We have respected the earth and tried to live without bringing harm to her skin. We have not killed more deer than we could eat or taken more fish than could be smoked. And yet, we fall before the white man like ancient trees before a storm. I see a time…" Cut-ta-ho-tha stared into the rising smoke, and Adam felt a prickle along the back of his neck and arms. "I see a time when the Shawnee will not hunt this land or sing their songs or hold out their hands to help a child learn to walk. We are a doomed people, Adam Rourke. A people of shadows."

"Enough of this gloomy talk," Rebecca said, coming to the fire. "There is a feast tonight for Sweet Water's new daughter. We must go and see the dancing and wish the child good fortune."

Cut-ta-ho-tha rose to his feet. "Yes—I promised Sweet Water I would come. It is a great joy for them. They have waited many years for a baby."

"Go ahead, Father," Rebecca urged. "We will follow. I will bring Adam his walking crutch. It would not do for you to be late. No one will begin the dancing until you are seated." She winked at Adam. It was rare enough that they were alone for any length of time in the wigwam. Tonight the older woman had already left for the celebration, and those in the next wigwam would go soon too.

"So be it. If you need help in walking, send a child and I will see that someone comes to help." With a knowing grin, he ducked low and left the wigwam.

"My father is a wise man," Rebecca said. She circled around the fire pit and snuggled down beside Adam, laying her head on his chest. "I do not feel much like dancing. Your child did not let me sleep much last night."

They shared a sleeping platform, even though the Shawnee did not consider them married. Rebecca had explained that since she was a widow first and then a divorced person, she could sleep without shame with any man she pleased. "And sleep is all I can do with you," she'd teased. "You could not harm a maiden in your condition."

Adam inhaled deeply, sniffing the odor of honeysuckle and pine that clung to her hair. She tilted her face up to his, and their lips met in a sweet kiss of shared pleasure. He let his fingers touch her throat, gently stroking the place where her pulse throbbed, and then dip to brush the top of a swelling breast.

"I'll envy our baby," he murmured. "He will taste your breasts before I will."

Rebecca laughed and pulled away from him. "Such talk from a father-to-be. Among the Shawnee, a woman does not lie with a man for many moons after her child is born, sometimes not until the child is finished nursing."

Adam groaned loudly. "And how long is that?"

"Two, maybe three years." She giggled. "Now you know why our men take a second wife." She rubbed his jawline. "I must shave you again, A-dam. It would be much better if you would let me pull out the hairs with a clamshell. They would not come back so quickly."

"No, thanks. I'd rather grow a beard." He caught her small hand in his bearlike paw. "As soon as I can travel," he said, "I'm taking you home to Sheffield. I want our child to be born there."

Rebecca sighed. "I have not said I would go with you," she answered, so softly he could hardly hear the English words. "I might be happier here with the child. Perhaps, when we are back on the Chesapeake, you will be angry with me again."

Adam brought her hand to his mouth and kissed her fingers, causing waves of sensation to travel up her arm. "Of course I will be angry with you. And you will be angry with me. But between those moments will be good times." He turned her hand over and licked the vein of her wrist with the tip of his moist tongue. "Come with me, Rebecca…please." Adam's voice cracked. "I don't want another woman at Sheffield. I want only you."

"My father may not let me leave," she parried. "He does not trust white men. Why would he give his only daughter to the enemy?"

Adam's eyes glowed in the firelight. "I am not your father's enemy. I never was, and I never will be. If you want me to, I'll give you my word never to raise a weapon against an Indian."

"No." She put her fingers over his lips. "There are good Indians and bad Indians. I cannot promise I would never—"

Her words were cut off by the thud of horses' hooves on the hard-packed ground and the roar of a musket.

CHAPTER 23

R ebecca covered her mouth with her hand to stifle a gasp of fear. Not again! For an instant she clung to Adam, then slipped from his grasp to pull aside the door covering. There had been no second shot, and that gave her courage to see what was happening.

"Rebecca!" Adam cried.

Shouting and a woman's wailing could be heard through the walls of the wigwam. At once, Rebecca was at Adam's side again. "Come quickly," she ordered, shoving the crutch into his hands. "We are in great danger. You must crawl outside. I will bring the horse." She grabbed a musket and shot bag, a container of dried meat and berries, a knife, and flint and steel for fire making, wrapping them in a deerskin robe and knotting it with a leather thong. "Go," she ordered, shoving him. "English soldiers come. Too many to fight. We must go!"

Outside, the camp was a mass of confusion. Men tried to assemble their families; children cried and dogs barked. Adam struggled to his feet, leaning heavily on the crutch as Rebecca darted away despite his demands for her to stay by him.

A brave whom Adam recognized as Rebecca's brother lifted the boy Amatha onto a horse behind a young woman and child and slapped the animal's rump. "To the river," he ordered in Shawnee. "You must put the river between you and the white soldiers."

"How far?" Adam called. "How long do we have?"

"Not long enough," came the harsh reply, and then Rebecca's brother was gone, running in the opposite direction, musket in hand. The braves would try to hold off the soldiers long enough to give the women and children time to escape. Shame ran through Adam as he realized he could not help.

"Here!" Rebecca cried. "There was no time to find the saddle. You must mount him bareback." She led the gelding close to Adam.

"Help me up and give me the gun," Adam said, seizing the animal's mane in his hand. Rebecca gave him a boost, then threw him the deerskin bundle, catching the gelding's reins almost in the same instant and pulling them over the animal's head. Leading the horse, she began to run toward the river with Adam's curses ringing in her ears.

"Damn you, Rebecca!" She looked over her shoulder, then turned her full attention to keep from running into something solid in the dark. "Let me go!" he insisted. "I should be with the men."

"You would be more of a danger to them. Besides, we may need your musket beyond the river."

The canoes were already full; one was halfway across the river. One woman led a pony down the muddy bank with two small children clinging to its back. Another mother stood sobbing with a baby in her arms.

"What is it, Mai-ah Dame?"

"My son! I can't find my son!" The baby began to wail, and the mother pinched the child's nose. Immediately, the infant was quiet.

"He was with Gimewane," Rebecca said. "I saw him." She looked up at Adam. "Do you think you can hold the baby? She can't swim and keep the child's head above water." He nodded and held out his arms. Hesitantly the mother handed the child over.

"We must go," Rebecca insisted, leading the bay into the water. Quickly, she flipped the reins over the horse's neck and shoved them into Adam's hand. "Don't try to fight the current. Let the animal swim with it. There's an easy bank downstream on the far side." She slapped the horse's rump.

"Rebecca?"

"Don't worry about me. I'll hold onto the horse's tail."

Shots rang out behind them from the direction of the camp; a man screamed in pain. Dark heads bobbed in the river as the women and children and old people crossed. The baby cried in Adam's arms, but he clung to it, trying to ignore the waving arms and feet. He didn't think the child could be more than a month old, and he was terrified that he would drop it in the water.

Rebecca gasped as the cold water closed over her head. She had meant to cling to the gelding's tail as she had promised Adam, but the animal was not a good swimmer and seemed to be struggling under his weight, and so she let go. She hoped they would be safe on the far side and that the English soldiers had no Iroquois scouts, against whom the women would be helpless. The moonlight made them all good targets.

She caught sight of the bay swimming beside the pony with the two children on its back. The river was swift and known for its floating logs and stumps beneath the surface. She prayed that the other swimmers would be lucky.

A canoe passed within a few feet of her head. Amatha offered her a paddle. "Let me help you," he called. "I'm going back to get the others."

"No, go ahead. I'm all right," she assured him. "Be careful." The far bank was in sight, and people were already scrambling up it. Rebecca's arms were tired, but she knew she was in no trouble. A few more yards and her feet touched bottom. Wearily, she waded ashore and began to look for Adam.

Anxious voices called out from the shadows of the trees as family members tried to find each other. Rebecca caught sight of gray-haired Gimewane with his little grandson on his shoulder. "Adam has the baby on the horse," she told the old man. "Mai-ah Dame should be with them."

To her relief, she was right. Adam was just handing a wet and screaming infant to her mother. Mai-ah Dame murmured a quick thanks and pressed the child to her breast to cease its crying. Gimewane hurried toward them with the boy.

"Rebecca!" Adam called, straining to see her among the dripping figures rising from the water.

"I'm here," she answered. Catching hold of his belt, she pulled herself onto the horse behind him. "We must get away from the river," she said. She pointed to the left. "That way. There are caves along the bluff. We can hide there."

"Are you all right?" Adam demanded. There had been a few more shots, and now the sky was red with flames from the burning village. Adam shivered, wondering how many of the braves had been killed and how many children had not made it safely across the river in the darkness.

Once they reached high ground, Rebecca slid off the animal and took the deerskin from Adam, pausing to unroll it and check the priming on the musket. "It's damp," she said. "Can you replace the powder without dismounting?"

Silent forms moved past them in the night. Now and then a child whimpered, but the cry was quickly cut off. Even the horses seemed to walk soundlessly, without even a nicker. An owl hooted in a tree over Adam's head, and he wondered if it was a real owl or an Indian.

As if reading his mind, Rebecca, laid a hand on his good leg and pointed upward. "*H-tow-wa-a*," she whispered. "Listen." He caught only a glimpse of the white of her eye in the darkness. "The owl spirit. He will protect us and make us invisible." She caught the bridle of the gelding and began to lead the animal forward again. "Keep the gun ready," she cautioned.

"I thought you said the owl would protect us."

"I did, but I trust you more than the owl."

At last Rebecca was satisfied that they were far enough from the river. She helped Adam dismount and spread the deerskin on the rocky ground so that he could sit. She tied the horse to a tree stump and came to sit beside him, laying her head on his shoulder and wrapping her arms around him. Instantly, she fell into a deep sleep.

But no sleep came for Adam that night. He stared into the blackness, straining at every snap of a twig and rustle of leaves in the wind, all the while cursing the broken leg that kept him from being a real protector of his wife and unborn child.

Dawn brought a gathering of the tribe and a count of their losses. One elderly woman had drowned crossing the river, and a child had been swept away but had been found in the morning playing safely in the shallows. One brave had been grazed by a musket ball, but his wound was not serious, and another had broken an arm when he fell from his horse.

Rebecca's father was safe, as well as the other members of her family, including Amatha. Two Iroquois scouts had been killed and another seriously wounded. Four redcoats had been carried dead from the village site. No accounting of the lost and strayed animals had been made, but one boy had captured the horse of a British officer, complete with sword and satchel. Another boy had the kilt of a wounded soldier and a drum.

The real disaster had been the loss of the village. When the wigwams burned, the people had lost their blankets and furs as well as the dried fish, corn, and beans they'd prepared for winter. It would mean hunger in the time of snow. Weapons and baskets and cooking implements had been destroyed, as well as many precious personal possessions.

The people turned to Cut-ta-ho-tha for guidance. Many had nothing but their open hands and hungry bellies. The decisions he made in the next few weeks could well mean the difference between death and life before the coming of spring, not just for one but for the whole tribe.

As self-assured as any European general, Cut-ta-ho-tha began to assign tasks to his tribe. New wigwams must be built downriver in the spot the people had intended to move to in the spring. Guards must be set day and night to be certain that another party of soldiers did not come to finish what the first had started. The women and children must fish and gather nuts and firewood and whatever roots and plants could be eaten. A band of old men was sent with whatever wealth remained to try and trade with the Delaware for supplies of corn and dried fish.

"Winter comes early to the Ohio country," Rebecca told Adam. "Before the attack, we would have lived well. Now"—she shrugged—"it will be a hard time in which to bear children."

Adam wanted to set out at once for home with Rebecca, but she refused. There was too much to be done for the tribe. Her hands were strong and capable, and even Adam's help was not to be scorned. He could fish and then cut those fish to be smoked, and he could take his turn at guard duty, freeing a brave with good legs to hunt. Besides, the swim across the river had done something to her body; she had begun to spot blood. It was a bad sign for their child, and she was afraid to tell Adam.

"We've got to get out before winter sets in," Adam repeated insistently. "At home they must think we're dead. God only knows what problems Isabel is having."

Rebecca turned hard eyes on him. "If we leave, a child might die for lack of food. I cannot go with that on my conscience. The tobacco is not that important."

"It's not just the tobacco! It's you! You should have a physician when the baby comes; you should be in a warm bed with plenty to eat and no fear of an attack by soldiers."

"I have heard of your English physicians," she said smugly. "Your godman said that a woman is supposed to feel pain when her time comes. That is not the Indian way. When our baby is born, the women will make a potion to send my thoughts away. My body will be able to work to deliver the child, but I will feel little pain."

Adam's face showed his disbelief. "I've heard of Indian women squatting beside the trail to give birth like animals," he muttered. He was uneasy with this talk of childbirth; it was a woman's matter. Surely, the Indians couldn't know more about such things than educated European doctors. "At least it would be clean in our bedroom at Sheffield," he added.

"Clean?" Rebecca snapped. "I would sooner be delivered by Amatha's hands than by that physician who came to see my grandfather. For all his satin and lace and fine horsehair wig, he smelled like a kitchen midden! How can you live among my people and accuse them of being dirty? Don't we swim in the river every day?" She attacked the deerskin she was scraping with a vengeance. "Dirty! Humph!" she sniffed. "And when the Delaware found you, they said you were walking with lice!"

Adam flushed and reached for his crutch. He'd not meant to anger her so; he only wanted to go home. He was worried about the coming winter. Women died in childbirth all the time. To go through so much and lose Rebecca now would be more than he could face. "The settlers were unclean. I told you that."

"And you didn't have enough sense to rub grease into your hair to kill the vermin, or to hold your clothes over a fire? Adam, sometimes I think you are as helpless as a child!" Rebecca held the hide up to the light and then folded it over and began to pull it back and forth around a sapling. The deerskin would make warm leggings once it was lined with rabbit skin. The winter would be hard, with much snow, and they would need to conserve heat.

Adam leaned on the crutch and hobbled toward the riverbank to check his fish traps. Rebecca's disposition had not become any sweeter as her pregnancy progressed. Somehow he had always imagined a mother-to-be sitting quietly and speaking softly. Rebecca's tongue was as sharp as a green-brier!

Cool winds from the north brought the country into full and glorious autumn. The leaves turned brilliant shades of red and copper and gold, and frost touched the forest with glittering magic in the hush of early morning. At night the stars sparkled with an unearthly brilliance, and Rebecca and Adam lay awake staring up at them.

"Do you see the star there?" Rebecca pointed. "The bright one that seems so close you could almost reach up and snatch it like a hazelnut. That is part of the belt of the Hunter. "

Adam pulled her close against him, tucking the wolf skin around her shoulders. They were only a few hundred yards from the camp, but they seemed to be alone. Of necessity, much of their time was spent in the midst of the tribe, and Adam treasured the private hours of night. Soon it would be too cold to sleep without shelter, and they would have to move back into the wigwam with Rebecca's family or build their own. It would be crowded if they chose the former. Rebecca's brother, his wife and child, and the boy Amatha shared Cut-ta-ho-tha's wigwam, as well as the old woman. It was a large house by Shawnee standards, long rather than round, but it was still close quarters for eight people.

"Long ago he was a real hunter," Rebecca continued, dropping into the singsong chant of the storyteller, "but he was not content to follow the trails of…"

Adam brushed the top of her head with his lips, content to let her rattle on in Shawnee. He didn't understand half of what she was saying, but it was easier to listen than to stop her every few minutes and ask her to translate. His Algonquian was getting better; children no longer laughed when he talked. But his language skills didn't extend to Indian fairy tales or astronomy.

He flexed his leg gently, glad of the aching; every day it was becoming stronger. He was putting weight on it, and the pain came from using muscles that had become lazy. If he regained full use of it before winter, he might still persuade Rebecca to return to the tidewater before the child was born.

The tidewater seemed far away, as distant as the gilded crescent moon that glittered over the trees. He missed Sheffield with an ache that went deeper than the pain in his leg, but had there been no plantation and all it stood for, he knew he could have made a new life here and been happy among the Shawnee.

Theirs was a primitive existence, but there were rewards that English society seemed to lack. He was utterly happy tonight with the woman he loved pressed close against his heart, without even a roof over his head. Rebecca and the child she carried were the most important things in his life; all else seemed insignificant.

If he stayed, he'd turn pure Indian. In a few years, he'd be painting himself with heathen symbols, wearing feathers, and strutting around as pompously as Meshepeshe. How strange to think that when the British had attacked the Shawnee village, he hadn't questioned which side he was on; he'd known. He would have killed any redcoat he'd seen, not just to protect his own life or Rebecca's but to protect the People.

"A-dam, you aren't listening to me," Rebecca chided. "How will you know the stories to tell our children if you don't listen?" She tugged on the stubble of his beard. "This is very important, what I tell you."

Adam's hand slipped under her tunic to cup her swelling belly and then to stroke her inner thigh provocatively. "This is more important," he murmured in English. "Are you sure we just couldn't—"

"No. We couldn't. It is not the custom," she lied. Rebecca felt a flush creep up her neck and cheeks and was glad of the darkness that hid her color. How easily she deceived Adam! There was more English in her than she liked to admit. She wanted to make love to him, and there were ways that would not have hurt his leg, but she was afraid for the child. It still kicked strongly, but every day there were traces of fresh blood on her breechcloth. It would do no good to tell Adam; he would only worry. And so, she must put him off with excuses.

"A decent Shawnee woman does not share pleasures with her husband at this time," she insisted. "Now is the time for talking and for sharing laughter."

"We could share a little laughter and a little pleasure."

"No, Adam! Now I know your leg is better, since you think of your manhood all the time. Tomorrow we must begin building our own wigwam. Or"—she turned her face up to his, her long lashes casting shadows across her features—"there is a thing I have been thinking."

"And what thing is that?" Adam pulled her to rest against his middle, savoring the warmth of her body despite his increasing desire.

"There is a cave, Adam." She pointed. "Just beyond those trees. Where the spring is."

"I saw it. I didn't climb up there."

"It is not a very large cave, but it goes back into the hill. Maybe we could live there. We would still have to make walls and build sleeping"—she switched from English into Shawnee—"places. But it wouldn't be as hard as building a wigwam, and you wouldn't need to cut as many poles. I'm not sure I could get all the bark anyway. If you want a place of our own, the cave might be better. We will need something before the snow flies."

"A cave?" Adam chuckled, thinking what his friend Jock would have to say about that. Would his son be born in a cave? "Why not, if you think it will be warm enough."

She snuggled against him. "I knew you would say yes, Adam, so I went up there today and began to clean away the dirt. We will not have to bring water from the river. I will be the only woman with water at her door. We will be close enough to the village for safety but far enough away so that Meshepeshe will not scowl at you everytime you step out into the sunshine."

"It sounds as if you intended to move into the cave no matter what I said," he observed, trying to keep his voice gruff.

"That is not true," she said. "We can still live with my father, but he has been saying that we should be married.

What do you think, A-dam? Will you make an honest woman of me before I bring you a son? Or do you want to wait to be sure it is not a girl?"

"We're already married, Rebecca. We've been married. Your throwing my stuff out the window didn't change anything. But if a few drumbeats and a little shaman magic will make you happy, let's get married again." He moved his hand to caress her breasts, thrilling to their lush fullness and the ripe, swollen nipples.

She twisted away and caught his wandering hand in hers. "The shaman will not marry us. My father will say the words."

"And Meshepeshe, will he carry the bouquet?"

"Adam, stop. You are silly. You must not make fun of him. It is not easy for him to see us together." She could not quite hide the hint of mischief in her voice.

"And I suppose you would have married him if I hadn't come after you."

"Maybe." She dug an elbow into his side. "Are you jealous, A-dam?"

"You're damn right I'm jealous! Why shouldn't I be? My back itches every time I'm in the woods. What's to keep him from putting an arrow in it, and then comforting the grieving widow?"

"He would not do that. It is not the Shawnee way. Meshepeshe is an honorable man. You are of the tribe now. He could not hurt you, at least not from ambush. He might challenge you to do battle with him if you do not marry me before the splints come off your leg."

"Why wait?" Adam's temper was rising. "Why not have it out now? Against a cripple, he'd be certain of winning you!"

Rebecca wiggled loose and stood up. "You know nothing, if you believe that. Now, he couldn't fight you. Now he would have to fight *for* you if another man challenged you. He is a warrior, a man of honor. You would do well to count him as a friend." She tugged at the wolf skin and wrapped it around her shoulders. "Since you are so contrary, I will go to my father's wigwam and sleep by his fire." Without another word, she turned and stalked toward the collection of wigwams.

"Go on, then!" he called after her. Damn! How was a man to figure a woman? Especially one who was breeding? He wrapped the remaining deerskin around his shoulders and curled into a ball. In the morning he supposed he'd have to speak to her father about performing some sort of Indian wedding for them. And he knew damn well he'd have to move into the cave with her. The thought of spending the winter inches from her brother and father, unable even to cuddle properly, was absurd. He was surprised they hadn't invited Meshepeshe to move into the wigwam, so highly was he regarded by the family! Maybe he, Adam, would ask the Panther to stand up with him for the wedding. That should delight their twisted sense of honor.

Rebecca pushed aside the skin that covered the entrance and crawled into the wigwam. Adam was angry with her again. She sighed. *Having a baby is very hard on a man. I should have more patience.* Her mouth turned up in a smile; she covered it with a hand and giggled. *Adam would marry her in the Shawnee way. He could not refuse.* And she knew he would be happier in the cave than in the village. For an Englishman he tried very hard, but he would be embarrassed if the others heard them quarreling. It would be much better for them to be alone.

She climbed onto her spot on the sleeping platform and wiggled into a comfortable spot. She didn't like to sleep alone anymore. Adam had spoiled her. *But he must not know that she cared so much. Let him sleep alone for the night. He would be all the more pleasant in the morning.*

CHAPTER 24

The soft throb of the drum seemed to call to the primitive urges in Adam's blood. He stood waiting in the center of the open space before the shaman's wigwam, adorned in the traditional garb of a Shawnee warrior. His thick brown hair was held back from his face with a beaded strip of leather, and wide armbands of native copper encircled his sinewy biceps. A white embroidered loincloth fell over deerskin leggings that Rebecca had dressed and stitched with her own hands. The high moccasins were worthy of a high chief, sewn so carefully as to be almost waterproof.

All fires in the village had been extinguished except those within the wigwams and the one that danced and flickered before him. The people waited, shadowy figures, almost one with the thick, swaying branches of the encroaching forest. Almost imperceptibly, the drumbeat was picked up by a second drum and then a third.

Adam was sweating despite the bite of the autumn wind and the fact that above his waist he wore only a fringed leather vest that left his chest and stomach bare to the elements. He had refused the paint; he was English, not Indian, and proud of it. He had worn the finery only out of love for Rebecca and respect for her people. This ceremony meant a great deal to the Shawnee, and he would not shame them or himself if he could help it.

The wind gathered strength, snatching leaves from the bending trees and whirling them about, dropping some into the fire and sending others skittering across the hard-packed earth. Winter would soon be upon them, and the threat added an element of portent to the cadence of the drums. Tonight the Shawnee would celebrate the beginning of new life, that of the joining of a man and woman and the public declaration of the intertwining of their souls. Tonight they would dance and feast and share the joy of the young lovers, and tomorrow they would face whatever fate decreed them, whether sorrow or joy.

Despite the threat of starvation hanging over the tribe, none had held back in the preparation of the ritual banquet. Women had vied with each other to create a tender roast or the most savory stew. Corn cakes had been prepared with maple sugar and dried berries, along with mixtures of corn and beans and squash baked with honey. Wild turkey had been roasted on a spit, then stuffed with rice and apples and garnished with cattail root and wild onion.

It was a mark of honor that the tribe would observe Rebecca and Adam's marriage, offering all they had without regard to the future. And if the portions of the feast were smaller than usual, none would have the ill breeding to say so. Every man, woman, and child would sample the good meat and bread and sweets, and the memory would help to ease the pain in the lean months to come.

Cut-ta-ho-tha materialized from the darkness like some pagan god, his face seemingly carved of the same ageless granite as the hills around them. He raised his arms high, and the drums fell silent. There was no sound but the whine of the wind and, from far off, the throbbing of the ever-changing river.

"A-dam Rourke." The old Indian's deep voice carried to the farthest member of the tribe. "You are of the enemy." An angry buzz rose from gathered warriors, and Adam's mouth went suddenly dry. "What is it you desire?" The ebony eyes drilled remorselessly into Adam's.

"I ask for the hand of your daughter Star Blanket in marriage. I have stood before the English and made her my wife. Now I ask your blessing on our union." The drums began again, challenging, questioning. Adam felt sweat run down his forehead and break out on the palms of his hands. Where was she? He hadn't seen Rebecca for two days, and no one answered his questions when he asked about her. Was this all some monstrous charade?

"You are of the enemy," Cut-ta-ho-tha repeated. "And yet, you are not the enemy. You have come alone into the land of the Shawnee to take away my only daughter."

A whispering grew among the women. The Englishman was brave. He had dared much for the daughter of Cut-ta-ho-tha. One woman nudged her neighbor and looked toward the warriors. Meshepeshe's face was pale despite the black and orange paint that streaked it. The Panther desired Star Blanket for his own. Would there be an open dispute?

"I have come to take her back to the land of the Chesapeake," Adam said. "I wish her to be the mother of my children and heart of my body." Bird woman had told him the words to say. They had sounded strange when he had repeated them to an empty forest; they sounded right in this time and place. "I would make a bond with your family, a bond that neither time nor man can break."

Cut-ta-ho-tha motioned, and an old woman stepped from the crowd. Her body was curved like a bow, and she walked with the help of a young boy. Only her eyes were young and alive. She raised her wrinkled visage and peered into Adam's face. "Star Blanket's mother, she whose name we may not speak, has gone ahead across the river. If she were here, it would be necessary that she give her permission. You have no clan, and so this is a serious matter." The old voice was high and reedy, as if played on an eagle-bone flute. "What do you give for the daughter of our clan? What do you offer for the most valuable thing we possess, the mother of our unborn children?"

"All I have," Adam answered softly.

The ancient woman waited for more than twenty heartbeats, then lowered her head in a quick nod. "So be it," she cried. "We give to you a gift without price." Quickly as a snake she caught his massive hand in her bony one. "Never forget the Shawnee gift," she crooned, "and you will prosper, and your children's children will hold this land where the People once walked." The fingers twisted into his flesh. "Forget, and you will repent your ways for many lifetimes, English-*manake*. Hahhah!"

A shout of joy rang out among the villagers, and they parted to let Rebecca step forward. She was smiling as she came toward Adam, a vision in white doeskin and red and silver beads. Silver bells dangled from her ears, jingling faintly as she walked.

The drumbeat changed, becoming frenzied, and was joined by other instruments and the chanting of the Shawnee. Rebecca laughed out loud, and her voice was drowned by the shouting. She held out her hand to Adam, and he took it; together they turned to face Cut-ta-ho-tha.

Shyly, Rebecca looked up into Adam's face. Did he feel her trembling? Their child was stirring beneath her heart. Did he know? A-dam, her heart cried. Is this right for us? Can you accept me as I am? Her knees were weak; she could hardly breathe. She wanted to trust him, to place her future in his hands. Her heart seemed to flutter like a caged bird.

She nodded to the question her father put to her, and her lips formed the correct syllables. Tears clouded her eyes, and she clung to Adam's hand like a drowning man to a bit of earth. "A-dam?" she whispered. He heard her and looked down, smiling. His heart was in his eyes—all could see it. "*Ki-te-hi*," she murmured and blinked back shining tears of joy. Now I am truly your wife, in this life and for all the lives to come. I pledge my life and my soul to you, A-dam Rourke. *Dah-quel-e-mah.* I love thee. Her lips moved. "I love you, A-dam."

"And I you, *keewa.*"

* * *

It was many hours before they could retire to their quiet place in the hill, many hours of dancing and feasting and story telling. The time meant nothing to Rebecca; she saw no one, heard no one, except her tall, broad bear of a husband.

They came at last up the slope, laughing and whispering together, followed by a band of merry villagers. As they entered the cave, hand in hand, the voices behind them grew faint. Rebecca laughed out loud and spun around as lightly as a child, her eyes gleaming in the light of the carefully banked fire.

In the time since Adam had been in the cave, it had been transformed into a snug nest. Walls of woven branches covered with bark and grass blocked off the drafts from the crevices that ran back into the hill, and a wide sleeping platform had been built along one wall. On it, branches had been laced together with leather thongs, cushioned with evergreen boughs, and covered with warm furs to form a comfortable bed. There were baskets and containers, and even a precious copper pitcher for water. Adam noticed that his musket and shot bag hung on pegs jammed into cracks in the rock wall, and his saddle lay near the entrance of the cave.

"You've made a home of it," Adam said. "I wouldn't have thought it could be so comfortable."

Rebecca beamed. "It wasn't just me. The other women helped, and my brother made the bed and put up the pegs for your gun. The furs and baskets are gifts. Bird Woman gave us the pitcher; her man brought it from Canada many years ago."

Adam sat down on the edge of the sleeping platform and held out his arms. "Come here, woman," he said with mock sternness.

She added another log to the fire and then came to sit beside him. "This will be a good place for our baby to be born," she said dreamily, resting her head against him. "Are you happy, A-dam?" She sighed. "I am very happy." She rubbed her belly. "I think our son is happy too."

Adam tipped her face up and kissed her lips tenderly. "Will you go back to Maryland with me and live at Sheffield?" he asked softly.

"Did you think I would not?" She looked deep into his brown eyes. "I am truly your wife now. Is it not the duty of a wife to go where her husband leads?"

He kissed her bottom lip, tasting the sweetness of her mouth, letting his fingers rub the back of her neck and hairline. "I want to hear you say it," he breathed huskily.

"I will go to Sheffield with you," she said. "After the baby is born."

"And you will live there with me?"

She giggled. "Of course."

"And will you miss this place?" He pushed her gently back against the thick fur covering as though she were made of fragile crystal that might shatter at a careless touch. His big hands were clumsy on her beaded belt, loosening it finally and pushing it aside so that he could pull her tunic over her head.

Adam caught his breath as firelight flickered on Rebecca's pale, full breasts with their ripe, red nipples. "I think you're the most beautiful thing I've ever seen," he said, bending to kiss the nearest nipple and then to moisten it with the tip of his tongue. "Do you love me?" he murmured.

"You ask too many questions, husband." Her hands reached up to stroke the hard, corded muscles on his chest and then to lock behind his massive neck and pull him down to pleasure her.

"I just want to hold you," he said gently. "I won't do anything to endanger the baby, I promise. I just want to lie next to you."

Shivers of anticipation ran through her body as she watched Adam strip away his clothing. "There are other things we can do," she suggested. "Ways to bring joy." She wiggled out of her skirt and raised herself on one elbow. With her free hand she untied the thongs that held her hair, letting it fall over her face and breasts. Her eyes made promises as old as Eve. "Come and lie beside me, A-dam."

He moaned deep in his throat, and her hand stroked the throbbing flesh that rose between them. "Rebecca," he cried, gathering her into his arms and pressing her against him. His skin burned where it touched hers; his heart was pounding so hard he thought it might burst through his chest. "Darling."

Trembling, she drew his hand to stroke her breast, and their lips met again. She would do nothing to risk the child, but the fire in her loins was as great as his. Her fingers tightened around his manhood, stroking, caressing, savoring its strength and sheer maleness. He shuddered with pleasure, and she let her mouth trail down his neck to kiss the nub of his nipple.

"Witch." He groaned. The hot, sweet scent of her mingled with the musk of the furs and the tang of the evergreen boughs beneath them. He wrapped his fingers in her glorious hair and covered her lips with his own, plundering her mouth with his tongue, seeking out the soft, dark recesses of her velvet flesh.

Rebecca entangled her limbs with his, losing herself in the magic of the night and the feeling of this man. There was nothing but the two of them and their unborn child— no past, no future, only this moment and the rapture of their passion. "I love you," she whispered. "More than life." And the sound of her name on his lips was the sweetest word she had ever heard.

Neither Rebecca nor Adam slept that night; there were too many things to say, too many kisses to give and accept, too many plans to make. The fire burned low, and they pulled the furs over them, unwilling to move from each other's arms to add more wood.

With the first pale streaks of dawn, the wind increased and a few flakes of snow drifted down. Rebecca smelled the snow and murmured sleepily to Adam, burrowing deep in his arms. "Snow. Winter comes quickly now."

Adam yawned and opened one eye. The air was noticeably colder in the cave. Shivering, he extricated himself from Rebecca's embrace and slid from the bed. Instantly goose pimples covered his bare skin. Quickly he added a few logs to the dying fire, then threw a wrap around his waist and walked to the front of the cave.

The sky was gray and angry; the trees looked bare and stark against the morning light. Crystalline flakes struck his face and arms. "Winter," he murmured, and a sense of uneasiness invaded his calm. There would be no returning to Maryland until after the child was born. For better or worse, they would stay here.

He looked down on the sleeping village; not even a dog was stirring. The people had feasted and danced until late into the night. There was no need to be up early. The icy winds coming down from Canada spoke plainly for any man to understand. It was a time of waiting, and soon, although no one wanted to say it, it would be a time of hunger.

The river froze from bank to bank hard enough for the children to play on, and although holes were cut daily to provide fresh water, those who fished through the ice had little luck.

Snow fell day after day, thick and bitter cold, piling in drifts around the wigwams and immobilizing the horses. The men had to cut evergreen boughs and scrape away the snow so the animals could graze. The cold deepened, trapping the land in endless winter, snapping branches with its intensity and driving men inside when their hands and cheeks turned numb.

Daily the hunters went out, seeking deer and turkey and smaller game. Often they came home empty-handed, although the sound of hunting wolves assured them that there were animals out there somewhere.

Providing enough firewood for the village became a chore almost as difficult as finding foliage for the horses. Adam brought his horse up the slope into the cave. "He might as well add his heat to this place as long as I have to gather grass and bark for him." Adam didn't mention that the wolves had become bolder and bolder, or that a yearling colt had been taken the night before. He only cautioned Rebecca to stay in the village. "It's too cold for you to gather firewood in your condition. I can do it."

"And hunt? And cut evergreens for the horses? I am not sick. I feel fine," she lied.

Adam looked at her suspiciously. Her face was thinner, her eyes a little too bright. He had lost weight himself; all the Shawnee had. The intense cold seemed to suck more out of a man than he could take in, no matter how much he ate.

He had taken off the splints. His leg was straight, although a little weak. He tried to favor it, but he had to hunt. Rebecca needed fresh meat, even if she did give away half of what he brought home.

"Everyone does not have such a hunter," she would say to quiet his protests. "How can we eat when others may be going without? I am already too fat."

Adam had taken to watching her closely when she ate, insisting that she finish all he gave her. "I know enough about having babies to understand you must eat for two," he said.

"You are the hunter. You must keep up your strength. I have nothing to do but sit by the fire and gather a few sticks."

She had melted snow to wash her hair; now she brushed it before the fire to dry it. Adam noticed that she moved more slowly now, more deliberately. He was afraid she was in pain, and he knew she would never admit it.

Sometimes the boy Amatha came to share their meal. He would sit shyly, his eyes lowered, saying nothing. Adam liked him and tried to teach him a few words of English. If spoken to directly, Amatha would answer, but only in Shawnee.

"I don't know why he won't try," Adam exclaimed to Rebecca one night after the boy had left. "He's not stupid."

"Take him hunting with you," she advised. "He has an eye like a hawk. My brother has not the patience to train a boy. I think it angers him that Amatha comes to our fire so much."

"He's got no other family?"

"He lives with my brother and his wife. Ordinarily, she would take him into her clan, but she is from another tribe and does not understand our ways. I think she resents Amatha, and my brother is caught between his duty to his wife and obligations to the boy. It would be a good thing if you would take him hunting."

"You said that already." Adam tightened the final cord on his snowshoe. "All right, I'll take him tomorrow if he wants to go. But don't get any ideas about him coming here to live. I like having you all to myself."

Rebecca giggled. "Soon we will have someone else here. Will you be jealous of him?"

"You'll have to wait and see, won't you?"

As the weeks passed, there was no letup in the cold. The snow continued to fall, and some of the people became ill. Adam insisted that Rebecca stay in the cave and away from the village. A child had died of coughing and fever, and he was afraid she would catch it.

"It is not the kind of sickness you catch," Rebecca insisted. "I cannot just sit here and stare at the fire. I will go mad! You are away hunting all day. I must talk to someone." She pulled his beaver-skin sleeve from a basket and turned it fur side in. When he put on his wolf-skin cape, she held out the sleeve for him to slip into, then pulled his beaver hat down over his ears.

"You bundle me up so I can hardly walk," he protested. "And I want you to stay here today. The slope is icy. I won't have you falling, with the coming of the baby so near. Bird Woman can come up and chat with you." He frowned. "I mean it, Rebecca. It is getting colder. Stay inside!"

"I hear you," she murmured. "But you talk like a foolish English-*manake*. I am fine. Strong as Meshepeshe."

"Good. I want you to stay that way. Be sure you keep a good fire going, and don't worry about me. I'll be back before dark."

He had seen deer tracks the day before. Even though the night's snow had covered them, he wanted to go in that general direction. Their meat supplies were low—not as bad as some in the village, but if the snow didn't let up, it could get serious.

Adam thought Amatha must have brought him good luck. It was only a little past noon when they came upon a wolf harrying a deer with a broken leg. The wolf took one look at them and fled, and Adam let Amatha kill the buck with his musket. It was a clean shot; they gutted the animal, cut it up, and carried it back toward the cave.

They were perhaps an hour's walk away when they met another boy from the village. "You must come," he called to Adam and Amatha. "Star Blanket's child comes now. She fell on the ice, and the women are afraid. Cut-ta-ho-tha has sent runners to find you."

Adam stifled a curse and began to run with long, loping strides. If she were...If she...Tears formed in the corners of his eyes, and he wiped them ruthlessly away with the beaver sleeve.

Despite his snowshoes, he sank almost to his knees in the snow with every step, and the wind stung his exposed face and burned his lungs with every breath. He heard the boys behind him and knew he should wait for them, but he couldn't. Every minute was precious. The deer lay heavy across his shoulders, but he couldn't leave it. It was too much for the boys to carry, and it would be devoured by wild animals if he left it for someone else to fetch.

His weak leg ached, and his hands were beginning to grow numb through the mittens. How much farther? Adam tried to remember. He knew where he was and which direction to go, but he couldn't be sure of the time. He was getting as bad as the Indians about time. They hardly used the concept, and so it had lost nearly all meaning for him too.

The snow turned to sleet, sticking to his eyelashes and caking the fur hat. He stopped to catch his breath, leaning forward to brace his hands on his knees as he sucked in air.

His heart was thumping like a drum. He looked back. The boys were moving specks in the distance, but he had already broken the trail for them; they would find it easier to run in his tracks.

After another minute's rest, he started out again, his mind as numb as his hands. Better if he'd never laid hands on her! If having this child cost Rebecca's life, he couldn't live with himself. It was so damned unfair. She was hardly more than a child herself. He began to sweat beneath the wolfskin cloak. She should be home at Sheffield with a proper physician instead of here in an icy cave in the wilderness! He must have been mad to let her stay.

He crested the last hill, and then the terrain dipped into a hollow. The snow was deeper here, and Adam was forced into a walk. Branches caught at the deer carcass and threatened to trip him. The wind shifted and brought the sound of a woman's high-pitched wail to his ears; a lamentation for the dead. Adam had been among the Shawnee long enough to know the death cry of the women. He stopped and let the deer fall to the snow. Were they weeping for his child or for Rebecca?

A groan of despair rose in his throat as he stumbled on through the snow and up the slope toward the cave. "Let it be the baby," he mumbled. "God forgive me, but if I must lose one of them, let it be the child."

CHAPTER 25

R ebecca opened her eyes when she heard Adam call her name. The women stepped aside to let him enter the living space. "Adam?" she said hesitantly. His snow-covered form looked even bigger than usual; frost clung to his beard and mustache and had turned the wolf skin white.

"Rebecca?" There was no mistaking the pain in his familiar voice. "Are you all right?" He dropped to his knees beside the sleeping platform and pulled off his mittens, reaching for her warm hands with his cold ones. "I heard the women crying."

She pulled his hands to her lips and kissed the stiff fingers. "They weep for another, husband, not for you," she whispered, smiling into his eyes. "Not for yours." She drew his fingers down to pull aside the fur beside her, revealing a small, twisting infant, eyes clenched shut and tiny pink mouth opening and shutting.

Adam stared at the baby, trying to control the flood of emotion that rolled over him. He'd never seen a newborn, never been around babies at all, but surely it shouldn't be this tiny. Something must be wrong, he reasoned. Nothing could be that small and live! His lower lip began to quiver, and he clamped his teeth over it. "Rebecca," he murmured hoarsely.

The minute human being in her arms began to mew, and she laughed.

"What do you think, A-dam?" She bent to kiss the dark wisps of hair on the baby's head. "Well, husband, did a forest ghost take your tongue?" She smiled up at him, her heart in her eyes, and Adam couldn't bear to shatter her happiness.

"You're sure you're all right?" His eyes sought out the older woman standing beyond the fire. If something was wrong with the baby, shouldn't they have told her? Desperately, he tried to find words to console her.

"English-*manake,* do you have a head of *h'kah-nih?"* Rebecca's laughter was like frothy water spilling over rocks. "Are you blind?" Her eyes danced with merriment. "I promised you a son. Is he not the most beautiful thing you have ever seen?"

Adam's brain refused to function. He wiped at his snow-encrusted face. "Isn't it…?" He struggled to find kind words, words that would not take the joy from her eyes. "Isn't it a little small?" He glanced at the baby again. It was definitely a male child, but as red as a skinned opossum, and ugly.

The women laughed. "Did you think he would be born with a bow and arrow in his hand?" called a wrinkled matron. "The only fault with this apetotha is that his eyes are blue, but even our children are born that way. Doubtless they will change to a human shade of brown in a day or two."

"He was big enough to pass between your woman's thighs," Bird Woman assured him. "See how he cries and waves his fist. He will be a mighty warrior, this one."

Adam looked hesitantly at Rebecca, the truth beginning to push back his fears. "It's all right? Nothing's wrong with him? He's normal?" Trembling, he reached down with one stiff finger and touched the tiny fist. To his surprise, the baby opened his eyes and stared up into his face as the little fingers tightened around the large one and held fast. Tears welled up in Adam's eyes and ran down his cheeks. "It's a boy?" he repeated dumbly. "A healthy boy?"

"What have I been trying to tell you?" Rebecca laughed. "All men are alike! He is but new hatched, this son of yours. Give him a few weeks and then decide if you will keep him."

"But...I heard the death wails and I thought..."

A frown crossed her face. "The old one, she who gave me away at our wedding, has crossed over. The mourning was for her."

"I was afraid it was you." Adam's lips brushed her cheek, then pressed gently against her lips. "I love you," he whispered, unashamed despite the women tittering behind him. He touched her cheek, cupping the curve of her chin in his big hand. "I..." His voice cracked. "I wouldn't want to go on without you," he admitted. "Are you...?"

"I am fine. The women say it was an easy delivery. I slipped on the ice. It must have helped him along." She kissed the hard, rough hand, tasting the salt of his skin with the tip of her tongue. "We are here, A-dam, both of us. Will you hold him?"

"Can I?" He arched a shaggy eyebrow doubtfully. "My hands are cold. I might hurt him. Maybe—"

"Pick him up, A-dam," she whispered. "Do you want the women to say you denied he was yours?"

The baby screamed in protest as Adam lifted him up and tried clumsily to wrap him in the rabbit-fur blanket. "My son," he mouthed silently. A grin spread across his face as he felt the strength in the tiny boy. He brought the squawling bundle against his neck and cheek and kissed the silken hair. A surge of protectiveness coursed through him as the baby nestled against him and began to make soft, happy sounds. My son. "He's beautiful," he said, not meaning it. "He's beautiful." What did it matter?

"He looks like you," Rebecca said proudly. "His hair is beaver brown like yours." She held out her arms to take the infant, and her blanket fell aside. Adam laid the baby against her naked breast and covered them both with the thick wolf skin.

He wished the women would all go away so that he could be alone with Rebecca. Suddenly he was tired. "Amatha killed a deer," he said in English.

"You are cold and hungry," Rebecca cried. "Bring hot broth for my hunter," she called. "He has slain a deer and there will be enough for all of us." She pushed herself up on one elbow, ignoring the pain. "His clothes are wet, and he must change them."

In less time than Adam would have believed possible, the fire began to take the bitter numbness from his body, and the hot soup brought new clarity to his mind. The voices of the women grew faint as they returned to the village and their own lodges.

"Better?" Rebecca asked, touching his arm with her fingertips. He nodded, and she smiled. "Sleep, husband. Tomorrow we will choose a name for your son. Come, lie beside me and sleep. The little one sleeps, but who knows for how long."

Gratefully, Adam lowered his weary body onto the sleeping platform. Rebecca was safe; the baby was safe. Whatever tomorrow brought, it could not be as frightening as today had been. He wrapped a strand of her dark, silken hair around his finger and slept, lulled by the soft sound of Rebecca's even breathing and the faint infant noises of his son.

In the night, the storm increased, whirling around the cave in a blind fury of howling wind and bone-numbing cold. As the temperature dropped, Adam rose again and again to add wood to the fire and to tuck the furs around his family.

The baby woke and nursed, tugging eagerly at Rebecca's full breast. He made soft, contented sounds and patted her with his tiny hands.

Adam watched them in the firelight, too full of joy for words. The baby had begun to look more human. Maybe newborns were supposed to look like that! God knows, he'd never paid much attention to babies before. Rebecca's cheeks were flushed with color, and his fear receded. She had been so pale before, as though her skin were made of wax.

"I did not try to be a good wife to you before," she whispered, cradling their little son against her. "I will do better, I promise."

"We'll both do better." He grinned down at them, secure in the circle of his arms. "We'll make new customs, combining your ways and mine. Our son will have the best of two worlds."

"Will you give him a name?" she asked shyly. Among the Shawnee, a name was chosen by an old one, but Adam had said they would make new ways. "If he is to be an English-*manake,* he will need an English name. You must pick a good one, a name that he can wear with pride."

"I was thinking on it, and I don't know of a better one for him to carry than your grandfather's." Adam laughed. "He tricked me in your marriage contract. I should have read the fine script. He was determined that the Bradford line continue at Sheffield. So, if you agree, we'll call him Rourke Thomas Bradford."

"Rourke Thomas Bradford," she repeated. "Rourke. It has a good sound, but what does it mean?"

"It's Celtic, a very old and honored name. It means great chief."

"It is a good name," she agreed. "Rourke. My father will be pleased." Rebecca moistened her lips with the tip of her tongue, and the invitation was too great for Adam to resist. He bent and kissed her. She sighed and snuggled down in the furs. "I hope it snows for three days," she murmured, "if it will keep you here by my side. I like having both of my men safe where I can touch them."

"I'll hunt tomorrow," he said. "Whether the snow stops or not. One deer won't last us long among so many. You need fresh meat."

She laughed. "And the fact that you will get to go out with the men and hunt means nothing." She pressed her finger against his lips. "We will not starve this winter; I know this, my mighty hunter. But neither will you hunt tomorrow. I know that too, as surely as I know that this little one has wet his wrappings. And I will have you both here with me, whether you like it or not."

Rebecca's words held the ring of prophesy. The storm raged for another forty-eight hours, dropping two feet of snow over what was already there. And when the wind died down and the sun came out, the forest had been turned into a fairyland of crystal boughs and bright, unbroken expanses of spotless snow.

Adam went out with a party of men to hunt, and although they did not return until well past dark, they found nothing but a few squirrels. Rebecca forced deer stew and some of the precious cornbread on her husband and assured him that the next day would be better. It wasn't.

Day after day, the men went out seeking game, and night after night they returned empty-handed to a village that was quickly depleting the stores its inhabitants had hoarded for the long months of winter. Adam's fears returned, invading his dreams, as he watched Rebecca's cheeks grow thin. What would happen if she lost her milk? Could they keep the baby alive on broth and honey?

Each day was like the one before. Adam waded through snow up to his chest or climbed the highest tree with cold-stiffened fingers to search out a squirrel nest. Boys shot birds when they could find them, and when a colt died, the meat was divided up and eaten by everyone in the village.

And then, one afternoon, Adam and Amatha struggled through a mass of intertwined pine boughs and came upon a herd of deer trapped in the deep snow. Adam froze, unable to believe what he saw. Mentally he began to count, stopping when he reached forty, nowhere near the total. He shouted and clapped the boy on the shoulders, sending the deer crowding to the far end of the natural compound.

"Aiye!" the boy cried. "So many!"

Adam knew that deer often banded together in a storm, and he had heard the hunters speak of such a find. But no one had ever told him that close to a hundred animals might be caught, unable to break out of the high walls of snow.

If it didn't melt, they would starve, but these deer were not destined for starvation.

Most of the animals were thin, but thin or not they would provide meat and hide and tallow. Their antlers and hooves would also be put to use and even the brains. Rebecca had told him that every animal had just the amount of brain needed to tan its own hide. Methodically, he fired off three shots, wasting precious powder and lead to summon the other hunters.

There was no need for guns to slaughter the deer. It could be done with bows and arrows or even by hand, using a knife. The killing of the animals was not a pleasant task, but it was a necessary one.

Joyously, the Indians gathered to harvest the deer. There was no bloodlust in their actions, no sport. Each hunter silently murmured a prayer to the spirit of the deer, telling of their great need and thanking the spirit for the gift of life. Not all the animals were slaughtered. More than two dozen of the strongest were left alive, and the men carefully tramped down a path out of the compound so that the animals could escape.

All night and into the next day human chains carried the life-giving venison back to the village. Drums carried the glad tidings, and women laughed and called out to each other. Meat! The men had found meat aplenty!

Rebecca's eyes glowed with the pride she felt for her husband. Adam had found the herd; white skinned or not, he was a hunter to match any of the Shawnee men. She wrapped the baby in a warm fur and tucked him into a cradleboard. Safely on her back, he rode down to the village to take part in the feasting and singing and dancing. And if the small boy slept through the festivities, at least his dreams were made sweeter by the happy sounds of the people around him.

Although Adam did not sing of his part in the deer hunt, others did. Thus the white man's name was added to the legend of the people, and a hundred years thence, some dark-skinned child would listen to the tale of A-dam the giant hunter and his magic whistle that called the deer to save the tribe from starvation.

Other storms came charging down from the north with snow and bitter cold, but the spirit of the Shawnee did not dim. They knew luck was with them and that spring would come again as it had come every year since the beginning of time. No more people died, and the babies that had been born in the winter grew fat and healthy, including the son of Sky Blanket and Adam Rourke.

"His eyes are green," Adam pronounced, rolling onto his back and lifting the baby high into the firelight. "Bradford green."

"They are not," Rebecca teased. "They are a proper brown. It is the light of the fire and your own weak eyesight that makes you think they're green."

Adam lowered the baby to his chest, marveling at how the child held his head up and stared around him with age-old wisdom. How could something that hadn't even existed a short time ago have wrapped himself around Adam's heart so completely? Every sound, every movement of the baby was a miracle. Adam found himself making plans for the boy, imagining the time when he could teach him to ride a horse or print out his letters. This was what Thomas had meant when he'd talked about his family. Soon it would be time to return to Sheffield and take up their lives, with the boy a symbol of their future.

"Weak eyesight?" Adam said dryly. "Have you forgotten so quickly who found the herd of deer?"

"And who could not tell a boy child from a girl?" Rebecca teased.

They laughed together, and Adam joined her in the furs, mentally counting off the days until he could make love to her again. He hoped they would begin no more children for a year or two, but Rebecca's silken flesh bewitched him, and he knew he couldn't stay away from her an hour longer than he had to.

They had become very close during this long winter, so close that one of them would often start a sentence in one language and the other would finish it in the other tongue. Rebecca seemed to read his mind. and he hers. Adam told her and the baby things he had never told another human being. For the first time since he could remember, he didn't feel alone and apart from the world. They fit each other like a hand and glove, and he knew that, despite their differences, that gift would last them through the years.

One morning they shared a simple breakfast, and then Adam walked down to the village to have the handle of his hunting knife rewrapped by a skillful Shawnee leatherworker. It was a bright day, warm enough to melt some of the snow, and Adam saw a flock of robins, bright-breasted spots of color against the monotone forest.

Rebecca joined several of the young women in gathering wood. Rourke was snug enough on her back in his cradleboard, and she believed the fresh air of the forest would do him good. The women had not gone more than a few hundred yards when they noticed that a man was following them. Rebecca turned to see Meshepeshe leaning against a tree.

"What do you want?" she called. The other women tittered.

"I would speak with you."

"What do you have to say to me that you could not say at my husband's fire?"

"I would talk with you alone."

Rebecca sighed. "Very well." Ignoring the arch looks of the women, she walked a little way apart from them. Meshepeshe took her arm and led her farther away to a spot where a fallen tree had formed a shelter from the snow. A bit of grass poked through in the center of the tiny clearing, and a bird was digging there for seeds or insects. Rebecca wondered at the boldness of the little creature, allowing them to come so near without flying away. "What do you want?" she demanded of the Panther. "You will ruin my reputation."

"You know what I want," he said, releasing her arm and moving a few feet away. "What I have always wanted." His dark eyes shone as fiercely as those of any bird of prey. "The talk is that you will return to the Chesapeake country with your man."

"That is what they say," Rebecca answered, meeting his gaze steadily with her own.

"Will you?"

"Yes."

The copper hands clenched into knotted fists, and a muscle jumped along his sharp-hewn jawline. "I do not wish you to go. Stay here and divorce the white man. Marry me. You are more Shawnee than English. I will take you and the child for my own."

Rebecca sighed. What could she say? She could not wound the ferocious pride of this savage warrior. He had come to her honestly and asked for her hand in marriage. Only the truth would do. "I do not love you, Meshepeshe. I love my husband." She lifted a hand to touch the sinewy forearm. "You are as fine a warrior as I have ever known, and you honor me by asking. My heart would weep if I could not count you among my friends. And if I loved you instead of him, none would part us…not in this life or in the next."

"I could kill him."

Rebecca shivered at his soft tone.

"I have killed other men, Indian and white, for less reason," he added. "What is one more?"

Rebecca's green eyes hardened. "Hurt a hair on Adam's head and I will hunt you down and kill you like a mad wolf, Meshepeshe. If he comes to harm, now or in the years to come, you will bear the blame. I will curse you to the seventh generation, and your children's children will spit at your memory." Swiftly, she undid the medicine bag at her waist. "In token of my promise, I give you a gift." She pulled forth a braid of blond hair and tossed it to him. "I cut this from the head of an English sea captain," she boasted. "He challenged my honor, and I swore to him that his scalp would hang from a Shawnee lance. Take it and remember." Her eyes narrowed menacingly. "Among the English I am called a witch, and I have great power. Do not force me to turn that power against one of my own."

Meshepeshe frowned in disapproval. "A woman does not take scalps."

"This woman does."

"He is not man enough for you, Star Blanket. I—"

Meshepeshe's words were cut off by an ear-shattering snarl as a huge form hurled itself from the thicket. Rebecca whirled to see a huge black bear charging directly at them. She screamed and tried to run, but the melting snow underfoot was slippery, and she fell to one knee.

Meshepeshe notched an arrow and let it fly, catching the bear in the neck and turning its attack toward him. He tried to fit a second arrow, but a massive paw snapped the hickory bow like tinder and tossed the warrior aside.

Rebecca scrambled to her feet as Rourke began to cry. She froze as the bear turned bloodshot eyes in her direction. One side of the bear's face was swollen out of proportion; it dripped with pus and decaying matter. Rebecca's stomach lurched as the smell hit her. A porcupine quill dangled from the sightless right eye and another from the nose.

Snuffling, the pain-crazed bear rose on his hind legs and stumbled toward her in a twisted parody of a man's walk. Meshepeshe staggered to his feet, bleeding from the face and arm, and threw himself against the bear's back. Rebecca screamed again as the bear twisted in its skin, grabbed Meshepeshe with a merciless paw, and threw him to the ground. She looked around her for a weapon and, seeing none, turned and ran. Rourke howled as the cradleboard banged against Rebecca's back. She looked over one shoulder to see the bear come charging after her.

Like a startled doe she ran, dodging trees and leaping over fallen stumps. She knew that no human could hope to match the speed of a maddened bear, but it was the only chance she had. The snow that dragged at her legs was nothing to the bear. His snarls of rage increased as he plunged after her. And then a tangle of greenbriar caught her ankle, and she plunged face down into the snow.

CHAPTER 26

A dam ran toward the source of Rebecca's agonizing scream, the mended hunting knife clutched in his hand. He had not believed that the Panther would dare to harm her, but jealousy had risen red-hot in his brain when Amatha told him that Meshepeshe had followed Rebecca and the women.

In the woods, a young squaw had lowered her bundle of sticks and smiled knowingly at Adam. "If Sky Blanket prefers another, you would be welcome at my fire," she had said softly in Shawnee.

"Which way did they go?" he had demanded.

Her laughter had mocked him as he ran in the direction she pointed, but then Rebecca's scream shut out all else.

A crimson haze danced before Adam's eyes as he tore through the low-hanging evergreens, a cry of fury issuing from his throat. If Meshepeshe had…Rebecca screamed again, and Adam caught sight of the charging bear.

It seemed to Adam as though he ran in slow motion. The white of the snow and the black streak that was the bear formed an image in his mind, an image of something not quite real. Rebecca's screams filled his ears, drowning out the crunch of the snow beneath his feet and the moans of a wounded man. The bear's growls were carried on the wind, blending with it, becoming a part of it. Only Rebecca mattered, and Adam's eyes followed her as she ran, his brain willing her to run faster.

"Rebecca!" he cried. "Run!" The distance closed between them, and then suddenly she was down, a splash of color against the snow. Adam heard the wail of his son as the cradleboard slammed against the ground. He saw the bear rear over them, his mouth a red maw, his claws and teeth shining like old ivory.

"Rebecca!"

She heard his cry and looked up. Adam ran toward the bear, knife in hand, a war whoop ringing from his lips. Her mouth tasted of copper; the baby's cries rang in her ears. Every instinct bade her run, yet a stronger power demanded that she stand and fight beside the man she loved.

"Adam!"

The bear turned away from the man toward the screaming infant. Rebecca gathered her feet under her and began to back away a step at a time. From the corner of her eye she glimpsed a tree, its branches weighed down with ice and snow.

"Ha! Bear!" Adam yelled. "Here!"

The huge animal swayed from side to side; slobber ran from the gaping mouth, and the beady eyes sought a target for its pain and anger.

Adam threw up his arms and growled, and the beast wheeled to face him. "Run!" he ordered, and Rebecca dashed toward the hemlock, seized a branch, and pulled herself hand over hand up the tree. Branches scraped her face and arms as she climbed beyond the reach of the bear, up to the smallest branches. The baby's face was crimson, his tiny fists beating against the sides of the cradleboard. Rebecca ducked her head and pulled off the band that held the carrier, twisting it around a branch. "Inu-msi-ila-fe-wanu protect you," she said, and then she was sliding and falling back down to the ground, toward the sounds of the snarling bear.

Adam circled the bear, dodging the deadly paws as they slashed and waved at him. He tried to keep to the bear's blind side, ducking under to jab with the steel blade of the hunting knife and then moving swiftly away in a macabre dance. Then, suddenly, the animal caught him and pulled him close, crushing him, the claws rending his back and shoulders. Adam heard a scream and wondered if it was his own. He was no longer thinking. Pain and terror had cut away everything but the primitive urge for survival. He thrust with the knife again and again. His brain was filled with the scent of blood, but whether it was the bear's or his own, he did not know.

Rebecca, armed only with a jagged stick, threw herself on the animal's back, seizing the plunging head and stabbing downward to try and blind it completely. A tooth caught her arm and ripped through the hide shirt and flesh, cutting her to the bone. Then the bear stumbled and fell, and all three went down in a heap. The bear gave a terrible groan, and a welter of blood gushed from its mouth, soaking Adam in gore.

Faintly, Rebecca heard the shouts of running men. Then someone was pulling her free. Her head rang, and spots danced in front of her eyes. She heard a baby crying and couldn't remember where he was. "Adam," she mouthed, but no sound came from her lips. She clutched at someone, her eyes focusing on the bloody figure, scarcely human looking, lying on the ground. A man began wrapping her arm with a bit of hide; she pushed him aside and fell to her knees. "Adam?" She stretched out her hand to the gruesome apparition, and it moved and called her name.

"Rebecca?"

Blackness closed over her.

Her arm hurt. It hurt so badly she wanted to leave her body to make the hurting stop. But something else hurt worse. The problem was she couldn't remember what it was.

She tossed with fever, fighting the bear over and over in her dreams. The nightmares came one upon another as she relived the charge of the bear and the stench of its hot breath. Sometimes Adam was in her dreams, feeding her and giving her sips of sweet, cold water from a birchbark container. Twice, she dreamed of the terrible day when her English family was massacred, and the dream world seemed to run red with blood.

Something cold and wet touched her lips. "Rebecca." A man's voice. A voice she knew. Was she dead? "Rebecca."

Her eyelids flickered. Adam's bearded face loomed over hers. The dreams faded, and the man became real. "Adam?" she murmured.

"Hush, darling. It's all right." Adam's scent enveloped her, pushing away the memories of the foul smell of bear. Adam's scratchy cheek brushed hers.

"The baby?" she whispered.

"He's fine. Not a scratch."

Adam's voice was strangely choked. She couldn't tell if he was laughing or crying. There was a deep scratch down one side of his face, and one hand was bandaged. "The baby's all right?" Was she speaking English or Shawnee? Her voice seemed to come from far away. "Where is he? Where is Rourke?"

In answer, Adam slipped the infant from his cradleboard and brought him close enough for Rebecca to touch.

"Meshepeshe?" The act of forming the words tired her, and she lay back against the sleeping platform, a wave of pain sweeping up her arm. It burned as if on fire, but she welcomed the pain; it pushed back the fog in her mind. "Does he live?"

Adam nodded. "He was hurt badly, but he'll recover."

Rebecca opened her eyes wide. "And you, my love?" she whispered. Her green eyes narrowed with suspicion. "The bear killed you. I saw...I saw the blood."

"His blood, not mine." Adam's lips pressed against hers. "What kind of a woman are you to take on a bear with bare hands?"

Rebecca closed her eyes and pulled his hand against her face. "I love you," she whispered sleepily. *"Ki-te-hi."*

"And I love you."

The first green leaves were beginning to appear on the willows when Adam and Rebecca prepared to leave the Shawnee village. Rebecca's father had given her a pinto mare to carry her and the child safely home, and the rest of the tribe had showered them with gifts, so many that the horses were in danger of being overburdened by the weight.

"I'll bring Star Blanket and your grandson back to visit you," Adam said, taking Cut-ta-ho-tha's hand in his. The stocky warrior looked older and sadder in the pale light of dawn.

"No." Cut-ta-ho-tha shook his head. "They must stay in the Chesapeake country forever." He sighed. "War is coming to the Shawnee. The Ohio will run red with the blood of my people and yours. She is the heart of my heart. If I know that she and the child are safe, I can face what I must unafraid."

For a long moment the two hands clasped and held, and then the Shawnee chief stepped back. "You are a warrior, English-man, one worthy to take my daughter. The Shawnee will not forget you, A-dam Rourke."

Rebecca sat beside him on her pinto pony, the baby tied securely to her back in his decorated cradleboard. Rebecca's face was pale, but she shed no tears. She had said her good-byes the night before, good-byes that must last a lifetime. Now she was ready to turn her face toward the tidewater...toward home.

Six heavily armed warriors stepped from the crowd, Meshepeshe among them. "They will shadow your trail," Cut-ta-ho-tha promised, "until you are safe in the land of the white men." He hesitated. "There is one more thing I would ask of you."

"What is it?" Adam asked. "Whatever I can do for you, Father, is already done."

The chief motioned, and Amatha led a bay pony forward.

"It comes to me that we should know the ways of the English. We must speak their tongue and know their thoughts."

"Amatha would go with you to the Chesapeake country and learn these things. Will you have him?"

"You wish to come home with us?" Adam asked the boy directly. Without speaking, Amatha nodded. Adam looked sideways at Rebecca; something in her eyes told him this was not a surprise to her. "Wife?"

"Yes," she said in English. "Let him come."

"I will watch over the little one," Amatha said eagerly. "I will protect him from eagles and wildcats and—"

Adam put up a hand. "Enough! I believe you. There is always a place at my fire for any of the Shawnee." A lump rose in his throat as he reined his horse about. "It's time, Rebecca. "

Her eyes swept over the village, and over the people she knew and loved, lingering on the carved features of her father. She would not see Cut-ta-ho-tha's face again; she would not taste of Bird Woman's corn cakes or listen to her brother's jokes. She inhaled deeply, wanting to remember the smells of the village, willing her eyes to remember the brown of the wigwams, the bright coals of the hearth fires, and the dark eyes of her people.

This life is over, she thought. But I follow A-dam into another. And in her heart, she knew the essential truth of the eternal circle. She smiled at Adam through her tears. "What are you waiting for, English-*manake?* The sun will be high, and we have many days' journeys ahead. Lead, and we will follow."

Adam dug his heels into his mount's side, and Rebecca urged her pony after him. The farewell chanting of the people sounded in their ears as they turned their horses east to the land of the rising sun. Adam turned toward her, and their eyes met for the space of a heartbeat. "You won't be sorry," he promised.

Her laughter rang out over the thud of the horse's hooves and the cooing of the baby. "I never thought I would."

EPILOGUE

Sheffield On The Chesapeake June 17, 1708

Green fields of tobacco and young corn stretched as far as the eye could see beneath the blue tidewater skies. Herds of sleek horses and cattle grazed in the pastures, and the meadow was dotted with the fluffy forms of white sheep. From somewhere far off came the cry of an osprey and the answering shriek of its mate.

Rebecca stood in the stirrups and shaded her eyes, trying to make out the figures on the beach. Yes, that was Amatha with a dark-haired toddler on his shoulders. Rebecca chuckled, knowing her daughter would be tugging at the young man's hair and demanding her horsey gallop even faster. At the water's edge stood another child, skimming stones across the surface of the waves. How fast her son was growing. He was tall and broad for his age, and she knew he would be a mighty man like his father, a slayer of great bears and a brave warrior.

And then, as if she had conjured him up by magic, she saw Adam galloping toward her. Her heart leaped, as it had each time since she had first seen him, and she rose in the stirrups again and waved.

The years had been good to Adam; Sheffield had prospered under his strong hand. They had shared in the life-giving of two children, and today she would tell him of the coming of a third.

"Rebecca." He grinned. "I decided they didn't need me at the prize house after all." He slid from his horse and came toward her, a great mountain of a man, his heart shining in his eyes.

"I would take you away to our secret place," she teased, letting him lift her from the saddle and throwing her arms around his neck. "Would it please you to lie a while with a Shawnee woman?" Their lips met, and Rebecca thrilled to the sweet, joyful sensations that spread through her body. "Just an hour, my husband," she said coaxingly.

Adam moaned deep in his throat and pressed her against him, savoring her fresh pine scent. "The children…?"

"Safe with Amatha." Her lips parted to accept his deepening kiss. The wind off the bay ruffled his hair, and she gazed up at his dear, familiar features. "I have laid fresh cedar boughs on your sleeping mat, husband." She cupped his chin in her hands. "It will cost you only a few beads."

Adam laughed, sweeping her up in his arms and cradling her against his chest as he walked through the knee-high wildflowers. "It will cost me more than that," he murmured.

She laughed again and pulled his head down to join her mouth to his. "A-dam, my *ki-te-hi,* my heart."

And he answered in soft Shawnee, *"Dah-quel-e-mah."* I love you.

*Turn the page for an
excerpt from*

TENDER

FORTUNE

The Triumphant Hearts Series

Book Two

Judith E. French

Maryland, 1741

The three-masted sailing ship moved silently through the dark waters of the Chesapeake as the vessel made her way toward the port town of Annapolis on the western shore of the bay. A light breeze filled the canvas and lulled the deck watch at his station. No one saw the slight form move toward the railing on the starboard amidship.

Trembling with fear, the girl dropped her shapeless woolen gown to the splintered deck. She scrambled up and stood naked in the pale moonlight, her bare feet clinging to the gunnel, her long flaxen tresses blowing about her.

Ever since the ship had entered the mouth of the Chesapeake, she had planned for this moment. By dawn it would be too late. There the convicted felons would be auctioned off to the highest bidder.

A sailor's shout stiffened her resolution and she dove into the dark waters of the bay. The cool waves closed over her head. She swam away from the vessel with the strong, steady strokes of one who had learned to swim in the treacherous currents of the Thames.

The cry of alarm spread. Charity took a breath and dove again. They must believe her drowned. Land was a thin blade of trees along the eastern horizon. Her naked body slipped through the water like a mermaid's. It had been an act of desperation to strip. For what real lady would wear such bug-ridden rags? She had set her mind to the task.

When she dove from the gunnel of the ship, she had transformed herself from a convicted prisoner to a person of quality.

Shore was farther than she had believed. She was beginning to feel cold; she kicked harder. The moon moved behind rolling clouds. She was no longer certain of her direction.

The trickle of fear along her backbone grew. When the judge had pronounced her guilty of murder, she'd taken it without flinching. But now she was scared. Sailors said drowning was an easy way to die. She didn't believe it. Not for her it wouldn't be. Drowning would be letting the water win ...giving up.

Arm over arm, that was the way. No need to push herself. No sense trying to fight the tide...just swim with it.

Life at the tavern had been soft compared to the streets where there were stray dogs and other street urchins to contend with. Cobblestones were cold, worse for a girl than a boy. It took a sharp eye and ready wit just to stay alive. She'd learned to run errands and dodge drunks by the time she was knee-high to the fishmonger's stall. She could run like a wharf rat and fight like a one-eared tomcat.

Her mind was wandering. A few more strokes...just a few more strokes. A dark shape loomed ahead. She strained to see. The clouds parted briefly, revealing the outline of a sail. "Help!" she cried.

For a long time it seemed as though they wouldn't hear, that they'd leave her to die in the black, black water. Then, easily, daintily, the little sloop altered course and circled toward her.

Strong arms reached out to pull her from the waves. "Where are yer clothes, girl?" The voice was very Irish and very masculine. "Don't tell me! The less I know of this, the better."

"Please...don't take me to Annapolis," she murmured. "I...I must go east," she insisted.

"No fear o' that, me girl. I'm fer the Eastern Shore, meself."

Exhausted, she allowed him to lead her below to the tiny cabin. He lifted her onto a bunk and left her to sleep.

"It's what ye need now, darlin', sleep. There'll be time an' time for talk in the mornin'." He dropped another blanket over her and went back on deck. "An' a fine story I'm sure it'll be," he said, chuckling to himself. "A fine story…an' a fine night's catch."

TENDER FORTUNE

available in print and ebook

THE
TRIUMPHANT HEARTS
SERIES

Judith E French is the bestselling and award-winning author of nearly sixty novels, including historical romance, contemporary, mystery, and suspense. Her books are translated into a dozen languages and sold worldwide. She has written for Avon Books, Dorchester, Kensington, Harlequin, and Ballantine Publishers. Judith is the mother of bestselling novelist Colleen Faulkner, and the recipient of Romantic Times Magazine's Career Achievement Award for American Historicals.

You can connect with Judith on Facebook at www.facebook.com/judith.french or via email through her publisher at JudithFrench@epublishingworks.com.

www.ingramcontent.com/pod-product-compliance
Lightning Source LLC
Chambersburg PA
CBHW022207010726
47493CB00002B/452